I0682358

GHELLOW ROAD

A LITERARY DIARY OF A YOUNG GIRL'S JOURNEY

T. H. WATERS

VEREFOR PUBLISHING COMPANY
MINNEAPOLIS

Copyright © 2010
T. H. Waters

All rights reserved. No part of this publication may be reproduced in any manner whatsoever without the prior written permission of the publisher.

Published by
Verefor Publishing Company LLC
Minneapolis, Minnesota

ISBN-13: 978-0-9828931-1-1

Library of Congress Control Number: 2010933224

Cover design by Anne Rokoski

Cover photographs: letters © Simon Ingate/istockphoto.com; sky © Kyu Oh/istockphoto.com; lightning © Jeremy Woodhouse/GettyImages.com; dove © Christopher Ewing/istockphoto.com; carnival © Don Davidson/ istockphoto.com; grass © zentilia/istockphoto.com; photo frame © Sharon Day/istockphoto.com; photograph by Richard Valentine Arnold

Please visit T. H. Waters at www.verefor.com

To order additional copies of this book visit Amazon.com

MY GREATEST HOPE IS TO BE A VOICE
FOR ALL THOSE OUT THERE WHO
ARE FUMBLING THROUGH THEIR OWN
TANGLED LABYRINTH

T. H. WATERS

This book is dedicated to my beloved
father~
Richard Valentine

To the love of my life, my believer~Michael
This book would not have been possible
without you

To my dearest Mom~
Forever in my heart.
You gave me the greatest gift of all . . .
The gift of love

To my brother Mark~
This one's for you & me

Grandma Julia-My young life was richer because of you. I was truly blessed to have your love. I love you.

Pam-Your friendship was like gold. I will cherish it forever.

Barbara-Thank you for providing shelter from my storm. I will never forget.

Uncle Bob-You are such a dear soul. I will never forget your kindness. I love you.

Aunt Louise-May this book shine a light on the beauty of your brother's spirit and all that he endured.

Grandpa Frank-A great man. You are one of my heroes. I love you.

John-Don't know what we would have done without you. I know how hard you tried.

Diane-One of the best friends I could've ever had. I love you.

Polly-You were like a second mother to me. So much gratitude for your caring & kindness.

Margo-You're one in a million, Girl. I will never forget all the fun we had. I love you.

Heidi, Mike, Peter, Bruce-You colored my world. I love you guys.

Donna-If ever a saint walked this world, it was you.

Uncle Jim & Aunt Shirley, Uncle Wally & Auntie Kay-Thank you for all the love and care you provided. I will never forget. I love you.

Auntie Kay-You saved me from my darkest days. A debt I can never re-pay. I love you.

All of my Falls Buddies-I couldn't have asked for better friends.

My high school counselor-A credit to your profession. You gave me the gift of self-respect. I wish you knew how much your kindness meant to me. I will never forget you.

All of my teachers-I had some of the best teachers on the planet. I will never forget you.

Curt-Thank you for being one of the best friends I've ever had.

Zap-My co-pilot. You are one in a million. Thank you for your love, comfort and precious purrs throughout the writing of this book. I love you, Punkin.

Anne-The best proofreader I could have hoped for. Thank you for everything, my friend.

Annie-An amazing artist & cover designer. You're the best, Girlfriend.

All the people of International Falls, Minnesota-It takes a village. I am truly blessed that you were my village.

† BOOK ONE †
Living in the Shadow of
The Invisibles

I was born in the arms of the City of Lakes. It was not a big city like New York or L.A.; not a city that had yet learned to swallow you whole. It was a place where the seasons never lingered long enough to tire of them, always having somewhere else to go; a place where majestic elm trees lined the quaint neighborhood streets, arching their woody tentacles to lend refuge from a multitude of elements; a place where the alluring beauty of the Minnehaha captivated all who walked beside her as her sensuous waters snaked through the urban landscape for miles, gliding toward her graceful demise over an ancient precipice and into the mouth of the thirsty Mississippi.

The year was 1965.

I was a tiny, toe-headed girl, the second child of two parents who were madly in love with me. I will never forget those early years before The Invisibles came to cast their dark, permanent shadows upon our unsuspecting walls. Mom would lovingly cradle me for hours in the mod 60s rocking chair that resided in a corner of our humbly furnished living room. "Hush Little Baby" she'd softly sing, or coo "This Little Piggy Went to Market" as she gently tickled my chubby, curled-up toes. In between performances, she'd smother my face with affectionate kisses, altering the peach hue of my delicate skin to that of a glowing blush.

Despite Mom's intense love, it was really through Daddy's eyes that I first discovered the splendor of my existence, and it was through his strength that I grew to embrace it. He had the passionate spirit of an adventurer, and because of him we were never a family to linger idly at home. If ever there was a parade to attend, well by God, we attended it; if there were fireworks to gaze at, we gazed from start to finish; if there were zoo animals to be adored, we lovingly adored them; if Santa Claus came to town, we were the first in line to welcome him with open arms. For a brief moment in time, our lives were full, as were our hearts, and the world was ours to receive without consequence.

The four-bedroom house we lived in wasn't much, but it was the nicest one in the working class part of town that Daddy could afford on his modest teacher's salary. A mournful, gray-colored paint clung to its interiors, and the once-beige carpet had gracelessly aged into a stained shade of brown. But, Daddy was never one to be conquered, and with the passage of time he transformed our simple dwelling into something the four of us could proudly call our home.

The postage stamp backyard was just as practical and unadorned as our house and harbored more dirt than the tired grass that withered beneath our maple tree. As we grew, my brother and I never used it much anyway, preferring to spend our time a few blocks away by the creek in Longfellow Park, not far from where Daddy had proposed to Mom beneath the watchful eye of a bronzed Iroquois warrior. Daddy had told us that story so many times . . . .

On a sunny afternoon in the summer of '61, Daddy had brought his beloved Rainy to a favorite spot upstream from Minnehaha Falls. Underneath a stately, old oak he laid out the blanket he kept in the back seat of his Volkswagen, and together they feasted on a picnic meal that his Ma had packed for the special occasion. After Mom and Daddy had eaten the last of their dessert, he took out two champagne glasses, poured a bit of bubbly into each, then raised his high in the air and toasted his future wife. "Here's to you, Honey! The prettiest girl in this whole city!" Daddy told us it took a while for Mom to discover the diamond engagement ring that was lingering at the bottom of her glass, but when she finally did she lovingly threw her arms around him and wept tears of joy.

Soon after the story's finale, my brother and I would often lose Daddy in a place unknown to the two of us as he gazed beyond the field's legions of pirouetting dandelions toward the statue of that fateful warrior, the one cast in an eternal embrace with his beautiful beloved. "Yep," he'd quietly muse in a hushed voice more to himself than to anyone else, "I got the prettiest girl in this whole city."

I will never forget my earliest traumatic childhood memory. I was only five years old. It was late in the evening, and the living room's night-light was the house's only illumination. Mom was lying on the sofa and softly crying, still garbed in her pretty evening dress and silver high heels. Her distress unsettled me, and I awoke. With sleep in my eyes and blankie in hand, I crawled out of bed, drowsily crossed the threshold of my room and shuffled over to her.

"Don't cry, Momma, don't cry," I urged, gently caressing her forehead just as she had done to me so many times before.

"I'm okay, Sweetheart. Toddle back to bed. Momma will be all right."

"Momma, how can I make you better?" I asked with great concern.

"I'll be better in the morning, Baby."

Mom slowly sat up and wrapped her arms around me. As she kissed my cheek, I could feel the dampness of her sorrow.

3

She turned me toward the direction of my bedroom and gently pushed me away. "Go on, Honey. Momma loves you more than anything."

Not sure of what else to do, I did as she instructed and headed back to bed.

"I love you, Momma," I told her earnestly.

"I love you, too, Baby."

When I awoke the next morning, the pleasing aroma of freshly baked cinnamon rolls was tickling my nose. As I lay half awake, the events of the past evening scurried to fill my head, urging me to get up and check on Mom. When I rushed into the kitchen, I began to gleefully exclaim, "Momma, Momma! You're all better!" before realizing that the person tending the stove was not my mother. "Oh, it's you, Grandmama," I said, giving her a toothy grin before walking up behind her and encircling her thigh with my small arms.

"Well hello there, Dear," she greeted in her thick German accent. She looked down upon me and returned my gaze with a weak smile before asking, "Are you hungry? I'm making breakfast. Would you like something to eat?" She then guided me toward the kitchen table and helped me into my booster seat. "Come. Sit down, Dear," she instructed, then returned to her post in front of the stove. My older brother, Mikie, entered the kitchen, still suited up in his Superman pajamas. I glanced at him before looking back at Grandma and asking, "Where's Momma and Daddy?"

Grandma kept a watchful eye on her task at hand and was slow to answer. "Your Daddy had to take your Momma someplace where she can get some rest. Yes, Honey, yes. God have mercy." She made a quick sign of the cross before grabbing a pot of freshly made oatmeal from the stove and pouring its contents into two colorful bowls on a nearby counter.

"Are they going to be back real soon, Grandma?" Mikie asked as he was saddling up across the table from me.

"You'll have to ask your Daddy about that when he gets home," Grandma replied as a matter of fact. "Right now we're going to have something to eat, and then I'll take you to the park." She placed our bowls of cereal onto the table, then poured each of us a glass of orange juice. "Say Grace, Kids." We obediently bowed our heads and rapidly rambled through our memorized prayers. While my brother dutifully dug in and began to fill his belly, I picked away at my food. Grandma gave me a disapproving look, so I gingerly swirled my spoon in the oatmeal, then licked the tip of it in a halfhearted attempt to appease her. I worried about Mom and Daddy.

Dear God,
Please bring Momma and Daddy back soon.

Daddy came back later that afternoon looking worn out and sad. He told us not to worry. In our world, whatever Daddy said was as good as gold, so we readily accepted that Mom's troubles were nothing more than temporary.

Grandma moved in with us, and we went on with our lives. Daddy continued teaching at Roosevelt High while Grandma stayed home and took care of us after school. She played all kinds of games with us, bandaged our owies and let us watch hours upon hours of afternoon variety shows while she churned out oodles of noodle casseroles and platefuls of homemade sweets from the kitchen. "Eat! Eat!" she'd cluck as fiercely as a devoted mother hen. "You kids need to keep up your strength!"

Mom's unexpected departure predictably took its toll, and I could sense the underlying sadness behind Daddy's forced smile. As time went on he gradually adjusted and resumed his active lifestyle, always quick to include my

5

brother and me in his adventures, always sure to shield the two of us from our painful reality.

It was during this period when Daddy decided it was time to teach us how to downhill ski. He took it upon himself to outfit us with the best skis, boots and poles that money could buy. To complete our ensemble he treated us to a rare shopping spree at an exclusive downtown department store. For me, Daddy selected a soft pink, cotton sweater with a matching turtleneck, while Mikie was given a white sweater of Scandinavian design embellished with red and blue snowflakes. Each of us received our own pair of black ski pants, and we were finally ready to storm the bunny hill.

Daddy often drove us to Theodore Wirth Ski Park on the weekends. Since he was quite an accomplished skier, he took on the task of instructing us personally instead of enrolling us in kiddy beginner classes. My brother took to the slopes immediately. He was stocky for his age and a natural daredevil, so a few tumbles in the powder posed no threat. Up he'd go to the top of the hill, and then bomb it all the way down with a huge grin on his face, poles never touching the ground. On the rare occasion when he did take a spill, he'd just laugh it off before repeating the entire routine until he was one with the snow.

I, on the other hand, did not possess a single "need for speed" bone in my body. I'd cautiously make my way over to the towrope like an old granny with a hip replacement, then firmly grab a hold of it. Once at the top of the hill, Daddy would encourage me to follow Mikie's carefree lead, but I wouldn't have any part of it. Instead, I'd painstakingly scope out the gentlest dips and bumps in the landscape, then slowly ease my way down the slope, always relieved to make it to the bottom in one piece. Because Mikie was so much braver and faster than I was, he'd lap me time and again, relentlessly teasing me as he whizzed past, "Chicken! Bak, bak, bak!!!" he'd yell while Daddy laughed at us from his bird's eye view above.

The three of us would ski for hours at a time, revitalized by the freshness of dense winter air and surrounding bustle. Only the incessant nip of the chilled breeze and our overflowing noses could urge us to retreat inside the lodge for a round of hot chocolate and marshmallows. When it was time to go home, Daddy packed up our gear and loaded it into the old Buick while Mikie and I competed for his attention, chattering like little magpies about all of the fun we'd just had.

As a special treat on those evenings, Daddy would swing by the drive-thru of our favorite fast food joint and pick up several grease-stained bags full of goodies before racing home in time to gather around the tube and watch *The Lawrence Welk Show* with Grandma. Our sweet granny was none other than a bona fide Lawrence Welk groupie. "Oh, isn't that Lawrence just so handsome!" she'd exclaim. "And those costumes . . . would you look at those beautiful costumes!" My brother and I would unfailingly roll our eyes, not caring much for Lawrence or the "beautiful" costumes, but whenever he uttered his famous "An-a one, an-a two . . ." line we sure had fun flailing our invisible conductor's batons enthusiastically in the air.

It was times like those that made me feel as though we still had some semblance of a normal American family life. It was times like those that now make me realize just how hard Daddy had tried.

~♦ ♦ ♦~

As the days turned into weeks, and the weeks turned into months, the essence of the mother I once couldn't live without

7

began to fade from my memory, and I hardly knew who she was on the day she returned from some faraway place.

It was during that following spring at the end of a bright afternoon. The sun was beginning its descent, forcing my brother and me to retreat home for dinner after spending several hours building a sand castle for a frog we'd found at the park playground.

"Messy! Why do you kids have to get so messy when you play?" Grandma scolded as we walked in the door. "Dinner's almost ready. Go change your clothes and wash up before we eat now, Dears."

We did as Grandma instructed, then made our way to the kitchen, sat down at the table and waited for Daddy to join us just as he always did. After several minutes he finally emerged with a gigantic smile spread across his face.

"Kids! You won't believe what a wonderful surprise I have in store for you!" he teased, knowing full well how much my brother and I loved surprises.

Mikie sat up straight, then happily clapped his hands and squealed, "Daddy, Daddy, what is it?!"

Mom's petite, pretty face appeared over Daddy's shoulder, and she slid past him to enter the room. She looked thinner and more pale than I'd remembered. Mustering a fragile smile, she glided over to each of us, bent down and affectionately hugged and kissed my brother and me, then took her old spot at the table. "I missed you kids so much!" she quietly gushed, suppressing fresh tears.

At first, I simply stared back at her, not knowing what to say. She'd been away for so long that I had forgotten what my life had been like with her in it.

"Momma?" I asked timidly. "Is that you?"

Mikie swiftly kicked me under the table and answered for her, "Of course it is, Dum-Dum."

Mom's expression transformed into a look of mild bewilderment. "Why . . . don't you remember me, Baby? It's

8

Momma," she explained. "I'm back. I'm home for good now. You don't have to worry about me anymore."

Still ill at ease, I turned to Daddy for reassurance. He was the happiest I'd seen him in such a long time. "It's true, Twink, Mommy is home for good."

I looked back at Mom. I had forgotten how good it felt to accept the warmth of her gaze. It took a moment for me to realize that our little family was finally complete once more. I smiled back at this strangely familiar woman seated across the table from me.

"I love you, Momma," I told her.

"I love you, too, Baby."

Things were never quite the same as they'd once been before Mom's unexpected departure. Although the gentleness of her spirit and genuine love for my brother and me never faltered, she often became listless and distant. I would notice how her eyes would momentarily drift away and focus on something that was outwardly unapparent to me. She'd shake her head "yes" or "no" and mumble inaudible words under her breath. This scared me and I tried to ignore it, but her odd, new mannerisms seemed to be here to stay.

After a while I began to ask, "Momma, what are you doing?"

My question seemed to startle her from her shallow trance, and she'd wearily explain, "I'm fine, Baby. Just fine." I never believed her.

After Grandma moved out of our house and back into her downtown apartment, Daddy was hell-bent on resuming the life we'd once led as if nothing unusual had occurred. No mention was ever spoken of what had happened to Mom or where she'd been. Mom simply took Grandma's place just as

9

Grandma had taken Mom's months earlier, and Daddy continued teaching at Roosevelt High.

Summer was fast approaching, and renewed hope filled the air. On those warm, sunny days Daddy would treat the three of us to picnics by the lake. Sometimes we'd go to Lake Harriet, sometimes Lake Calhoun, and occasionally we'd make the drive out to Lake Minnetonka. Daddy absolutely loved the water. It didn't much matter which body of water we were near, he found joy in the endless smell of coconut suntan oil and the silky, smooth feeling of sand underneath his bare feet . . . and, of course there were the boats. Daddy couldn't get enough of them. Sometimes before hitting the beach, he'd trot down to the boat launch, pull out his favorite camera and snap a whole host of photos . . . close-ups, artistic shots, and sometimes he'd even ask my brother and me to pose next to one of the particularly nice vessels. All types of watercraft intrigued Daddy, to be sure, but there was one in particular that had captivated his heart, and that one just happened to be the Catamaran. Whenever he'd spot one at the launch he'd wave us over and flood our small minds with the minute details of its capabilities as we tried to pretend like we knew what he was talking about. "Kids," he'd say pensively, "someday we're going to have a Cat of our own."

The summer festival known as the Aquatennial soon was upon us, and every year Daddy took us to several of its events that, naturally, all focused around water. Daddy knew how much Grandma enjoyed the water skiing show at Lake Nokomis, so he invited her to go with us that year. It was a lovely July day. Not a cloud hung in the sky as the pretty, female skiers rode upon the backs of their muscular counterparts, performing spectacular tricks behind a large powerboat. Being as small as I was and unable to see over the crowd, Daddy hoisted me up and planted my small frame squarely on top of sturdy his shoulders.

10

After the show's dramatic conclusion, we were in the car driving Grandma back to her apartment when we were suddenly shaken by an enormous explosion. Our conversation halted as we nervously looked around.

"Look, look! Over there!" Daddy shouted as he pointed toward an enormous billow of smoke hanging in the sky just one short block to the right of us. We all snapped our heads in that direction. That is to say, all of us snapped our heads . . . except for Mom. She was sitting quietly in the back seat, in between my brother and me. Her eyes were half closed and a bit glazed over. She appeared to be lost in a state of mind that Daddy would later refer to as a "catatonic condition."

Daddy was too intrigued by the explosion to notice anything else around him. You could see the wheels turning round and round in his head as he tried to drive closer to the source of the blaze.

"Richard!" Grandma squealed nervously. "Richard, don't you dare drive me anywhere else but home—this instant!"

Daddy chuckled, holding his course, then replied with a sly smile, "Oh Ma, all you do is worry. Don't be such a scaredy cat. Let's go check out the action!"

"Oh, Vixadunavettle!" Grandma shot back in frustration, using her infamous German swearword that nobody else knew how to properly pronounce, let alone spell.

Daddy ignored Grandma's fury and addressed Mom, "You doing all right back there, Rainy?"

It took Mom a minute to realize that someone was speaking to her. "Yes, Rick. I'm fine," she responded apathetically, completely unaware of the surrounding excitement.

Daddy maneuvered the car to within half a block of the blast. "Richard! God have mercy!" Grandma dramatically shouted as she clung helplessly to the passenger's door in the front seat.

11

Daddy just chuckled again as if he were playing some kind of espionage game while staring at the scene that lay before us. A gigantic cloud of dusty, black smoke hovered ominously in the air above a Sinclair gas station. As it was making its slow ascent toward the heavens, it ignited without warning, mercilessly spewing its blistering breath below. People were sent screaming, and there was absolute chaos as everyone in the direct path of the fireball ran for their lives. Daddy had kept us at a safe distance, yet still close enough to scare my brother and me. As the two of us sat on the edge of our seats with our mouths agape, I had to stifle a scream. I had no idea how my brother was feeling, but I was in complete agreement with Grandma and wanted to get out of there . . . pronto!

Leaving the scene was the furthest thing from Daddy's mind. He was like one of those crazed storm chasers, hungering to catch a buzz off the excitement. It was only when he realized that Grandma's panic attack was getting worse that he finally eased the Buick around. As soon as Grandma sensed we were heading away from the fireball and toward the safety of her apartment, her shoulders slackened into a more relaxed position and she took a deep breath. "Please take me home, Richard," she quietly requested, clearly drained of all emotion.

Daddy reached over, reassuringly patted her thigh and teased, "Oh, Ma-a! You know I'd never let anything happen to you."

Grandma gave him a weary smile.

As we drove the remainder of the way back to Grandma's apartment in silence, Mikie and I instinctively sought protection from our mother, huddling as close to her as we could like two newborn puppies. She didn't seem to notice. "Momma?" I said. "Momma, are you okay?"

Neither the oddity of the explosion nor the sound of my young voice was an antidote for her catatonic state. She simply stared out the window at the blurred images fleeing past.

~♦ ♦ ♦~

Mom continued seeping in and out of reality. On those days when she was faring well, she'd desperately try to fulfill the role of the wife and mother she'd long dreamt of becoming. She'd frequently join Mikie and me at the park, clean our house from top to bottom, and cook or bake anything her family requested, even if she didn't care much for it herself. Daddy enjoyed food almost as much as he enjoyed the water, and it wasn't unusual to hear him sweet-talk Mom into culinary pursuits. "Hey Rainy, maybe you could fix us that famous hot dish of yours tonight?" or "Honey, how 'bout whipping up a batch of homemade onion rings?" Mom was especially thoughtful whenever a birthday rolled around. She could always be found in the kitchen lovingly preparing our favorite cake. Mine was a German chocolate number with extra coconut frosting, no exceptions. Mikie chose white topped with chocolate fudge, and Daddy opted for angel food smothered in whipped cream and strawberries.

During the heart of each autumn, Mom would unfailingly bake us an all-American apple pie, and the tantalizing smell of cinnamon and sugar would fill our entire house. The instant it drifted past my nose, I'd stop whatever I was doing and race into the kitchen to beg for the leftover, sugarcoated crust I knew Mom had prepared especially for me. The radio was usually on, and if I happened to catch her when one of her favorite songs was playing she'd gently grab hold of both my hands and encourage, "C'mon, Baby, let's dancie dance." She'd lead me out into the center of the kitchen where the two of us would bop and groove together for a few blissful minutes. Mom would always giggle while enjoying my performance. "You are the cutest little thing, Baby Girl!" she'd say. "Just look at you. Why, you could be on *American Bandstand*!"

13

I so dearly cherished tender moments like those. They were rare exchanges of nothing but utter joy between just the two of us, mother and daughter. Mom's unconditional delight with that of her own creation bathed me in the purest kind of rapture, a treasure that would forever remain untarnished deep within my heart.

During the times when Mom's mind became paralyzed and unreachable, she would retreat to her bedroom and simply disappear. She would often be gone for only a few hours, but occasionally her absence lasted for days. If she were clearly in dire straits she'd end up back in the hospital, at which point Grandma would move back in with us until she returned. Her life's rhythm was unpredictable, even to herself.

As I look back on it all now, I realize just how hard Daddy tried to buffer my brother and me from the seriousness of Mom's illness. He spent countless hours taking us on canoe rides and patiently sitting on sandy, city beaches while we blissfully fluttered in the cool waters. He would often chaperone a tribe of our friends to enchanting places like the Conservatory, where limitless merry-go-round rides were enjoyed and scores of chocolate chip ice cream cones were avidly devoured. Daddy carefully colored the empty spaces of our world with so much laughter and fun that we never had time to grasp the true weight of our circumstance.

On a cool, crisp October evening in the fall of 1972, Mikie and I were sprawled out on our living room floor in the midst of creating homemade Halloween costumes. We'd rounded up a couple of large, beat-up cardboard boxes and were attempting to transform them into fake television sets with a little help from some tinfoil and black magic markers.

"Hey, Mikie, where's the scissors?" I asked. "I need to cut out my TV screen."

Mikie scanned the floor, thinking he'd already grabbed a pair. As soon as he realized his mistake, he got up and sifted through a nearby desk.

"That's weird," he said. "I thought they were right here."

"I'll go upstairs and check with Momma," I said. "Be right back."

I pushed myself away from the floor, passed through the dining room, then mounted the stairs and headed for Mom's bedroom at the end of the second floor hallway. I noticed that her curtains had been drawn, and only the flicker from a small lamp on the dresser lit the dark room. I could hear an angry, muffled voice as I approached, and the hairs on the back of my neck stood up. It sounded unfamiliar to me, and I wasn't able to place it. I cautiously slowed my pace.

"You don't know!" The angry voice shouted in a scratchy whisper. "You don't know anything! Go straight to hell!"

I was scared now. As I moved forward, my lower lip began to tremble. "Momma? You there?" I asked as bravely as I could.

There was no answer.

The angry whispers continued.

Once I reached the threshold of Mom's room, I could see her lying in bed underneath the covers, still fully dressed. Her pale, agonized face twisted and contorted as she carried on her delusional conversation with an unknown being.

"Momma?" I said in a soft, trembling voice.

She didn't realize I was calling her name, so I stepped closer. As I passed her dresser something unusual caught my eye, and I glanced over at it. On the mirror was a message erratically scrawled in dark, red lipstick that read:

Demons Be Gone! Leave Me in Peace!

15

The blood rushed from my face. I couldn't comprehend what was happening and was so terrified that I began to cry. "Momma!" I shouted as tears streamed down my face. "Momma! Are you all right?"

My anguished cries jousted Mom from her trance, and she glared at me with bloated, resentful eyes.

"Get out!" She yelled at me.

"Momma, what's wrong with you?" I was sobbing now.

"Get out of my room . . . this instant!" She started to get out of bed, so I turned and ran back toward the stairs.

"Momma, please don't do this! You're scaring me, Momma!" I yelled over my shoulder. I ran down the stairs and back into the living room.

My brother looked concerned. "What's wrong?" he asked, clearly having heard all the commotion.

"Something's really weird with Momma this time!" I stuttered as I tried to get my explanation out in between sobs.

"Slow down, I can't hear what you're saying," Mikie instructed.

Just as I was trying to calm down and retell my story, Daddy walked in the front door. "Hi, Kids," he greeted as he began to take off his coat. It didn't take long for him to notice my distress.

"What is it, Twink? What's wrong?" he asked as he hung up his coat, then quickly strode toward me.

"It's Momma! Something really bad has happened!" I told him.

Daddy gently guided me over to the couch, sat down next to me and put his arm around my slender, heaving shoulders while Mikie plopped onto the floor next to his half-finished cardboard TV set.

As I unfolded my bizarre conversation with Mom, Daddy's face became completely expressionless. He kept on sighing and shaking his head from side to side. Mikie looked as scared and confused as I was.

Daddy tried to reassure my brother and me, just as he always did, and then became uncomfortably silent for what seemed like a long time, his breath deepening as the minutes took their toll.

"Now, you kids stay right here," he uneasily instructed. "I need to go make a call to Grandma." Mikie and I exchanged wary glances. We both knew exactly what that meant.

The next morning, Mom was gone and Grandma had moved back in.

Up until this point, neither Mikie nor I had ever visited Mom while she was away. Daddy finally decided that it was time for the four of us to reunite, despite the supernatural forces that poisoned the well of our existence.

The drive from our house out to the County Hospital was well beyond the city limits. A forested landscape and several family farms dotting the route were our only relief from boredom, except for an occasional herd of heifers. Each time my brother and I spied one of those large, gentle creatures, we exuberantly greeted it in our own, special moo-language until Daddy couldn't take it anymore and made us roll our windows back up.

As we neared the hospital, Daddy tried to prepare us for what lay ahead as he described the facility where Mom was staying. "And Kids," he cautioned, "don't expect Mom to be the mother you're used to. She may be very tired or in a catatonic condition or overmedicated. It's hard to say at this point."

I took my eyes off the scenery and momentarily stared at the back of Daddy's seat. I suddenly felt overwhelmed at the loss of my mother and wanted someone—anyone—to put her

17

back together again . . . just like it was before when she used to hold me tightly in her arms on our red rocker and tickle my toes.

As we pulled into the hospital grounds, we drove past a lone woman who walked feebly down the street in our direction. The enduring lines of agony that were etched across her face were a constant reminder to all of the battle within, and a clear indication that her demons had been victorious. Her haunting gaze followed us until we were well beyond its reach, leaving me uneasy about the condition of my mother.

I can still vividly recall the place where Mom was staying. Several lovely, turn-of-the-century, brown brick cottages collectively speckled a circular street that wound its way around a little park as serene creek waters flowed nearby; the deceptive charm of it all masking its painful reality.

As Daddy maneuvered the Buick over to cottage number 8, it felt as though we were pulling up to a mansion in the rich part of town rather than a home for the ailing. Inside the cottage, however, was a much different story. It was divided into several small rooms, providing each occupant the security of their own private space.

Mom's room was located up one flight of stairs and to the left. As the three of us ascended, we passed a nurse who gave Daddy a tired greeting, dark shadows encircling her eyes. Mikie and I started to chatter until Daddy glanced back at us, quickly drew a forefinger to his mouth and whispered, "Shhhhh . . . we don't want to disturb anybody." My brother and I immediately came to attention and fell in line behind him, now sheepish and silent.

Mom's austere, spotless room was dimly lit. She was lying in bed with her eyes closed, propped up against a few pillows. The three of us approached her side, then Daddy lovingly touched her arm and whispered, "Rainy, it's Rick. How ya doing today, Kiddo?"

Mom became aware of someone beside her and groggily replied, "Oh, Rick. Is that you?"

Daddy said, "I've brought the kids this time, Honey."

Mom struggled to open her eyes. They fluttered several times in an attempt to squint at us. "My dear little ones," she whispered before closing them again. Her effort to connect with us seemed to sap her strength.

"Daddy? Is Momma having another catama-tonic condition again?" I asked fretfully.

"Not this time, Twink. Momma's just very, very tired. She's been through a lot these past few weeks."

"Dad?" Mikie asked. "Is Mom going to be able to come back home soon?"

Daddy didn't answer at first, solemnly staring at his young wife's drained face. She was only thirty-four yet looked decades older. "I'm not sure, Son," he said after a while.

We lingered in the room for a few more minutes before Daddy felt it was time to head back home. He took my hand in his, and the three of us slowly exited cottage number 8, each heart as heavy as a boat anchor.

After we piled back into the Buick, I stared up at Mom's window in earnest, hoping she would show us a sign of life and wave goodbye, but her pretty, delicate face was not destined to appear.

It would be several more weeks before I would see that face again.

Mikie and I were restless when we arrived home later that afternoon. We didn't feel like being with our friends or going outside, so we just sat around my brother's bedroom and played Parcheesi while listening to the local bee-bop radio station.

19

I was winning and excitedly teased, "Bet you wish you were me, Loser!" Mikie gave me a dirty look. "Shhhhh. Listen," he said as he cocked his head, trying to concentrate and silently pointed at the radio.

Initially, I took this as an attempt to outmaneuver me, but as he became more insistent I stopped teasing him and paid attention to the chipper voice of the radio announcer.

KS97 was having a contest with a Payday of $10,000 big ones! All my brother and I had to do was keep listening to their station and identify whichever song accompanied the chime of a cash register. Mikie and I got really excited about our big break. Mom constantly had the radio on, and the two of us could recognize just about every current hit there was.

"Mikie! Are you thinking what I'm thinking?" I gleefully asked.

"Ahhh..." stammered my brother. "Well . . . that's a ton of money. We could buy lots with it. Get some primo hockey gear, a super cool stereo . . ."

"We could get a kitty!" I interrupted, and then began to imagine shopping for all the toys I'd dreamt about, and the possibility of a new pink banana bike. After several minutes, my thoughts steered me back to Mom. I looked over at my brother and asked, "Wait a minute. What is the-e-e one thing we've wanted more than anything else?"

Mikie thought about it for a while and then astutely responded, "We've always wanted Mom to never get sick again."

"Exactly! And if we won the 10,000 bucks, we could send Momma to that one place she's always talking about." I crinkled my nose as I tried to remember the name of it. I asked my brother, "What's it called again? Loads? No, wait... Louds!"

"Lourdes, Dum Dum."

Whenever Mom told us the story of the tiny French town where a young, peasant girl named Bernadette had several recurring visions of the Virgin Mary, she would get a faraway look in her eyes. Since that miraculous event, just a century before, tens of thousands of pilgrims have fervently flocked to the surrounding baptismal waters. As soon as they immersed their burdened flesh into the soothing, aquatic arms of salvation, something powerful happened, something rather miraculous. Their earthly wounds, both physical and metaphysical, vanished, and they became whole souls once more. No more tears to be shed. No more agony of mind and spirit. Just a gloriously radiant being who was free once more to give love and to receive it. Mom was certain that the waters at Lourdes were the conduit between heaven and earth.

My brother and I were true believers. We were so convinced that if Mom could get enough money to make the quest, all her troubles would be gone, and . . . all our troubles would be gone.

We were now on a mission. When we weren't in school, we burrowed ourselves in Mikie's room, flipped on the radio, and played board games until we got the signal that it was time to call in and win the $10,000 prize.

We were shocked when we didn't win on the first try. We didn't even win on the second. We dialed our little hearts out, but someone else beat us to the punch every single time. Saturday sped by, then Sunday. We tried again all night Monday, Tuesday and Wednesday. No luck. The weekend rolled back around and we were plumb sick of playing games and waiting by the radio. We finally realized that there were just too many other people in the city who were also trying to get their paws on the prize. It was time to give up. Any hope of being able to reclaim our mother from her murky, catatonic state was gone. We were crestfallen.

We slumped up to Daddy's bedroom on the third floor, and told him we had decided to abandon our scheme. He gave us a comforting look, then kidded, "Is that why you two have been holed up in Mikie's room all week?" He leaned forward to lovingly tweak my nose and pat Mikie's shoulder. "You're good kids, you know. Never forget that. Your mom would be real proud of what you tried to do for her. She'd be real proud."

Mom came home from the mental hospital a few weeks after Halloween, just as the leaves were beginning to change from deep, earthy greens to burnt reds and cornhusk yellows. She'd never gotten to see the cool TV sets that Mikie and I had concocted out of the cardboard boxes we'd scavenged from the corner grocer, so Daddy found a Polaroid he'd taken of us on Halloween night and stuck it on the fridge.

"What's this, Honey?" Mom asked of me one morning as I was sitting at the kitchen table eating breakfast.

"Don't you remember, Momma? Those are the costumes Mikie and I made."

Mom stood in front of the fridge and stared at the picture for a long time. "Why, I'm sorry, Dear . . ." she began before briefly pausing, ". . . that I wasn't able to be here with you."

I stopped crunching my cereal and reflected on our visit at the mental hospital, then somberly replied, "Me too, Momma."

As the days passed, I could sense Mom's relief to be back home. In the evenings, she could usually be found in her room quietly reading the Bible in bed. I longed for her company and often sought her out before going to sleep. On one particular evening she smiled at me when I entered her bedroom and patted the side of the bed, silently beckoning me to sit beside her. She set her book down and lovingly caressed the side of my face.

"You are a beautiful, little girl, Baby. So beautiful," she said tenderly.

I'd forgotten how long it had been since the last time she'd spoken to me like that.

I wrapped my slender arms around her neck, shut my eyes and hugged her as tightly as I could. "Please don't ever leave again," I silently pleaded, wishing to cast a spell upon her.

But, time would come to prove that whatever mortal powers I held would soon be doomed against those of The Invisibles.

After she'd been home for a couple of months, Mom was transforming into the mother we so desperately needed. She was laughing that wonderful Irish laugh of hers, and appeared connected to her outside world again . . . connected to us again. She took great pains to ensure we were always freshly dressed in clean clothes and packed our lunches each morning in crisp, brown paper bags that had our names penned across the top. When my brother and I arrived home from school in the afternoons, she was eager to greet us with a big hug and kiss.

One Saturday morning while Daddy was away, Mom decided she was long overdue for a visit with the man of cloth.

"Kids," she declared, "we'll be going downtown to St. Olaf's after breakfast."

"But Mom, it's only Saturday," Mikie replied.

"Yeah," I whined, "can't we go to the candy store instead?"

Mom looked at me disapprovingly.

I knew her answer was a resounding, "No! No candy today." She didn't even have to use her vocal cords.

"Okay, fine. Can I just wear my jeans then? I don't feel like getting all dressed up like we usually have to for church." I was pushing her buttons now, and I knew it.

Another disapproving glance . . . this time the eyebrows went up.

23

Mom always made us dress up for church whether it was for Sunday sermon, Sunday school, Christmas Mass, Ash Wednesday or some screaming baby's baptism. You name the saintly occasion, and it was one that called for uncomfortable hairstyles and tights that were far too tight.

After Mikie and I had finished our breakfast, we excused ourselves and headed up to our rooms to change clothes. On our way out of the kitchen, Mikie complained under his breath, "But there's not even going to be anyone else there."

"What was that? What did you say, young man?" Mom asked authoritatively.

"Uhhh . . . nothing Mom," my brother cautiously replied.

Once properly attired we went back downstairs and plopped onto the living room couch, then waited for Mom to finish the last of her primping in the bathroom.

When she finally came to retrieve us, we thought we were ready to get our coats on. No such luck. She had the dreaded bottle of Johnson's No Tangles in her hand. I sighed, knowing exactly what was in store for me.

"C'mon, Baby, I need to do your hair," she encouraged.

I sighed again, this time louder.

I was unlucky enough to have been born with curly hair. Not just wavy, pretty hair, not even pretty wavy hair. I got socked with crazily curly hair, Buckwheat-style. Sure, all the grannies loved it and would coo at me in restaurants or at church exclaiming, "What a little Dollie!" I think they mistook me for a pet toy poodle. I hated my hair. It was so much work to take care of that I rarely ever did, and unless Mom or Daddy or Grandma came to my rescue, I preferred to walk about with wild, toe-headed locks, looking tribal.

Mom sat down on the couch. An "Ah, man!" escaped my lips as I took my appointed position on the floor directly underneath her, my head in between her nyloned knees. She doused my hair with the no-tangle potion until I coughed, and then began to pull through it with a black, plastic comb. She yanked and yanked at it until she got all the snarls out. It hurt so much that I wanted to blast out a few swear words but thought better of it, knowing full well that I would have gotten grounded had I let them fly.

After the hard part was done, she fashioned my hair into two pigtails, tying a short, pink bow made of yarn around each one.

"Don't you just look so cute!" she exclaimed. "Doesn't she look cute, Mikie?"

My brother didn't even bother to look at me. He merely shrugged his shoulders as if to say, "Doesn't make any difference to me."

"How do you like your hair, Baby?" Mom asked as she handed me a mirror.

I cringed as I peered into it and tried to sound appreciative of her stylistic efforts.

"Oh, you look just like Buffy!" Mom exclaimed. "Don't you think she looks just like Buffy, Mikie?"

"Who the heck is Buffy?" he asked, clearly annoyed.

"You know, that sweet little girl on TV. What's the name of the show she's on? Is it *Family Affair*?" Mom didn't wait for an answer. "Yes, that's right. I think it's *Family Affair*."

My brother shrugged again.

Personally, I preferred to look tribal. It was a lot less work.

We were finally ready to be on our way. Mom opened her purse and took out two dimes, one for me, one for my brother. She placed a single, silver coin into each of our palms.

"Money for the bus, Kids," she explained.

We donned our winter garb and headed out the door.

25

Mikie walked on one side of Mom while I walked on the other as the three of us marched toward the metro bus stop located only a few blocks from our house. It had been a cold, snowy season and mounds of winter wonderland flanked the sidewalks. Several long, smooth patches of ice occupied the pavement along our route, and whenever one came into range, Mikie and I took turns sprinting full speed ahead and sliding its length.

We didn't have to wait long before the bus rolled up. Mom gathered the two of us in front of her and checked our palms to make sure we hadn't lost our fare.

"C'mon, Kids, let's get on now," she directed.

The warmth of the bus welcomed us inside. Mom chose the side seats at the front so the three of us could sit next to each other. Mikie sat beside Mom, and I sat beside Mikie. He asked me if I wanted to play Bloody Knuckles, that game where you hold both of your clenched fists directly up to your opponent's and each combatant attempts to whack the other's knuckles first.

"Naw," I responded irritably, flicking my hand at him as if shooing away a fly. "Maybe later." Mikie always won that stupid game anyway.

As the bus was winding its way downtown, an elderly man boarded and sat directly opposite from us. His hair was sparse and white, sharply contrasting the brown age spots that lightly speckled his face. His worn jacket was torn in a few places, and some of the fiber filling was trying to escape its polyester prison. He woefully gazed down at the rubber-matted floor. I kept looking at him, wondering what made him so sad. Finally, I leaned over toward my brother, cupped the side of my mouth with one hand and whispered, "Ask Momma if that man over there can come with us to see the priest."

Mikie bent toward Mom and relayed my message. She leaned forward to get a better look at me, then reached over and patted my knee while shaking her head, "No."

26

"But Momma," I loudly whispered back, brows furrowed.

She patted my knee more urgently so that I would stop talking and again shook her head, "No."

As we were approaching our destination, Mom pulled the stop cord. After the bus had come to a halt, she stood up and grabbed each of our hands to steady us while we exited. As I passed the sad man, I purposefully caught his eye and smiled. He didn't smile back. I don't think he had any more smiles left to give.

St. Olaf's church was only a short distance from our bus stop. We walked the first block in silence as Mom seemed to be thinking of other things. After crossing a busy intersection, with only one more block to go, she started softly singing under her breath. I couldn't hear her very well at first because of all the background traffic noise, but as she got further into the melody, I realized it was one I'd heard her play on the piano hundreds of times. She was never able to finish a performance without crying.

♫♫♫ "Like a Bridge Over Troubled Water"

A single tear slid down Mom's face as we entered the church. Once inside, she turned to the two of us and whispered the rules. "You'll be good for me, right Kids?" she asked while earnestly searching our eyes.

We eagerly shook our heads, "Yes."

Mom smiled approvingly and extracted a few more objects from her purse, then held them out for each of us.

"I'd like you to say the rosary while you're waiting for me. Do you both remember what I taught you?"

"I do," Mikie proudly whispered.

"Yeah, me too!" I said.

"Okay, good. Now when we go inside the chapel you'll be very, very quiet, won't you?"

"Yes, Momma," replied Mikie.

"Yeah, we'll be really, really, really, really, quiet for you, Momma," I playfully assured her as I gave her a toothy grin.

Mom ushered us into the chapel where there were but a few other souls seated throughout the pews. The room was so dimly lit that I had to wait several seconds for my eyes to adjust to the darkness.

Mom led us over to the row of pews that was closest to the confessional booth. We tried to extract ourselves from our winter wear as quietly as we could, but the echoes scattered. An old lady in the front pew turned around and looked at us with annoyed curiosity. Mom knelt down, rosary in hand, and then glanced at my brother and me. This was our cue. Mikie held his dark brown rosary in his right hand and cradled the first bead with his free forefinger and thumb. He began to whisper his first prayer.

I never understood the rosary thing. To me, it was just a bunch of memorized words strung together to form a bunch of religious chants about hailing Mary, praising the Lord, and something about Art. I didn't know what they were talking about when they said Thou Art this and Thou Art that. Hell, I didn't really know what they were talking about . . . ever. But, since my big brother was making me look bad I, too, cradled the first bead of my rosary and began to pray:

Hail Mary . . .
The Lord . . .
Thou Art . . .
Amen.

Next bead.

The lady who'd been in the confessional when we first arrived had finished, so Mom stood up and took her turn with the awaiting clergyman. While Mom was away, I tried as hard as I could to concentrate on saying my prayers but started getting bored and looked over at my brother. His fingers were on the seventh bead, and he was struggling to stay awake. His lips moved a few times, then his eyes fluttered and his head began to bob. As soon as his chin hit his chest, his eyes flew open and he gently shook his head from side to side, trying to become more alert. Within seconds, he was once again lulled by the comforting darkness and heady smell of incense and burning candles. His eyes started fluttering a second time.

I leaned in closer to him and mischievously whispered his name, "Mikie."

The sound of my voice nudged him back to reality and he sleepily replied, "Yeah?"

Instead of saying something, I giggled mischievously, then lifted my buttock and let a fart fly out.

Mikie tried not to laugh and elbowed my shoulder. "Stop that, Dufas, you're going to get us in trouble."

I couldn't stop giggling and let another one rip.

Mikie lost his composure this time and started to snicker right along with me.

The old lady in the front pew turned around and eyeballed us again. Now she was really annoyed and let us know it. "Shhhhhh," she hissed at the two of us as she menacingly drew an arthritically crooked finger to her lips.

Mom came out of the confessional booth just then. I thought my brother and I were doomed for sure. Either Mom would be giving us a tongue lashing on the bus or, worse yet, she'd tell Daddy when we got home, and he'd give us the belt. The two of us froze immediately and scoured Mom's face for any signs of anger. Much to our surprise, her expression held no hint of disapproval whatsoever. In fact, she didn't even seem to notice we'd been horsing around. She had this wonderfully serene look about her; a look of absolute peace.

Usually I didn't stare at Mom, but I was staring at her now. She looked angelic, almost as though she were akin to the

29

majestic statues we'd passed earlier when we entered the church. Her eyes met mine as she smiled sweetly down upon me. Mikie elbowed me and said, "C'mon, Dufas, get your coat on."

I punched him in the arm and annoyingly replied, "Stop calling me Dufas, would you, Dufas."

"*You* are a Dufas," Mikie responded.

"You're the one who's the Dufas, Mikie!" I argued.

"I know you are, but what am I?" my brother quickly snapped back.

Mom put on her black wool coat and glanced down at the pew to make sure we hadn't forgotten any of our hats or mittens.

As we were about to exit through the chapel's giant, wooden doors, I gently dipped my fingers into the bowl of holy water and lightly dabbed it onto my forehead. I wondered if this clear liquid really was divine. I re-immersed my hand into the copper bowl and let a few of my fingers skim the water's surface a second time, then firmly grasped Mom's hand. I prayed that it was.

On the bus ride back home, my brother asked me if I wanted to play Bloody Knuckles. I rolled my eyes and replied, "Geezzz. All right already!" Mikie always won that stupid game.

Winter crawled on. By mid-February we'd had a warm spell, if that's what you can call it. The thermometer crept up to a whopping 38 degrees for four straight days; warm enough to reduce any remaining snow piles into crusty sheets of ice. With my outdoor options dwindling as fast as the melting snow, I turned my attention to that favorite all-American pastime . . . watching the tube. My daily social life began to revolve around episodes of *Bewitched, The Beverly Hillbillies, Mission*

30

Impossible, and, whenever I could get away with it, *Love American Style.*

One day Daddy asked, "Why've you been watching so much boob tube lately, Twink?" Daddy always referred to the television set as the "boob tube."

"Nothing else to do, Daddy," I replied matter-of-factly.

He didn't seem to like that response, and I could hear a loud "Hmmmm . . ." escape as he walked away. Faster than I could spit out the words "Black Gold, Texas Tea," Daddy had enrolled me in Camp Fire Girls, a youth group whose mission was to build confident, future leaders. Boob tube problem solved.

At first, I didn't want to go, assuming most of the other girls would know each other and I wouldn't fit in.

"You'll make some new friends," Daddy encouraged.

I wasn't buying it.

He forged ahead, "The troop leader told me you'll make lots of neat crafts. You know, like pinecone feeders for the birds. You want to help the birds, don't you, Twink?" Daddy ignored my shoulder shrug. "And you'll go on fun field trips. Hey Kiddo, maybe they'll even take you skiing."

"I only want to go skiing with you!" I replied in the poutiest voice I could muster.

"Oh, c'mon now, Twink. You don't really mean that," Daddy gently insisted.

My lips pursed even tighter.

I eventually succumbed to Daddy's persuasive rhetoric and agreed to let him take me to the first Camp Fire Girls meeting, trying not to whine too much on the drive over.

Meetings were held every Thursday evening at 7 p.m. sharp in Longfellow Elementary. At 6:45, Daddy maneuvered the Buick up to the school's main entrance, then stopped to let me hop out.

As I was reaching for the door handle, he instructed, "Be back at this same spot no later than 8:30, okay? It's dark out, and I don't want to have to worry about you."

"Yes, Daddy. I'll be here," I responded halfheartedly.

"Remember to have fun, Kiddo," Daddy told me as he was slowly easing the car away.

I said I'd try.

I'd never been to Longfellow Elementary before and was a bit disoriented when I entered the front doors. I stopped to study the beige-tiled walls, searching for direction before coming across a handwritten poster with a flaming arrow on it that said, "Camp Fire Meeting This Way." With some trepidation, I gradually made my way down the locker-lined halls to the designated meeting room. Daddy had penned the numbers 2-3-1 on the palm of my hand so I wouldn't forget where to go.

The room's sunflower-yellow walls and bright, florescent lights were in stark contrast to the unending blackness of the night that peered through the large glass windows. Most of the other attendees were standing in clusters, chitchatting about their new Barbie Doll accessories and scenes from the hit kid movie, *Escape from Witch Mountain.*

My face began to radiate more heat as it reddened with anxiety. I mustered a bit of nerve, then meekly shuffled over to the largest clique of girls and stood just outside their outer ring, attempting to make it look like I belonged. Every time one of the other girls looked my way, I offered a shy smile with the hope that the clique's parameters would widen, thereby officially letting me in. But they didn't seem to notice me, and I became more and more uncomfortable as the minutes passed.

Finally, our leader clapped her hands to get our attention and cheerfully greeted, "Welcome, everyone, welcome to the winter session of Camp Fire Girls troop number 437." She wrote the troop number on the chalkboard behind her, then smiled enthusiastically as she scanned her half-pint audience.

"I see a lot of familiar faces, but a couple new ones as well, so let's begin this evening by going around the room and taking turns shouting out your names." She quickly lifted her hand and pointed at one particular girl in the front, then nodded encouragingly in her direction.

"Tina!" the chosen girl shouted.

One by one the others randomly obliged:

"Lisa!"

"Cindy!"

"Tammy!"

"Kathy!"

When my turn came around, I shouted my name as courageously as I could, masquerading as a lion but feeling far more like a goat.

"Great!" said our leader after each of us had taken our turn. "My name's Ruth and this here's Barb and Donna," she said as she pointed to each of her co-leaders. Ruth seemed genuine and sweet and earthy, like someone you could trust with one of your biggest secrets. I was drawn to her from the get-go.

Ruth playfully asked, "Okay all you old-timers, are you ready to teach the newbies our song?"

"Yes, Ruth!" several girls said in unison.

"Here we go, then." Ruth led the chorus:

♫♫♫
You are my friend
I'll stand by you
Through thick and thin
I will be true

Ruth caught my eye and winked as she said, "Okay newbies, now it's your turn!"

The spotlight was on the remaining four of us as the other more seasoned girls shushed in order to let us have a go.

Although the lyrics were easy, we stumbled through our lines and sounded off key. I sensed the other three were as nervous as I was.

♫♫♫
You . . . you are my friend
I'll stand . . . stand by you
Through thick and thin
I will be . . . true

"All right!" shouted Ruth as she vigorously clapped her hands, "Way to go! Now, old-timers AND newbies, let's gather 'round in a circle. That's right. Grab onto one another's hands. All together now. Ready?"

The whole troop, 17 in all, sang the simple yet tender song of sisterly fellowship.

As we stood in that circle, hand in hand, I studied the faces of my youthful compatriots. Some were boisterous, some were silly, some were shy like I was, but all were harmonious at that single moment in time. I decided that I was going to like it here after all.

~♦ ♦ ♦~

I faithfully attended my troop meetings every Thursday evening, not only because it made Daddy happy, but also because I truly loved going. Playful camaraderie soon replaced my obsession with the fanciful lives of Jeannie and Master, Jethro, Granny and Miss Jane.

Ruth and her co-leaders put their hearts and souls into the brood they called Troop number 437. Among the many activities they had cleverly devised were the ever-popular art projects. Daisies blossomed from multi-colored pipe cleaners; cotton balls and construction paper gave way to three-dimensional bunnies; hues of pink, yellow and purple dye transformed plain old hard-boiled eggs into beautiful Easter figurines. We even made pinecone bird feeders, just like Daddy had said.

I was proud of my budding creations and ever so carefully divvied them up. Sometimes Daddy was the lucky recipient, and at other times it was Mom. I loved the way she would gently cradle my treasure in her hands, as though it belonged in a shiny, glass case. She'd place it on one side of her bedroom dresser next to all the others until a raging battle ensued between the perfume bottle army and the kitsch brigade.

Winter's seasonal closure signaled the approaching dismantlement of our troop, at least during the summer months, but our final and most challenging task still lay ahead. The night Daddy picked me up after the annual Candy Drive rally, I was eager to tell him all about it.

"Ruth says we're suppose to make goals and think up a, um, stragegy."

"Strategy," Daddy corrected.

"Yeah, a strategy for what we're going to do, and then Ruth said to get out there and sell, sell, sell! Will you help me, Daddy?" I pleaded.

"You know I will, Kiddo."

Satisfied with his answer I leaned back against the car seat and pondered Ruth's directives at the rally. "Daddy?"

"Uh, huh?"

"Do you think I'll be able to sell enough candy to get the Super Seller patch?" I earnestly inquired.

He gave me a knowing look, and then said, "Have I ever let you down before?"

I beamed back and silently thought . . . no. In all of my young life, Daddy had never let me down.

~◆ ◆ ◆~

35

I was raring to test my strategy that following Saturday. It was a partially cloudy day, and the air remained cool and damp. It wasn't winter weather, but it didn't feel like springtime either, so Daddy bundled the top half of me in a navy, wool pea coat and stuck rubber ducky boots on my feet.

Armed with my blank, candy sign-up sheet and a pen that Daddy had tied around my wrist, I was ready to pound the pavement.

As I stood near the front door waiting for my goodbye hug, Daddy prompted, "What's our team name?"

"Supersonic Sellers!" I enthusiastically replied as I lifted my hand high into the air and curled my fingers into an *I'm number one* symbol.

"And what's our team motto?" Coach Daddy asked again.

"Camp Fire candy is the Feel Good candy!"

"Because why?"

"Because you can enjoy several flavors of chocolaty goodness while supporting the future leaders of tomorrow." I looked at him sideways, hoping that I'd said it right.

"That's my girl!" he encouraged as he playfully tussled my hair. "Now, go get 'em, Super Seller!"

I threw my arms open, and he bent down to give me a hug and a peck on the cheek.

"Are you sure you don't want me to go with you?" he asked.

"Naw, it's okay," I told him.

Daddy smiled down at me then opened the front door. At the ripe age of seven-and-three-quarters, I was headed out on my first entrepreneurial endeavor.

36

After a few hours and hundreds of footsteps later, I arrived back home just as dusk was beginning to mask the sky. When I opened the door Daddy was waiting for me and helped me out of my coat and rubber ducky boots. "How'd you do today, Twink?" he curiously inquired.

"Well," I began, "I sold 5 boxes of Caramel Whirls, 10 boxes of Almond Roca Buttercrunch and 6, no I mean, 7 boxes of Mint Meltaways."

"That's fantastic! How come you don't sound too happy about it?"

"Daddy, you don't understand," I explained, gesturing wildly with my hands. "I need to sell a total of 100 entire boxes before I can get the Super Seller patch."

Daddy sat down on the piano bench in the living room and slapped his thighs with both hands. As I hopped up onto his lap, he said, "We'll get you your patch, Kiddo. You have the whole week left to make your goal."

"Yeah, I guess you're right," I said, my hope resurfacing as I realized that I still had a shot.

With renewed resolve, I was out every day the next week selling my little heart out. Some people weren't home, others had already bought candy from someone else, and some just plain didn't want any . . . period. "It gives you cavities and zits!" one crabby, old man snapped before slamming the door in my face.

Nevertheless, I persevered in the face of adversity, and at week's end Daddy tallied the results.

"I'm proud of you, Kiddo, you sold 82 boxes of candy!"

"Only 82?" I moaned.

"Not just ONLY, that's a heck of a lot," Daddy encouraged.

"Yeah, I guess so," I said disappointedly as I shrugged my shoulders, realizing the Super Seller Patch was now out of reach. I'd have to wait another year before trying again.

"Thanks, Daddy," I said over my shoulder as I turned and began to slouch my way up to my room.

It was about a month later when I arrived home from school to find boxes and boxes of Camp Fire Girls candy piled neatly in a corner of our living room next to the radiator.

Daddy had heard me come in and met me at the front door.

"Wow! Look at all this candy!" I exclaimed as I stared at the treasure trove.

"Let's see just how much you sold," he said.

"But Daddy, I already know how much . . . 82 boxes."

"Why don't we double check, okay?" he playfully insisted.

With eyes wide open, I looked at Daddy, then back at the boxes. I started to count. One, two, three . . . twenty-seven, thirty-five, fifty-four, seventy-three, eighty . . . ninety . . . one hundred. Wait, one hundred? My jaw dropped open.

"Something's not right," I declared and carefully counted each box a second time only to discover the same result.

"I believe you counted right," Daddy said mischievously. "Here." He handed me my sign-up sheet that was blanketed with surnames, addresses and phone numbers. Starting at the top, I began scanning the long list of names. When I got to the very last one, I stopped and looked up at him in disbelief. It said R.V. Waters. Daddy had ordered 18 boxes of P-Nutties from the Supersonic Sellers team.

He grinned and said, "I told you the Super Seller patch would be yours."

I was jumping up and down now, hugging him and whooping, "You are the best Daddy in the whole, wide world!"

And just like he said, Daddy never let me down.

Before I knew it, the days were getting longer. Whatever was left of the vanishing snow finally melted once and for all, turning to liquid and fueling minute, icy rivers along the sloping curbs of our boulevards. The neighborhood kids all took turns racing the cheap, plastic boats we'd exhumed from the depths of cereal boxes.

One morning in early June, Daddy was in the mood to celebrate summer's arrival with a picnic by the lake. As soon as the Coleman cooler had been planted firmly in between my brother and me in the back seat and Mom had slid into the passenger's side, the Buick was approved for takeoff.

"Where're we going to today, Daddy?" Mikie asked cheerily.

"Why, I thought we'd go check out Lake Calhoun. How does that sound?"

"Yeah!" Mikie said. "They have super good ice cream at Calhoun."

I licked my upper lip at the thought of my all-time favorite food, then spontaneously started bobbing back and forth. "You scream, I scream, we all scream for ice cream," I chanted. Before long, Mikie joined in. The two of us must have blurted out that ditty about ten or twelve times before Daddy finally turned around and gave us the *simmer down* look.

Our drive to Calhoun was expectedly short, and we could see the tops of the colorful boat sails gently flapping in the wind as the lake came into view. Daddy slipped the Buick into an empty spot in the public parking lot, then hastily got out of the car without bothering to extract the Coleman. "C'mon gang. I've got something I want to show you," he said as he motioned for us to follow. He led us down toward the water, past the refectory, past the herd of lifeguard boats and rental canoes. We could tell by the way Daddy was walking that he was excited, and our anticipation was building as we followed closely behind.

39

We gathered around him at the end of one of the long, wooden docks. Daddy pointed toward a white Catamaran that resembled so many others I'd come to know in summers past. "Well, what do you guys think about that Cat over there?" he asked, grinning widely.

Mikie and I attempted to feign fascination, but Daddy could sense our confusion.

"Why, that's not just any Cat, gang. That just so happens to be *our* Cat!"

The three of us looked at him in amazement.

"Wow, really?! Cool!" Mikie exclaimed.

"When do we get to take a ride, Daddy? Now? Can we go now?!" I squealed, unable to contain my excitement.

"Rick, when did you buy that boat?" Mom asked, a little stunned. "I didn't think we could afford it for another year."

Daddy was too hopped up on adrenalin to bother with what he considered an insignificant detail, so he quickly sidestepped Mom's questioning glances. "We'll talk about it later, Honey. Just sit back and enjoy the ride."

Once on board and adorned in life preservers and our favorite eyewear, we were raring to hit the high seas.

"I'm Sinbad," Mikie said as he retrieved his invisible sword from its sheath and began slicing it through the air. "Sinbad of the Seven Seas! Take that and that and that!" Apparently, he was dueling for gold.

As Daddy was maneuvering the craft away from the shoreline, he instructed us to keep a lid on the horsing around and, most importantly, to be wary of what he referred to as "the boom."

"Listen up, everyone," he began. "This boom is going to shift from one side of the boat to the other and when it does, what are you going to do?" he asked as he tapped the long, horizontal pole affixed to the bottom of the sails.

Mikie and I gave each other "heck if I know" glances. Mom didn't say anything at all.

"Duck, gang! You'll need to duck," Daddy explained. "It's important that you pay attention, okay? Because if this little hummer hits any of you, I'm going to have to fish you out of the lake."

We all agreed that we didn't want to be fished out of the lake.

At the onset of our maiden voyage, the sun shone brightly above bejeweled waters. Daddy was uncommonly carefree as he skillfully captained the U.S.S. La Reine, inhaling all this aquatic kingdom had to offer. My brother and I were equally enthralled.

"Hey, Mikie," I said. "This is even more fun than skiing!"

I craned my neck skyward to gaze up at the tall, white sail cloths. A pair of ducks flew overhead and skidded into the water, bobbing in our wake as we passed. "Quack, quack, quack!" I mimicked back.

"Anybody up for some grub?" Daddy asked as he flipped open the lid of the Coleman.

"Me!" I chirped.

"Yeah!" said Mikie.

Daddy looked over at Mom, "How about you, Rainy?"

"What . . . oh sure," she answered distantly.

He took out a stack of homemade peanut butter and jelly sandwiches and a couple cans of Shasta, then handed them to Mom who handed them to us. Mikie and I put our opened pop cans next to us on the hard, plastic seat, but they kept on sliding away, almost toppling to the ground. Daddy pointed to the can he'd strategically positioned in between his legs and motioned for us to do the same.

Just about the time we were finishing our noontime snack, a platoon of daunting clouds rolled in from the west. The water, once gentle, began to slap against the boat's hull, while the sail cloths rebelliously whipped in the wind, as if tired of obeying their new master.

41

Concern replaced serenity on Daddy's face. "Shit," I heard him swear under his breath. "Looks like some bad weather's coming our way, gang. We're going to have to head on in." At that moment Daddy became a one-man-crew, feverishly reeling in this rope and loosening up that one, trying to shift the Cat back toward shore's safety before the rain fell.

A bolt of thunder cracked in the distance, giving my brother and me a case of the shivers. We tightened our preservers, slid off the seats and crouched down in the center of the boat. The air was thick with moisture, and we knew it was going to start pouring any second. Just then, the boom started to shift. Daddy saw it head toward Mom and yelled, "Rainy, get down! Now!" But, Mom had been engulfed in the fog of anti-hallucinogens all afternoon and was slow to react. As the boom grazed the back of her shoulder, Mikie and I screamed. Daddy lunged toward her while desperately trying to stay in control of his vessel. Mom reeled toward the edge of the boat, but the force of the blow wasn't strong enough to send her overboard. Daddy grabbed on to her arm, allowing her time to regain her balance and crawl into the Cat's depressed bottom alongside my brother and me.

As the rushing rain ruthlessly pelted our skin, Daddy steadily sailed across the small lake and back to the dock in a matter of minutes. "Wait in the refectory while I tie up the boat!" he shouted above the wind as he hurried to extract us. As soon as Mikie and I hit the dock, we raced across the aged, wooden planks as fast as we could toward the shelter of the Mediterranean-style beach bar while Mom struggled to keep up, extending one arm across the side of her face to shield her from the elements.

"Hurry up, Mom! Hurry! Come on!" my brother and I hollered from beneath the bar's protective canopy until she was safely beside us.

A few minutes later, Daddy found the three of us huddled together in a semi-circle, shivering more from the ordeal than from the cold rain.

"We're okay, gang, everyone's okay," he assured as he approached, handing each of us a dry towel that he'd taken from the car.

He looked over at Mom. "How are you doing, Rainy?" he asked as he gently wiped away her running mascara with his thumb.

"All right, I guess," she wearily replied while staring at a smashed piece of popcorn on the ground. "I just need to rest for a bit."

Daddy's eyes lingered on her ashen face, and then turned his attention to me. "C'mon, Twink," he said as he gently grabbed a hold of my damp hand. "Let's go get some of that ice cream you've been itching for while we wait this thing out."

My spirits rose as soon as I saw the "open" sign near the ice cream window, and in true competitive spirit I raced my brother to be the first in line. As the rain battered the ground, the four of us sat on a wooden bench in the covered courtyard, protected from the storm's breath by our tattered beach towels. My brother and I eagerly devoured our fast melting confection before it oozed onto our fingers while Daddy kept a vigilant eye on his prized vessel as it rocked to the rhythm of the stormy beat. And Mom, well, she just stared out toward the direction of the lake, surrounded by her family yet completely alone, lost in a world that belonged only to her.

We still went sailing after that day, but it would never again be a family affair. Daddy often took my brother and me along, and sometimes he just went by himself. Mom's maiden voyage, however, would prove to be her last.

~ ♦ ♦ ♦ ~

43

The last licks of summer's heat were fading fast, and Mikie and I would soon be faced with a brand new regimen of lessons to be learned and homework assignments to be completed. The end of summer wasn't exactly all that bad because it also ushered in our second favorite holiday . . . the annual Minnesota tradition known as the state fair. Daddy knew the explosive joy it brought and never let a September pass without at least one visit to this ghetto-fied version of Disneyland.

We loved the fair far more than we loved Santa Claus or even Christmas presents, for that matter, revering it as the gateway to a place where all was right with the world. The streets, once mummified by winter's touch, were now more alive than a fireworks display on the Fourth of July. One concession booth after another dotted the sugar-lined avenues, brimming with cinnamon coated mini-donuts, buttery caramel apples, beehives of silky cotton candy and artificial fruit-flavored Sno Cones in a variety of colors. Hovering vendors sporting burnt tans hawked red and orange and lime-green stuffed animals and shiny, silver souvenirs that no kid could live without. There were sky rides and carpet rides and water rides galore. And, a fistful of balloons was a mere appeal away.

Our fair itinerary was always the same, and this year would prove to be no different. The concession booths were our first stop, where we charged up our engines on all the crystallized speed we could handle. Next came the livestock barns, awash in smells so distinctive that we'd wisely learned from seasons past to gobble the last of our food before entering. Because horses were the favorite of both my brother and me, we never had to argue about where to go first. Once inside the building, I dashed up and down the aisles, searching for the handsome steed whose head was pressed against the stall's bars. As soon as I spied him, I skidded to a halt and longingly stared up into his glassy, brown orbs, wishing I were tall enough to stroke him. Daddy came up beside me and gently took my hand, then led me away toward the exit.

"There's plenty more to see, Twink," he reminded as I hesitantly obeyed, craning my neck backwards for one last glance.

"Can we get a pony, Daddy? Pleazzze??? Can we, Daddy???" I begged. My brother started to neigh as we left the horses behind and headed for a nearby cattle barn.

Once we'd had our yearly fill of farm animal sights and sounds, we plowed through the sea of gluttonous humanity to the other side of the fairgrounds, several blocks away. Our hard-won reward was the most enchanting parcel of terra firma in the entire world. It was there, at Kid-e-Land, where my brother and I could truly live out our fantasies. We could fly a jet plane or drive a sports car without ever toting a license; we could even captain our very own boat, just like our Daddy.

Daddy patiently followed behind, paying for one ride after another, and snapping Kodak moments in between bites of his corn dog or cheese dog or whatever dog was close at hand. After a few hours, Daddy told us that we should think about calling it a day. "But Daddy," I pleaded, "just one more ride? Pleazzze?" He easily gave in, knowing I couldn't leave the fair without a final go-round on my most treasured amusement . . . the carousel.

Mikie thought the carousel was for sissies and opted to wait on the sidelines with Daddy. This, I didn't understand. How could he not be as entranced as I was by the alluring sounds of the calliope?

Daddy's wallet readily opened again for my final admission ticket, then he followed behind as I raced up to the painted ponies, frozen in mid-pose, and carefully selected my companion. "Look how pretty, Daddy!" I said as I pointed to the chosen one, a cream-colored beauty with alert, black eyes and an elaborate mane of pinks and purples. Daddy lifted me onto the saddle, then snapped a photo for posterity before

45

stepping away and walking back to my brother's side. As the carousel began spinning, something akin to a wet kiss brushed my cheek. It was a solitary bubble in a parade of many that began floating past. I reached out to catch another as it grazed my shoulder. Turning my attention to the crowd, I searched for Daddy, then gave him a big, happy grin and vigorously waved his way. A light breeze kicked up and caressed the side of my face, as if trying to lull me into another world. I tightened my grip on the golden pole in front of me, then closed my eyes and let my pony guide me to a place of warmth and light and comfort, a place of unexpected peace.

After the calliope had hit its last note, and the beautiful beasts slowed to a stop, a state of melancholy suddenly washed over me. I kept my eyes tightly closed and my slender hands fastened to the pole, not yet ready to leave behind this magical place of distraction.

As the hot, humid days drifted past, Mom drifted right along with them, retreating deep into the chasm of her own mind in the company of her queen-sized bed. I wanted her to feel better, to *be* better, but the ghostly shadows blocking her path to a normal life ominously loomed, causing her to stumble and lose her way.

I continued to seek her out, yearning to capture her elusive attention. Often awaiting me was a stranger in the dark, underneath the covers, conversing with her assembly of angels and demons. Sometimes, Mom's interludes were bizarrely seductive as she caressed her pillow and whispered sweet nothings, while at other times, venomous voices and crazed, fluttering eyes were what infiltrated the stillness of her refuge.

The stark reality of who my mother was becoming frightened me out of my wits. As her ever-changing faces more frequently revealed themselves, the unrelenting madness began

46

eerily weaving into the daily fabric of my life. It was during that period when I started to withdraw from her, realizing that the woman holed up in the dark, corner bedroom was never going to be the mother I so desperately needed. She simply belonged to something else.

A few weeks after the beginning of the new school year, Mom's unremitting descent finally caught up with our little family. Mikie and I had been outside, playing kick-the-can with our friends before dinnertime. I had to go number one real bad, so I ran inside the house and up to the second floor bathroom. As I approached, I could hear loud voices coming from Mom's bedroom down the hall. At first, I assumed that she was just having another of her episodes, but soon realized that not all of the voices were hers. This time one of them was Daddy's. I could tell by his tone that he was angry. I became really nervous, and that made me have to tinkle even more. Standing with my legs crossed, I weighed my options, then squeezed my thighs together as tightly as I could. Ever so quietly, I bypassed the bathroom and awkwardly waddled down the hall in the direction of my parents.

"Are you ever going to get out of that goddamn bed?!" Daddy spat. "All you do is sleep, piss, smoke and read the damn Bible. Don't you realize that we have a family to take care of? Bills to pay?"

I didn't hear Mom say anything back.

Daddy kept on going, "Is there ever one second in that ridiculous, little brain of yours when you think about me and all that I've sacrificed for you? For the kids? I wanted so much more than this pathetic life. It's fucking pathetic! Don't *you* ever want more than this?!"

After several seconds of silence I heard Mom apathetically respond, "I'm sorry, Rick."

47

My lip started quivering and I thought a sob was going to bust out, so I clenched my teeth as hard as I could.

"You're the one who wanted these kids, not me," Daddy continued. "I wanted to teach for a few years, save enough money to start my own business . . . Hell, maybe even buy my own goddamn plane someday. How am I supposed to do that now? Can you tell me?! Huh?!"

I couldn't listen to any more of it. My lip was shaking really hard, and I was pretty sure I was going to pee my pants. I backed away toward the stairs, turned and ran down to the bathroom on the first floor. I quickly closed the door and locked it. My chest was heaving now as silent sobs began to escape. Hot tears cascaded down my face as I hopped up onto the stool and did my business. Long after the last drop of liquid had drained from my body, I remained seated on the toilet, staring at the floor and sobbing as quietly as I could. I cried until my tear ducts ran dry, then redressed myself and washed my hands.

"How could Daddy say those things? Didn't he love me anymore?" I mournfully thought to myself.

Throughout all our troubled times, Daddy had been my rock, my very reason to believe that, in the end, everything really was going to be okay. Now nothing, not even Daddy, made sense to me anymore.

Mom and Daddy were nowhere in sight when Mikie and I arrived home from school the next day. Grandma was sitting on the living room couch talking to someone who we couldn't yet see. As we got closer, a woman with her coat still on came into view. She stood up and quickly walked over to greet us.

"Hi kids, my name's Jeanine. I'm a social worker with the county, and I'm here to help you out." She politely shook our hands and tried to smile. "Your mom's not doing so good right now, so she had to go to the hospital. Now, don't you worry, okay? She is going to be just fine." Jeanine searched our faces for sufficient signs of comprehension.

My eyes fled to Grandma. She was staring at the blank television screen and sporadically mumbling, "Mercy . . . mercy . . ." as she remained seated with her hands clasped together in her lap.

Jeanine continued. "Your dad requested that we take you to a safe place, so you'll be staying in a temporary foster home until your family situation can be resolved. It's a real nice place . . . lots of other kids to play with, and the people who will be taking care of you are just super."

Mikie and I weren't buying Jeanine's feigned consolation and exchanged fearful looks, then stepped closer to one another.

Grandma was now slowly shaking her head from side to side, and I could still faintly hear her chanting, "Mercy . . . mercy . . ." underneath her breath.

"Grandma?" I said with panic in my voice, "why do we have to go away? Couldn't you take care of us until Daddy gets back?" I went over to the couch and sat down next to her.

She put her arm around me but continued staring at the blank television screen. "No, Honey, I can't. Not now. I don't know what is going to happen." She squeezed me a little tighter then said despondently, "I'm sorry, Dear. I really am."

Jeanine continued the dialogue of her purpose, "Your grandma has already packed your bags, so why don't you kids go ahead and grab them so that we can be on our way."

At first, Mikie and I were shell-shocked and unable to move. Things had gotten pretty rough for us at times, but through it all we'd never had to live with anyone else besides our Mom and Dad, and sometimes Grandma—this was a first. We finally pulled ourselves together, then went to our respective bedrooms and collected our belongings. Neither of us said anything to the other. We were terrified and on the brink of bawling. There really wasn't anything worth saying anyway.

With teardrops as big as freshwater pearls welling up in the corners of our eyes, we kissed our Grandma and told her how much we loved her. She hugged us hard as she said her goodbyes and told us that she loved us, too.

From that point forward, everything seemed to be moving in slow motion. We slid into the back seat of Jeanine's Corvair, then she drove us in weighty silence to a suburb on the other side of the city.

After what felt like a very long car ride, we pulled into someone's driveway. My brother and I remained seated as we emptily stared at the gray-sided rambler that was to be our temporary home.

Jeanine escorted us to the front door, and then rang the bell. A woman sporting a plastic smile who looked to be in her early 40s answered. Virginia introduced herself, then Jeanine gave each of us a pat on the shoulder and told us she'd be back in a few weeks.

There we were and that was that.

Plastic Smiling Virginia was a big phony baloney . . . that much I'd gathered right away. As soon as Jeanine had left, Virginia became detached and expressionless. She was a somewhat frumpy and dumpy woman, short with a pale, puffy face and coiffed, red hair that failed to be trendy.

"Fred! Fre-ed!!" Virginia squawked. "The new kids are here. Fre-ed!!"

Fred didn't answer.

"Hmmmm," she muttered absently, "he must be in the basement again."

"Come in, kids," she said as she motioned with her arm. "I'll introduce you to the others."

"K," I said, my eyes earnestly searching the floor.

"K," Mikie said.

Eight other kids, ranging in age from 7 months to 16 years, were going to be our new housemates. One of the eight was Vanessa, Virginia and Fred's sole, biological child. They called her Nessie for short, but I would later refer to her as the Loch Ness Monster. The rest of the kids were basically in the same sad situation as Mikie and I, and each had a sobriety about them that most their age didn't even comprehend.

After Virginia had showed us to our appointed spaces, we dropped off our belongings. "Well now, you're just in time for dinner. We'll be eating in a bit," she said lethargically before nodding her head in the direction of the living room. "Go ahead and watch TV while I get everything ready, and I'll call you when it's time."

Mikie and I, still in shock, silently obeyed and shuffled into the living room where we shyly looked around, then sat down next to one another on the sofa. The minutes slowly passed as we halfheartedly watched *Gilligan's Island* until we heard Virginia yell, "Dinner! Time for dinner!" At that moment, everyone in the house stopped what they were doing and saddled up to the dining room table. Virginia soon brought forth platefuls of hot dogs, creamed corn and unnaturally orange, government cheese. This would serve as our meal several times a week.

After seating herself, Virginia clasped her hands together and began to speak with authority, "Let us pray," she said dramatically, then closed her eyes. All present obediently bowed their heads and, in unison, recited the mealtime prayer:

"Bless us oh Lord for these thy gifts which we are about to receive through thy bounty o Christ our Lord. Amen."

This was my own, personal prayer that I said in my head:

"Dear Lord,
        What have you done with my Mommy and Daddy? Please bring them back. From now on, I will be extra good . . . I promise."

51

~♦ ♦ ♦~

The days literally dragged on. In the past, I'd always managed to wade through my family's river of dysfunction. But now, for the first time, I started to lose interest in life and shifted into a mode of survival. I got up when I was supposed to, brushed my teeth at my allotted time, and didn't speak unless someone else started a conversation first. It was during that time when I began to love school more than ever. It became my sanctuary. I sought solace in multiplication tables and gym class and *Charlotte's Web*.

At lunchtime, I didn't bother with infiltrating any of the cliques that populated the cafeteria. Instead, I kept to myself, sitting quietly at the end of a vacant table and focusing on my food. During that particular time, the government had come out with an innovative way to entice school children to consume more dairy by encasing milk in clear, plastic sacks that mimicked small breasts. Each day during the noon hour, I'd delicately pierce my miniature boob bag with my miniature straw and pray that its contents wouldn't spurt out all over the table. Then I'd separate the small mounds of food on my tray so that the canned vegetables were unable to mingle with the fruits.

Mikie and I would ride the school bus home together every day, and sometimes Nessie would be on it. Most of the time she ignored us and would respond with a sneer if we ever dared say, "Hi." I can vividly recall one particular day on that bus. Mikie and I were seated together as usual, I next to the window and Mikie near the aisle. Loch Ness had boarded after the two of us and was forced to sit across the aisle from my brother for lack of any other empty seat. As was her usual manner, she pretended like she had no idea who we were. Once the bus had reached our exit, my brother hopped into the aisle ahead of Loch Ness and got off. He wasn't trying to one-up her, but that's exactly how she took it. While my brother was waiting for me outside, Loch Ness passed by and punched him in the arm. "Better not do that again, Fat Boy," she hissed. Mikie grimaced, "What'd you do that for? Geez . . ."

Loch Ness didn't bother answering, arrogantly flicked her long, blond hair in the wind as she sauntered all the way home in front of us.

My favorite time of the day was when Mikie and I arrived home from school. It always felt like that feeling you get just before you open a birthday present. We'd walk in the front door, and I'd race to the room I shared with two other girls. My heart would beat a little faster whenever I'd find a small, white envelope with the words "Hennepin County Hospital, Ward M" printed in the top left-hand corner lying on top of my bedspread. I'd snatch the already opened letter from its casing and quickly scan Mom's barely legible scrawl. Short quips like, "Momma loves you, Sweetheart" and "God is smiling down on you, Honey" rested in my hands, but word of my release was never mentioned. As quickly as you can pop a black balloon, my private birthday party would end.

As promised, Jeanine came to see us every other Wednesday after school. On those particular days, I'd anxiously wait close to the big, bay window in the living room so that I could easily spot her Corvair. I whiled away my nervous energy by coloring animals onto blank pieces of paper and daydreaming of the life I once knew. Jeanine would eventually pull into the drive, and Plastic Smiling Virginia would answer the door acting just as sweet as farmer's market strawberry pie.

Virginia would lead Jeanine, my brother and me into the formal dining room, which *just so happened* to be strategically adjacent to her kitchen, then remain within earshot as she

53

tended to some nearby, opportune task, like washing the dishes or cleaning out the fridge.

Jeanine had such caring, brown eyes, and I knew her heart went out to us each time she rolled through her scripted dialogue to ask how we were getting along. Whenever it was our turn to respond, I wanted to yell and scream at the top of my lungs and tell her how horrible this place was. I wanted to tell her about all my opened letters, and about the time Fred pushed Mikie down the basement stairs after he'd tried to retrieve his comic book from Loch Ness, or the time Virginia and I were in the van with the unbuckled 7-month-old who was thrown face first onto the floor at a sudden red light, or how I sat outside for hours on the grass in the backyard, searching endlessly for that ever-evasive four-leaf clover that was going to be our ticket out of this hell hole. But, the harsh reality was that I could never say what I so desperately needed to say because I was well aware that Virginia would hear me, and I simply couldn't afford to live with the consequences.

Our bi-weekly visits with Jeanine never lasted more than half an hour. Each time she closed her manila folder and got up to leave, my eyes would silently beg her to help us, wishing through some miracle that she possessed the power to read minds. She'd kindly smile and tell us to take care of ourselves until next time. "Thanks, Jeanine," my brother and I would solemnly answer in unison.

Every other Wednesday, as she made her way back to the front door, I'd swallow hard the bump that had swelled in my throat.

Each day bled into the next. Curriculum, routines and daydreams became the oxygen of my life. As no word of freedom emerged, I began to fear that my brother and I had become abandoned for good. Mom's incoherent letters from

54

the mental hospital continued to appear on top of my bedspread from time to time. We never received any letters from Daddy. He didn't even call. He must have finally lost his grip on the family tree and was somewhere out there in the wind, hanging by a thread.

Jeanine's visits seemed to be the only thing left to look forward to. I will never forget what happened on one particular Wednesday as I was waiting for her in my appointed spot, watching her approach the house after she'd gotten out of her car. Something was considerably different about her expression. She wasn't looking at the pavement as she normally did but, rather, her eyes were clearly focused on the front door, and her strides were longer and faster. I couldn't be sure, but I thought I'd even detected a slight smile on her lips. Virginia met her at the door and let her in, but this time Virginia's phony baloneyness didn't surface. Instead, her sober gaze greeted Jeanine robotically. As soon as my brother entered the room, Jeanine told us the news we'd been waiting lifetimes to hear. WE . . . WERE . . . GOING . . . HOME. Mikie and I beamed at each other uncontrollably.

"Do we go get our things now? I mean . . . Or what should we do?" Mikie asked.

Jeanine directed us to pack our bags right away. I ran to my room as fast as I could, and grabbed my suitcase from the closet. As I frantically scooped out the contents of my dresser drawer, something caught my eye, dissolving my commotion. Lying at the bottom of my clutter was a small figurine of Mother Mary, one that Grandma had slipped into my coat pocket on the day we'd said our goodbyes. As I cradled it in the palm of my hand, I wondered if there really was a God after all. Maybe he was smiling down on me just like Mom had said. Maybe there had just been too many other people who needed saving before it was our turn. I grabbed one of my socks and gently inserted the icon, rolling it up to give her extra protection and surrounding her in the cushion of my under

55

garments. I closed the lid of my suitcase, took one last look around the room, then ushered my cargo out to the front door.

Mikie had beaten me to it and was waiting with Jeanine in the entryway. Virginia shrilly called out "Fre-ed ! Fre-ed !" who eventually emerged from the basement to help carry our bags to Jeanine's car. As my brother and I were hurrying out the front door, Virginia went through the motions of telling us that she'd surely miss our company. I could see in her eyes that the more likely sentiment was that of displeasure in losing two of her nine meal tickets.

While Fred was busy loading our things into the trunk, Mikie and I bolted down the steps toward the getaway vehicle, sweet relief embedded in every muscle. Jeanine passed by him on her way to the driver's seat and told him she'd be in touch. He just said, "Yep," then shut the trunk and walked back up to the house.

Time was no longer running in slow motion as my brother and I ecstatically hopped into the backseat of the Corvair like a couple of bandits fleeing the scene of a bank heist.

As the engine turned over and began to hum, I felt with overwhelming gratefulness that the darkest of my days had finally passed. I grabbed my brother's hand and tightly squeezed it all the way home.

Home. I was home at last. I wasn't sure if I would ever see this place again. My room was exactly as I had left it, furnished in the gold-gilded bedroom set that Daddy had bought at Sears especially for my 7th birthday. Laid out beside my pillow was my favorite white blankie, the one I dragged behind me everywhere I went until it turned a purple shade of gray. Teddy was lying on top of the covers at his appointed

56

post, arms outstretched, patiently waiting to be hushed into slumber once more by my side.

Everything felt surreal when I crawled into bed that night. Had I gotten tangled up in one of my many daydreams? Or, had the foster home been nothing more than a long and scary nightmare? The faint light from the hallway drifted into my room, assuring me that time was here and now. I tried to keep my eyes open for as long as I could, wanting to capture this moment as if it were a beautiful butterfly. I could hear Daddy across the hall in the bathroom, rustling about as he readied himself for bed. To feel his presence so near once more was powerful comfort indeed. My first minute passed in bliss as I skimmed the edge of unconsciousness; my second, in serenity. I never made it to the third.

Mikie and I easily stepped back into our old lives, and it seemed as though Mom and Daddy had picked up the pieces of theirs. No explanation was ever given as to why my brother and I had been sent away. At the time, we never really thought much about it, preferring to bury it deep within and praying it would never happen again.

Whenever Daddy wasn't around I spent my free time with girlfriends, choosing to leave Mom to her own devices. It was true that I had lots of them, plenty to keep me occupied, but there was never one special enough to bestow upon her the prized title of "best." Never, that is to say, until the day I met Sammie.

It was early May, 1974. I was outside playing hopscotch with a couple of other girls when this sweet looking kid with brown, curly hair tied back in a ponytail walked up to us and introduced herself. She told us that she'd just moved into the neighborhood and asked if she could join us. My friends and I looked at each other, shrugged, then said, "sure thing."

57

As dusk eclipsed the day, we all agreed that it was time to head for home. I looked over at Sammie to get her attention, then pointed to my house halfway down the block. "Mine's number 2221," I said, "the blue one. Come and get me if you ever want to play again." She told me she would and we shyly exchanged smiles as we said our goodbyes. From that day forward we were like blood sisters.

Sammie was the only child of a budding, young lawyer and her live-in lover, Les. The three of them resided in a newly built townhouse located just a block away, which soon became my favorite hangout. I loved the fresh way it smelled, like cloves and lemon, and how it warmly welcomed golden sunlight into every corner.

Whenever I would visit, Sammie's mom, Chana, was usually reading a book on the couch with her feet propped up or in the kitchen cooking. The notion and commotion of life never seemed to weigh her down, as was the case with Mom. She never once excused herself to retire to her bedroom, and I most certainly never caught her whispering dark secrets to invisible strangers. She was spirited and strong, and I liked her a lot.

Their spacious townhouse occupied three separate levels, the lowest of which had long since been surrendered to the whims of my new best friend. The completely finished space was a preteen's dream haven, featuring a mammoth, brown sectional that Sammie and I mercilessly jumped upon until the cushions had so many rips and lumps that it was no longer fit for company.

Sammie had her own TV, her own stereo, her own phone. Man, she even had her own electric organ, which we set up in the far corner of the room next to the stereo. That prime piece of real estate became our official recording studio. To authenticate our band, we concocted microphones from marshmallows glued onto pointed pencils, and Chana bought us a used tambourine at a garage sale. Les' contribution was an old, electric guitar from his college gigs with The Fender Benders. Sammie and I each took a turn strapping it around our bony, little shoulders, but it was far too heavy and practically sent us spiraling into a face plant, so we kept it on a stand in the corner just for looks.

I was lucky that Sammie was an only child. There was room for me here.

Sammie and I had slumber parties at her house almost every weekend. She had these neat, wooden bunk beds in her room and always called dibs on the top bunk, relegating me to the bottom, but I never minded. After our evening bubble bath, we'd crawl into the warmth of our freshly laundered sheets and watch weekend family night specials until the news came on.

One night, well into the wee hours, I was awakened by the muffled sounds of giggling and laughter. I wiped the sleep out of my eyes, then lifted my head from the pillow and looked around the room. I could hear Sammie's even breathing above me and knew that she was still sound asleep. Moon shadows danced in the glow of the hallway, eventually giving way to Chana and Les who were heatedly mingling and commingling, caressing and kissing a naked path from their bedroom to the bathroom that was just outside our door. The soothing sound of gently flowing water spilled into the tub. They paid no mind to modesty as they moved their forum from the bathroom back to their bed, and soon, soft moans readily replaced giggles in the room next door.

Long after lunar stillness had crept back into the darkness, I had a hard time shedding those erotic images. At eight years old, I hadn't the slightest desire to participate in such foreign acts of adult behavior, yet couldn't help but be captivated by a few, wayward sparks of that marvelous, vibrant energy. I swore that someday, when I grew up, I was going to have that, too, and the blood running through my veins would flow into a valley where the scent of despair never dared permeate.

~ ♦ ♦ ♦ ~

The summer months of 1974 were unbearably hot and humid. Every time I played a game of neighborhood kickball, beads of sweat would slither down my face while my ankles turned bloody from failed attempts at warding off all of the mosquitoes.

July, the month of my birth, was merely weeks away, and Daddy promised to take me wherever I wanted to go as a special treat on my big day. I gave his offer some serious thought before finally choosing the Let-Er-Rip Go-Cart Track.

"Yes-s-s-s," Mikie said, showing his approval with an arm pump and a grin.

About a week before my birthday, a letter addressed specifically to me arrived in the mail. It was a birthday card, colorfully decorated in pastel balloons that flew from the tails of smiling giraffes and elephants. Inside it read, "Best wishes for a lovely birthday! Sincerely, Nancy."

"Nancy?" I thought. "Who the heck was Nancy?"

I wandered into the kitchen where Daddy was busily painting the pantry doorframe.

"Daddy?"

"Yeah, Kiddo," he replied as he dipped his paintbrush into the can.

"Who's Nancy?"

"Nancy?" he pondered. ". . . Nancy. Hmm, don't know. Why do you ask?"

"Cuz, this card says it's from her."

"It does? Let's have a look." I walked over to his stepladder and held my card up to him as best I could. "I'd say it looks like you have more friends than you know about," he told me.

"Think so?" I innocently asked.

"Think so? I know so!" he said as a matter of fact.

The next day, I received two more birthday cards, each from someone I'd never heard of. One was from a girl named Peggy, the other from Karla.

I asked Daddy about Peggy and Karla.

"Not sure who they could be, but I do know one thing," he told me.

"What's that, Daddy?"

"Young Lady, you are very popular," he answered as he tweaked my nose.

I lit up. This got me to thinking that maybe Daddy was right. I was popular, wasn't I?!

I had never before been this excited about receiving mail. I anxiously waited for the postman to make his drop the next day, and the day after that and the day after that, with hopes of receiving more celebratory greetings. I was not to be disappointed. It didn't matter that I knew none of these well wishers, I simply looked forward to all the brightly animated cards.

The sun streamed into my bedroom window on the morning of my big day, tickling my senses awake as aromatic tendrils of a baking birthday cake wrapped themselves around my bedposts. Mom was feeling good . . . happy day! I dressed myself and went downstairs, eagerly anticipating a few velvety licks from the mixing bowl beaters that I knew Mom had saved especially for me. When I walked into the kitchen, Daddy asked if I still wanted to hit the track.

"Course I want to go, Daddy!" I responded cheerily.

He looked over at Mikie, then back at me again. "How about your brother over there," he asked as he nodded in Mikie's direction. "Does he get to come?"

I crossed my arms in front of my chest and silently studied Mikie with feigned seriousness.

"Aw, come on!" my brother pleaded, a concerned look spreading across his face. "Don't you dare forget that I let you come along on *my* birthday when Daddy took us skating at Rollin' Right Along!"

I broke into a smile and confessed, "I know, I know. I'm just kidding! You know you can come."

Within the hour, the three of us had piled into the Buick and were off to conquer the carts, while Mom stayed home to put the finishing touches on my cake.

Daddy drove us to a newly opened go-cart track on the edge of a nearby suburb while my brother and I giddily bounced up and down on the back seat. Mikie looked over at me and teased, "Don't even think about trying to beat me 'cuz you know you can't win anyway."

"How do you know?" I sassily countered. "I can do anything I want because today is my birthday, remember?"

"Yeah, right. Just don't count on it."

Daddy pulled into an empty spot in the parking lot, and then Mikie and I bolted from the backseat and raced over to the admission window. As we were waiting for Daddy, we peered through the chain-link fence at all the corralled, empty go-carts that were itching to take us for a ride.

"Hey, look at that shiny yellow one!" I chirped as I pointed at it. "I get that one."

"Okay," agreed my brother. "Well then, I get that black one right next to it, the one with the orange stripe."

"Which one do you want, Daddy?" I asked as he walked up beside us and paid our admission fee.

"Well Kiddo, I've got some bad news for you . . . looks like you and I will be sharing a cart today."

"What do you mean, Daddy? Why can't I get my own?" I asked, disappointed.

Daddy pointed to a white, horizontal stripe painted on the side of the admission booth that stated, "Parental guidance required for any child not meeting height requirement."

My brother started to laugh as I raced up to the white stripe and stubbornly stood beneath it, fully aware that the top of my head didn't even come close to reaching.

Daddy strolled over to me and tousled my hair then took my hand. "Come on, Kiddo," he said light-heartedly. "Now let's go beat the pants off your brother!"

The distinct smell of gasoline drifted through the air as I waited for Daddy to properly position himself in the cart. As soon as I was seated in front of him, he looked over at my brother and asked, "How ya doing over there, Mikie? Are you ready to hit it?"

Mikie flashed Daddy the "thumbs-up" sign. "Ready, Daddy!" he rowdily yelled while firmly gripping his padded steering wheel and revving the engine before easing off the brake and navigating toward a sign that said "Let Er Rip Here."

Two other go-carts manned by a father and son team flanked us at the starting line while we waited impatiently for a gangly, teenage boy dressed in shorts and a muscle shirt to wave the large, white flag he held in his hand and send us speeding down the dirt track.

As I sat on the go-cart seat in front of Daddy, my curly locks flying straight backward in the wind, I tightly held onto the tops of Daddy's knees and pretended to be a famous racecar driver trying to outdistance my three opponents. Every time we began to pass my brother, Daddy would ease up on the gas and let Mikie catch up. "Don't let him beat us!" I'd whine. We lapped the dirt track time and again, laughing and whooping until the gangly teenage boy came alongside the finish line and began waving a large red flag this time.

"Can we do it again, Daddy? Pleazzzze?" I squealed.

Daddy let us zoom around the track until we were breathless from laughing so much. When it was time to pack it all in and head back to the car, Daddy stopped at the concession stand and bought Mikie and me a couple of strawberry Popsicles for the ride home.

"That was soooooo much fun, Daddy! I wish we didn't have to go back home now," I said as I skipped back to the Buick in front of my brother who was making loud zooming noises.

"Yes, yes that was a good time. Yes . . . but, your birthday isn't over just yet. We still have to go home and have cake, remember. And don't forget about your birthday presents, too, Kiddo."

"Did Mom make me my favorite chocolate cake with that coconut frosting I love so much?" I dreamily asked. "I'll just eat chocolate cake for dinner, too, okay Daddy? I really don't want anything else."

"We'll see about that when we get home," he replied.

Despite Daddy's easy-going response, I was pretty sure he was going to make me eat more than just cake for dinner.

Cheerful, suntanned faces greeted Mom when we returned home.

"Did you have a good time, Kids?" she asked sweetly.

"I was ahead, Mommy!" I exclaimed, recounting my Let-Er-Rip thrills.

"Yeah, for about five seconds until you ate my dust," Mikie said with a smirk.

"Well, you never won because me and Daddy passed you about five seconds after you passed us, so there!" I replied triumphantly, not wanting to let my big brother get the best of me.

Turning my attention to Mom I said, "You should have seen it, Mommy! You should have been there!"

Mom walked over and kissed me on the cheek then said, "Maybe some other time, my Little Sweetheart." She took hold of my hand and led me into the dining room, "Let's go have some cake. I baked your favorite, you know."

While we'd been away, Mom had wrapped all of my presents in pretty pink tissue and matching iridescent bows, thoughtfully placing them in a small pile on top of the dining room table. Beside my gifts sat a luscious chocolate cake, adorned in pink, edible letters that spelled out "Happy Birthday."

One by one, I jubilantly tore into all of the packages, oblivious to the delicate care that had gone into their lovely presentation. From Mom I received a short-sleeve blouse and a pair of Cinderella underwear. From Daddy came a new tennis racket and a can of balls, and Mikie gave me the portable transistor radio he knew I'd been wanting. "I saved some of my paper route money," he proudly said as I was opening it.

Daddy chose that moment to reach across the table and swipe a tiny glob of frosting from the top of the cake, then playfully plop it onto the tip of my nose. "Time for some grub," he said as I giggled.

It was a happy birthday for me that year, indeed. When it came right down to it, it was just a happy day . . . period. And, that's the best gift I could have wished for.

I never found out who sent me all of those birthday cards, at least not in a conventional way. Much later, when I was in high school, I was sorting through some old storage boxes and came across them, fifteen in all. The memory transported me back to that hot and humid summer so long ago. While I scanned each greeting anew, I was struck with utter amazement by a clue that had bypassed that little, nine-year-old child. The handwriting in each card was exactly the same . . . it was Daddy's.

That sweaty summer dripped away. August was ending, and I was getting excited about going back to the fair. I couldn't wait to show Sammie all the fun rides at Kid-e-land. In years past, Daddy had gotten my brother and me all charged up about the whole affair well beforehand, but this year was different—he hadn't yet said a word about it.

65

About a week before the fair's commencement, Mom and I were on our way to get her hair styled at the beauty salon when I noticed a big, colorful advertisement plastered on the side of our bus. It depicted an oversized dairy cow that was staring into the blue sky above as swirling chocolate, vanilla and strawberry ice cream cones danced just out of reach. The bold caption read, "Don't miss this year's Great Minnesota Get-Together." It got me to thinking that I'd better set a game plan with Daddy, pronto.

As soon as Mom and I returned home later that afternoon, I immediately ran up the stairs to the second floor and approached the door that led to Daddy's "apartment." That's what we called his bedroom in the attic. I'd never been able to recall a time when Mom and Daddy had shared the same sleeping quarters. As far as I was concerned, parents were meant to operate as separate entities rather than a unified front.

Daddy's apartment was what I'd call a bona fide bachelor pad. At the far end of the rectangular room was a utilitarian, twin-sized bed tactically positioned next to a desk and matching bookcase. At the opposite end was a hip lounging arrangement, complete with two yellow, funkadelic chairs, a futon and a Kenwood stereo system. And propped up near the window in the center of the room rested a shiny, silver telescope that Daddy used, on occasion, to ponder the heavens.

I opened the door to his apartment and yelled up the stairs, "Daddy? You up there?" No one responded, so I began to ascend. Once at the top, I could see him seated on his futon with a letter clasped in his hand. He didn't look up as I approached, but instead stared at the floor as if he were the only person in the room.

"Daddy?" I said again. "Are you okay?"

After a second or two, he broke his trance and told me that he was all right. He didn't look all right.

"Everything's going to be fine, Twink," he said with a hint of sadness in his voice.

I didn't know what he meant by that.

He took a deep breath, as if breathing in life itself, and then finally looked up at me. "Come over here," he said as he set aside his letter, "and sit across from me in that chair." He gestured toward one of the yellow funkadelics.

We sat together for a few moments in silence, and then out of the blue he asked, "Want to hear something that will blow your mind?"

"Sure, Daddy," I replied, always interested in what my father had to say.

His gaze drifted toward the far corner of the room then he slowly asked, "Do you remember what I taught you about Albert Einstein, one of the greatest minds in history?" Daddy didn't wait for my reply. "Well, he had this amazing theory about the concept of time called the Special Theory of Relativity."

"But, Dad-deee," I whined, "I don't want to talk about Einstein. I want to talk about the state fair-r-r."

Being a teacher and all, Daddy was constantly trying to instill within me lessons of mathematical and scientific importance. Once, he'd even tried to teach me how to use an abacus, but I was more interested in the cute, albino squirrel that was bounding past our park bench. Sometimes I knew what Daddy was talking about and sometimes I didn't.

"Everybody," Daddy continued, unaffected by my annoyance, "even Einstein's colleagues, thought that time was a constant. And . . . why not?" he said as he shrugged his shoulders. "I mean, a minute . . . is a minute . . . is a minute, right? But, Einstein proved that a minute experienced by a traveler in one vacuum of space may be quite different from a minute experienced in another, depending on the traveler's velocity."

Daddy's eyes momentarily lingered elsewhere. He shifted the toothpick in his mouth with his tongue, then finally

67

looked back at me. "Do you know what that could mean?" he asked reflectively.

I shook my head "no" and sat with my arms crossed over my chest, playing the role of a half-hearted audience.

"It means that the speed in which time passes here on Earth may be different from how it passes elsewhere in the universe," Daddy continued, his voice taking on an enigmatic air. "Let's pretend that I have a secret spaceship that can travel at a rate of half the speed of light. *Half* the speed of light," he said a second time as he snapped his fingers to emphasize the great swiftness of his craft. "I decide to take off and explore the cosmos. What happens to time in my newfound vacuum of space? Slows down. Time . . . slows . . . down. You see, Einstein calculated that the time interval between events for me in my ship would be fifteen percent shorter than the time interval between events for you back here on Earth."

His eyes once again rested on mine, and then he asked, "Given that, how old would you be if I came back in five years?"

I furrowed my brow and began my simple calculation. "Um, I'm nine right now, so nine plus five is fourteen. I'd be fourteen." I looked back at him for approval.

"Yes. And how old do you think I'd be?" He tapped his index finger over his heart.

"You'd be . . ." I paused for a second, then asked quizzically, "Well, I guess I don't know. How old are you right now, Daddy?"

"Forty," he replied. Just then, he got really quiet and looked away, then spoke as if he were talking about someone else. "Richard V. Waters is forty fucking years old."

Oblivious to this nuance, I worked through my answer. "That's an easy one," I said confidently, "you'd be forty-five."

Daddy was still swimming in the depths of his mind's eye, then resurfaced and looked over at me. "What was that?" he asked.

I repeated my answer.

"No," he said as he shook his head, "I would only be forty-four. You see, since I've been traveling at half the speed of light, *my* real time would be passing more slowly than yours back here on Earth. What Einstein theorized is that time passes slower at speeds approaching the speed of light."

"Daddy, I don't even know what the speed of life iz-z-z," I complained while giving the armrest on my chair a good whack.

"Think about this for a second," he said, brushing past my incomprehension, "Time would theoretically stop *if only* one could find a way to travel at the speed of light."

Within that split second, a shimmering nugget of insight revealed itself to Daddy. Suddenly, he was no longer looking at me. In fact, he didn't seem to realize that I was still in his apartment.

"If time stops," he said, now speaking to himself, "then, theoretically, light can be everywhere all at once." Daddy got this faraway look in his eye as he sat back against the futon and pondered his statement in silence. When he began speaking out loud again, he'd emerged onto a different plane of existence than when our conversation had first begun.

"Son of God loves pure light," he declared, as if it were a revelation.

He began verbalizing the puzzle that was quickly piecing itself together in his mind. "Pure light. Son of God loves pure light. Son of God . . . *is* pure light." Just then, Daddy stopped talking and stared intently out the window past his silver telescope and whispered, "God . . . is light."

We never made it to the fair that year.

69

The next time Grandma came over to babysit, she told my brother and me that we needed to be extra good because Daddy was going through some hard times.

"Why is he so sad right now, Grandma?" I asked, oblivious to the severity of my father's situation.

"Things have been very difficult for your Daddy lately, Honey," she answered, then began to wring her hands. "You see, he doesn't have a job right now. Try not to get into any trouble, will you? And be very good kids. Your father doesn't need any more headaches. No more headaches."

That's when I remembered the afternoon not so long ago when Daddy had been philosophizing about Einstein, the same afternoon that had changed him forever. The hard times in his life became the hard lines on his face. He didn't smile anymore, didn't talk as much, and no longer embraced the world around him. It had become his tomb.

He started buying powdered milk instead of fresh, and gave us lessons on how to conserve toilet paper. He even asked his father, who worked as a bellboy at the Radisson, to save discarded hotel soap, which piled high in one-gallon ice cream buckets underneath our bathroom sink.

Daddy tried to land as many substitute-teaching jobs as he could. When those began drying up, he drifted from Electrolux salesman to machinist to bus driver. In his spare time, he brought home wood framing from the lumberyard and mysteriously carted it into our basement. "You kids are going to be in big trouble if I ever catch you messing around down there," he warned my brother and me as he pointed down under, then told us that he was building a wooden boat especially for Easter Sunday.

One day after school I was bored, so I went up to my brother's room to harass him. As soon as I breached his inner sanctuary, he peered at me from behind the latest issue of his Spiderman comic book.

"Wha cha doin'?" I asked.

"What's it look like, Dum Dum?"

"Hey, want to go down into the basement and check out Daddy's boat?" I prodded.

"N-o-o-o-o-o way. You've *got* to be kidding me! Now, you know darn well he doesn't want us down there."

"Yeah, so?" I said impishly.

"So?! So, we're going to get our butts kicked if he finds out."

"We won't get in trouble. Come on!" I begged.

"No way," Mikie responded defiantly. "You can go all by yourself and tell me about it later . . . that is, if you make it out alive."

I dug in my heels and continued to argue, "Daddy went to the hardware store, and you know how long he hangs around that place."

Mikie studied me for a moment, mulling over my logic, then set his comic book down on the nightstand. "Suit yourself," I taunted before turning and heading back toward the stairs.

My brother was soon trailing right behind me.

The two of us descended the stairs, lingering at the landing on the first floor to peek out the back door window for any telltale signs of Daddy.

No Daddy . . . We scurried into the kitchen and cracked open the door leading down into the basement. Illumination glared back, and my heart skipped a beat. Maybe Daddy had already returned and was once again feverishly working on his secret project?

Mikie tugged at the back of my sweatshirt. "C'mon, let's get out of here!" he said, clearly panicked.

I put my index finger over my lips and beckoned him to ssshhh. "Don't blow it for us," I warned. "Maybe Daddy just forgot to turn off the basement light."

We stood completely still at the top of the stairs and listened for any laborious noises rising from the depths below.

71

As soon as we were confident that our plan was still in play, we crept down the basement steps, trying hard not to make them squeak. When we got to the bottom, we scanned the room for signs of Daddy's handiwork.

"Do you see anything, Mikie?" I whispered.

"Not really."

We moved closer toward the forbidden zone.

"Look in that corner over there," Mikie said as he pointed to the far end of the basement. "I see some stuff on top of that table."

I focused on the area in question, but that part of the room was too dark for me to make out any details. It just looked like a big pile of junk to me.

Despite the consequences, curiosity got the best of us, and we began inching toward the table, hair standing up on the backs of our necks. That's when we heard the back door open, and then footsteps creaking on the floor directly above. We froze in our tracks and looked at each other with eyes as big as silver dollars.

"Oh, shit!" I shrieked.

"Hurry!" Mikie spat.

We turned and raced up the basement stairs, but it was too late. Daddy was already waiting for us in the kitchen when we reached the top.

"What in the hell were you two doing down there?" He demanded, mad as a hornet.

"Nothing, Daddy," we said in unison.

"Nothing, huh? What did I tell you?!"

"We're sorry, Daddy! We won't do it again!" Mikie pleaded.

"Who's idea was this?" Daddy angrily asked.

"Mikie's!" I blurted as I pointed an incriminating finger at my brother.

Daddy turned to him and demanded, "Is that right? Was this your idea?"

"No, Daddy, no! I swear. It wasn't!" Mikie defended as he started to shake.

"Well, I'm just going to have to teach you a lesson now, aren't I?"

As Daddy began taking off his belt, Mikie started to scream, "It wasn't me, it wasn't me!" A tidal wave of fear washed over my brother's face as his eyes locked with mine. He heatedly glared at me as if to say, "I'll get you for this!"

I was overcome with remorse as soon as the violent echoes of my brother's cries began bouncing off our living room walls. I couldn't stand listening to it any longer and had to get out of there . . . fast. "Sammie," I thought. "I'll go to her house!" I raced out the back door without even grabbing my coat and headed toward the direction of safe harbor.

Chana answered their door and greeted me, "Well, hi Hon, come in. It's cold out." She gave me the once-over and then asked, "Where's your coat?"

"Um, I forgot it at home. Is Sammie around?"

"She's upstairs on the phone with Grandmamma. Feel free to go on up. You want some water or Ovaltine or something?"

"No thanks, Chana," I said as I began climbing the stairs.

"You look flush, Hon. What's the matter?"

"Nothing," I lied. "I ran all the way over, so I guess maybe that could be it."

"Well, all right," she said hesitantly. "You come down and help yourself to a snack when you feel like it."

I smiled and told her "thanks" as I continued up the stairs.

I found Sammie in the family room, still on the phone. After waving my hand to get her attention, I turned my thumb in a downward position and shook it a few times, signaling that I'd be waiting for her in our recording studio in the basement. She smiled, then placed a hand over the phone's mouthpiece and whispered, "Be there in a sec."

73

My brother's pain kept playing over and over in my head, as if the echoes had tracked me down and infiltrated my secret burrow. I put my hands over my ears and yelled, "Stop!" I needed a quick remedy, something to transform me, so I walked over to the stereo and started leafing through Sammie's album collection. What could I spin?

The Carpenters? Naw, too mellow.

Barbara Streisand? Too melodramatic.

The Monkees? Not in the mood.

Ah-ha! Found it.

I took the album out of its slipcover and placed it onto the turntable, then grabbed my tambourine and got into position.

One, two, three, four . . .

♫♫♫ The Partridge Family

I closed my eyes and sang my little heart out, pretending that I was up there on that stage, right alongside Shirley, Lori, Danny, and none other than Keith Partridge himself. For a few cherished moments in the depths of my mind, I was no longer a lower-class kid living a life I didn't really want. No, no, no. Not me. I was the center of adoring attention. The fans loved me, Keith loved me and, hell, I even loved me. When it was Keith's turn to sing, he wasn't singing to the frenzied horde of enraptured teenage girls. Oh, no! He was, without a doubt, singing to yours truly, looking me right smack dab in the eye with his gorgeous hazel come-on. I adoringly stared back, repeatedly slapping my secondhand tambourine against my hip.

The only thing I wanted to do right then and there was "get happy" . . . just like the song said.

I eventually went home that night, much later than usual, avoiding my brother while I got ready for bed. In the darkness, thick with unease, I tossed and turned, thinking about the life that plagued my family and me. "Why did I have to sneak into the basement to see that stupid thing anyway?" I angrily mused to myself. "And, why was Daddy making a boat in the first place? I mean, we already had the Cat. Wasn't that good enough?" I let my thoughts race around in my head like a bunch of old, beat-up cars at a summertime derby, then eventually decided that I needed to apologize to my brother and tell him that I never, *ever* wanted to see that damn boat again.

But, as destiny would have it, I would indeed see that damn boat again, one last time, and it would sear upon my soul a haunted memory to last a lifetime.

The following week, after our third supper of scrambled egg sandwiches in as many days, Daddy decided that it was time for a trip to the supermarket. I looked forward to those excursions, simple as they were. They gave me what I ached for in our ever-present times of family crisis, a sense that somehow we were all still normal.

"Rainy, Twink, get your coats. We need to make a food run," Daddy told us.

"But Rick, don't you think someone should be here when Mikie gets home?" Mom protested.

"He can take care of himself for an hour if he has to," Daddy flatly replied.

Mom grimaced at Daddy's callousness, then looked down at the floor. "I don't feel all that well," she moaned. "Why don't you just go without me?"

"I don't want you staying by yourself tonight," Daddy insisted, then grabbed the car keys off the kitchen counter and put on his jacket. "I'll pull the car out while you two get ready."

Realizing that she had little choice, Mom tried to pull herself together and reluctantly succumbed to Daddy's command.

She and I were bundled up and shivering out in the alley, waiting for Daddy to back out of the garage, when her eye happened to drift across some nearby graffiti on the ground. She stepped closer to it and bent down to get a better look, but the orange spray paint was a bit cryptic and hard to read. Mom started getting panicky, "What does that say?!" she demanded.

"I'm not sure, Mommy," I replied as the muscles in my neck began to tighten.

"Does that say . . . bitch?" she asked. "Who is calling me a bitch?!"

I sighed and shook my head from side to side, not knowing how to respond.

When we got into the car, Mom turned to Daddy and barked, "Who is calling me a bitch, Rick? Did you write that?"

Daddy got this perplexed look on his face then asked, "What in the world are you talking about?"

"Those orange markings in the alley. You wrote that didn't you!" she accused.

"Rainy, I didn't write anything," he responded defensively. "I'm sure it was just a bunch of punks who didn't have anything better to do than vandalize the neighborhood. Don't worry about it."

Daddy's words hadn't put Mom at ease. They rarely ever did lately.

Mom started shrieking, "Punks! Who do they think they are calling me a bitch?!"

As we drove to the food mart, I silently sat in the back seat, staring at all the everyday people who were passing us by. When we got to the first stoplight, I noticed a young female driver and her male companion in the car next to us. They were looking at each other and laughing as the boom-boom of the bass vibrated in the background. I pressed my forehead against my windowpane and sat there wishing I had the guts to open my car door and climb into the backseat of their Chevy Nova. I wanted to be laughing along with them, right that very minute. The light turned green, and my eyes remained glued to them until their car turned out of sight at the next corner. Once again distraction-less, the weight of my circumstance bore down hard, and I slumped lower in my seat. I had a pretty good idea of what was coming.

"Do you think I'm a bitch, Rick? Do you?!" Mom continued.

"Rainy, please! Will you stop?!"

"I'm not a bitch!" Mom screamed then turned away from Daddy and appeared to be looking out the window. She began asking the same questions over again, her voice huskier and more violent. "Do you think I'm a bitch?! *You* wrote that didn't you?! *Didn't you*?!"

The levee of Daddy's patience had finally been breached. He glanced over at her and angrily hissed, "God dammit, I told you it wasn't me! How many times do I have to say it! Now shut the hell up, would you!"

"I'm not talking to you, I'm talking to Satan," Mom spat back. "Satan hates me. He's out to get me, aren't you Satan?!" She then began slapping herself in the face over and over again while continuing her argument with the ruler of Hell.

Daddy lost it, "Jesus Christ! I have had it. Shut the fuck up!"

Mom's dagger-filled glare turned to Daddy. "I knew you never loved me, Rick. I knew it!" Mom spat back.

"What are you talking about?! I don't know what you're talking about anymore!" Daddy shouted.

By the time we got to the next stoplight, Daddy's jaw was severely clenched, and his hands were gripping the steering wheel so tightly you'd have sworn he was going to snap it right off. Mom kept screaming at him, telling him that he didn't love her. Telling him that he was on Satan's side. Telling him that they were both against her. Before the light turned green, she got out of the car, slammed the door shut, then hotly walked away with no regard for where she was or where she was headed.

"Where in the hell are you going?!" Daddy shouted after her, but Mom kept walking farther and farther away.

Daddy's face started to get really red, and he looked like he was about to blow. He flopped his head down onto the steering wheel and let it rest there momentarily. When he didn't see the light turn green, several cars behind us starting honking their horns. One guy yelled, "Move it, you fuckin' idiot!"

A feeling of gloom permeated our car as just the two of us continued our journey. I thought about Mom and halfheartedly wondered where she was at that moment, tired of being held hostage by her perpetual state of instability.

Daddy muttered expletives under his breath as he parked the Buick in the grocery store lot and walked with me into building. Once inside, he impatiently grabbed a cart, then extracted a shopping list from his pants pocket. As we walked the aisles together, he rattled off what he needed from whichever section we happened to be in, and I, in turn, collected the item then threw it into our basket.

My favorite aisle was the one that displayed a dazzling kaleidoscope of breakfast offerings. As Daddy and I turned the corner with our cart and began walking through it, I was reminded of a TV commercial I'd seen one Saturday morning that starred a singing and dancing leprechaun. I carefully scanned the display for my heart's desire, then excitedly grabbed the cereal box and presented it to Daddy.

"Please Daddy," I begged, "can I have some Lucky Charms?"

"Sorry, Twink, not this time. We don't have the money for it."

"Please, please, please, Daddy," I said as I put on my most charming smile.

"Next time, okay?" He firmly took the box from my hands and placed it back on the shelf.

When we lined up at the checkout, Daddy laid his coupons on the conveyor belt, unloaded our groceries, and took out an envelope with some cash in it while we waited for the clerk to tally our total bill.

"That'll be seventy dollars and fifty three cents," she said robotically.

Daddy started counting his money. Instead of handing over the appropriate amount when he'd finished, he began counting it a second time.

"I only have sixty three," he awkwardly explained.

The young clerk looked back at him with a blank expression as she snapped her gum.

Daddy slowly put the envelope with the sixty-three dollars back into his coat pocket. Now utterly humiliated, he explained that he'd need to put a few items back.

"Wait here, Twink," he said to me as he began sorting through our sundries and grabbing those deemed less critical. " I'll be right back."

I had never seen Daddy shaken before. I'd seen him irritated, impatient, even infuriated, but never shaken. Daddy was finally beginning to unravel beneath the weight of his burden.

Thanksgiving that year was a repeat of so many from my past. Mom spent the day upstairs in bed while Daddy, my brother and I, and Grandma gorged ourselves on turkey and mashed potatoes while we sat around the tube in the living room.

That following Saturday, I was playing in my bedroom with our cat, Rusty, when Daddy came in and asked if I had any plans for the day. I told him about the new ice skating rink that had recently been installed at Sammie's townhouse complex. "Me and Sammie are going to practice our Peggy Fleming moves today, Daddy!"

"How about going to the museum with me instead?" he encouraged.

"But Daddy, you're always working on your boat every weekend," I replied as a matter of fact.

"Boat can wait. What do you say?"

"Well, I guess I can call Sammie and see if she'd be able to skate tomorrow instead," I said hesitantly. My desire to slice the ice far outweighed that of pursuing the arts.

"I'll be waiting for you in the kitchen," he calmly told me.

The Institute of Arts was a short drive down the parkway, then northward toward the center of the city. I'd been to a museum only once before when Miss Smith had taken us on a school fieldtrip, but this was my first outing to the fanciest fine arts establishment in town.

Daddy parked the car on a side street, then we walked half a block to the museum's entrance. As we passed through the atrium, I couldn't help but glance up at the ceiling where a stunning, glass octopus gracefully floated above us. I stood there, momentarily transfixed, until Daddy put his arm around my shoulder and guided me up the staircase to the second level.

The spacious, marble tiled hallways escorted the two of us past elegantly attired walls draped in royalty and religion; a Madonna scene here, a Duke of Windsor portrait there. Loveliness abounded. At the end of the long hall we found ourselves in the presence of a beautiful, Italian fountain. Its peaceable water dance beckoned, and I couldn't help but bend down, wanting to dip my hand into the mystery. Daddy was one step ahead and stopped me short. He placed a penny into my palm and pointed at all the other coins on the bottom. "Close your eyes and make a wish," he whispered. I didn't have to think long before splashing it down next to all the other contenders.

We moved on toward the special exhibition gallery that was down another long hall to the left of us. Before we could enter, Daddy had to buy us two tickets at the admission booth. As I waited, my restless side got the better of me, and I began tickling the naked toes of a nearby wooden deity. A museum guard approached and kindly requested that I keep my hands to myself.

Daddy came back to retrieve me, then we entered the exhibit rooms. Goose bumps sprang to life on my skin after a few, cautious steps, and I craned my neck, peering back at all the hand-painted coffins that seemed to be closing in on me. Although there were many, each depicted the anciently departed identically, with long, straight, jet-black hair and matching cat-like eyes generously bathed in eyeliner and mascara. "Where in the heck was I?"

Mystified, I stepped closer to Daddy and asked, "What is this place anyway, Daddy?"

"It's an ancient Egypt exhibit," he replied. "Haven't they taught you anything about the pyramids and mummies in school yet?"

"Nope," I said, still confused and a little creeped out.

We meandered through the rooms, curiously studying the many artifacts of antiquity. There were hunting weapons of all shapes and sizes, jewel-encrusted knives, necklaces crafted from the finest gold and silver, and handsomely carved pottery. Daddy quietly read aloud the description paired with each object of interest as we drifted from one to the next. Toward the end of our tour, Daddy stopped to deeply regard a stone relief of the Egyptian god Osiris that was hanging from the wall.

"What does it say?" I asked inquisitively.

Lost in his own thoughts, he didn't answer me at first, then finally replied, "It says that Egyptians, perhaps more than any other civilization, wished to live forever. They were the first people known to have formulated definite ideas regarding the immortality of the individual human soul."

Directly beside Osiris hung a second relief. Daddy stepped toward it, then voluntarily read aloud the paired caption, "The tomb provided the place where a man could continue his existence for eternity."

"Huh, that sounds a lot like what Mr. Arnold teaches us in Sunday school." I looked up at my father with a most serious expression on my face then stated, "But Daddy, sometimes I wonder if people say those things just because they're scared to die."

Daddy solemnly turned away from me and stared back into the eyes of Osiris, then replied, "Yeah, maybe."

We moved on to an adjacent room where we reached Daddy's primary purpose for visiting the museum. Straight ahead laid the mummified remains of the boy king, Tutankhamen. The room was crowded with curious onlookers, and we couldn't get close enough to the display until several of them finally wandered away, opening up a front row spot. The bandaged body was lying horizontally on top of a Plexiglas bed, giving the eerie impression that he was floating in mid-air. I couldn't see above Tut's chest and was unable to absorb the significance of what rested before me, so I glanced up at Daddy and yanked his jacket sleeve.

"I can't see much, Daddy," I said, speaking in full volume.

A few of the other patrons gave me a harsh look, so Daddy put his forefinger to his mouth to remind me of my promise to be quiet.

"I forgot," I whispered.

He picked me up and held me next to him. I quietly studied King Tut, feeling unnerved in the presence of death. I started to fidget, and almost asked Daddy to put me down, but I couldn't keep my eyes off the mesmerizing beauty of one thing . . . the golden death mask that covered Tut's face. Daddy was staring at it, too. Tut's features, frozen in time, were like those we'd seen earlier on the other coffins, but this one was so much richer, and its depth, exquisite. The king's solid gold visage held painted, lifelike eyes that scorched the abyss of eternity, and atop his gilded head slithered a foreboding, coiled snake that had wrapped itself around a stunning, regal headdress.

The two of us stared at the mask for several minutes until something resting nearby captured Daddy's attention. He set me down and walked over to the third of three wooden, nested coffins in which the king had been buried and studied its intricately carved detail, scanning it up and down, then letting his eyes rest on Tut's engraved expression. His brow furrowed, then he reached into his jacket pocket to retrieve a small notepad and began sketching a rough outline of the figure before him. "Features show great serenity, symbolizing the pharaoh's fortitude as he awaited resurrection," he wrote beneath it as he whispered the words aloud, then placed the notepad back into his pocket. He gazed intently at the coffin for what seemed like a long time until I became restless and once more yanked on his jacket sleeve.

"Daddy, I have to go to the bathroom," I whined.

"Okay," he said. "I guess it's time for us to leave anyway."

He took hold of my hand and began leading me back to the atrium where the women's bathrooms were located. I started walking faster as we neared the lavatory, anxious to relieve myself, when much to my dismay, Daddy abruptly veered off track.

83

"Hang on, Twink," he told me, "this will take just a minute."

He let go of my hand, then strode into the museum gift shop and systematically scanned the memento-filled tabletops. Before long, I saw him hastily grab a small object from one of the displays and take it to the cashier counter.

I met Daddy back in the atrium after finally taking care of my business, then pointed to the gift shop and asked, "What'd you buy in there anyway?"

He opened the small, black paper bag in his grasp, then extracted a tiny replica of King Tut's death mask, one that had been cleverly transformed into a souvenir key chain.

"For good luck," Daddy explained as he held it in the palm of his hand for me to see.

His comment puzzled me and I naively asked, "Is it like a rabbit's foot or something?"

"It is for me," he replied distantly before placing the souvenir back into the bag.

After we'd left the building and gotten back into the Buick, I glanced at the museum as we drove past and wondered why Daddy was so fascinated with King Tut. After all, the Egyptian ruler was no more than a bony, lifeless soul who'd departed this earth years ago. "Maybe this outing had been nothing more than just another one of Daddy's many lessons," I mused to myself.

Yeah . . . maybe.

I didn't see much of Daddy during the next few weeks. Now completely jobless and lost, he became even more obsessed with his secret project in the basement. Mom remained burrowed in her bedroom, occasionally taking a break from The Invisibles to savor a few smokes at the kitchen table. My brother and I? We did just exactly what we *always* did when the road felt like Jello . . . we left. Mikie enrolled in a karate class while I retreated to Sammie's house whenever I could.

It was now mid-December, 1974.

Every year between the Thanksgiving and Christmas holidays, the most popular department store in town would celebrate the season by showcasing a spectacular holiday display in their flagship auditorium. "Cinderella" was this year's theme, the story of my most beloved fairytale character. Since I'd already missed a chance to enjoy the state fair, I wasn't in the mood to skip this big show. I began nagging Daddy to take Mikie and me, but he claimed he needed to finish his boat on schedule and didn't have the time. After getting fed up with my persistence, he finally threw in the towel and phoned Grandma.

The following Sunday after mass, Daddy drove us to Grandma's apartment on the edge of downtown and idled the Buick in the circular drive alongside the main entrance. Grandma eventually popped from the belly of the building, sporting a fashionable pair of dark sunglasses and her favorite brown wig. As she slowly made her way toward us, Mikie and I got out of the car and waved goodbye to Daddy, then obediently followed her across the street to wait for the next bus that would cart us into the heart of the city.

The short ride went by in a flash, and before I knew it, Mikie and I were crammed behind Grandma in one of the store's many revolving, glass entrance doors. Shiny, red Christmas balls suspended from the ceiling merrily greeted us inside, while pretty, lip-glossed girls lined the green carpet runway that guided all patrons toward the escalators. One of them caught my eye as I passed and furtively misted the back of my hand with the perfume bottle she cradled. "Chanel," she said silkily. I bashfully pressed my wrist against my nose and inhaled the lovely scent, feeling that surely I was the better for it. My brother couldn't help but stare longingly at the sexy Chanel girl. Her brown, velvet eyes and flawless, honey-colored complexion swallowed him whole. "Your neck is going to snap off your head!" I teased.

As Grandma ushered Mikie and me along the runway, my thoughts drifted as I imagined myself to be a top fashion model, even more beautiful than the perfume I was wearing. The waiting escalator carried the three of us beyond the bustling crowd of well-dressed shoppers and up to the eighth floor auditorium, where the spiced aroma of gingerbread saturated the air. I asked Grandma if my brother and I could each have a quarter to buy a Christmas cookie. "After we're done, Dear," she gently directed.

The auditorium entrance overflowed with families of all shapes and sizes. Attentive mothers pushed baby strollers, toddlers tried in vain to free themselves from parental bondage and fathers balanced wide-eyed youngsters upon their shoulders. Unable to see above the dense crowd, I tried to perch my weight upon my tiptoes with little luck. I had no beast of burden to transport me in luxury since Daddy wasn't around.

The crowd eventually began to enter, enabling us to follow and escape inside the world of holiday magic. Chronological stages flanked our pathway where mechanized mannequins acted out the roles for which they were born beneath colorful mood lights. Far beyond anything else, I was magnetically drawn to the delicate, young girl with the mournful, blue eyes, dressed in tattered rags. In the opening scene on stage number one, she was seated in her room at the edge of her dilapidated bed, tediously mending her evil stepsister's torn gown. Her arm moved slowly to and fro as she toiled away the hours, while her weepy eyes pleaded with the audience before turning her attention back to the chore at hand.

I leaned close to my brother and exclaimed, "Oh, look how neat this is, Mikie!" By the look on my brother's face, I could tell he was just as enchanted as I.

Ever the watchful matriarch, Grandma patiently shuffled behind as Mikie and I slowly progressed from one scene to the next through this three-dimensional storybook. Unfolding before us was the tale of a young girl hopelessly trapped by circumstance in a world that cared nothing for her song. Aimlessly she drifted through a life full of thunder and shadows, fearing Sorrow would remain her master forever. But somehow, by luck or by destiny, Fortune kissed her brow and led her to the one who could instinctively play all the chords of her heart.

When we came upon the final scene, the one where the handsome prince bows before his princess, then tenderly kisses her hand, my brother and I were saddened to see it all end.

"Can we go through it again?" we begged.

"Oh, Honeys, I can't," Grandma firmly replied, making an impatient gesture with her hand. "My legs. They ache so. This has been enough now. Maybe your father can take you next week."

I was pretty sure Daddy would be too busy working on his boat, but at least I got a chance to meet the beautiful Cinderella, a magical encounter that I would never forget.

Daddy picked us up at Grandma's apartment later that afternoon. On the drive home, he told us he needed to stop at the Holiday store and pick up a few Christmas gifts. He was in his usual somber state, the same one he'd been in since losing his teaching job at the high school.

The parking lot was filled to the brim when we arrived, forcing Daddy to drive up and down the rows of cars until he found a space at the very back end of the lot, just as someone else was leaving.

Controlled pandemonium reigned inside the store where throngs of frenzied shoppers rifled through displays, searching for satisfaction. Few were in a jolly good mood. Mikie made a beeline for the sporting goods, and Daddy said he wanted me to follow him to the electronics department. Along the way, we began walking past a camera display before he hesitated then went back to ponder the selection before grabbing a box off the shelf. He extracted the Polaroid from within, then held it to his face and pretended to shoot my photo. "Say cheese," he said mechanically. After I dutifully smiled, he lowered the camera and began examining a few of its features before unexpectedly handing it to me. As I nervously cradled it in my hands, Daddy pointed to one button after another, patiently explaining each of the functions.

"Looks pretty cool," I said sincerely.

"It's for your mother," he told me. "Think she'll like it?"

"Like it?" I said. "Not only will she like it, Daddy, she'll think it's absolutely neat-o."

"Neat-o, huh?" he mimicked, putting the camera back into its box then placing it in our cart. "We'd better go find your brother and get home," Daddy said as we began heading in the direction of the sporting goods department.

It was snowing by the time we left the store, the kind of heavy snow that comes down in full force and instantly melts to liquid on your face from the heat of your skin, as if it had decided it would rather not be there after all.

We jumped into the car, and Daddy began to back out of our spot when he noticed that a nearby vehicle had lost its traction, rendering it paralyzed. Daddy pulled forward and let the Buick idle while he retrieved something from our trunk. He knocked on the backseat window and asked my brother to get out, then placed one of his many inventions into Mikie's hands. "Now Mikie, I want you to walk over to that car and provide assistance with this traction mat in exchange for a few bucks. Do you think you can do that for me?"

Mikie began to protest, telling Daddy he didn't want to do it because he felt stupid talking to people he didn't know.

"Just do it!" Daddy irritably demanded.

My brother begrudgingly took the grooved mat over to the stranger's car and stood beside his frosted window. I watched from our backseat as the driver opened his door and listened to my brother's pitch then got out and walked to the back of his vehicle where he inserted the mat underneath the left, rear tire. The vehicle's passenger slid behind the steering wheel and rhythmically fed the car some gas while the driver rocked it from behind. After a few back and forth passes, they'd managed to free themselves from winter's icy grip. The driver brushed away some of the slush that had splattered across the front of his coat before reaching into his pocket. He placed something into Mikie's hand and waved, then got back into his car and cautiously drove away.

Clutching Daddy's traction mat, my brother raced back to us and handed Daddy a one-dollar bill through the half-opened car window before joining me in the back seat.

"I told you to get a *few* bucks from them," Daddy snapped, emphasizing the word "few."

"I'm sorry, Daddy," Mikie responded. "I just took whatever the guy gave me."

"Next time, get more than just one lousy buck. Understand?"

"Yes, Daddy," Mikie said disappointedly as he lowered his head and stared into his lap.

We drove home in the dark with only the sound of the popular radio station keeping us company. Just as we were rolling into our garage, the perfectly pitched voice of a well-known tenor began streaming over the airwaves. I thought Daddy was going to shut it off and park the car, but he didn't. He just sat there, transfixed, listening to that song.

♫♫♫ O Holy Night

89

I looked at my brother, knowing exactly what he was thinking. He didn't want to move a muscle for fear of upsetting Daddy again, so the two of us sat completely still while Daddy finished listening to that pretty Christmas song. When it was over, he slowly reached for the ignition and turned it off before stepping out of the car. I could tell that something was weighing heavily on his mind.

The winter sun had long since set, bathing our yard in blackness. Daddy had forgotten to turn the floodlight on before we left and was now fumbling with his house keys. When we entered through the back door, all the lights were off except for the one in the second floor bathroom.

"Rainy!" Daddy shouted up the stairs. "Are you home?"

A feeble, mumbled response of what sounded like, "Oh Rick . . . I need . . . some rest," came from the depths of Mom's bedroom.

Daddy slowly shook his head then stepped away from the stairs. "Looks like it's another Mac & Cheese night," he said, more to himself than to my brother and me. He walked into the kitchen, flipped on the light, then set the grocery bag on the counter and pulled out the Polaroid.

"Twink, come over here," he said to me. I followed him to the pantry where he stuck the camera behind a jug of apple cider. "Promise that you won't tell your mother where it is, okay?"

I promised.

"Cross your heart?"

I vigorously shook my head "yes" and painted an invisible "X" on my chest with my index finger.

"Alright Kids," he said with a sigh of fatigue, "I need to take care of a few things. I'll be up in my pad."

Daddy headed upstairs, leaving my brother and me to face an empty table. I looked at Mikie and whined, "I'm hungry."

"Yeah, me too," he said, then walked over to the pantry and grabbed a jar of dry roasted peanuts from one of the shelves. He turned to me and asked, "Hey, want to play a round of Monopoly?"

"Monopoly? Yeah, sure," I readily agreed, wanting to do anything to escape the trappings of boredom and hunger.

My brother and I went into the living room and turned on the tube, then spread out our favorite board game on the floor. Our cat, Rusty, flopped down next to us and began taking swipes at the plastic hotel pieces with one of his orange-striped paws.

"I get to be the shoe!" I yelled.

"You always get to be the shoe!" my brother protested.

"You can be the shoe next time," I said defiantly as I tightly cupped my miniature prize.

"Fine," said my brother. "I'll be the iron, then."

So around the board we went, passing GO, collecting $200, going to jail, then buying our way out. We played the game once, then played it some more until our Daddy finally came back down to fill our bellies.

Christmas Eve morn. By the time eleven o'clock rolled around, Mom was still in bed with no sign of wanting anything more. I don't think she even knew which day it was, let alone that it was a holiday most families eagerly anticipate and celebrate together.

Daddy became more and more restless with the passing of each hour. By four o'clock that afternoon, he went upstairs to try and coax Mom out of bed only to return defeated a half an hour later. He strode into the kitchen without hesitation, picked up the phone receiver and called his sister.

Mikie and I were in the living room watching *It's a Wonderful Life* when Daddy told us we would be spending Christmas Eve with Aunt Lois and Uncle Rob.

"What's wrong with Mommy?" I asked. "Is she going crazy again?"

"She's having trouble," is all he would say.

It was a quick trip to our aunt's house. Uncle Rob met us at the front door and firmly shook Daddy's hand. "Merry Christmas, Rick," he said. "Sorry to hear about Rainy." His sincere, blue eyes fleetingly held Daddy's before he turned his attention to my brother and me. "Come on in, Kids!" he said with a welcoming, jovial air. "We've just finished eating, but there's still plenty of time to dive into some Christmas cookies later. You like cookies, don't you?" he asked good naturedly as he gathered our coats and hung them in the closet.

We shyly told him that we were ready to eat some Christmas cookies.

Daddy solemnly stood in the entryway with his coat still on and handed my brother and me the presents that he'd carried in from the car. "You can open these tonight," he told us with noticeable sadness in his voice.

"Where are you going, Daddy?" Mikie fretted.

"I won't be able to stay," he answered as he knowingly glanced at Uncle Rob. "You guys have fun, okay? Uncle Rob, here, will take real good care of you." With that said, he and our uncle warmly shook hands again. "Thanks for everything," Daddy told him before bending down to give my brother and me each a hug. "Merry Christmas, Kids," he told us, momentarily masking his heavy heart with feigned cheerfulness before opening the door and heading back into the dark, crystal void.

My brother and I must have looked like two petrified, porcelain dolls as we stood motionless in the entryway staring at Daddy's back, fully aware that he was leaving us behind. My lower lip started to quiver and I wanted to run after him, but

Uncle Rob's gentle hand on my shoulder held me back. "C'mon, Kids, let's go have some fun!" he said, as he closed the front door and ushered us into their living room.

All four of our cousins were seated next to one another on the sofa, oblivious to the new arrivals as they feverishly anticipated the impending fulfillment of their North Pole wishes. My brother and I awkwardly walked through the living room toward the bay window and sat across from them on the floor, placing Daddy's gifts atop our laps. As soon as we were seated, Uncle Rob knelt beside the Christmas tree like a crazed elf and began tossing presents to each of his children, igniting frenzy. Torn gift wrap and shiny, store-bought bows were haphazardly pitched aside to reveal Santa's secrets while gasps of surprise and rowdy laughter pierced the air. My brother and I watched the unfolding joy from afar, wanting to join in but not really knowing how.

Amidst the chaos, Mikie leaned toward me and timidly asked, "Do you think we should open our presents from Daddy now?"

"Guess we should," I said. "You go first."

My brother started to unveil his single gift. He carefully took off the bow and wrapping paper, then set them next to him on the floor. When he lifted the box lid, disbelief spread across his face. Inside was a brand, spanking new, Spalding leather baseball glove. "Oh, man!" he exclaimed. "This is the exact one I wanted so bad. I was looking for it when we went to the Holiday store that day! Remember?"

I nodded and clapped my hands, happy that my brother had gotten his wish. "My turn," I said.

"What do you think you got?" my brother asked as he excitedly pounded his fist into the webbing of his new treasure.

"No idea," I answered as I discarded my big green bow.

When I opened my box and looked inside, my mouth fell open but no words could escape.

Mikie nudged me, "What is it?"

93

I lifted the Polaroid out of the box so he could see it.

"Wow!" said my brother. "You got a camera! I can't believe you got a camera!"

"I can't believe it either," I said under my breath, feeling like I'd just gotten the wind knocked out of me.

Taped to the camera was a small card. I set the camera down and opened it.

"So that you will always remember. Love, Your Father," was all it said.

"So that you will always remember . . . so that you will always remember . . . so that you will always remember . . . ," I kept saying out loud, over and over again, as I was trying to understand Daddy's message. It wasn't clear to me *what* Daddy had wanted me to remember. There had never been a time in my young life when Daddy wasn't carting around his own camera. Sometimes he'd even bring along a tape recorder, too. He was compelled to document the timeline of his life, as if he feared it would soon slip away. Maybe this was just another one of Daddy's lessons. I positioned the camera in my hands so that I could review its features and tried to remember what he had taught me back at the Holiday store, then gently placed it back into the box and set it on the floor in front of me. Although unable to unravel the riddle of Daddy's gift, I was certainly sure of one thing I had to remember . . . ask Daddy why he had chosen to give the Polaroid to me instead of Mom.

Later that evening, after Mikie and I had downed so many Christmas cookies that we were starting to feel sick, Uncle Rob diverted our attention by asking us kids if we wanted to join him on a moonlit stroll. "It's a beaut out there tonight," he told us. "Maybe we'll get lucky and see old Santa himself! C'mon, what do you say?"

Chris and John passed, opting instead to head for the attached heated garage and check out their new automotive tools on the muscle car they just bought. Rachel remained seated at the kitchen counter, playing with her Lite-Brite.

"Naw, too cold out," she said before wrapping a blanket around her shoulders. That left Randall and my brother and me. We retrieved our coats, then followed Uncle Rob outside.

It was mystically still that evening. The snow twinkled a light blue hue in the darkness underneath the lampposts. Ambling along, we listened intently as Uncle Rob dispensed a story for each of the houses we passed. He told us about Pharmacist Tom in the white split-level and Attorney Dennis in the brown bungalow. While walking by a newly built tan rambler, he explained, "Now that lady who lives over there is a teacher, just like your father."

When we reached what Uncle Rob called a cul-de-sac at the end of the street, the four of us stopped to look up at the twinkling stars.

"Can you see the Big Dipper, Kids?" our uncle enthusiastically asked. I shook my head "No," able to discern only a random cluster of bright white lights against a sea of darkness.

He pointed into the sky and drew an outline of the constellation in question with his index finger.

"I still don't see it," I said softly.

He stepped closer to me and bent down until he was at my level. Once again he drew the outline, lining up his hand directly in front of the center of my face so my eyes could more easily follow the movement of his fingers.

I squinted for a moment, waiting for the constellation to reveal itself, then finally exclaimed, "I think I can see it now, Uncle Rob! There it is!"

"Fantastic! Now you know where the Big Dipper is. And over there, Young Lady, is the Little Dipper." Once again, Uncle Rob used his finger to outline the constellation above.

"Yes, I can see that one, too!" I squealed with delight.

"I see it, too," said my brother, who was standing directly behind me.

95

We gazed at the stars a little while longer, then turned around and headed back to the house. My uncle started to softly sing "O, Holy Night," and it made me lonesome for Daddy. I wondered if he was celebrating Christmas Eve all by himself. I wondered if he was even celebrating at all. I wondered about Mom, too, and suddenly wished to be home again.

After the four of us returned from our stroll, Aunt Lois threw together a makeshift bed for Mikie and me on the living room couch. I burrowed beneath the layer of blankets on one end while my brother claimed the other. Uncle Rob lovingly tucked us in and gave us each a kiss on the forehead then turned off all the lights except for those on the Christmas tree. I stared at the softly glowing shades of red and green, hoping they would lull me beyond my melancholy to the brighter side of daybreak.

"Mikie? Hey, Mikie," I whispered.

"Yeah?" he answered sleepily.

"Make a wish on the angel at the top of that tree," I pleaded.

"No, I don't want to. What if it doesn't come true?"

Unaffected, I ignored my brother's question and composed my own wish, "Please, oh please let Daddy be okay," I begged. "Please let him pick us up in the morning. I will die if I have to go to another foster home. You don't know how terrible those people were to us. Please take care of my brother and me. Pleazzzze."

And for once, the angel listened.

During Christmas recess in the winter of '74, my brother and I somehow got it into our heads that we needed to acquire another pet. Maybe it was because we'd watched *101 Dalmatians* too many times on TV, or maybe it was because

96

our cat Rusty preferred the comforts of Mom's blankets to ours and rarely ever came out to play with us. Whatever the case, we were convinced that our lives wouldn't be complete without another furry companion. A member of the rodent family seemed the obvious, least unobtrusive choice since we already had a cat and were smart enough to know that a dog would simply be out of the question.

A few days after the New Year, Daddy finally submitted to our begging and drove Mikie and me to the local pet shelter where we selected a gerbil from one of the large, glass holding pens.

"Oh look at how cute that one is right there," I cooed as I pointed to one in the far corner who was sleeping on top of his sibling's head.

"Yeah, that one seems nice," my brother agreed.

After we brought him home, Mikie and I pleaded with Daddy to let us keep our new, little critter inside the house. He refused. "Don't you dare let that rat in here," he curtly responded, forcing us to set up residence for Harvey out on our three-season back porch.

The bitter cold sorely tested the human condition that January. Night after night, the temperature dropped well below freezing, and it was a rare day when the weatherman didn't forecast a record breaker.

I was getting ready for bed one cold and drafty evening when my thoughts drifted to little Harvey. I began to worry about his welfare and decided to sneak downstairs in my pajamas and bare feet in an attempt to smuggle him inside. I opened the back door that led to our porch as quietly as I could, bent down and firmly grasped the handle on the top of Harvey's orange, plastic cage. Daddy must have heard me and caught me red-handed then demanded that I place the tiny, helpless rodent back into the clutches of Bitterness herself.

When I awoke the next morning, Harvey was the first thing on my mind. I scrambled downstairs to see how my furry friend had fared. With trepidation, I opened his cage and cautiously pawed through the wood shavings, only to stumble upon his cold and lifeless body. Still kneeling on the floor, I hung my head in defeat and began sobbing uncontrollably. My grief soon turned to rage, and I raced back into the house then started screaming at Daddy. "How could you let him die like that!" I ranted. "He was just a helpless, little gerbil, Daddy, and he needed us to keep him safe!" I couldn't talk to Daddy for days afterwards.

Coldness clawed at our frost-framed windowpanes and seemed to be feasting on the fragile heart of our family. A much-welcomed winter thaw arrived by mid-March, and the sun seemed to smile again. With spring at our doorstep, I felt a bit cheerful, maybe even hopeful. I was convinced Daddy would feel better after he finally finished his secret project and could once again dock the Cat near the shores of Lake Calhoun. And maybe, just maybe, Mom would return from Planet Oblivion.

It was early April when Daddy took a call from Sammie's mom who asked if I could join her family for their Passover celebration. Daddy readily agreed and marked the date on his secular calendar. I had never before experienced Passover. In fact, I'd never even heard of it. "What was it, anyway?" I wondered. "What exactly was passing over? And why did it sound more like a freeway maneuver than a holiday?" In the end, it didn't really matter; any type of social gathering at my best friend's house was always something worth anticipating.

The days passed agonizingly slowly until the festive date had finally arrived. It was Wednesday, the 12th of April. When I came home from school that day, Daddy was nowhere in sight. It wasn't hard for me to guess where I could find him. I walked into the kitchen and opened the basement door. "Daddy, I'm home!" I yelled down the stairs. "I'm going over to Sammie's tonight, remember?"

I could hear gritty sandpaper rhythmically stroking the body of his boat.

"What should I wear for Passover?" I asked, genuinely wanting to know.

"Something nice!" he yelled back without even missing a stroke.

His answer wasn't much help, but I didn't want to push my luck. I turned around and went upstairs to my bedroom, then rifled through all the clothes in my closet, carefully studying the possibilities of each selection. "Passover must be sort of like Easter," I deduced, and eventually settled on a pastel number.

After donning my holiday duds, I walked down the hallway to Mom's room and sunk my head into the murkiness. "I'm going over to Sammie's tonight, Mama. It's Passover Day," I explained. Knowing she wouldn't answer, I whispered, "I love you," then went downstairs and said my goodbyes to Daddy. He told me he'd pick me up around nine o'clock later that evening. "I don't want you walking home in the dark," he said sternly.

The atmosphere at Sammie's that day was filled with its usual warmth, but something was different, something I couldn't quite put my finger on. There was an added element of excitement. Chana and Les were there, dressed in stylish party attire, as were Sammie's Grandmamma and Grandpapa, who had flown in all the way from New York City. Chana's brother, David, and his Lutheran wife, Lisa, rounded out the list of adult attendees.

The dining room was aglow with flickering, golden candles that brilliantly illuminated the elegant table. Fine bone china paired with pretty, crystal goblets graced each place setting atop a fancy, linen tablecloth. Chana had fed me hundreds of times, maybe even thousands, but this was the first time I'd ever had the good fortune of eating anywhere other than in their kitchen or on the basement couch.

Les took my coat, then Sammie led the way into the living room where the two of us sat on the couch. Les joined David and Grandpapa in the surrounding Danish modern lounge chairs. The men sipped scotch from low-balls and talked about the Watergate mess while Chana, Grandmamma and Lisa busied themselves in the kitchen making last minute meal preparations.

I had no more than settled in when Grandmamma announced it was time for the Seder to begin. After we'd all taken our appointed places at the table, Chana entered with a bottle of wine and began circling her guests, pouring generous helpings for all the adults. Sammie and I giggled when she neared and brazenly held our fancy, crystal goblets high into the air. "Adults only, girls," Chana said playfully as she passed us by.

"Can't we have just a *teensy* bit of wine, Mom?" Sammie begged as she held her hand up and displayed what she meant by "teensy" with the distance between her forefinger and thumb.

"Maybe next year, Hon, when you're a *teensy* bit older," replied Chana as she winked at her daughter. "Nice try, though."

Grandpapa stood and held up his cup, then ceremoniously recited a blessing over the wine, "And there was evening and there was morning, the sixth day. The heaven and earth were finished . . ." He raised his vessel higher and concluded, "A reminder of God's first promise," then partook in a long sip. More blessings followed, matzo was passed and the drink of the gods flowed freely.

Riveted, my eyes focused upon Grandpapa as he prayed and told his stories of struggle and hope. I soon began to understand the Seder's rhythm and anticipated the blessings that allowed me to drink my grape juice "wine." Everything about this celebration was vastly different from what my own family holidays were like. It held an abundance of purpose and meaning, a far cry from the beastly feasts and gift exchanges I was used to.

Before I knew what had hit me, I was taking part in a Seder ritual that frightened me out of my wits. Invisible people were suddenly being acknowledged! No one else seemed unnerved as Grandpapa filled a special chalice with water and proclaimed that it was for a spirit named Miriam, then passed it to the person on his left and encouraged each of us to pour water from Miriam's cup into our own. This made me nervous. I didn't want any part of The Invisibles. As far as I was concerned, all they did was torment the hell out of my mother. "Wasn't Sammie's family aware of the consequences?" I wondered to myself as I warily eyed Miriam's cup while it glided from person to person. After it had made its way into Sammie's hands, she took her turn, then firmly held the goblet before me. I froze.

Sammie's brow furrowed. She leaned toward me and explained, "You have to do just like I did. Pour some of the water into your glass." I was just about to shake my head "no," then thought the better of it. These people were like family to me, and I didn't want to make them sorry they'd invited me to their nice party. I cautiously grasped the goblet, did what was expected of me, then passed it over to Uncle David so hastily that one would have thought it was searing my flesh. My shoulders reflexively hunched as I surveyed the room with suspicion for any outward signs of abnormalities. Luckily, there weren't any. Not yet, anyway.

Then, to my utter amazement, Grandpapa instructed Sammie to open the patio door behind her and let in a second spirit named Elijah. Prickly tingles sprung up on the back of my neck. I wondered why these people chose to freely mingle with the spirit world, and willingly, no less. Were they all mad? Just as the door opened, a slight breeze blew in, ruffling the sheer, white drapes as it passed.

"OH my gosh!" I shrieked inside my head. "Elijah just came in!" I wanted to shut my eyes or, better yet, make a break for our recording studio in the basement. I tried as hard as I could to act as though nothing was wrong with me.

Out of the blue, everyone started to softly sing in unison. The tranquility of the moment pierced through me, and I no longer had the urge to run. I surveyed the room once more, cautiously letting down my guard. The expressions of Sammie's family looked so serene, without a trace of fear. No one started slapping themselves in the face. No one shouted in horror. I determined that the spirits surrounding us were of the friendly variety, and my shoulders began to relax as I sat up straight, eager to once more enjoy the festivities.

The Seder concluded that evening with a poem about peace; peace for those of us present at the table, and peace for all others throughout the world. Uncle David began to sing "We Shall Overcome," and then everyone else joined in. I looked at Sammie who was half smiling at me as she sang. It was clear that she had sung this song many times before. I joined in after hearing the chorus a few times and sang along as best I could.

I left Sammie's house that evening with a renewed sense of faith in my future. The Passover celebration had made me realize that my family was not the only one to have struggled through turbulent times. People everywhere, regardless of their burden, embraced hope, even during the roughest of life's storms. And, where there was hope, its sister, joy, would surely follow.

After returning home that night, I hung my Passover outfit on the backside of my closet door, knowing it would be the same one I'd wear a few days from now on Easter Sunday.

I hurriedly brushed my teeth and put myself to bed, wishing I didn't have to wake up early for school the next morning.

Friday soon rolled around, and I was getting excited for the weekend to begin. When I arrived home from school that afternoon, I headed straight for the kitchen to get myself a snack. While nibbling on a cookie, I pondered my fun-filled options, then wiped my mouth with the edge of my shirtsleeve and walked over to the basement door.

"Daddy!" I yelled. "What are we going to do tonight? Can we go out to a movie or something?" I stood at the top of the stairs with my hand on the doorknob, waiting for an answer.

"I'm too busy," he yelled back.

"How about sometime this weekend, then?" I pressed.

"Why don't you ask one of your friends."

Since I wasn't in the mood to argue, I let his disappointing reply stand. I momentarily rested my head against the basement door before closing it, then walked to the opposite end of the kitchen and picked up the telephone receiver.

"Wha cha doin'?" I asked Sammie when she answered, trying to sound cheerful.

Our conversation rambled from the latest Partridge Family episode to the topic of Sammie's crush in fourth hour gym class. I asked if she could hang out with me over the weekend, but she already had plans to visit a friend who lived in the northern suburbs.

"I'm going to Cindy's house after my ballet class at the Y on Sunday," she told me. "Maybe you could meet me at the mall after and go with. My mom could drive us."

"That'd be so neat-o," I chirped. "But, how do I get . . ." I stopped before finishing my sentence, realizing that I needed Daddy. "One sec, okay? I'll get my dad and he can get directions from your mom."

I placed the phone on the kitchen counter, then walked back over to the basement door and yelled, "Daddy? Could you come up here and talk to Chana?"

No answer. "Are you even still down there?" I screeched. "Leave me alone. I told you I was busy, didn't I?!"

"But Daddy, I need you. Will you pleazzzze come up here?!"

I heard his tools thump down onto the workbench, and soon he was trudging up the stairs. "What on earth do you want from me?" he petulantly asked.

"Well, since you're *so* busy this weekend, Daddy, I asked Sammie to do something with me instead," I answered ever so snottily as I handed him the phone. "Now you need to get directions from her mom and drive me to the mall on Sunday."

Daddy gave me an incensed look, then motioned for me to retrieve a pencil and notepad. "Yes, Sunday at 1:00. Roseville Mall. Not a problem, we'll see you then," he said with all the politeness he could muster while writing down the instructions.

After hanging up the phone, he turned to me and irritably asked, "Do you realize, young lady, that this Sunday is Easter?" After a slight pause he continued, "It doesn't matter. We won't be celebrating it this year anyway."

"Oh, no!" I said, sincerely apologetic. "I forgot all about Easter!"

"It's just that you're always working on your *stupid* boat, and you never have time anymore for anyone but your *stupid* self," I abruptly spat.

My stinging insult had finally pushed Daddy over the line. He forebodingly walked toward me and lifted his hand high in the air, then slapped me across the face. Hard.

Never before in all my life had he ever laid a hand on me. I shrieked from the shock, then started crying uncontrollably. More than anything else, I wanted to be released from the cacophony that permeated our family's opus. I kept telling Daddy over and over again how sorry I was, but he didn't want to listen and retreated down-under to the quiet recesses of his workroom.

That night I parked myself in the corner of our living room, far out of Daddy's way, and licked my wounds as I watched the tube. When the head-bobs started setting in, I shuffled upstairs and got ready for bed. While I was passing from the bathroom back to my bedroom, I could hear my parents' voices drifting down the hallway. Daddy kept asking Mom to read him a passage from the Bible. "Just this once, Rainy," he pleaded.

"Leave me alone, Rick. I don't feel like it right now. Can't you let me be?" she hissed, her speech slurring from heavy drug usage.

Their exchange was completely out of character. Daddy hadn't had any meaningful interaction with Mom for months, as though he'd finally given up on her. And why was he so interested in her Bible studies, anyway? "Just another day at the Funny Farm," I pessimistically thought to myself.

I slipped underneath the covers that night feeling hollow and raw. Daddy's love for me was so distant these days, and I wished with all my might that I could make him smile again. "But how?" I wondered. Deep down, I knew that the answer was sliding away and light-years beyond my reach.

I had been asleep for just a few hours that night when Daddy came into my room and woke me up. Immersed in the strong pull of slumber I struggled to open my eyes, then looked at the clock on my nightstand. 12:13 a.m.

"What's going on, Daddy?" I asked groggily. "Is everything okay?"

105

"C'mon Twink, we need to take a ride," he told me, as if a midnight car ride were nothing out of the ordinary.

"A ride? In the car? But Daddy, isn't it still dark outside?" I protested from beneath my warm covers.

Daddy just stood there looking down at me, saying nothing. Although his anger had subsided he seemed strangely intense. Something instinctively told me that I should get out of bed and go with him.

I don't remember much about getting dressed, getting into the car or any other of the finer details for that matter. I don't even remember much about the actual ride itself. I only remember how damp and foggy it was outside that night as the saturated clouds spit a jumbled mix of rain and snow onto the Buick. Daddy started the car and turned on the wiper blades. They sharply squeaked as they slid back and forth across the front windshield, loudly declaring that they, too, wanted to return to where it was warm and dry.

I rested my head against the car door and tried as hard as I could to keep my eyes open. "Daddy, can we turn on the radio?" I asked.

He said "no," then told me to pay close attention to where we were going.

"Where *are* we going, anyway," I asked.

He explained that we were driving to the mall, the same one where I was to meet Sammie on Sunday. His answered seemed as foggy as the evening air, but I was too tired to think much about it at the time.

We pulled into the mall's empty parking lot. Daddy maneuvered the Buick toward the entrance of the Sears store, shifted into park and turned off the headlights. I felt his strong hand on my shoulder as he gently shook me awake. "Twink," he said in earnest, "this is very important. Now, pay attention, will you?"

The chill of the evening air was seeping deeper into my bones. I folded my arms across my chest to fend it off, then tried to sit up straight. The dull glare from the store's neon letters above caught my attention. The lights in the "S" had burned out, giving the false impression that the name of the store was "ears." "Where are we again?" I drowsily asked as I lifted my small hands to my face and tried to wipe the sleep away.

"We're at the Sears store in Roseville Mall," Daddy answered, eerily calm. "This is where you'll be meeting Sammie on Sunday. Do you think you can remember how to get here?"

I told Daddy I'd try, then glanced over at him. He was staring straight ahead, fixated on the architecture of the Sears building. I slid closer to the passenger door and eased my back against it so I could focus on him. He didn't say anything for a long while so I tried to urge him home. "Daddy?" I said quietly. "Don't you think . . . I mean, maybe we should . . . why don't we just go home now?" He was so deep in thought that he didn't hear me. After a while, my eyes began to flutter, then slowly closed again.

"Did I ever tell you about the times when I was a kid?" Daddy offered, breaking his silence.

I kept my eyes closed and whispered, "No Daddy. Now that I think about it, you haven't."

"When I was just a kid," Daddy continued, "right about your age, life was a beautiful thing. I had it all ahead of me, just like you do now. The world was absolutely amazing, you know, like this magnetic paradox of riddles and knowledge." Daddy slid a little farther down in his seat and continued. "For as long as I can remember, my old man was constantly on my ass, always harassing me about taking care of the house and making me do all kinds of chores. Whenever I could get the hell out of there, me and my buddies would sneak down to the river and climb all over the place. Sometimes we'd do a little fishing, maybe catch a crappie or two or a few crawdads. Once in a while I'd even go down there all by myself and lie in the

107

sand along the riverbank, just soaking in that hot, summer sun. I felt so free there, like nothing could ever go wrong again."

I lifted my heavy lids and peered over at Daddy. I could detect the tension on his face. I wanted to ask him why he didn't feel free anymore but thought the better of it, opting to remain close-lipped.

"You're such a curious, little thing, Twink," Daddy said to me without looking my way. "I can see it in your eyes, you know, whenever I take you anywhere. You're so hungry to learn, constantly searching for answers . . . you got that from me, you know. I was exactly like that when I was your age." He briefly stopped speaking to survey the parking lot, then continued. "My old man never wanted to teach me anything, never wanted me to learn. He'd get pissed whenever I messed with his things. But once in a while, when that asshole wasn't around, I'd sneak into our garage where he kept all his tools and study them, one by one. I'd pick them up and hold them in my hand, trying to figure out how to use them." Daddy stared down at the open palm of his hand as if he were cradling the worn handle of one of his father's tools, then abruptly curled that same hand into a fist and snorted angrily. "He never took one fucking minute to teach me a goddamn thing about those tools. Not one fucking minute," he shouted, then clenched his teeth and shook his head from side to side. "One time, that S.O.B. caught me and hit me so hard that it knocked the wind clear out of me. He took his belt to me until I peed my pants and told me to take it like a man. That fucking son of a bitch. All because I was screwing around with his damn tools. He was never any kind of a real father to me, and I wish Ma would have left him years ago. Me and Sis, we tried to convince her to walk out on him, but she wouldn't hear of it, telling us that divorce was a sin, and she wasn't about to be sent to hell. Yeah . . . well . . . being a fucking asshole is a sin, too. I was going to prove it to the old man that I was stronger than anything he could dish out. I left home as soon as I could and enlisted in the air force." Daddy's voice became a little lighter as he reflected on that memory, "It was the best thing I ever did. Those planes were quite a sight, quite a sight. I had big plans to be a pilot. Yep. That was my dream. I was going to fly one of those metallic beasts come hell or high water. I had a lot of smarts back then. Still do, I guess . . . that was about the only thing my old man gave me that was ever of any value. After my four years were up, I got discharged and moved back to Minnesota for a job at the flourmill. That's when I met Rainy. Your mother." Daddy became really quiet as he thought about Mom for a moment. "Did I ever tell you what a beautiful thing she was, Twink?" he asked. "She was, without a doubt, the prettiest girl in this whole city. We had so many plans, your mom and I, so many things that we were going to do together." Daddy bent his head and stared into his lap. "They all just passed us by, one by one. And now . . . they're all gone." Daddy looked up at the Sears store again, then shook his head from side to side as if in complete disbelief of what his life had become. Melancholy seeped into his voice as he said quietly, "She's not the same woman I once knew. Not by a long shot. That woman is gone forever."

Daddy let the car idle a little while longer as he tilted his head back and peered into the sky. "You know something, Twink," he said, "look at all those stars shining up there. Look at how huge the universe really is." To emphasize its vastness, he raised his open hand and fluidly moved it from right to left, as if erasing a word on a chalkboard. I narrowed my eyes and peered in that same direction, but all I could make out was an empty sky full of haze. Daddy gazed a long while, as if mesmerized by something I couldn't understand, then suddenly pressed his forefinger onto the front windshield and intently scribbled several letters in the formed condensation.

I leaned closer to the glass, trying to decipher his spelling, then scooted toward the center of the front seat to get a better look. Slowly, I began to verbalize each individual letter

as I decoded it: s... u... r... r... e... c... t... i... o... n.
"Surrection? Daddy, what does surretion mean?"

Daddy silently used his finger to underline the first two letters that I had missed then instructed me to decipher it once more: R... e... s... u... r... r... e... c...

Before I could finish spelling it out again, Daddy turned the headlights back on and shifted the car into drive, then somberly declared, "Resurrection . . . ."

After we arrived home that night, I slid my coat off and laid it on one of the dining room chairs. Daddy walked over to the radiator and rested his back against it. I tried to read the features of his face but the room was too dark, and all I could make out was his profile against the glow of the kitchen night-light. "I love you, Daddy," I told him before ascending the stairs. "See you tomorrow morning."

I thought I heard him reply, "Yeah, maybe . . ." but decided I must have been mistaken.

As I drowsed in bed, trying to get back to sleep, I felt Daddy's uneasy presence in my bedroom doorway. Silhouetted by the hallway light, he stood quietly in the gloom, observing me from afar. Soon thereafter, as if an illusion caught between two worlds, Daddy was gone.

I awoke slowly the next morning, basking in the bright sunshine that bathed my face. My first thought was how good it felt to be safe and warm. I lay there for a while with my eyes closed, listening to the robins chirp outside my window, then my mind began to wander. I started thinking about the park down by the creek. Maybe Daddy would take a break from his secret project and go with me. Suddenly I remembered our peculiar escapade just hours before. Blood rushed from my face as the light of day brought revelation to the midnight car ride that now seemed like a Twilight Zone episode. My heart pounded erratically as I bolted out of bed then ran downstairs. I raced into the dining room, then into the living room. Daddy wasn't there. I sprinted into the kitchen where Mom was making muffins and flung the basement door open.

"Are you there, Daddy?" I cried.

When he didn't answer, I started to panic. "Mom!" I screeched, "Do you know where Daddy is?"

"I haven't seen him yet this morning," she replied, oblivious to my erratic behavior. "Maybe he's out in the garage."

"The garage!" I rationalized. "That's it! He's in the garage." I raced outside, still in my pajamas and bare feet, and frantically tried to open the garage door. It was locked.

My heart was pumping like a train engine as the realization hit me that something was terribly wrong. I raced back into the house and up the stairs to the door that led to Daddy's apartment. With a trembling hand, I opened it and yelled "Daddy," just as I had so many times before. I kept saying his name over and over again, but there was no answer. With no other choice but to go up there, I warily placed one foot onto the first step and took a deep, nervous breath before slowly stepping up onto the next. I was terrified of what I would find. In the pit of my gut, in the very center of my soul, I knew that the fateful car ride I'd taken with Daddy would prove to be the last time I'd ever see him alive.

I reached the top and stepped into Daddy's apartment. There he was, on the floor at the edge of his bed, his lifeless, bloody body splayed out before me.

Daddy was finally free at last.

111

I stood at the top of those stairs screaming my head off. Before I knew it, Mom was screaming right alongside me. I started to hyperventilate and nearly collapsed, but somehow instinctively knew I had to pull myself together and find somebody to help Daddy. Maybe he wasn't dead yet. Maybe someone could put him back together. I raced downstairs to our phone in the kitchen and dialed 9-1-1. Each time I put the receiver to my ear, there was complete silence. I kept frantically repeating, "Hello? Hello?" I couldn't understand what was happening, so I hung up the phone, and then tried to redial. No matter how many times I tried, I couldn't get a dial tone. Frustrated and angry, I threw the receiver onto the floor, and that's when I remembered that our neighbors' son was home from medical school. I ran next door and furiously rang their doorbell until Mr. Olson answered. I started blubbering incoherently, trying to spit out my words. "My Daddy!" and "Please Help!" were the only two expressions I could reasonably articulate. Mr. Olson ushered me inside and led me into the den. "Have a seat, Dear, everything is going to be all right," he kindheartedly assured.

I sat shaking uncontrollably in a lounge chair next to a window that faced our house and nervously peered out. "Please help my Daddy," I begged one last time before Mr. Olson left to retrieve his son. A few minutes later, I saw the two of them enter my house. I lowered my head into my hands and began sobbing and shrieking again. I cried so hard I thought my lungs were going to explode. I began to hear the faint sound of sirens and knew they were coming for Daddy. I stopped crying and looked out the window again. I saw my brother approaching our front door as if it were any other day. He was arriving home from a sleepover at a friend's. Mr. Olson, who had been nervously pacing around our front yard while waiting for the paramedics, approached my brother and gently put a hand on one of his shoulders as he delivered the dire news. My brother stood completely still, clearly in shock, and then tears began streaming down his face. Mr. Olson put his arm around Mikie and guided him inside to join me in their den. Mikie sat on the edge of the couch and let his face rest on his propped-up hands as hot tears sped down his cheeks. We didn't say anything at first; we just sat there and bawled for what seemed like an eternity. Mikie broke our dark spell when he turned to me and asked, "Where's Mom?"

My mind went blank. I didn't have an answer. I began retracing the sequence of events from the moment I'd felt Mom standing next to me in Daddy's apartment. I suddenly realized that I hadn't seen her since. Perplexed, I replied, "I honestly don't know."

Mikie wiped away a handful of tears, and then said with false bravado, "You know, maybe Daddy's still alive. I mean, he has lots of guns and one of them is what they call a Saturday Night Special. They're not very powerful, you know, so maybe it just hurt him real bad and the doctors can still fix him."

"Do you think so, Mikie?" I asked desperately.

"Man, I hope so," he said, suddenly sounding despondent.

We sat in that small, brown-paneled den, feeling as if we were losing oxygen by the minute as we watched Mr. Olson and his son converse with one of the paramedics on our front lawn.

"Please bring Daddy out alive. Oh, please, please, please," I kept repeating as one of my hands nervously clutched the other in my lap.

My brother and I suspended our breath as soon as one of the paramedics emerged from our house walking backwards, carrying the bottom end of Daddy's stretcher. As soon as Daddy's form was fully revealed, all hope instantly vanished; a snow-white cotton sheet covered him from head to toe. In that split second, it became crystal clear that whichever gun Daddy had used the night before had fulfilled its intended purpose. He was never coming back to us. Not this time, not ever. In that split second, we forever left behind our Daddy at that juncture on Ghellow Road.

It is disturbing how the emotion from a single event, frozen in time, can conquer you so completely. It gnaws at your innards like a starved coyote, always wanting more than you have to give. We all became victims of Daddy's assault upon himself that day, my brother and I, Mom, even Grandma. And the burden of all the pain that Daddy had carried so closely for all those years did not cease at the moment of his final breath; on it would live, multiplying and becoming stronger as it serpentined its way through the hearts of those of us who loved him, fueled by the grief that we could never escape.

A crucial piece of myself remained back in the bloody aftermath at Daddy's apartment that day, slashing a wound that the hands of time would never be able to mend.

Mom was re-admitted to the mental hospital, so Grandma came to stay with us for a few days. Relatives on both sides of our broken family soon arrived to dismantle what remained of our household. Since Mom's relatives accused Daddy of causing her schizophrenia, and Daddy's relatives accused Mom of causing his suicide, the two camps took great pains to avoid each other while they cleaned up the messy details of our lives.

I was at the kitchen table trying to choke down some Corn Flakes one morning when I thought I heard a noise in our basement. At first I thought it was Daddy's ghost and became a bit scared. After all, he was the only person with official clearance to enter the basement. I set my spoon down and walked over to the door that led to Daddy's workroom, then mustered the courage to descend.

Aunt Lois was standing with her back toward me at the opposite end of the room, deep in the forbidden zone, silently studying Daddy's secret project. I impulsively moved closer. When no one tried to stop me I felt safe enough to find out once and for all what had kept Daddy so distant during the last few months of his life. My mind's eye was expecting a masterfully carved, wooden boat, just like the ones Daddy had always talked about. But, as I neared, I realized that my expectations couldn't have been further from the truth. What Daddy had crafted wasn't a boat at all. Instead, resting before me on a large, makeshift worktable was a life-sized, wooden sarcophagus, similar to those he and I had seen at the museum.

Aunt Lois gasped when she realized that I was standing next to her, and put her hand over her chest. "Oh Dear, it's only you," she said with a sigh of relief. "My goodness, you scared me."

"Aunt Lois?" I asked, my body trembling with fright, "What's that?" I already knew the answer.

"Now Honey, that's not for you to worry about," she said as a matter-of-fact before composing herself and ushering me out of the basement. "Let's go on upstairs. I have something of your father's which I'd like to give you." I craned my neck backwards to examine Daddy's sarcophagus, but my aunt steadily strode toward the stairs with a firm grip on my shoulder, and led me up through the kitchen then parked me in our living room. "I'll be right back," she said as she helped me onto the couch. When she returned, she handed me a small envelope with my name written in Daddy's handwriting. "I found this in your father's belongings. Be sure to keep it in a safe place now, won't you, Dear?" she encouraged.

I tenderly perched the envelope on my lap. Darkness enrobed me, and I wanted to burst out crying again.

"I suppose I need to get some more things accomplished today. I've still got to pack up your father's things from his apartment," my aunt said before pecking me on the cheek. "I'll see you in a little while."

115

I watched her walk away, then picked up the envelope and started tearing it open. "No," I thought as I stopped myself, "I'll put it in a safe hiding place and read it later." I went upstairs to my bedroom and reached underneath my bed for the pretty jewelry box that Daddy had given to me after I'd come back from the foster home. On the backside of the case was a tiny knob that opened a secret compartment. I gently pulled it, then slipped the envelope inside and slid the box back underneath my bed.

That night I had a dream. I was standing in the street in front of our house, wearing a long, white velvet dress. It was pitch black outside. No one wandered the streets, no one haunted the houses. The winter wind broke the silence with her howling, chilly cackle. I shivered in the cold and flung my arms about me, trying to keep warm, then struggled to turn and run back inside, only to discover that my feet were frozen to the ground. Out of desperation, I twisted my body to the left and was confronted by a vast tunnel of surly fog. To my right was more of the same. I tilted my head back toward Sister Moon and cried, "Won't somebody please help me!!!" The echoes laughed as they fled.

No one ever came.

†BOOK TWO†
Fumbling through the Tangled Labyrinth

As I now look back upon those tragic events, I stand astonished at how quickly my young, shattered mind was able to piece itself back together, at least long enough to christen the next chapter of my life. The destruction from within would patiently lay in wait amidst a dense cluster of cattails and delicately painted butterflies until the last one migrated southward, never to return again.

After Daddy's funeral, the county sent someone to our house to take care of my brother and me while Mom's relatives checked her back into the mental hospital. We never knew what the county worker's real name was, so we simply referred to her as "The County." Whenever my brother and I were unsure of her whereabouts at any given time, we'd ask each other, "So, where's The County?" This new intruder made me nervous. It wasn't that I was fearful of her, not in the least. It was more that her mannerisms were most peculiar, indeed. She was a middle-aged woman of average height and build with electrified short, brown hair that had seen its share of too many home perms. She frequently applied cheap, Drugstore Orange lipstick to her aged, thinning lips even though she rarely left our house, and was a cigarette company's chain-smoking dream, leaving behind vibrant hues on the beaver dam of butts in Mom's ashtrays. For the most part, The County ignored my brother and me. On the rare occasions when she did speak to

117

us, she was never able to maintain eye contact for long, preferring to glance at assorted objects scattered around the room. She mumbled so softly that we often couldn't understand what she was saying, and would then make a quick dash into an unoccupied part of our house. It wasn't immediately clear to my brother and me if the government had sent a bona fide employee or one of Mom's escaped roommates from the mental hospital.

During this period of my life, time slowed down for me, as if I were quickly approaching the speed of light in one of Daddy's physics riddles. It felt as though I couldn't grow up fast enough, longing to be in control of my own life and leave behind all this mayhem once and for all.

Mikie and I rarely saw each other, seeking refuge with our own set of friends until Mom finally returned to us several weeks later, coherent but far from healed. Uncomfortable with her newly appointed head-of-household status, Mom struggled to remain focused and in control, often opting to leave my brother and me to our own devices while she cried away the hours next to Rusty underneath the soft comfort of her warm bedroom blankets.

On the last day of the school year, Mom made a determined effort of greeting us when we arrived home and informed my brother and me that we would soon be moving far from the only way of life we had ever known.

"Where are you taking us to, Mommy?" I asked fretfully.

"Up north to International Falls where Grandma and Grandpa Hansen live. Do you remember when we visited them there a few years ago?"

"Yeah, sort of," I uneasily replied as I stared at the ground, biting my bottom lip.

"I need help raising you kids," she explained, her voice sounding as fragile and pained as the look in her eye.

At the time, I felt little sadness at the prospect of moving, perhaps because I'd always considered myself imprisoned anyway. Time and again, the fate of my future was never my own, and I was continually forced to succumb to a higher power.

International Falls was a tiny, industrialized town of 10,000 people perched deep in the heart of the northern Minnesota pine forests along the Canadian border. Its blue-collar population of European descent worked damn hard and drank even harder, but their handshakes were deep and genuine. The golden goose that attracted only the heartiest of souls to this rugged country was a prosperous paper mill positioned on the banks of the Rainy River. It incessantly belched a thick, black foggy breath past the rooftops of the town's aging business district, mercilessly crucifying this once-stunning parcel of God's Country in exchange for hefty profits.

The year was 1975.

The day before we left, Grandma came over to say goodbye. The two of us sat together in the living room as we waited for my brother to get back from his afternoon paper route, I in the red rocking chair and Grandma on the couch.

"Grandma?" I said earnestly as I stood up and walked over to sit beside her.

"Yes, Dear."

"I just want you to know that you are my most favorite Grandma. I'm never, ever, never, ever going to love my new Grandma the way that I love you," I exclaimed as I swung my head from shoulder to shoulder in an exaggerated fashion.

She chuckled softly then put her arm around me. "Oh, Honey," she said, "You will love her just the same." She paused and looked down at me, "Maybe even more."

"No, Grandma, I won't! I just know I won't!" I told her indignantly. "You are like a Momma to me!"

She held me closer and then said, "Always remember that no matter how far away you are, I will be thinking of you."

119

She put her soft, wrinkled hand underneath my chin and gently nudged it in her direction so that I would look her in the eye. "You'll remember, won't you?"

A few tears started to slide down my face and I couldn't say anything at all, so I just nodded my head "yes" and tried to smile.

"Don't you cry," she said as she broke eye contact and looked straight ahead. "You can write me lots of letters and tell me all about your new friends and how you are getting along in the fifth grade."

My tears started to flow harder and I trembled slightly.

She looked back into my eyes and said with intent, "I have known you all of your life. You are such a smart little girl, and you will find your way. Yes, Dear, yes you will."

"Not without . . . out you," I said as I started sobbing. "Now Daddy's gone and if I don't have you, then I don't have *anyone* to take care of me," I moaned, then plopped my teary face into the center of her bosom.

That must have struck a chord with Grandma because she remained silent for a long time. Finally, she bent her neck and softly kissed me on the top of my head, then gave me one last squeeze before gently pushing me aside and extracting herself from my desperate grasp. She stood up, then turned to me and said, "Never forget that I love you, Honey."

She started to make her way over to the second floor stairs. "I need to say goodbye to your mother now," she told me. "I'll be back down as soon as Mikie gets home. Tell him to wait for me in the living room." Then slowly, she turned away from me and left.

The emergence of summer that year brought forth the emergence of a new life for me. I entered the streets of my newfound hometown with a heart as heavy as a lost puppy's, poised to beg for love from anyone kind enough to give it.

Mom, my brother and I were fresh off the Greyhound when a beat-up yellow taxi deposited a disheveled threesome in front of Grandma and Grandpa Hansen's house on a hot, June day. We waited beside the cab as Grandpa strode over to meet us. He handed the driver a ten dollar bill and said, "Thanks, Jerry," then gave the side of the car door a few friendly thumps, sending the driver on his way. Since Mom was basically penniless and didn't have a job, we had no other choice but to live with her parents until our fortunes turned around.

"Wull, Hullo there, Rainy, how was your trip?" Grandpa asked Mom in his north woods dialect as he briefly but warmly hugged his daughter.

Mom sighed and said, "Fine, I guess. We made it," then concocted a quizzical expression with her face and hands as if to add, "Believe it or not."

Grandpa then turned to my brother and me and said affectionately, "Wull Hullo, Kids! It's good to see you again. It's been a while. C'mon in." Then he bent down and grabbed two of our suitcases, leaving my brother to wrestle with the third.

Mom's parents owned a small, one-story dwelling in the center of town. It was a humble, Depression-era house furnished in the bare-boned essentials. Under foot rested an outdated, multi-colored shag that smelled of hard living from days past. Their sole expression of extravagance was a wooden, upright piano that stood forgotten against the wall in the corner of their tiny dining room. Softening the drabness of the brown, paneled walls were a few artful decorations, among them a cluster of six high school graduation photos that proudly hung in the entryway. Grandma and Grandpa had raised all six of their kids in this house, seven if you count the oldest, who had died unexpectedly in her youth. On the opposite side of the room, above the television set, hung a

121

solitary photo of a delicate, 10-year-old girl, hauntingly reminding all who entered of love, lost.

As soon as we crossed the threshold, Mom walked over to New Grandma, who was seated in the living room on her favorite orange and brown, floral high back chair, and lovingly kissed her on the cheek.

"Well, well, Rainy," New Grandma said to my mother as if she'd just seen her the day before, "So you're here."

"Yep, I'm hanging in there," Mom replied, attempting to reassure herself more than New Grandma. She then walked over to the unoccupied matching high back and sat down. Dark circles hung beneath her eyes, and she appeared especially pale without the false glow of blush upon her cheeks.

Grandpa told the three of us to make ourselves at home, and informed Mom and me that we'd be sleeping on the hideaway in the living room. Mikie would be using the extra twin bed in Grandpa's room, and Grandma would continue sleeping alone in the room that shared nothing more than a wall with her husband. Somehow, it all seemed completely normal.

After we'd settled in and unpacked our belongings, Mikie and I plopped ourselves on the living room couch while Mom and New Grandma retired to the kitchen table for a smoke.

I turned to my brother and asked, "What should we do now?" We didn't have any friends yet, and didn't even know if there was a playground nearby. I was pretty sure that Mom wouldn't take the time to show us around town. She'd often treated us more like pets than children, bringing us along if it was convenient. And if it wasn't? Well, we were pretty much on our own.

Mikie shrugged his shoulders then said, "Want to watch the tube?"

"Sure," I replied as I got up and switched it on.

About the only thing of interest was a Mutual of Omaha program. It started out innocently enough as the camera zoomed in on an unsuspecting herd of zebra that were calmly grazing on the African plains. Minutes later, they unexpectedly scattered as one lame soul was singled out and stalked, then eventually dismembered by a hungry pride of lions. I sat wincing in silent horror, my knees recoiling toward my midriff.

Grandpa came out from his bedroom several minutes later. "It's a beautiful day out there," he said to us as he nodded toward the door. "Don't you want to go outside and play?"

We told him that we didn't know where to go.

"Well, I'll fix that," he said pragmatically as he reached into his pants pocket and extracted a few bucks, then handed the money to Mikie.

"Here you go," he said. "Now, I'd like you to go down to the Bridgeman's and get yourselves a couple of cones. How does that grab you?"

Cones? As in ice cream . . . cones? Our eyes lit up like a fistful of firecrackers. Neither of us had ever been to a Bridgeman's before. Fact is, we'd never even heard of it, but one thing was for sure, if they had ice cream there it had to be some place worthwhile.

From where he was standing, Grandpa turned his head and yelled into the kitchen, "Mother! Rainy! The kids are going on down to the Bridgeman's. What kind of ice cream would you like?"

They both answered they weren't hungry so Grandpa turned back to us and said, "All right, well they don't want any, but I'm not going to pass it up. I want you to get me a good old-fashioned vanilla."

"Vanilla, Grandpa? That's boring," I told him.

"Yep," he said firmly, "If God would've wanted ice cream to be any other flavor, he'd have made cow's milk a different color."

Grandpa then proceeded to give us directions to the ice cream shop. "You go out the front door, then you make a left, you see. Go down the street three blocks, and then you'll get to a shopping center. That's where the Piggly Wiggly is. Now, Bridgeman's is right next door to the Piggly Wiggly. Grandpa studied the two of us for a moment, then asked, "Are you following me?"

My brother and I both shook our heads "yes." It seemed easy enough. We left the house, happy to have something fun to do.

"Hey, how come Grandpa gave the money to *you*?" I asked my brother.

"*Obviously*," Mikie answered, clearly emphasizing his word of choice and rapping his thumb on his chest, "because I'm the one in charge." Then added as an afterthought, "And the smartest one, too!"

"Yeah, whatever," I replied.

We arrived at the ice cream parlor a few minutes later and walked inside. The artificially cool air felt pleasantly refreshing. We slid in real close to the glass-topped freezer and lustfully peered down at the array of multi-colored choices.

"What kind are you going to get?" asked my brother.

"Um, I think I want orange sherbet," I told him.

Mikie nodded as he continued perusing the selection until a waitress came over and courteously asked, "How can I help?"

Mikie said, "I'll have one chocolate, one vanilla and one . . . ," then he looked over at me.

"And one orange sherbet," I declared, emphasizing my choice by tapping on the glass above my chosen flavor.

After my brother had paid the nice lady, we hurriedly walked back to our new home while begrudgingly taking turns holding Grandpa's cone, fearing it would turn into sweet soup if we didn't walk fast enough. Along the way, I studied the pleasant, working-class homes. People were shooting the bull with their neighbors while their kids raced bikes up and down the dirt alleyways. Things seemed friendly and safe in this new place.

I looked into the sky at the unfamiliar sight of paper mill exhaust that was billowing past, and prayed that the communal arms of this foreign land would wrap themselves around me.

In the weeks soon after our arrival, my brother made fast friends with a boy who lived down the street from my grandparents, leaving me to spend most of those early days either alone or with Bucky, our resident brown-eyed beagle. He and I would often walk downtown together or over to Smokey the Bear Park, intentionally ambling past the community playground with the hope of making some friends of my own.

I was standing at the kitchen counter one afternoon, picking apart a piece of stale banana bread, when I suddenly became aware of New Grandma staring at me past the tip of her ashy cigarette. "Why don't you go outside and find yourself some friends?" she blurted while seated against the wall at the marbled Formica dinner table.

Her bluntness took me by surprise. I gazed steadily back at her and defensively replied, "I don't have any."

"Well, why not? Doesn't make any sense. All kids your age have friends."

I started getting annoyed and narrowed my eyes as I returned her intrusive stare.

She seemed undaunted and took a long drag off her cigarette. "You can talk, can't you?" she asked rhetorically.

"Of course I can," I snottily replied.

"Well then, what's the problem?"

Uncomfortable with where this conversation was headed, I scooped up the remainder of my banana bread and stomped out to the backyard, finishing it off in silence on the broken down picnic table.

I didn't like this cantankerous, old lady one bit. She was as abrasive as a jagged shard of glass on a sandy beach and

125

would slice clean through you if you didn't watch your step. It wasn't that I was afraid of her really; it was more that I preferred taking the side streets rather than risking a gory accident on the freeway. From that day forward, I avoided her whenever I could, and as time went on, we formed an unspoken agreement that if she didn't get in my way, I wouldn't get in hers.

That night, after everyone else had retired, I confessed my true feelings about New Grandma as Mom and I were lying in the dark on the living room hideaway.

"Momma?" I said as we lay there back to back.

"Yes, Honey," she softly replied.

"I don't like living here," I told her. "I don't like my New Grandma."

Mom didn't get mad at me like I thought she would. Instead, she asked sleepily, "Why not, Dear?"

"She's mean," I heatedly whispered. "She's a mean, old witch!"

Mom started to stir from my fussing and said to me, "Shhhh, you don't want her to hear you." She rolled over so that her torso pressed against my back and began to stroke my forehead with her soothing, motherly caress.

"She's mean, all right," Mom confessed. "I spent eighteen years of my life with that woman, and I know how she can be. I never thought I'd have to live with her again, but here I am." She sighed and then continued, "Right now, we just don't have any other option." She gently brushed the hair out of my eyes. "I interviewed for a job at Pearson's Bakery yesterday. If they hire me, I'll be able to save up some money."

"Does that mean we'll get to move away from here soon?" I asked hopefully.

"We'll move as soon as we can, okay Baby? Now close your eyes and go to sleepie."

Her affectionate hand against my brow felt so comforting. I wanted to believe her, so I tried not to think of any other outcome. I closed my eyes and snuggled in closer, letting her embrace me away to Dreamland.

Midsummer quickly rolled around. The morning of the Fourth of July was bright and sunny that year, waking me especially early as the sparkling rays of light sped their way past the opened brocade curtains and into the living room where I slept.

As Grandpa was helping me take the blankets off the hideaway, he told my brother and me that we would be heading over to Smokey the Bear Park after breakfast. "Today's Independence Day," he jovial declared. "And it's about time for us to do some celebrating, don't you think?"

"Oh Goodie, Grandpa!" I exclaimed, always keyed up for a party.

As the three of us readied to leave the house, Grandpa began walking out the front door instead of heading for the garage out back. "Aren't we going to drive?" I asked.

Grandpa got a confused look on his face then started to chuckle. "Drive? Why, there's no need to drive, Young Lady. The parade is only six blocks away as the crow flies, right over there at the edge of the downtown," he explained, calmly pointing toward his north living room wall as if I could see through it.

I was astonished that an entire, citywide celebration was within walking distance of our house. From where I'd come, you would never have been able to hop-skip-and-jump your way to merriment. Daily living had always been far more complex in the big city.

The parade had not yet begun when we arrived at the park. A few of the local vendors were in the process of setting up their food trailers along the park's perimeter, blanketing the air with the familiar aroma of grease and sweet sugar as they

127

hawked the usual carnival fare. Clusters of families milled about the football-field sized grounds like schools of fish in a pond, as friendly, costumed clowns tried to eke out smiles from timid children. In the center of it all, an oversized statue of Smokey the Bear loomed above the crowd, stoically welcoming all visitors while reminding them to "Prevent Forest Fires" with his brightly painted yellow sign.

I patted Grandpa's arm to get his attention and asked, "Where is everybody?"

He chuckled and replied, "Wull, what do you mean? This here's a pretty good turn out."

I looked around in disbelief. This was nothing at all like the beloved fair I had known all my life. Gone were the sea of faces, the lavish food concoctions on a stick, the shiny trinkets that no kid could live without. Gone was my beloved Kid-e-land. I felt deflated. So far, this celebration seemed meager and incomplete.

Not knowing what else to do, I asked Grandpa if we could get a raspberry Sno Cone. While I was slurping it beneath the shade of a nearby birch tree, I noticed some commotion in front of the outdoor bandstand where a crowd was starting to gather and multiply. A select group of young kids began to muster nervously as they lined up next to each other behind a thick, white chalk line on the ground. Then a man directly beside them lifted a megaphone to his mouth and proclaimed, "On your mark . . . get set . . . GO!" The kids took off in a blur down the 50-yard grass track, all dashing for the coveted silver-dollar first prize.

I started getting anxious and excited all at the same time. "Grandpa!" I exclaimed. "Do you think I could be in one of those races?"

"Wull, I don't see why not. Why don't we go over there and see what we can do."

The two of us trotted over to Mr. Megaphone, and Grandpa asked him if the ten-year-olds had raced yet.

"You'd better hurry!" Mr. Megaphone replied. "It's the next race on deck."

"But Grandpa," I fretfully said to him as we were walking over to the starting line, "I'm not ten yet, I'm still only nine. My birthday isn't for three more days, remember?"

Grandpa gently patted my shoulder and told me that was irrelevant. I didn't know what he meant, but since we were still headed for the starting line, I figured he wanted me to compete against the ten-year-olds anyhow.

My heart started beating faster as I left Grandpa behind on the sidelines and positioned myself in front of the white chalk line. Directly to my left was a tall, thin girl wearing a Mickey Mouse t-shirt. Since I didn't know her name, I decided to nickname her Daddy Long Legs. To my right was a cute, athletic-looking girl with long, blond hair. When I looked her way, she leaned closer to me and asked what my name was, then said that hers was Kelly. I nodded politely and said, "Hi Kelly." She then turned away from me, looked straight ahead and intensely studied the track before us as she tied her hair into a ponytail with a rubber band that had been dangling from her wrist. She turned to the girl on the other side of her and whispered something into her ear. Up until now, I'd been so distracted by Kelly that I hadn't even prepped for my upcoming event. Before I knew what was happening, I heard Mr. Megaphone instruct, "On your mark . . ."

"Holy crap!" I thought, "I need to get into position!"

"Get set . . ."

I could hear Grandpa cheering for me from the sidelines, "C'mon Theresa, show us what you got!"

I looked over into the crowd and tried to single him out, but before I could find him Mr. Megaphone yelled, "GO!"

Off we flew, all dozen of us. Tennies were tearing into the ground, arms were spastically flailing about, and grimaces of cutthroat determination dominated every contestant's face.

I desperately wanted to win this race and was giving it all I had. Sure, I wanted the silver dollar, no question about it, but more than anything I wanted this newcomer to be known as a winner. I was pumping my scraggly arms as fast as I could and digging my shoes into the grass with each stride. Before I knew it, I was one of the leaders of the pack. Daddy Long Legs was half an arm's length ahead while Kelly trailed slightly behind. I kept on saying to myself, "If I can just pass Daddy Long Legs, I'll have it made." We were nearing the halfway point when I felt a hand from behind pull back on my t-shirt, causing me to lose my balance. I stumbled and nearly fell as Kelly passed me with a smirk on her face, but I was able to regain my balance before falling completely to the ground. Kelly may have slowed me, but this game wasn't over yet. With more resolve than ever, I kicked my short, skinny legs into high gear and focused on Kelly instead of Daddy Long Legs. "I'll show that little brat," I said to myself. "I can do this . . . I can do this . . . I can do this." With only a fourth of the race left, I was gaining on Kelly. I was now so close to her that I could have pulled out a healthy chunk of those long, golden locks, but I stayed focused and kept my cool. I was running full tilt and could feel my neck muscles straining to their full capacity when I saw Kelly look at me with surprise from the corner of her eye. We were now neck and neck, shoulder to shoulder. Just a few more strides left to the finish line. I can do this . . . I can do this . . . I can, and before I knew it, I'd passed her. I'd passed that little brat! I'd been concentrating so hard on Kelly that I hadn't even realized I'd raced right through the victor's string and beaten everyone else. I had won!

Grandpa met me at the finish line, smiling fondly as he held my Sno Cone. "That was some race, you little whippersnapper. Now I wish I'd have brought my camera. You should have told me you could run like that. Why didn't you say something?" he asked.

I was bent over, facing the ground with my hands on my knees. I could feel the heat beating out of me as I tried to catch my breath. I looked up at Grandpa and grinned from ear to ear as I puffed out my reply, "Guess I didn't know I had it in me."

I had proven more to myself than to anyone else that day that I was a winner, indeed.

The rest of that summer dragged on, and I dragged right behind it like a bunch of empty beer cans tied to a trailer hitch on the Charter Bus to Boredom. I still hadn't made any real friends and was looking forward to a change with the beginning of the new school year.

Much to my surprise, Mom landed a job at Pearson's Bakery, just like she said she would. She waitressed or bused tables most of the time, but occasionally ran the till whenever a co-worker didn't show up for their shift. On the days when I didn't have much else to do, I'd leash up old Bucky and we'd walk the few blocks to the bakery. I'd tie him to a nearby tree, then go inside and sit at one of the torn, black vinyl booths. Mom always instinctively knew what I'd want without ever taking my order and was quick to pluck a homemade, frosted cinnamon roll from the deli case and place it on the table in front of my longing eyes. It was so large that I had to hold it with both hands as I eagerly devoured it in no time flat, barely savoring its pleasant combination of sugar and spice. I'd lick my fingers with satisfaction and beam at the other patrons as I scooted out from behind the booth, waving goodbye to my mother and shouting, "Thanks, Momma!" on my way out the door.

A few weeks before the first day of school, Mom told my brother and me that she had some good news.

"Guess what, Kids?!" she asked exuberantly.

"What is it, Momma?" I replied.

131

"We'll be moving into our very own house next week!"

"Wow! Really?" exclaimed my brother. "Where?"

"Yeah, where's the new house?" I chimed.

"Next door."

My brother and I furrowed our brows simultaneously and looked at each other, then back at Mom.

Mikie hesitantly pointed toward the east wall of Grandma and Grandpa's house and asked, "Next door? You mean, like over there next door?"

"Yep," Mom replied. "Grandpa owns that house and said we could move in just as soon as the old lady who's there now moves out. Lucky for us, she gave her notice last week."

"Yee-Haw!" I exclaimed.

"You mean, no more sharing a bedroom with Grandpa?!" Mikie yelled excitedly. "I mean, I like Grandpa a lot and everything, but he snores like you wouldn't believe, and I'm talking loud!" Mikie then began to mimic Grandpa by sucking in deep mouthfuls of air and letting them ripple over his tongue to recreate the annoying sound of snoring.

That made Mom laugh. "We should be all moved in before school starts," she stated.

"What a relief," I thought to myself. "I'll finally have my very own bed, and I can unpack all my stuffed animals. And best of all . . . no more creepy stare-downs with New Grandma."

"Yes, Kids," said Mom with an air of drama, "We're on our way. I pulled myself up by the bootstraps, got myself a job, made a little money. And now . . . we'll have a house to call our own again."

"Amen to that!" Mikie said, just as dramatically.

I looked over at Mom and pondered this new turn of events. Things seemed to be looking up for us. Even though Daddy was never coming back, maybe everything really was going to be okay.

~♦♦♦~

The move went about as smoothly as it could have. Grandpa rounded up a couple of his old buddies to dig out of storage the few possessions we'd brought with us from the city, mostly sentimental furnishings that Daddy had acquired in our other life and several gifts my parents had received on their wedding day just thirteen years before. Later that afternoon, Mom scanned the Want Ads for garage sales and used furniture while Grandpa phoned Mom's siblings, asking them to loan our family some much needed cash for household essentials.

I remember sitting on one of the unpacked cardboard boxes that day and eating a peanut butter sandwich as I studied the flaking, pea-green colored walls in the living room. Our "new" house was pretty run down, there was no mistake about it. Grandpa was pushing seventy-five by that time, and his ability to lord the land wasn't what it once had been. Even so, I knew it was the best house Mom could afford and found solace in knowing that our little family was still together under the same roof.

The first day of school that year found me wide awake, even before my alarm clock went off. Normally, I would have slept right through it, but on that particular morning I had a pretty bad case of the jitters.

I went downstairs and poured myself a bowl of peanut butter Captain Crunch, then set the cereal box on the table in front of me and tried to absorb myself in The Captain's Crazy Code Breaker. Nauseous and unable to concentrate, I gave up on eating after only a few spoonfuls and set the bowl down on the floor for Rusty to finish off, then went back upstairs and got ready for the school day.

Mom was still dozing in bed and wasn't able to give my brother and me the much-needed cheerful send-off we needed. Caring for us in her own, unique way, she'd left some change and a note on the table. "For hot lunch," it said. I placed the change into the zipped pocket of my backpack, then walked the three blocks to Alexander Baker Elementary alone.

All the kids were hanging out on the school playground when I arrived, waiting for the bell to toll. Some were playing foursquare, others were swinging wildly from the monkey bars, and some were simply catching up on gossip after a long summer's hiatus. Since I didn't feel like talking to anyone, I sat down on the school steps and pretended that I had on my super-secret invisible cloak as I observed from the sidelines. I felt unsure and shy, hoping that everyone would like me. I worried they wouldn't.

That morning, I uneasily settled into my creaky, wooden chair for the first few agonizing hours of English, Science and Social Studies. The loud "ding, ding, ding!" of the highly anticipated recess bell sent kids flying out of their seats so fast you'd have sworn they were on their way to Willie Wonka's Chocolate Factory. In a wholehearted attempt to fit in, I galloped right along with them.

Once outside, everyone migrated to their respective cliques. Since I didn't yet have one of my own, I made a serious attempt at infiltration. First, I went over to a group of boys who were playing kickball. It was immediately apparent that I'd never blend in, so I walked over to a cluster of girls who were jumping rope. I timidly stood nearby, waiting for them to invite me for a turn, but they didn't. "Not last night but the night before," they chanted as the skipper took center stage. "Twenty four robbers came knocking at my door! One . . . Two . . . Three . . ." Several uncomfortable moments passed without the slightest acknowledgement of my existence, so I walked back to the same steps where I had begun my school day and once more sat down. It just so happened that the foursquare game was only a few yards away, so I pretended to be enthralled with the competition: Daddy Long Legs was playing against a boy I'd never before seen, and a sweet, freckled brunette named Dana who I'd met one day just last summer

134

when I'd ridden the community bus to City Beach all by myself.

After the game ended, Dana and a friend of hers walked over to where I was sitting.

"Hi Theresa, remember me?" she asked.

"Yeah. I met you on the beach bus," I said bashfully as the forthcoming width of my smile equaled that of a crocodile's.

"This is my friend, Cheyanne. She lives over there, across the street and down the block." Dana turned and pointed toward Cheyanne's house.

"My dad's a forest ranger," Cheyanne proudly announced. "What does your dad do?"

Her innocent question caught me off guard and placed me at a loss for words. I stared at the ground, trying to rebound. It had never occurred to me that anyone would ask about Daddy. I didn't know if I should tell Cheyanne and Dana the truth, or if I should make something up. In the end, I chose the latter.

"He died in a car crash a few months ago," I lied.

The words had no more than slipped from my tongue when I wondered why I'd even said them. I didn't want to state that "my dad killed himself" because it would have sounded brutally callous. I didn't want to use that "committed suicide" line that all of my relatives were throwing around because it sounded more like an illegal act that warranted a prison term rather than the tragedy it was. Maybe deep down I just didn't want to go back to that dark place, the one in which Daddy had left me through his own free will rather than by accident.

Now Dana and Cheyanne were suddenly at a loss for words as they stood beside me, uneasily looking at the school building, then at the ground, then at each other.

Finally Cheyanne said, "So sorry . . ."

"Yeah, really sorry . . ." chimed Dana.

135

A teacher walked by, providing the three of us with a much-needed distraction.

"Hey," said Cheyanne mischievously after the teacher had passed, "want to go get some candy?"

"Candy?" I said, a little confused. "Where can you get any candy around here?"

"We sneak off to the gas station at the other end of the block," explained a seasoned Dana. "You see that lady over there," she continued as she discreetly pointed toward an unintimidating, geriatric woman.

"Yeah," I replied, waiting for her to give me the lowdown.

"That's Mrs. Burnet, but we call her The Lady. She's supposed to watch all us kids on the playground and make sure we stay in line," Dana explained while making quotation marks with her hands as she said the words, "stay in line." "Every once in a while at recess, someone poses as a decoy and distracts her so that a bunch of us can make a run for it to the gas station and load up on candy. See, we're not allowed to leave the schoolyard, but we do it anyway." Dana then put her hand over her mouth and giggled before adding, "Whenever we can get away with it, that is."

I was genuinely intrigued. "Does anyone ever get caught?" I asked.

"Nope!" said Cheyanne confidently.

"Not yet, anyway," corrected Dana.

"Count me in," I told them as I smiled mischievously.

Cheyanne then turned and cupped her mouth, yelling over to a boy who was waiting to play foursquare, "Eric! Hey, Eric!" When Eric turned around, she motioned him over.

He gave up his place in line and hastened to her side. "Yeah?" he asked. "What's up?"

"Can you be our decoy today?" Cheyanne asked sweetly while flashing a toothy smile and fluttering her fiery hazel eyes.

Eric knew exactly what she wanted. "Sure thing, Chey," he said as he casually grabbed a stray foursquare ball and began bouncing it on the schoolyard pavement in the vicinity of The Lady. The closer he got, the harder the ball bounced. As soon as he was behind The Lady, he began bouncing it at lightning speed while dribbling it in between his legs. At just the right moment, he took a dive and hit the pavement, screaming in false pain, "Oh, my leg! My leg!"

The Lady whirled around and was down by his side faster than you could say Mary Poppins. "Oh, Dear!" she exclaimed with true concern.

The rest of us were too busy scurrying behind The Lady's back to catch the rest of their exchange. I started to snicker, but Dana gently dug an elbow into my side and gave me a look that said, "Keep a lid on it."

After blowing most of my lunch money on a Marathon Bar and some Pop Rocks, the three of us hurried back to the playground. We sneaked behind a corner of the school building and waited a few minutes for an opportune chance to blend back in with the crowd. Soon afterwards the bell rang, and it was time to finish out the remainder of my first day at school.

I was lucky that day. My two new friends seemed pretty cool, and things were finally looking up for me.

The days unfolded quickly as my life entwined with those of my two new pals. Before I knew it Halloween had arrived once more, summoning forth plenty of mischief and spirited glee. My brother and I were giddy with anticipation on the evening of the big event as we hauled out a pair of worn pillowcases from the linen closet and added the fright factor. Mikie stood in front of the bathroom mirror, smearing blood-red cosmetic paint all over his face, then tied a pair of cheesy, black plastic horns to the top of his head while I sat at the

137

kitchen table with Mom's lighted makeup mirror and drew whiskers on my face with her eyebrow pencil, then carefully smudged some of her frosted lipstick onto my pale cheeks for added effect. In dire need of a tail, I sneaked upstairs and smuggled a pair of Mom's black, waitress pantyhose from her bedroom dresser, then stuffed one empty leg with crumpled newspaper before tucking the other into the backside of my jeans. For the final touch, I donned my brother's black ski cap, and voila! We were ready to mingle with the ghouls.

That night turned out to be the most fun my brother and I had experienced in months, maybe even a whole year. We tore through the pumpkin-adorned neighborhoods in our cheap, makeshift costumes, ringing any doorbell in sight and unabashedly begging for more candy than we'd ever be able to eat. With no busy streets to speak of and no strangers to fear, we were free to roam the town as we pleased . . . and roam it we did.

Mikie and I arrived home later that evening, entering through the back door. I could see the backside of Mom's head poking up above the rocker in our living room and ran over to see her, eager to showcase my treasures. "Look, Mommy! Look at all the candy I got!" I screeched excitedly, swinging my plump pillowcase off my shoulder and emptying its contents onto the floor. As I beamed up at her, I suddenly realized that I was in the presence of a complete stranger upon whose lap my mother was seated. I stopped smiling and pointed to the man with the missing front tooth. "Who's that, Mommy?" I asked uneasily.

Mom remained seated on the stranger's lap while making the introductions, "Kids, this is Steve. He works with me down at the bakery." She then pointed to my brother and me, "Steve, this is my daughter, Theresa, and my son, Mikie."

"How you kids doin'," said the ill-groomed Steve, giving us a slight wave with the hand that wasn't holding a beer.

Before my brother and I had time to react, Mom told us to go over to New Grandma and Grandpa's house.

"I want to stay here!" I pouted. "I want to arrange my candy into piles!"

"I told you to go next door, now go on and do it," Mom said sternly. "I'll come and get you when it's time for bed." She made a motion with her hand as if to shoo us out faster.

I begrudgingly squatted onto the floor and re-bagged my candy.

"Who's this Steve guy anyway?" I asked Mikie once we'd left the house.

He shrugged, "Don't know, but I can tell that I don't like him already."

"How can you tell?" I inquired.

"I just know," he said stoically.

Mikie and I stayed up for a few more hours and watched the tube at New Grandma and Grandpa's until we couldn't stop yawning. Deciding it was finally time to go to bed, we trotted back home without Mom's blessing. We found Mom and Steve seated closer together on the living room couch than I would have preferred, well under the influence of several more beers.

Mom acted surprised when she saw us. "I thought I told you two I'd come and get you when I was good and ready," she snapped.

I rubbed my eyes and snapped back, "Don't you even know what time it is?"

Mom gave me a dirty look then glanced at her watch. "Midnight," she said absently. "Guess you two ought to get to bed."

"I *told* you," I said over my shoulder as Mikie and I turned and made our way upstairs to our bedrooms.

Lucky for us the next morning was a Saturday, allowing my brother and me a few extra hours of sleep. Mom was still in bed when Mikie and I slipped downstairs; God only knows where that Steve character was.

139

When Mom finally did present herself, my brother and I were seated at the dining room table, engrossed in a game of Chinese checkers. She looked tired and hungover as she sat down next to us and lit a cigarette.

Mikie eyed her apprehensively then bluntly stated, "Steve can't be our dad."

Mom looked at him as though she were looking through a fog. "What did you say?" she asked.

My brother stated his position more loudly this time, "I said . . . Steve is not going to be our dad!"

"I can go out with whoever I want, you little snot!" Mom retorted. "I'm not about to let a little 12-year-old boy tell me how to run my life!"

Mikie, typically the most mild mannered in the family, now stood up and yelled back, "Daddy hasn't even been gone a year! And that guy's a creep! Why would you even like a creep like that?! He doesn't even have all of his teeth!"

Mom was out of her chair in a flash and held her face so close to my brother's that they would have licked each other had they both stuck out their tongues. "Listen, Mister!" Mom shouted back. "You are not going to tell me what to do! Undastand?"

Mikie stepped away from her, then turned and walked briskly toward the back door. "No, I don't understand! I'm getting out of this hellhole!" he shouted as he slammed the door behind him.

Still seething, Mom picked up the phone receiver on the dining room wall and started dialing several numbers.

When someone on the other end answered, Mom inquired, "Hello? Is this Sarah? I think Mikie is on his way over to your house to see Charlie. Listen Sarah, I was wondering if you and Buck could take him off my hands for a while . . ."

Mom talked to Sarah for a few more minutes, but I never heard the rest of their conversation. My mind was too busy reeling from the prospect that Mom was kicking her only son and my only sibling out of our house. And for what? Understandable rebellion?!

Mom hung up the phone, then snubbed out her cigarette in the ashtray. "I'm going back to bed," she moaned. "Ahhh, I just can't take this anymore."

And that was that. The lesson of the day was that exile was a simple phone call away.

A few weeks later, Mikie stopped by our house to pack up the few belongings he wanted to take with him, and unceremoniously left us behind. I would never live in the same house with my brother again.

I easily adjusted to my brother's involuntary disappearance, at least for the time being. Up until that point, Mom and I had been sharing the larger of the house's two bedrooms, if that's what you could call it. After Mikie left, Mom decided it was time to give me some much needed freedom and allowed me to take over my brother's space. Those two tiny rooms were all that would fit into the upper level of our crammed and dilapidated old house.

As the days began to darken, so too, did Mom, just as she had so many times before whenever the likes of Tom Turkey and Old Saint Nick reared their ugly heads. Instead of anticipating the holidays, I learned to dread them and leaned heavily on basic coping mechanisms to see me through.

New Grandma and Grandpa traditionally prepared all the festive fixin's during that time of the year, and welcomed family and friends to gather near when the chilly, northern winds summoned all to seek shelter and warmth. In the early morning on Thanksgiving Day, I slipped over to their house to escape Mom's brewing misery and sneaked handfuls of Ritz

141

crackers and stuffed, green olives from the kitchen counter. Grandpa playfully encouraged me to stop snacking, "You're going to turn into one of those chubby chipmunks, Theresa."

After everyone else had long since finished their feast and vacated the dinner table, I licked the remainder of my cranberry sauce from my spoon, then obediently brought my empty plate into the kitchen and began helping Mom, New Grandma and the rest of the women clean up the dishes. Halfway through my chores, when I was confident no one would notice, I sneaked into the back hallway, slipped into my winter coat and enticed Bucky the beagle to follow with a leftover dinner roll that I'd smuggled off the dining room table.

The neighborhood was so quiet and still on that holiday evening. Bucky and I walked for blocks alone, as though we had the night all to ourselves. Underneath the soft glow of the streetlights, Bucky and I climbed to the top of a massive, white heap of fresh snow that the city had plowed onto the corner of our block. "Look Bucky!" I cried. "We're King of the Mountain!" He looked up at me with his big, droopy eyes and energetically wagged his tail as if to let me know that being King of the Mountain was his ultimate dream, realized. I leaned down toward him while pointing into the frosty, northern Minnesota sky and said, "There's the Big Dipper, Little Buddy. Can you see it?" I drew an outline of the constellation just like Uncle Rob had shown me. After a few minutes of silent meditation, the two of us climbed down and headed back home.

Strange as it may sound, I found true peace on those cold, winter nights in the company of my trusted friend.

February 24, 1976. It was Mom and Daddy's anniversary; the first one Mom had ever spent solo. I woke up that morning to her pitiful cries coming from our downstairs bathroom.

"You bastard!" she shrieked. "Why did you do it, Rick? Why?!" Her anguish sounded as fresh as the day we'd discovered a lifeless Daddy in his secluded, upstairs apartment. Mom's guttural, one-way argument lasted for several minutes until it was overtaken by an eerie silence. Suddenly, I heard the toilet flush. "And you can take your goddamn ring back, too!"

I threw my covers back, leapt out of bed and ran to the top of the stairs. When I looked down toward the bathroom directly below, I could see Mom kneeling at the base of the toilet with her head in her hands, sobbing. "Mom?" I said. "Mom, you okay?" There was no answer, only more sobbing. By this time in my life, I knew that nothing I could say or do would comfort her, so I walked back to my bed, slipped beneath the covers, and waited for the tide to turn once more.

Later that afternoon I conducted my daily tour of New Grandma and Grandpa's house. Grandpa was in the living room, serenely listening to Herb Alpert and the Tijuana Brass, while a tearful Mom expelled her woes to New Grandma at the kitchen table.

I bypassed Mom and New Grandma, opting to hang out with the mellower Grandpa.

"Wull Hullo there, Theresa. How are you?" he asked.

"Good," I quietly replied before sitting next to him on the couch.

"How's school?"

"Good."

"Are you making any new friends?"

"Some."

"Are you still running like the wind?"

I looked over at him and smiled, then proudly acknowledged, "I won the Presidential Physical Fitness Award last fall."

143

"Good for you, Kiddo," he said as he closed his eyes, then folded his arms behind his head and leaned slightly backwards, resting against the wall behind him. "Ain't that Herb Alpert something?"

"Yeah, I like it, too," I replied. I studied Grandpa's pose. He looked appealingly relaxed, so I decided to give it a try.

I had just closed my eyes and begun to lean backwards when turmoil erupted in the kitchen, disrupting my reverie. Mom and New Grandma were no longer talking peacefully, but were brawling like a couple of roller derby girls.

"He was a terrible husband to you, Rainy," New Grandma railed, "and you were just about as bad a wife!"

I could barely see the two of them from where I was seated in the living room but was able to witness Mom's fist wind up and crack New Grandma across the face. "Why, how dare you!" Mom screeched as New Grandma's glasses went flying onto the floor, sending New Grandma lunging after them. As Mom began striding away, she seemed unfazed by what she'd just done. "You witch! You're an awful woman!" Mom angrily fumed before slamming the door behind her.

I ran after my mother, wanting to lend comfort, but she was not to be consoled. "Leave me alone," she scolded.

I knew exactly where she was headed. Although it was still mid-afternoon, any time of the day was always a good time for Mom to hit the sack; leaving her street clothes on was optional.

Since Mom didn't want me around, I let her be and walked over to Dana's house, remaining there for the rest of the day. When I returned home later that evening, I ascended the stairs to check on Mom. Although her back faced me as I entered the room, I could tell by the extensive pillow burn on her hair that she'd spent the better part of that entire day exactly where I'd left her.

"Momma?" I gently cooed. "Are you okay?"

I stepped closer and peered down at open, unresponsive eyes and a face that was muddied with despair. "Momma?" I said more anxiously a second time. "Please tell me that you're going to be all right."

The hair on the back of my neck stood up as I felt the electric charge of The Invisibles all around me. Mom had summoned them forth in full strength. In her deluded state, she ignored me and began demanding that they deliver a message to Daddy. "Tell that bastard I hate him for leaving me!" she yelled, then zeroed in on the leader and screamed even louder as she beat her fist into her pillow, "I hate this life! Do you hear me, Jesus?! Jesus! I don't want to live anymore!"

A five-alarm fire started blazing inside my heart, and I started to cry. "Stop saying those things!" I screamed. "Momma, please stop!" The Ferris wheel of pharmaceuticals on top of her nightstand caught my attention, sending me running for the closet where I grabbed one of Mom's empty shoeboxes, then dashed back to her nightstand and frantically started plucking the drugs from her reach. All the while I was crying and pleading with her, "Momma, please don't do this to me. Please!"

I took the box of drugs into my room and hid them underneath my bed, then went back and sat at the edge of Mom's bed while she continued her tirade. I silently wept for what must have been hours until I was sure that she had wound back 'round into the slumber phase of her psychotic cycle. Only then did I let myself leave her side. I went back into my room and robotically changed into my pajamas, then sat on my bed with my legs folded in front of me and began to rock back and forth. I was in that limbo place of being so exhausted that I was too tired to sleep. I tried to calm down by telling myself that Mom would snooze her way out of this, but the longer I thought about what she'd said to Jesus, the more frantic I became. I looked at the clock; it was closing in on midnight. I wanted to alert Grandpa but, in the end, decided against it. There was nothing he could do about it anyway.

My mind started to replay what Mom had said about life . . . maybe it really wasn't worth living. I put my face in my hands and started bawling again. My eyes were burning with fatigue and despair. Some days I hated this life, too.

The darkness began to surround me, but not with its usual, comforting embrace; more like a thief that was rapidly robbing my mind of reason. The adrenalin inside began flowing again, pushing me to find a way out of this purgatory. I momentarily stopped bawling and took the box of drugs out from underneath my bed. I picked up each opaque, plastic bottle and held it in the moonlight next to my window then read the label as best I could, one by one – Lorazepam, Sinequan, Benztropine, Sectral, Norvasc. Could these tiny tablets be my ticket out? The notion of losing my life within a matter of minutes washed over me, and I started to shake, then the tears came harder than ever and it became my turn to yell at Daddy's ghost. "Why did you leave me with her, Daddy?!" I screamed underneath my breath. "I don't want to live like this anymore! Why would you do this to me?!"

This was the first time I would contemplate suicide. At ten years old, I was burned out. It wasn't that I wanted to die; it would never be about that. It was more about shedding the skin of this perverse lifestyle. Maybe that's all Daddy had really wanted.

I picked up the bottle of Sinequan and opened it, then slowly poured its contents into the palm of my hand. A flurry of questions rushed through my head, "How would the drugs make me feel after I swallowed a handful? How many should I take? Would I die quickly? Would it be painful? What would it feel like when my heart stopped beating?"

After staring at the specter of death for a few more minutes, I decided I didn't have the courage to go through with it. I carefully put the pink and white pills back into their container, then snapped the lid shut before angrily throwing the bottle against the wall. Full-blown exhaustion was now diluting what remained of my adrenaline surge. I stared out my tiny window as I let the final wave of anger roll through me, then crawled underneath the covers and asked the darkness to once again be my friend. Within a matter of minutes, the temporary relief of slumber distanced me from one more day.

I dragged myself out of bed the next morning and looked in on Mom before going downstairs for breakfast. She was snoring pretty hard, so I knew she'd be down for the count indefinitely.

As I left the house for school later that morning, I felt unusually queasy. My instincts told me that Mom had headed out to sea in a canoe and was right smack dab in the middle of a hurricane with no help in sight.

After classes had finished later that afternoon, Dana asked me if I wanted to stop by her house. Still uneasy about Mom, I lied and told her I had some *stuff* to take care of. I rushed back home as inconspicuously as I could and scampered up the stairs to Mom's bedroom. That's where I found her. She was slumped sideways on top of her bedcovers, face up, with her feet still on the ground, as if she'd once been seated in an upright position. A bunch of pills that hadn't hit their mark were haphazardly scattered on the floor. Mom wasn't moaning; she wasn't snoring; she wasn't even talking to The Invisibles. It was just lights-out. At first I didn't know if she was simply unconscious or had expired, permanently.

I ran over to her and placed my small, trembling hands on her shoulders, then started to gently shake her. "Momma? Momma?! Oh no! Momma! Oh no!!!!!!!!!!!!!!!" I backed away, suddenly overcome with the urge to throw up. Everything about this was too eerily familiar. Within a matter

147

of seconds I got my head together and ran down the stairs, then over to New Grandma and Grandpa's house. I found Grandpa in the living room, browsing through one of his *National Geographic* magazines.

"Grandpa! Grandpa!" I yelled at the top of my lungs, as though I were blocks away from him rather than just a few feet.

Startled, he glanced up at me then calmly instructed, "Now just settle down there, Theresa, I'm sitting right in front of you."

"But Grandpa!" I said as I started to cry. "Please help me!"

"What seems to be the problem?"

"It's Mom! She's taken all her pills, and I don't even know if she's breathing anymore!"

Grandpa promptly laid down his magazine, then quickly trotted toward the back door and over to my house, leaving me to scramble behind as he hurried up the stairs to Mom's bedroom.

As soon as he saw his daughter, he started hollering at her, "Rainy, get up!" He rushed to her side and shook her, just as I had moments earlier, but harder. "Do you hear me, Rainy?!" When she didn't respond, he began slapping each side of her face, each smack repeatedly failing to revive her.

All the while I stood nervously in the doorway. My heart was racing. How could Mom do this to me after everything that had already happened?! Tears began streaming down my face as I watched Grandpa trying to unsuccessfully resuscitate Mom.

Grandpa soon realized that professional help was needed. He turned to me and said, "Looks like we're going to have to get your mother to a hospital. Come over here and take hold of her feet while I get the rest of her."

I suddenly locked up, and all I could do was stare blankly back at him.

148

Demanding a quicker response from me, Grandpa commanded, "There's no time to waste, Theresa! You're going to have to help me carry your mother to the car."

That's what it took to snap me into action. I grabbed Mom around the ankles as Grandpa scooped her up from behind, and together we lifted her limp body out of bed. With Grandpa in the lead walking backwards, we cautiously eased our lifeless load down the stairs and over to his garage.

Once we got close enough to his car, Grandpa instructed me to set Mom's feet on the ground and open up the back passenger door. Then the two of us clumsily struggled to pour my mother into the back seat of his Ford.

"Are you going to call the ambulance now?" I naively asked.

"No," he replied, matter-of-factly, "I can get your mother to the Emergency faster if I do the driving." Before sliding into the driver's seat, he looked over at me and said stoically, "Why don't you go in the house with Grandma. I'll be back as soon as I can."

I despondently leaned against my grandparents' rickety, old garage, and watched Grandpa's white Ford furiously kick up dust as it sped down the dirt alleyway and out of sight. At that very moment, my ability to feel anything simply vanished. I was so tired of being angry, being sad, being overwhelmed. I was just plain tired of being tired.

Daddy was gone. Mom soon would be. What was going to happen to me now?

Miraculously, Mom survived her near-fatal suicide attempt, but would soon pay a hefty price for her revival. The local medical community had exhausted all potential avenues of outreach and made the necessary decision to send her to Moose Lake State Hospital, a reputable institution in central Minnesota that treated mentally ill patients in crisis. I, in turn,

149

would be sent next door to once again live with New Grandma and Grandpa until she could sufficiently recover.

Mom's journey to the sanitarium in early March strangely coincided with Moose Lake's annual Ice and Slice winter golf tournament. As the smiling, happy crowds were cheering the tournament's first foursomes, Mom was being checked into the institution on the other side of their small Minnesota town. She would never be allowed to fish the town's namesake or ramble the heavily wooded walking paths along the city park. She would never even sample a brew at the Moose Droppings Pub down on Main Street. Locked in her newfound reality, she would be placed on suicide watch for forty-eight hours in mind-numbing isolation with only a bed, a nightstand and The Invisibles to keep her company. With time and caring treatment, she would integrate into a more social setting with some of the other patients and begin a rigorous therapy program, eventually bringing home more than just better coping skills.

While Mom was away, I spent hours and hours listening to the stereo with Grandpa and playing rounds of solitaire at the kitchen table. During the stillness in the dead of the night, it felt so strange to sleep on New Grandma and Grandpa's hide-a-bed all by myself without the warmth of Mom's body merging with mine as it once had all those months ago right after Daddy died.

I tagged along with Dana after school whenever I could and found asylum at her house; she had become my new Sammie. Dana's parents were far from the hip and urban couple of Chana and Les, but they kindly welcomed my ever-present presence nonetheless, and for that, I was eternally grateful.

Dana's first duty upon arrival home was her daily piano lesson. I'd quietly sit by her side on the wooden bench in her basement and admire her long, nimble fingers as they gracefully plucked the keys. Afterwards, her mom would treat us to a rib-sticking meal, then I'd snatch a treat or two from their well-stocked cookie jar before retiring to Dana's bedroom for one last bout of fun. The two of us would laze about on her quilted, double bed and talk incessantly about the boys in school. When we were in a particularly rowdy mood, we'd make crank phone calls to random, unsuspecting townspeople. Dana would pick a number from the phone book and I'd bravely dial it, then hold the receiver slightly away from my ear, allowing the both of us to hear my forthcoming interview.

"Is your refrigerator running?" I'd ask, feigning innocence.

"Well, of course it is!" my victim would reply.

"Well, where's it running to?!" came the punch line. Dana and I would laugh and laugh at our silliness until we just about peed our pants.

One night while lying on Dana's bed, after we'd run out of entertainment ideas, Dana rolled onto her back and stared up at the ceiling. Bored, she asked, "What should we do now?"

"Hmmmm . . ." I said as I tapped a forefinger against my upper lip and looked around her room for possibilities. When I spied her stereo, I asked, "Hey! Want to listen to some mewww-zak?" as though I were some kind of '60s hipster.

She looked over at me and lazily replied, "Sure, why not."

I rolled off the bed and went over to the stereo. Just as I was about to flip on the radio, I noticed a forty-five sitting on the turntable. "What's this, Dane?"

"What's what?" she replied.

"This?" I said as I gently extracted the small disc and elevated it for her to see.

"Don't know," she told me. "I can't remember what I was playing."

I looked down at the psychedelically colored label and read it aloud. "It says, 'Life is a Rock' by some band I've never heard of called Reunion."

151

"Haven't you ever heard that song before?" she asked.

I shook my head "No."

She rolled toward me onto her side and propped her head up with her arm. "Put it on," she instructed.

When I set the disc in motion, spinning it through the first lines of the track, I was having trouble making out the words of the fast-pumping, funky beat. After the first chorus had played, I lifted the needle off the record and placed it back on its cradle.

"What was that?!" I asked, laughing.

" 'Life is a Rock, but the Radio Rolled Me.' I mean . . . Duh!" Dana said as she looked at me with an "I already told you" glance.

"Do you even know what they're saying?" I asked.

"Not really," she said. "I just basically know the chorus."

"You know what we should do?" I asked excitedly, "Let's write down the lyrics!"

"Write down the lyrics? How are we going to do that?"

"One of us will man the record player and the other will write the lyrics down," I explained.

Dana sat up and folded her legs in front of her. "Okay," she said, finally buying into my idea. "Get me a notepad and pen from my drawer," she instructed as she pointed to her nightstand.

We got into position, I next to the stereo and Dana with pen poised in hand.

"Okay . . . go!" she said.

As the lyrics flew from the speakers, she frantically tried to capture them all on paper, but they were about as elusive as a first place teddy bear at the county fair. "Stop, stop! Back it up!" she said with frustration as soon as the words got too far ahead of her pen.

I gently lifted the needle and held it on the tip of my forefinger as the disc continued spinning around.

"Okay, here's what I have so far," she said to me as she listed a handful of words.

I stared back at her in disbelief. "That's it? That's all you got out of that?" I asked.

"It's hard, man! You try to write all that down."

"Are you sure those are even the right words?" I asked.

"Okay, Smarty," she declared. "We're switching."

So Dana manned the record player while I sat on the bed and readied myself.

"Action!" I playfully directed.

Within a matter of seconds I quickly realized that this task was much harder than it looked. After several lines, I said, "Whoa . . . Wait. Stop!"

"What cha got?" she asked.

"Besides what you got, I got this . . . ," I stated with pride, listing several lyrics that were completely wrong.

"Cool!" she said exuberantly. "Let's keep going."

We must have run through the first section of that song for about an hour or more. At around 8:00 that evening, Dana's mom defied my friend's "Keep Out" sign and knocked on her door, then entered. "Time to go home," she said to me. "Go get your coat on so I can give you a ride."

I looked over at the clock to verify the time, then looked back at her and sheepishly appealed, "Mind if I stay another half hour?"

"I promised your grandparents I'd get you home early. Besides, Dana has some homework to finish." Then she gave me a knowing look and added, "I bet you do, too."

I slowly stood up to retrieve my coat, "Yeah, I guess you're right." I looked over at my best friend and sadly waved. "See ya later alligator."

As Paula and I stepped out onto the cold, crunchy snow, she said to me, "Tomorrow's another day, Kid. You can come back then, okay." Indeed, I would.

153

Throughout the course of the next several weeks, Dana and I made numerous attempts to decode "Life is a Rock." We never did get it right.

With her meds properly readjusted and a new lease on life, Mom had returned home, happy as the sunny, spring days that were now surrounding us. To see her smile again gave me hope that we'd left behind the downhill leg of the roller coaster ride that makes you feel like you're going to die and leaves behind lingering screams that reverberate inside your head. She seemed locked in a temporary state of bliss and rambled on incessantly about the wealthy easterner she'd met while at the sanitarium.

"The last thing you need, Rainy, is another cuckoo on your hands," advised New Grandma.

Mom sourly looked back at New Grandma and explained, "He's not cuckoo, mother. He was at Moose Lake for chemical dependency problems."

"Cuckoo problems, chemical problems, what the hell's the difference?" asked New Grandma sarcastically.

Mom rolled her eyes, "His wife and mother died within months of each other, and he had coping issues." Then Mom intently stared New Grandma down and dramatically added, "Isn't anyone, in your opinion, allowed to be human?"

"It's your life, Rainy," New Grandma conceded insincerely.

Over the next several months, Mom's affair with her new beau blossomed. Numerous love letters were exchanged and long-distance phone calls seemed never ending. A day didn't pass without some sort of reference to Arthur. As the mystery man eased into my consciousness, I began to like him more and more, and secretly began wishing for an introduction. My fantasies included a pair of first-class airplane tickets to New

York City and a weekend stay at the finest hotel. Living the high-life felt giddily close at hand.

That summer, Dana and I landed dream jobs at the boys summer hockey camp concession stand. Our pay was only fifty cents an hour, but free pop and unlimited ogling were essential employee benefits. We used most of our earnings to buy matching handkerchief-patterned girlie Hee-Haw outfits of red and black, donning them whenever we felt there was even the slightest chance of running into some cute boy from school.

One Saturday afternoon, Mom asked me if I wanted to accompany her downtown. She was going to Penney's and needed help looking for a new dress. "You can pick out something nice for yourself, too," she said, sweetening the pot.

In the store's small but adequate women's department, Mom tried on several eye-catching outfits: a brown and white Hawaiian floral number, a sleeveless navy dress, a white cotton blouse with a matching skirt that was just sheer enough to make things interesting. Each outfit complemented her not-yet-faded-into-oblivion beauty queen good looks.

I wasn't sure what to make of it and remarked, "Those are all pretty fancy, Mom. Are you going somewhere special?"

"Arthur's flying in next week," she explained. Then thoughtlessly added, "Oh, didn't I tell you?"

"Arthur? Arthur's coming?" I replied, slightly surprised.

"Yes. From New York. You remember me talking about the man I met at the hospital, don't you?" she asked as she coyly observed herself in the dressing room's three-way mirror.

How could I not?

So . . . the Mystery Man was finally coming to town. The prospect was more than exhilarating. It's not that I yearned for a Daddy replacement, not exactly, anyway. No one would ever be able to fill the deep void that forever lingered. What I really wanted at that point in my life was the buoyancy of a lifeboat

155

named Security, and a buffer to shield me from Mom's extremes.

Arthur was scheduled to fly in from the east coast on a beautiful July day. Grandpa asked me if I wanted to ride with him to the airport to pick up Mom's new boyfriend.

"I've never been to the airport before, Grandpa," I told him excitedly. "In fact, now that I think about it, I didn't even know we had one."

Grandpa playfully patted my head and replied, "Well, now's your chance, Kiddo."

While Grandpa backed the Ford out of the garage, I called out for Bucky and we both jumped into the back seat at the same time.

"How 'bout a Dairy Queen stop along the way," Grandpa inquired.

My look told him, "Why bother asking."

We picked up a couple of cones, then headed south toward Airport Road. Along the way, on a side road less traveled, Grandpa slowed the car, then pulled over and stopped. "Would you let Buck out?" he asked.

"Sure," I said as I opened the back door that was closest to the weed-infested ditch, letting Bucky the beagle gleefully spring out with as much athletic gusto as a champion swimmer.

"Is he ever coming back?" I asked an unworried Grandpa, who began slowly driving on the shoulder alongside his pal.

"Oh, yaw," he replied. "I take old Buck out every now and again. He'll run around for a while and come back when he tuckers."

After about ten minutes, Bucky was begging to jump back into the car, just like Grandpa had said, and the three of us continued on our way toward the airport, passing an occasional hobby farm along the nearly deserted, two-lane road. The slight inclines of the pine-blanketed terrain eventually gave way to barren, leveled ground that housed a simple, utilitarian building alongside a long strip of concrete. A United States flag flapped in the wind, greeting us as we approached. Grandpa eased the Ford into the nearly empty parking lot and told me, "Well, this is it, Kiddo."

I studied the scene, and then commented indifferently, "It's not really what I expected."

Grandpa started to get out of the car and replied, "It's nothing fancy, that's for sure, but at least we got ourselves an airport."

I suddenly remembered why Grandpa and I had come here in the first place and started getting nervous as I tried to think of what I'd say to Arthur. "Be funny," I told myself. "No, no, be clever. Yeah, clever. Everyone loves a clever, little girl. Well, if you try too hard that might be weird. He'll be able to tell. Yeah, don't try so hard. Just relax." I couldn't decide which side of my brain to listen to, so I took a deep breath and hoped with all my might that the mystery man from New York would be the *something good* that would help heal our fractured family.

Arthur. A man who would soon enter my life to become both friend and foe.

He was well educated, well groomed, well mannered and wore expensive cologne that smelled like fresh, wild water. He was a gentleman's gentleman, to be sure. He was also old enough to be my grandfather.

Since Grandpa and I were the only ones in the airport waiting area, it wasn't hard for Arthur to figure out who was picking him up. He confidently strode over to the two of us and extended his bronzed hand to Grandpa, then fondly squeezed my shoulder and observed, "Why, you must be Theresa."

Suddenly shy, all I could do was shake my head "yes" and beam back.

157

"How was your flight, Arthur?" Grandpa asked.

"Oh, just fine, really. Fine," he replied. "But quite a funny thing happened when I booked my reservation."

"What was that?" asked Grandpa.

"You'll never believe this, but my travel agent assured me that International Falls, Minnesota, does not exist."

The very thought made Grandpa laugh. "You don't say? Well, I'll be," he exclaimed.

"How did you get here, then?" I curiously inquired as I walked in between the two men toward the exit.

"I politely requested that she reference her atlas," he replied.

Grandpa nodded in agreement, a grin lingering across his freckled face.

"What's an atlas?" I pressed.

"An atlas is like a map," he explained.

"How can somebody say that we don't exist when so many people live around here?" I said indignantly as I hunched my shoulders, positioning the palms of my small hands skyward in disbelief.

"My thoughts, exactly," chimed Grandpa.

Bucky was anxiously waiting for the three of us in the front seat of the Ford and leapt into Arthur's lap as soon as he slid onto the passenger's seat. Grandpa apologized, "You'll have to excuse old Buck. He gets a little excited now and again."

Arthur gently stroked Bucky's head and assured Grandpa that he didn't mind the company of the shaggy, unexpected passenger.

"C'mon Bucky. Come here," I softly encouraged until Grandpa picked the defiant dog off the front seat and set him next to me in the back, then started the car and slowly drove toward Airport Road. As we were heading home, I quietly observed the two older men as they talked with ease between themselves. Arthur was relaxed and personable; I felt instantly comfortable around him. Arthur likes dogs? Check. Arthur likes Grandpas? Check. "Yup . . . I think I'm going to be fond of the Mystery Man after all."

Over the next few days, when the summer sun lazed in the northern evening sky before the crickets had yet to emerge, Arthur would come 'round in his shiny silver rental car and take Mom and me to dinner at the fanciest place in town. In the darkest alcove of the town's sole supper club, he'd light a cigarette and let the smoke caress the side of his tanned face as he recounted tales from his colorful past. He was warm and kind and genuine, and it never seemed to matter much that Mom and I lived in a broken-down shack, owned an unreliable car and subsidized our grocery runs with government food stamps. He treated us as though our world and his had been and always would be one and the same.

Arthur stayed in town only a few days during that first visit. After he flew back to Oyster Bay, he wrote kind, thoughtful letters to me on fancy, personalized stationery. I, in turn, promptly replied, revealing personal musings on the world around me and begging him to visit again soon.

Shortly after our pen-pal relationship had firmly taken root, I received a thick, bulky postal package wrapped in brown paper. It was sitting, unopened, on our kitchen table. Curious, I began walking toward it, then stopped short as soon as I saw my very own name written in bold, black letters. "For me?" I wondered to myself. It wasn't even Christmas or my birthday! My heart began to race as I carefully lifted it off the table and awkwardly transported it into our dimly lit living room. I placed it onto the floor and knelt down beside it, gawking a moment more before carefully tearing off the paper. Inside, a small, white note card was taped to the front of a thick, black book. I peeled off the envelope and read the enclosure. "To aid

159

in a bright future for one smart, little gal," it encouraged. I stared at the priceless gift that lay unwrapped on the living floor. It was a brand new Webster's unabridged dictionary. No one besides Daddy had ever given me such a present. My lips slowly moved up and down as I whispered the book's title to myself then gingerly opened its thick cover and penned my name on the inside page in purposeful, capital letters. Ever so tightly, I hugged my treasure to my chest as I carried it up the stairs and placed it in a special spot next to my bed. "Maybe Daddy wasn't really gone after all," I thought to myself. "Maybe he brought this nice man to take care of me?"

"Mom," I said to my mother later that day.

"Yes, Dear?"

"I like Arthur," I firmly stated, then quickly corrected myself. "No. You know what? I think I even like him *a lot*."

She stepped closer and enveloped me in her arms. "I think I like him a lot, too, Dear. Maybe this is just what the doctor ordered."

By the summer of '77, Mom had grown weary of New Grandma, or perhaps it was the other way around, so we packed up our belongings and moved about a mile away to the other side of town.

Mom and I would call a one-story, avocado-green duplex "home" for the next few years. The kitchen was so tiny you could barely spin a circle in it, and the counter space so limited that what few gadgets we owned were crammed next to one another by the sink, as though waiting to be reclaimed from their miniature junkyard. Mom, clearly in need of sharpening her appliance management skills, accidentally set an overhead cupboard on fire the first time she used the toaster. The good news was . . . I still had my own room.

A family of four mentally disabled folk lived on the other side of the duplex wall, a mother, father and two teenage boys.

160

After running into them several times, I resentfully whined to Mom behind closed doors, "Why do we have to live next to a bunch of retards, anyway?"

Mom glared at me and corrected, "They aren't retards, Sister, they're children of God. Don't slander them that way."

I kept on calling them *The Retards*, anyway.

Always eager to flee the homestead, I remained diligent about keeping my social calendar jam-packed. One warm evening at the end of June, I met Dana at Smokey the Bear Park. "You'll never guess what!" she exclaimed as we were sitting on top of a picnic table, eating raspberry Freezie Pops.

I stopped licking my Freezie Pop and glanced her way. "What?"

"Guess."

"No idea," I answered truthfully.

"C'mon. Just guess, would you."

"Um, you got your first period?"

"Gross! No-o-o-o-o."

"You . . . started shaving your legs?"

Dana looked down at her bare legs and asked, "Does it even look like I have any hair worth shaving?"

I shrugged my shoulders and defended myself, "I don't know. You told me to guess."

Losing patience, Dana canned the guessing game and explained, "You know that one hockey player I've had my eye on?"

I affirmatively shook my head. "How could I *not* know," I thought to myself. "Yeah, you mean, Chip?" I said out loud.

Dana raised her eyebrows up and down and seductively replied, "Uh huh."

"Luscious Lipped Chip?" I said again, without any real purpose except to make his name rhyme with something.

"That's the one. Uh huh, uh huh. Well . . . he asked me to go with him up to Lang's cabin on the Fourth. I really, really, really want to go. Will you come?" she pleaded.

Her face had "pretty please" written all over it. I didn't know what to say at first, so I glanced over at a young couple that was playing tennis on the nearby courts. "It'd be fun, I guess . . ." I let my voice drift off then added, "But what am I suppose to do when you're off with Luscious Lips?"

"They'll be lots of other guys there. You'll have fun, Ther. I swear."

When I kept avoiding eye contact, she added, "If you don't go, then there's no way my mom is going to let me go alone. C'mon . . . please?"

Dana was my best friend in the whole wide world. I was about as loyal to her as Ed McMahon was to Johnny Carson. I just couldn't let her down.

As soon as I reestablished eye contact, a big smile spread across her face. She already knew I was going to agree even before I'd said anything. "We're gonna have a blast, Ther! You're the best!"

Back in those days, just about anyone could afford a parcel of pine forest heaven upon the lake that embraced the eastern edge of our town. Rainy was her name, and she was surely Poseidon's most bewitching freshwater mistress. She was abundant yet not all-consuming, flirtatious while careful not to overwhelm. To look upon her was to look upon paradise itself. The deciduous trees that called her shores their home clustered so thickly that, from afar, they looked like the Chosen Ones, standing unabashedly tall and proud. From within her bosom, islands aplenty sprouted to the surface like fuzzy, moss-ridden sea monsters, and the water was so clear and pure it could soothe the ailing as it gently massaged her beige, sandy beaches.

The Fourth of July that particular year was the most glorious day imaginable. The sky was filled with a soft blue hue and dotted with filmy clouds as thin as Swedish pancakes. The temperature climbed quickly in the company of gentle, soothing breezes before relaxing at a perfect 82 degrees, making it ideal for our forthcoming adventure at the lake.

Dana's mom dropped the two of us at the cabin around three o'clock that afternoon. Giggling nervously, we hurried along the pebbled path toward the back screen door.

"You go first," insisted Dana.

"No way, are you kidding me? This was your idea. You go first," I replied defiantly, gently nudging my best friend to get in line ahead of me.

"All right, fine," she said with feigned annoyance, then approached the door and decisively rapped on it a few times before entering. "Hi everyone!" she exclaimed with a wave to accompany her cheery greeting while I hovered close behind and smiled as widely as I could.

Our two female chaperones were comfortably seated at the kitchen table, drinking CC and water in their one-piece bathing suits as they played a round of cribbage. Through the bay window on the far side of the rustic room, I could see several boys outside on the dock, each preparing to dive-bomb one of their buddies in the water.

"Come on in, Girls," said Mrs. Lang as she glanced at us from behind her cards, then smiled sweetly and waved us in. "Make yourselves at home. We have pop and sandwiches in the fridge." She then gestured toward all the opened cookie boxes and potato chip bags that littered the countertop. "And, if you want a snack, we have plenty . . ." Her annoyed facial expression implied, ". . . as you can see *by this mess!*"

All that talk of refreshments was making me hungry, and I wanted to dive right into the Nutter Butters, but Dana had her mind set on loftier ambitions and single-mindedly walked past the snacks, then past the table of tipsy, tanned women and out the lakeside door. Purely by default, I was forced to bypass Mrs. Lang's generous offer.

Chip immediately spied the two of us and darted over to where we were standing on the back deck. "Hey, how's it going, Dana?" he asked coolly.

"Good," she replied, smiling nonchalantly in hard-to-catch fashion.

"Hey, you guys want to go for a swim or something?" He asked, then looked in the direction of the dock. "We got inner tubes."

"I don't think so," Dana said firmly, her lips pursed. "I really don't want to get my hair wet."

I looked longingly over at the boys who were having so much fun in the water. I didn't see the point in coming all this way and not even taking a dip. Besides, my hair always looked tribal anyway, so why *not* get it wet?

Dana and Chip continued their childish, infatuated banter, boring me to tears, so I excused myself and walked down the grayed, wooden steps to the dock. I grabbed an unused inner tube and flung it into the lake, jumping after it, then dove underneath the water and up through the center of my floating, black doughnut, flinging my arms and legs over the hot, rubber sides in an effort to keep my torso afloat. My rowdy companions seemed completely unaware of their new visitor, so I ignored them right back by closing my eyes and listening to the water strike a soft rhythm against the dock while the sun's warmth licked the moisture from my skin. Moments passed, then many more as I drifted in and out of my silent reverie, only to realize much later that I was the only remaining body in the water, bobbing atop the gentle waves like a forgotten fishing lure. I lazily looked across the lake. Not far from shore was a small fishing boat carrying a crew of two bronzed buddies, and their loyal black lab that was seated at the rear. Slowly but surely, their boat drifted closer. The two men jubilantly waved in my direction, then one cupped his mouth with his hands and yelled, "Happy Fourth of July!" I returned their gleeful greeting by raising both of my arms straight up in the air and moving them toward each other then back again, crossing and re-crossing them. I couldn't help but laugh when the black lab started barking at me, as if he, too, wanted to send a summer salutation.

The fishing crew eventually drifted out of sight, leaving my gaze to drift up the cabin's wooden steps and rest upon several of the boys who were sitting on the deck next to the railing with their feet hanging over the side, busily replenishing the calories they'd burned while horsing around in the water. I scanned the chattering crowd for my best bud. Nope. She was nowhere in sight . . . and neither was Chip. Mrs. Lang emerged from the cabin with a six-pack of Coke dangling from one hand and started distributing it amongst several of the boys, then proceeded to light a nearby barbeque on the opposite side of the deck. "Must be dinnertime soon," I thought to myself. As I continued drifting alone in the water, I pondered my options. Sure, I wanted the boys to like me and was anxious to latch on to my very own hunk just as Dana had, but my shyness and insecurities regarding the opposite sex kept me from actively mingling. Besides, nothing could have been better than exactly what I was doing at that moment in time. It was pure bliss.

I looked up and spied Mr. Lang bounding toward me down the wooden steps. He walked over to a small patch of sand on the narrow beach next to the dock, then tossed a Styrofoam bait pail into the lake. "You doing all right over there, Missy?" he asked.

I grinned, then eagerly waved and told him I was doing great. "Thanks for having us out to your cabin, Mr. Lang! This is sooooo cool!" I glanced down at the kaleidoscope of sunbeams shimmering on top of the water, then lowered my hand into the lake and softly caressed it. On that beautiful Fourth of July, I was doing more than just great . . . I was golden.

~♦ ♦ ♦~

For as crazy as Mom was, she had an uncanny knack for making friends, and she had lots of them, too. Some were from church, some were friends of friends, and some were just lonely barflies she'd drag home from The Buzy Bee. Many would stick around for only a few weeks or months, quickly tiring of Mom's peculiar ways, while a handful possessed the patience to see past her many flaws and understand the beauty from within. One of those life-long companions was a kind and gentle spirit named Sheila.

A devout Catholic in every way, Sheila loved the Lord as though he had personally opened up her beating heart and breathed life directly into it. To her, God was Good and God was Great. No questions asked. From the very start, Sheila had sensed a weary soul within my mother who was in dire need of God's mercy, and had tucked Mom safely beneath the downy folds of her wings, offering her unwavering friendship each moment the Lord Almighty so graciously allowed her to serve.

Schizophrenia ran deep within Mom's veins, often coursing through her in twisted ways; the very power of the Christian horror movies that plagued her mind were enough to render her delusional. During those occurrences, night or day, she'd pick up the phone and call upon Sheila, who'd show up at our doorstep within a matter of minutes, bestowing her trademark hugs with a heart of solid gold. She'd patiently take a besieged Mom by the hand and lead her into the bedroom where the two of them would lie down together on top of the rumpled covers, Sheila cradling Mom in her protective embrace as she rocked her fast asleep.

Since I never knew when Mom was going to slide into one of her episodes, it was a rare occasion for me to invite anyone to our house, including my best friend. One late summer morning, after Dana and I had done a little window shopping downtown, I daringly asked my best pal over. I realized my big mistake the moment we walked in the front door. The curtains remained unopened in our small, cramped quarters as Mom sat listless at the kitchen table with a church friend of Sheila's named Ruth. "Rid yourself of evil, Rainy," Ruth encouraged. Promptly obeying her orders, Mom leaned forward and opened her mouth as widely as she could in an effort to spew forth her inner ghosts, then coughed uncontrollably and dabbed at her tear-filled eyes. Ruth sympathetically rubbed Mom's back while holding her hand. "That's it, Rainy," she whispered loudly in the tone of a divine healer. "Good. You're doing it! They're leaving your body now."

Ashamed, embarrassed, confused, I turned to Dana and stammered, "Hey, Dane, I'm, I'm . . . I'm really sorry about this! I didn't know my mom wasn't feeling well." I nervously looked over at Mom who began chanting in tongues. "I guess you better go," I persuaded. "Maybe I'll call you later?"

After Dana left, I stormed into my room full of rage and flopped onto my bed. "Why was Mom so freaking weird?!" I thought to myself. "Why couldn't this bizarre stuff end once and for all?!" I rolled onto my back and stared at the ceiling. I could hear Mom and Ruth engrossed in their cultic ceremony. The longer I lay there, the angrier I got. The whole thing gave me the creeps. Finally, I'd had enough. I got up and burst into the kitchen then yelled, "Stop! Would you just stop it! Right now!"

Startled, Ruth snapped her head up and glowered at me while Mom, now in the throes of another vomiting session, bobbed unsteadily and moaned, "My illness, oh my illness."

"I just can't take this anymore!" I screamed uncontrollably. "Will you just stop all this craziness?! I don't care about your stupid illness. In fact, if you want to know the truth, I HATE your stupid illness!"

Mom's dull look of incomprehension ever so slowly boiled over into one of absolute fury, just as it had with Mikie not long before he'd left us for good. As if a switch had been

167

turned, she stood up and marched to within a few feet of me. "How dare you talk to me like that, you little snot!" she barked.

"You are out of your damn mind, you know that?" I barked back.

"Why, you little . . . !" Mom hissed as she raised her hand up high, preparing to strike.

I stopped her on the downturn and held her wrist in a deadlock grip. We glared at each other with eyes of hatred as Mom's guest sat in bewilderment with her mouth agape.

I finally broke the thick silence by screaming, "I hate you! I hate your guts! I hope I never see you again!" I cast her hand aside, headed toward the door and ran outside. At first, I didn't even know where to go, my pent-up rage pounding from the inside out like a bucking bronco at the rodeo. "Run," said a small voice inside me. "Run!" I started sprinting toward the paved path that would take me all the way to Beach Road. My arms and legs pumped effortlessly together in synch, releasing my fury and quieting the anger within. Tiny raindrops patted my skin, alerting me to an approaching storm, then thickened and pulsed stronger with each beat on the pavement. I didn't care. I didn't FUCKING care! LET IT RAIN!!! And rain it did. The faster I ran toward Beach Road, the faster it came down, strangely quenching the turmoil inside me. I ran and ran and ran, immune to the fire in my lungs.

My pace slowed as I neared the beach where I sought shelter under a nearby tree. I could feel the heat of my skin collide with the coolness in the air as my chest heaved up and down. I took a deep breath and looked out upon Rainy Lake. She was just as enraged as I, her waters thrashing in the storm, unwilling to surrender, her whitecaps roaring to shore. I let my lungs regain their balance before slowly sitting down on the wet sand, then wrapped my arms around my bent knees to fend off the oncoming chill and waited for the tempest to subside.

~♦ ♦ ♦~

168

As the storm's severity eased, I wondered where to turn. I didn't want to go to my grandparents' house because Grandpa would have just sent me back to Mom anyway. I didn't want to go to Dana's and face the demoralizing task of explaining my mother's odd behavior. Having no other options, I reluctantly returned home later that evening. Mom was sitting alone on the couch, anxiously awaiting my arrival. She stood up as soon as I walked in the door, a mixed look of relief and anger scrawled across her face.

I didn't say anything as I hurried past her toward my bedroom, wanting nothing more than to rid myself of my waterlogged clothes.

I could feel the heat of Mom's glare as she forcefully stated, "You are never going to do that again, Young Lady!"

I turned toward her and glared back but held my tongue.

"I was worried sick!" she told me, her voice coated with genuine angst. "Where have you been all this time?!"

"Does it really matter?" I spat.

She walked over to the kitchen table and sat down. "I called Sheila," she huffed.

My heart started racing. By the tone of her voice, I already knew what was coming.

" . . . and, she said you could live with her for as long as you want." Mom reached for her pack of smokes, pulled a fresh one out then lit it.

Overcome with so many colliding emotions, I stood frozen in place, not knowing what to say or how to feel. Sure, I hated Mom sometimes, but mostly I really loved her. Plus, I wasn't exactly prepared for my turn at exile. I guess I'd always thought I'd be smart enough to outmaneuver her, avoiding the entire dilemma altogether.

"Why'd you go and do that?!" I demanded as my throat started to thicken with fear.

"If you hate me so doggone much, then I just don't know how to take care of you anymore," she replied in her signature high-pitched shriek. "You'll just have to get along with someone else. You'll be better off."

The tears started to come now. "But, Mom," I whimpered. "You don't understand how hard it is sometimes. You're so crazy, and you do all these weird things all the time. Why can't you just be normal for once?"

"Normal? I am normal," she screeched. "I go to church, I have lots of friends, I have a job . . ."

I wiped my nose with the back of my hand and looked at my mother in complete disbelief. How could she not know just how crazy she really was?

"None of my friends have moms like you," I countered weakly. "They don't talk to demons and they don't consider Jesus a personal friend. They don't have to go to mental hospitals and they're not sick in the head all the time! You . . . are! You're sick in the head all the time!" I yelled as I slammed my fist into the nearest wall.

"I don't know what to do with you, anymore. You're just going to have to live with Sheila," Mom said dismissively. Without fail, this was how my mother dealt with the world around her, instinctively operating on impulse with no regard for the unintended consequences of her actions.

Feeling an intense desire to get away from her as quickly as possible, I stormed into my bedroom and slammed the door shut, got out of my soaking clothes and put on my pajamas without bothering to towel dry my hair. Before getting into bed, I flipped my radio on and turned it up, trying to drown out the noise coming from the opposite side of my bedroom door.

Now it was my turn to get kicked out of the nest . . . ready or not.

170

Sheila lived just eight blocks away with her husband, Brad, in a small and humble, yet well-manicured Tudor. All but the two youngest of their abundant brood had long since moved away by the time I came into the picture. Although more than willing to open up their home, Sheila and Brad's three bedrooms were currently occupied without a vacancy in sight, leaving me no place to call my own. Sheila tried to convince her 17-year-old daughter to share a room, and when Kathy flatly refused, Sheila tried to ease the sting. "You know how moody high school girls can be," she lightheartedly joked while hugging me close. "Don't take it personally, okay?"

My default alternative happened to be the living room couch. I didn't really mind it, except that I had to wait until after the 10 o'clock news before I could catch any shuteye.

In her gentle, maternal way, Sheila cared for me as though I were an orphaned kitten she'd found roaming the midnight streets. She encouraged me to keep up with my friends and readily drove me to my many social events, always ensuring I never went hungry by providing after school and bedtime snacks that were on-demand and plentiful. On the nights when I couldn't sleep, she'd stay up late into the evening hours and fix me hot apple cider and graham crackers as I sat at the kitchen table with a blanket wrapped around my shoulders. "Give your troubles to God," she'd advise.

For as kind as Sheila and Brad were toward me, their two children were equally nasty, making it difficult to adjust to my new life. Early on, the siblings made it crystal clear that I had invaded their territory. Whenever I got within range, their eyes would flash, "Intruder Alert! Intruder Alert!" and I quickly learned to steer clear. After enduring this for several weeks, I decided it best to bide my time elsewhere during the daytime hours until I had little choice but to return when evening fell.

I yearned for the life my brother now had, a normal stepmother and father to love and call his own with a brother, sister and family dog thrown in for good measure. They took camping trips together in the summer, and vacationed at Disneyland every winter. Most importantly, they seemed like a bona fide family unit. As time passed at my new house on Eighth Street, it was looking more and more as though I'd simply never attain that same kind of storybook ending.

One night after the ten o'clock news, I retrieved my sheets from the linen closet just as I always had and began assembling my bed. Everyone else had retired for the evening except for the youngest boy. I walked over to the TV and clicked it off. David glared at me from the La-Z-Boy, then resentfully demanded, "Why'd you do that?"

"Um, it's time for bed," I replied, a little confused. Wasn't this the same old routine we'd gone through every night since my arrival six weeks prior?

David got up and turned the TV back on, then folded his arms in front of him and said to me, "I'll turn the TV off when I'm good and ready, got it?"

My eyes began darting around the room as I nervously clenched my teeth, sensing a brewing atmosphere of confrontation and wanting no part of it. I felt ill at ease as I made my way to the bathroom where I began brushing my teeth.

David followed. "Who do you think you are anyway? And why are you even here?" he snapped.

I started getting anxious, unsure of what this fight was all about. At first I ignored him, hoping this was all just a bad dream and he would soon disappear.

He stepped closer to me, using his height to intimidate. "If I want to watch TV, I can watch it anytime I want. Got it?!" he insisted.

I was afraid now. "Shut up and get out of my face . . . Jerk!" I said without meeting his stare.

That's when he pushed me. My toothbrush somersaulted into the air and landed on the floor as I went sailing down onto the toilet. Lucky for me, the lid was shut. I gripped the wall next to me, trying not to slam down onto the tile. I steadied myself, then stood upright again, consciously making an effort not to shake for fear David would sense my weakness. His face was beet red, and so was mine.

A concerned Brad came in from his bedroom and asked, "What's all the commotion, Kids?"

David stared me down, as if daring me to tattle.

For a split second, I wanted to spill the beans and tell Brad what an ass his son was, but bit my lip instead. "Nothing," I tersely replied.

David said the same.

One last dagger flew my way before David turned and went upstairs to his room.

"You sure you're doing okay there, Theresa?" Brad asked with genuine concern.

"Fine," I lied as I vigorously shook my head up and down and gave him a false grin like that of a tense chimpanzee, then bent down to retrieve my soiled toothbrush.

Brad told me to "sleep good," then he, too, turned and left.

With toothbrush in hand, I sat down on the toilet seat and began to quiver. I retraced what had just happened in my mind, trying to figure out what I had done that was so wrong. No matter how many times I replayed that scenario, I just couldn't find an answer. As I sat staring at the pink and purple seahorses floating on the plastic shower curtain, I began wishing I could somehow submerge myself into their playful waters. Through the fog of my daydream, I gradually began to realize that I was now left with only one viable alternative . . . Mom. At least when I lived with my mother, as screwed up as that situation was, I lived in a world where I didn't have to walk on quicksand all the time. The next morning I called her up and pleaded to go back home.

My first foray into another life had failed miserably.

~ ♦ ♦ ♦ ~

By the time I moved back into the duplex, Mom's anger had long since subsided. She welcomed me with open arms and seemed happy to have me in her life again. We hugged and kissed each other in the doorway while she cooed, "My little angel" and stroked the hair out of my eyes. After our warm exchange, I retrieved my suitcases and lugged them to my room. A brand-new, striped cotton blouse lying on my bed was the first thing that caught my eye. Delighted, I clapped my hands, then quickly shed what I was wearing so I could try it on.

It felt good to be out of the quicksand and back into the mire.

Arthur continued drifting in and out of our lives, preferring the comfort of his Oyster Bay apartment to the lifestyle of small town U.S.A. Even still, he loyally maintained contact by phone and mail, flying back for trouble-free visits every once in a blue moon. I asked Mom why Arthur wanted to live so far away. "He doesn't want to part with his apartment out east. I suppose the good ones are hard to come by," was her simple explanation. I figured the more likely reason was to avoid getting driven off a cliff the way the cowboys used to do to the buffalo.

Despite the ebb and flow of Mom's holy tirades, we peaceably coexisted for quite some time. She clung to loyal friends, leaning hard on them when she had to, and carried close to her heart an undying devotion to the Lord. It was around that time when she became obsessed with the PTL Club, also known as Praise the Lord Club, owned and operated by the infamous Bakker televangelist empire. The program featured Jim and Tammy Faye, the enthusiastically devout couple who touted personal religious experience as the panacea for all of life's problems. Having an overabundance of problems, Mom bought their shtick hook, line and sinker.

She'd sit riveted on the couch with a blanket on her lap, listening to testimonies of how the glory of God could bring persons such as herself a more fruitful and fulfilling life.

"Sing the song of abandonment to the will of God and you will be unafraid of anything!" advertised one well-heeled, custom-suited, diamond-sporting faithful who was preaching to a cameraman in the center of the L.A. studio. "All of heaven will stop. All the angels will sss . . . ttt . . . op. All the saints will stand still . . . as you begin to sing your hymn of praise!"

"Amen!" chimed Jim Bakker, who was seated next to him behind a studio desk.

"All the mistakes, sins, imperfections will be taken off," continued the preacher in rapid fire. "Yes! I said, taken off you, children. And you will be wrapped in gladness."

"Praise the Lord, Billy!" added Jim.

"And now my heart will sing and praise you forever, my brothers and sisters!"

"Glory be to God, Billy!" said Jim as the camera closed in on Tammy Faye, who brought a fragile hand to her brightly colored face and wiped away what was supposed to have been a tender tear.

"Give generously to the Lord, my children!" encouraged Billy persuasively as the toll-free PTL phone number flashed continuously at the bottom of the screen.

"Oh, that Tammy Faye!" Mom exclaimed while reaching for her checkbook. "She's just beautiful. Don't you think she's beautiful, Theresa?"

"Not really," I replied honestly. "She looks like she has a pack of black bubblegum stuck to her eyelids," I said as I lifted my hands in front of my eyes, protruding all ten of my slender fingers and wiggling them vigorously to visually emphasize my point.

Mom ignored my derogatory comment as she faithfully wrote out her twenty-dollar contribution and absently commented, "Tammy's from International Falls, you know."

It didn't much matter to me where the heck Tammy was from; I still wanted nothing to do with her.

Aside from turning to religion for strength, Mom also turned to the bottle. She began drinking more and more, forcing Grandpa to wisely recommend, "I think you should join Alcoholics Anonymous, Rainy." After too many mornings of ferocious headaches and stumbling through a Budweiser-littered kitchen floor, Mom finally took her father's advice and started attending weekly meetings. That's where she hooked up with Peggy G.

Peggy was the wackiest of Mom's friends to date. Most of them danced to the tune of their own drummer, to be sure, but were mild mannered, nonetheless. Not Peggy. Oh, no! She was tall and loud, and wore lots of red rouge and lipstick, making damn sure everybody knew when she walked into a room. She had frizzy, crimson hair that she purposely combed outward to exaggerate its thickness, making her look more like a worn-out rock 'n roll groupie than a Betty Crocker baking mom from The Falls. Despite her eccentricities, I liked her a lot. She had a kind heart. When she was feeling fine, she'd roar with laughter at even the smallest things, as though life had written a prime-time comedy special just for her. Her mirth was infectious, and I often found myself laughing right along.

Mom started going out on the town with Peggy on a regular basis. They'd make their usual rounds, driving up to the bars on the lake before ending their evening on the sloppy, beer-stained dance floor of the smoky Border Bar. In spite of their good intentions and a solemn AA oath to never more touch the devil's brew, they'd land back home in an intoxicated state of mind, time and time again.

Spring eventually rolled around, heralding its usual agenda of high school graduation parties. Mom received an invitation that year from her eldest brother and his tall, attractive wife who were celebrating their son's plunge into the pool of adulthood.

Mom insisted on buying the young graduate a gift and outwardly mused about what would be appropriate to give an 18-year-old.

"Why don't you buy him a Billy Joel album?" I recommended.

"Well," Mom hesitantly replied, "I don't know who that is."

"You know, that one singer . . . 'The Stranger,' 'Scenes from an Italian Restaurant.' "

Mom stared blankly back.

" 'Piano Man'?" I said with befuddled disbelief.

When Mom still didn't respond, I began to croon lyrics from "Piano Man."

Still nothing.

Frustrated, I decided to switch directions. "Okay, how about getting him a jackknife. You know how Mikie always carries one of those things around with him wherever he goes."

"Nawwwww," Mom replied. "I'm not going to get him any jackknife. If he wants one, he can go out and buy it for himself."

I shrugged and resigned myself to the fact that she was clearly not in the mood to entertain any of my ideas.

"I'll think of something," Mom passively declared.

Although Mom was generous, her intentions were often misguided. I had a sinking feeling she would end up giving my cousin something strange, so I took one last crack at persuading her. "You know, Mom, you probably don't have to get him anything. I mean, I bet he already has everything he needs, know what I mean?"

"Ahhhhhh, Lord love a duck," she replied, slightly annoyed. "Let's not talk about it anymore."

Parties at Uncle Willie and Aunt Mae's were always a kick. The two were a popular pair who mixed with the town's working class crowd. Liberal-sized cocktails flowed freely from my uncle's hand behind the bar, and every guest's appetite was satisfied with fresh deli trays from the local Piggly Wiggly. Colorful conversations flourished, becoming more uninhibited as time touched the midnight hour, reflecting the amount of alcohol that had been drained from the caramel-tinted bottles.

On the night of the festivities, Peggy came by our house around seven o'clock. She was wearing a loud, orange and white pantsuit that screamed, "Look at me!" and had accentuated her kisser with a matching shade of lipstick. Six thin, golden bangles graced her weathered, suntanned wrists, matching the long, decorative chains that hung around her neck.

"Hi, Hon!" Mom cheerfully greeted as Peggy walked through the front door and into our tiny kitchen. The pungent smell of her drugstore perfume pummeled my senses, and I tried not to cough.

"Are you ready to have fun tonight, Rainy?!" asked a high-spirited Peggy as Mom prepared herself in the nearby bathroom.

I could hear Mom chuckle in affirmation.

Peggy took a seat at the kitchen table and began tapping her well-manicured nails to the beat of a song that was playing in her head. I smiled at her from a safe distance and leaned against the stove.

"Get down, get down, get down tonight, baby . . ." she grooved while impatiently waiting for her drinking buddy.

When Mom finally reemerged, her green eyes sparkled above peach-perfect, blushed cheeks, and her frosted, brown hair was styled to perfection.

"I'm ready, girls!" an elated Mom proclaimed as though Peggy and I couldn't be more fortunate, then grabbed the graduate's wrapped gift from the top of our buffet.

"What'd you end up getting Danny, Mom?" I asked as we walked along the sidewalk to the party.

"Oh, just a little something."

"Like what?" I pressed.

"An ant farm," she said as casually as if she were giving him a sweater.

I stopped dead in my tracks. "Mom?! You didn't say what I thought you just said. Did you?" I asked in complete horror.

"Uh huh," she answered as she and Peggy kept walking straight ahead.

I squeezed my eyes shut and said to myself, "Don't panic, don't panic, don't panic," then raced to catch up and did some fast talking. "I have a better idea," I began, making up a story as I went along. "I have another present we can give him. Why don't we just save the ant farm for another day?"

"This is a nice present," Mom said defensively, emphasizing the word, "nice." "I bought it, and I'm going to give it to him."

My worst fears had been realized. "Please don't give him an ant farm, Mom!" I desperately pleaded.

"What's the matter with you?" she asked. "There's nothing wrong with giving someone an ant farm."

Knowing Mom all too well, I reluctantly surrendered. No amount of persuasion could stop her. "Well, at least it will be something no one else has thought of!" I sarcastically contemplated to myself.

When we arrived at the party, several of my aunt and uncle's friends were already there. Uncle Willie met us at the door and gave Mom a one-armed side hug while gripping a lowball in his left hand. "Well, how ya doing there, Rainy?" he cheerfully asked.

Mom hugged him back and said, "Oh, Willie . . . do you know my friend, Peggy?" Before he could answer, Mom planted the wrapped ant farm in his drink-free hand and remarked, "Just a little something." She looked around their pleasantly appointed house and gushed, "Your house is just

179

beautiful!" then turned to her friend and rhetorically asked, "Isn't their place just beautiful, Peggy?"

"Well, I'll be a son-of-a-gun if it ain't!" Peggy flamboyantly replied as she smiled widely, revealing a smudge of orange lipstick on her front tooth.

Uncle Willie set down the present and his drink then saddled up behind the kitchen counter that doubled as a bar and asked his latest customers, "So, what can I get you gals?"

"Whiskey soda," Peggy plainly replied.

"Comin' right up!" said Uncle Willie as he began filling a silver-decaled glass, then handed it to the thirsty party girl whose bangles clinked softly together as she took the offering from my uncle's hand.

Riveted by the glass and its bubbling contents, Mom oozed, "Mmmmm, looks real good. I think that's what I'm gonna have too, Willie!"

As the night flowed along, Mom and Peggy fluttered from one social group to another before ending up back at the kitchen counter where Uncle Willie was deep in conversation with one of his long-time buddies. Peggy smoothly moved in and placed both elbows on the countertop then leaned over just far enough to reveal her ample mounds of womanhood. She smiled flirtatiously and introduced herself to Ivan. "I'm Peggy," she said. "So nice to meet you, now."

Ivan swirled the booze around in his glass then quizzically glanced at my uncle as if to ask, "So, what's this broad all about?"

Peggy reached past Ivan and grabbed an open bottle of whiskey. "Can I freshen up your drink, Hon?" she asked, eyebrows slyly raised.

Before she had a chance to apply her best moves, Mom innocently grabbed the bottle and mistakenly replied, "Thought you'd never ask!"

Peggy lunged for the whiskey, trying to retrieve it. "No, Rainy, I wasn't talking to you!"

Mom held her ground and demanded, "I want some more, too!"

Before I knew it, the two of them were smothering the whiskey bottle, trying to yank it out of one another's hands like a couple of grade-schoolers in a playground brawl.

Uncle Willie jumped into the mix and managed to reclaim the booze, then set it back on the counter. He turned toward Peggy and firmly stated, "Ivan's just fine. He doesn't need anymore, and if he did, well then, I'd get it for him." Now it was Mom's turn, "And, Rainy, you've had enough for now, don't you think. You should probably be calling it a night anyway."

Both Peggy and Mom were speechless from the raw sting of their scolding. Mom's eyes sobered as she said, "I'm sorry if I embarrassed you, Willie." She left to retrieve her purse and met her brother at the back door while Peggy and I waited outside on the patio.

Mom profusely apologized to her brother once more. He gave her a hug, then gently said in his older brother tone, "Ah now, don't you worry about it, Rainy. Just do me a favor and go home and get some sleep. All right?"

"Okay, Willie. I will," she replied with the innocence of a young child.

Unusually quiet, Mom stepped onto the patio in the warm, humid air, and walked past Peggy and me as if she hadn't seen us.

Peggy caught up with her and asked, "You okay? You want to go over to the Border Bar or something?"

Wrapped up in her own thoughts, mom didn't answer.

"Rainy?"

By this time, we'd reached the front door of our duplex, a mere half block away.

"Talk to you tomorrow, Peggy," Mom said with an air of sadness without even bothering to look in her friend's

181

direction, then ascended the two wooden steps that led to our unlocked front door and stepped inside.

Peggy stood motionless for a moment, just staring at the door, then folded her arms in front of her and sneered, "That's it?" She abruptly withdrew her right arm from its cradle and slapped it against her thigh. "That's it?" she said again, befuddled. "You just leave me like that? No 'goodbye'? No 'thanks for a fun night'?"

"That's just the way she is," I interrupted. "She'll feel better tomorrow."

Peggy turned and thought about my comment for a moment. "Well, all right. I guess you're right," she said, her east coast accent beginning to reemerge. She pulled her car keys from her purse then gave my shoulder a squeeze and told me, "Take it easy now, Hon."

I promised I would, then waved as she strode over to her shiny blue Buick and got in.

I entered our duplex and walked through the dark kitchen over to Mom's bedroom. Her door was still open, so I peered inside. She was lying on top of the covers with her clothes still on, snoring and fast asleep.

She would sleep off the booze, she would sleep off the pain, she would sleep off all the sorrow that had haunted her throughout the years. Tomorrow could offer a *brand new* day and a fresh start. But Mom would never see it like that. Instead, she would move through it just as she always had, just as she always would. Living the moments of her life as though she had no past . . . or future.

Just a hair shy of the legal working age, Dana and I managed to get hired as a couple of carhops that summer at the local A&W Root Beer Drive-In. The boss wasn't willing to pay us minimum wage, but at least what we did pocket topped the fifty-cents an hour job we'd held last summer at the hockey school. Now fourteen years old and eager to earn some cold, hard cash, we felt like we'd hit the big time.

The joint's owner was a tall, middle-aged man who slicked back his dark, thinning hair, Grecian Formula-style, and sported one of those mistrustful, skinny mustaches on his upper lip. His beer belly bulged from far too many greasy burgers, and his once-muscular arms were plastered with faded tattoos like the one of a skull and crossbones that roared, "Live and Let Die." Dana and I begrudgingly wore the ugly, brown polyester uniforms that he provided and reeked of lardy French fries, no matter how often we washed them. Even so, we gladly toiled away the warm, fleeting days in anticipation of our prized Friday afternoon paychecks.

It was during that time, right before ninth grade, when an ear-piercing frenzy spread like wildfire among the popular girls in our grade. Forever absorbed in teen mags and pop culture, Dana and I were not to be left out of this latest craze. On a day when neither of us was scheduled to work, Dana called me on the phone and asked, "Hey, Ther, my mom just said I could get my ears pierced. Do you want to go with me?"

"You've got to be kidding me, right?!" I chirped excitedly. "I've been wanting to do this for only forever! I was talking to Patty yesterday, and guess what?! She and Tammy just got theirs done at the drugstore, and I mean, we so have to do this!"

"Ask your mom if it's okay then call me back."

"Naw," I said confidently. "She doesn't really care what I do. It's really no big deal anyway."

We walked into the neatly organized store and strode with purpose past the candle display toward an oversized poster of a bronze-faced beauty in the cosmetics department. Dana flagged down one of the young clerks and informed her of our intentions. "Are you sure you girls are up for this?" the

183

clerk lightheartedly teased before excusing herself to retrieve the piercing technician.

"Go first, go first," Dana anxiously coaxed while we waited.

"No. Uh, uh," I protested, vigorously shaking my head from side to side. "You go first! Please?" I begged. "I hate needles!" Then I made a face as if one had just poked me. "You have to tell me if it hurts or not."

My best bud and I still had not yet decided who would be the brave one when the piercing technician arrived. Dana could sense I wasn't going to budge as I looked at the technician with feigned innocence. "Fine. I'll just do it," she said impatiently, hopping onto the metal stool and pinching her eyes shut as the technician gently dabbed rubbing alcohol onto her earlobes while calmly instructing her to relax. "Click!" snapped the piercing gun as Dana's shoulders twitched in reaction. She looked as though she were about to reopen her eyes when the gun clicked a second time. The whole process was over within a matter of minutes.

As a relieved Dana eased off the stool, she proclaimed, "Didn't hurt a bit. Your turn!"

I slid into position and clenched my teeth. "It's not a big deal, Ther. Really," Dana reassured right before the "Click!" I felt a slight sting that quickly passed. Almost done.

Proud owners of newly bejeweled ears, Dana and I skipped down the town's side streets in the mid-afternoon sun singing, "I Am Woman, Hear Me Roar!" at the top of our lungs.

Dana dropped off at her house, while I started prancing back to mine, one block away. As an afterthought, she yelled, "Hey! Wanna go see a movie tonight?"

I gave her the thumbs-up sign and told her I'd call her.

We later made plans to check out *Heaven Can Wait* that was screening at the Cine 2-Plex. When Dana stopped by to pick me up later that evening, she was wearing a new pair of

Levi's and a pastel, cotton shirt that she'd borrowed from me weeks before.

"Chip called," she revealed en route.

I snapped my head sideways to look at her and asked, "Really?! What'd he have to say?"

"W-e-l-l-l-l-l . . . He's going to be at the show tonight."

"Uh!" I gasped. "Do you think he's going just because you are?"

Dana slyly smiled then shrugged, "Dunno. I guess." She looked at me from the corner of her eye and confided, "I hope so."

"You *so* know he has the hots for you," I frankly stated. "Sooooo . . . that's why you're wearing your new jeans."

"No it's not!"

"Yes it is!"

"It is not!" Dana hotly defended. "My mom just got paid the other day and gave me a little money."

"Right," I said sarcastically, unconvinced.

The lights were just beginning to dim by the time we made our way down the theater aisle, squinting in the dark as a trail of popcorn fell onto the floor. We managed to find two good seats, front and center, then sat down in the half-empty theater. We could hear someone behind us clearing his throat and calling Dana's name. My best bud suspiciously turned around, trying to pinpoint the source. Once she realized it was coming from none other than her charming, young flame, seated a few rows behind us, she excitedly whispered, "He's here! He's here!" then slid lower into her seat.

She didn't seem to notice that I wasn't nearly as joyful.

We munched on popcorn as we watched Mr. Sexy on the big screen, distracted by the commotion behind us. About halfway through the comedy, Chip called Dana's name. When she turned around this time, he motioned for her to sit in the recently vacated seat next to him.

185

She looked at me and asked breathlessly, "Oh my gosh. He wants me to sit with him. What should I do?"

"Don't do it," I selfishly advised, mortified at the thought of being left all alone.

She didn't seem to hear me and again asked, "Should I go sit by him?"

"No way," I said in my most convincing voice

"I'm going over there. Don't be mad, k, Ther?"

"Aw, c'mon, Dane," I whined.

Before I could protest any further, my best bud was up and out of her seat, helplessly seduced by the wild call of puppy love.

I panicked. There I sat, all by myself. What would people think? Feeling like a big, fat loser, I angrily turned around to stare at the newly united lovebirds. Dana smiled back as if she'd just been crowned homecoming queen, completely oblivious to my discomfort. I tried to regain my composure and concentrate on the movie but soon lost interest. I finally got up and started walking out of the theater, but not before giving Dana a contemptuous "thanks a lot!" glare.

Outside, the sun was just beginning to fade. I forlornly began my journey back home, kicking every rock I could find along the way and aiming it straight for Chip's big, fat head.

Mom was gone when I arrived, most likely out with Peggy again. Although it was too early to go to sleep, I went to my bedroom and changed into a pair of light cotton pajamas anyway. As I took off my shirt, I looked down at the small duo of cocoa-colored knobs protruding from my chest and anxiously wondered when they were ever going to blossom. I proceeded to the bathroom to wash my face. Standing motionless in front of the mirror, I stared back at myself. I took a long look at my eyes and nose, then my lips. They all seemed plain and oversized. I started to run a brush through my short, blond hair, adjusting it this way and that in an attempt to better frame my face. Nothing seemed to help. Ugly! That's what I was . . . just plain ugly. What boy would ever find me attractive, let alone want to love me? Even my newly pierced ears couldn't lead me into the arms of happiness.

Over the next few days, I didn't bother calling my best bud. It hurt too much to think about how she'd laid down her loyalty and chosen some stupid, smelly boy she hardly knew over me. I finally started missing her and decided it was time to make up, so I walked downtown to Woolworth's and picked out a record that seemed to fit my mood. When I went over to Dana's house to drop off my gift, I found her sunbathing in her backyard.

I walked up beside her and sheepishly said, "Hey." I waited for her to say something, but she didn't. "I bought you a record," I continued. "Can we be friends again?"

Shielding her eyes from the sun, she looked up at me. "Why'd you get so mad?" she asked.

"Cuz you left me all by myself," I explained.

"But it was Chip, Ther. What was I supposed to do? Blow him off?"

"I guess not," I reluctantly replied, then changed the subject. "Anyway, let's go inside and listen to this. I heard it on Casey Kasem."

Dana grabbed her beach towel and bottle of baby oil before the two of us headed into the house. Her bedroom appeared dark in contrast with the bright glare of the sunshine. Standing in her yellow bikini, she took the record from my hand, then read the label. "'Bluer than Blue.' How does that go again?" she asked. I hummed a couple bars for her. "Oh, I love that song!" she said, then placed the record on the turntable and pushed the "Play" button.

After the song ended, Dana looked over at me and giggled, then simply said, "Oh, Ther, you're so dramatic!"

We were best buds once more.

187

A few weeks before beginning the ninth grade, Dana and I took the last of our summer job savings and headed downtown to do a little school shopping. After we'd purchased the usual kitten-covered notebooks, Elmer's glue and no. 2 pencils, Dana told me she wanted to check out the latest fall shoe collection at The Bootery.

When we walked into the store, a tall, thin woman with short, neatly combed hair approached. "May I help you?" she kindly asked. Dana glided over to the central display island, then picked up a pair of funky, red and white shoes with striped, rubber soles and a vibrant brand emblem stitched onto each side. "I'll try these," Dana requested. "Size 6."

"Oh my gosh, those are so cute!" I squealed. "We so have to get those!"

The clerk retrieved the shoes, and then Dana promptly put them on, lifting her pant legs as she walked over to one of the wall mirrors. I enviously stared at her newfound treasure while she maneuvered her foot to the right, then to the left. I reached into my pocket to pull out what remained of my summer earnings. Four crumpled, one-dollar bills, two quarters and a lousy penny were all I had left. "How much are those?" I asked the clerk.

"Those are . . ." she began, as she strode over to the display shoe and flipped it over to reveal the price, "Eighteen, ninety-nine."

Dana removed the shoe from her foot and placed it back in the box. "I'll go ahead and take these," she requested matter-of-factly.

"You're so lucky!" I said, trying to conceal my jealousy as I shoved the remnants of my earnings back into my pocket.

"You can borrow them anytime, you know," my best bud generously offered.

Sure, I was grateful for borrowing rights, but it just wouldn't be the same as having my very own pair. With no more than a few bucks left to my name, the only other legal means of obtaining shoe gold was, well . . . Mom.

When I returned to the duplex, Mom had already drawn the curtains and was lying sideways on the living room couch, watching none other than the PTL Club. Her usual twenty-dollar check was resting on the kitchen table, ready to be shoved into a pre-paid, pre-addressed envelope and mailed off to the Bakker mansion.

I suppressed my irritation and cheerfully asked, "Mom? I need twenty big ones, please."

"What for, Honey?" she asked absently, remaining engaged with what was happening on the tube.

"There are some really cool shoes downtown at The Bootery that I've just GOT to have."

"We don't have the money right now. You'll just have to wait until some other time."

My mood took a downward turn as I glared at the twenty-dollar check.

"But, Mom," I began to argue, "What's this stupid check for?"

"Now, you leave that alone!" she hotly replied as she swung her feet onto the floor and sat up. "That goes to our Lord." Apparently Jim and Tammy Faye had more control over Mom than I did.

I started getting agitated. "Mom, why do you always have to give our money away to other people? Can't you see that this is important to me? All my friends get shopping sprees before school starts, and you can't even buy me one stupid pair of shoes!"

"Oh, I don't know," was her exasperated answer. "That's just the way things are. Can't you undastand?"

"No, I can't undastand!" I mockingly replied. "Can't YOU undastand! Can't YOU undastand!" I yelled like a trained parakeet to emphasize my annoyance with both this

189

displeasing predicament as well as Mom's unorthodox pronunciation of the word "understand."

Mom stood up, grabbed her glass from the coffee table and indifferently explained, "Well, you won't have to put up with me much longer because I'm moving out to New York in a few weeks to be with Arthur."

Kaaa . . . Booommmm!!!!! Another detonated bombshell blast was headed straight toward me.

I jerked my head in her direction. "What?!" I desperately asked, hoping with all my might that I hadn't heard her correctly.

"Yaw," she calmly stated as she walked to the fridge and refreshed her Kool Aid. "Arthur called me the other night and said he wants me to come out there."

A flood of questions came rushing from my mouth, "Well, how long will you be gone? Who will take care of me? I mean . . . Why can't I go, too?"

"Oh, you'll be just fine, Honey," she answered. "Arthur has made arrangements for you to stay with my brother over at the trailer park." Mom set her glass on the counter, then walked toward me and lovingly wrapped her arms around my shoulders. "Oh, Baby, you'll be all right," she said in consoling tones, as if the only thing I'd lost at that moment was a favorite stuffed animal. "I'll be back before you know it."

Burning tears started streaming down my face as I blubbered, "But when?! When?! When will you be back?!"

"Before you know it . . ."

I moved into the Ridgeview Mobile Home Park with Uncle Slim, Aunt Cindy and their 2.5 kids a few days before the new school year. Their doublewide was nestled among nineteen other broken down units on a flat, barren parcel of land that flanked a dusty, dirt road. No ridge was in sight and the only existing view was that of an occasional car on its way to the local strip joint.

Once again, I'd been plunked into the middle of a makeshift family, and felt the strong pull of my tendency to withdraw. My uncle and aunt continually reminded me to "make myself at home" and tried to break my habit of tiptoeing around the house and politely requesting simple things like snacks, water or use of their phone. "You are part of our family now," they'd reassuringly tell me. "You don't have to ask." But I could never shake the need to apologize for my existence.

Days turned into weeks, then weeks turned into months. Mom would occasionally call from New York to talk about her new wealthy friends, shopping trips to Saks, and the weekly lunch special at the Waldorf Astoria. "We're just having a ball out here!" she'd gush. During one conversation, she crowed, "Arthur golfed with Perry Como this morning!" There was news of marriage plans and a trip to Tiffany's in Manhattan to pick out the engagement ring.

Before we'd say goodnight and hang up the phone, she'd always tell me how much she loved me. "You're my little, shining star, Baby Girl," she'd coo. I felt more like an imploding supernova.

"I love you, too, Mom," I'd mechanically reply. She never seemed to detect the numbness in my voice.

A few, final seconds of silence would seep beneath my heart's secret door, the one where I'd hidden away my trust, my vulnerability. "When are you going to come home?" I'd ask in quiet desperation.

The answer was always the same.

While Mom was away out east, I'd often seek Grandpa's company after school, searching for consolation. Without fail, he'd greet me with a warm, "Well, hullo there, Theresa!" and ask how I was doing. If I seemed exceptionally down, he'd put on his coat and walk out back to the garage, pull out the Ford, then treat me to a drive around town until dinnertime.

During one of our town patrols, I complained, "Grandpa, why'd Mom ditch me like that and run off to New York?"

"Why, you can't feel too sorry for yourself there, Young Theresa," he replied from behind the steering wheel. "Your Mom's doing the best she can, you know. You got a roof over your head and good folks who are willing to take care of you. That's about all you can hope for. He then glanced in my direction out of the corner of his eye and added, "You've got to remember that there are a lot of kids out there who are worse off than you."

I looked past him out the driver's side window and paused before replying, "Yeah. I guess I know what you mean."

I clung to Grandpa's words with the hope that he was right. Maybe Mom really was doing the best she could. But, then again, why wasn't "her best" back at home taking care of me?

My limited understanding of Mom's true capabilities always seemed so hazy and gray, like one of those foggy, spring mornings on the lake when you could never tell where the water ended and the mist began.

During the summer of '79, a new kind of sound hit the airwaves in my hometown, flooding our local radio stations with requests for the novel, top forty bands that were dominating the charts. It was a time when K. C. and the Sunshine Band was on fire, Donna Summer was smokin' hot and the Bee Gees were downright outta sight. It didn't take long for me to catch the chill of Disco Fever. And, I wasn't alone. Just about every kid in school was trying to perfect their own, smooth style of the Hustle, whether they were willing to admit it or not. The New York City hit machine had netted us, one and all . . . hook, line and sinker.

Music was my secret spaceship, an imaginary vessel of transcendence. Happy times were multiplied by the funky groove of a song like Summer's "Hot Stuff," and the crooning cries of the Brothers Gibb indulged my adolescent fantasies as their rich, falsetto harmonies wove a tapestry through my imagination. Mom knew about my spaceship; she even had one of her own. In the years before she'd hightailed it for The Big Apple, we'd often crank up the Borderland radio station and dance with abandon around the living room floor, like two footloose, mountain gypsies.

As the boogie pandemic spread, our high school band teacher capitalized on this new money making prospect by transforming the Catholic Church gymnasium into a discotheque. Every Saturday night, a mere two bucks gained admittance into an carnival of sights, sounds and teenage lust that was not to be found anywhere else in town.

On the days leading up to those infamous disco parties, boring class lectures became prime breeding grounds for penning secret friendship notes that would later be passed between classes. On one such Friday morning, the fallen Czar of Russia was the furthest thing from Dana's mind:

"Theresa, Hi, what are you doing? I'm sorry, but I forgot to ask you to bring your money in case you wanted to go up town tonight. I almost died yesterday in Chorus when Tommy gave me that note, UGH! YUK! BARF! I went skating last hour, and guess who came in the arena? Twice! Just to embarrass me, Cindy told Jody that I said when Chip comes into the arena I wanted them to tell me 'cause I wanted to

193

know. Guess who Jody sits with on the bus? All the way to Grand Rapids! I'm so fired up for the disco tomorrow night. I hope Cheyanne can go with us. If Chip has a hockey game, I'll be so mad 'cause maybe that will be my chance!!!!!!!!!! Did Ch__ come (just breathe hard) to your English class? You lucky bum, you see him more than me. It is now 8:50 in the morning. I think I'm going to die! Why did I wear this stupid dress?"

Friends Forever, D____

P.S. Write Back (A long one!)

"Hi, Dane (or should I say, Princess Diana)!

I'm in American History right now. We're watching a movie about the Revolutionary War, and when they started playing the Star Spangled Banner at the beginning Mr. Ross stood up and put his hand over his heart. In front of the whole class and everything! Can you even believe it?! What a goofball. I forgot to tell you that Barbie told me that Tommy told her that he has a big crush on you. I guess now you know! Better stop wearing those cute painter's pants. Ch__ was in English today and he told me to tell you that he loves you like he's never loved another. He even used the word L-O-V-E instead of "like." I'm totally serious. No, just kidding! But I really did see him in English. He said he doesn't have a game until next week. I asked him if he was going to the disco but I never told him you wanted to know (I swear!). He said that it depends on if the other guys go. I passed a note to Cheyanne before this class. Ask her what she's wearing to the disco when you see her at lunch. Can I have your Fritos?"

F/F, T_____

P.S. I'll write another note next hour (Longer!)

Saturday afternoon finally arrived. I called Dana to see if she wanted to head to the church gym early and take the free disco dance class that was being offered. She decided to pass and told me that she and Cheyanne would meet me later.

When it was time to get ready for the big night, I dug my coolest pair of bellbottoms out of the closet I shared with my cousins, then purposefully selected a dark-colored blouse, hoping it would mask the sweaty circles bound to pool underneath my arms. I grabbed my makeup bag from my dresser drawer, took it into the bathroom and plugged in my curling iron. Several minutes later, with a cosmetically altered face and sprayed hair as big as Farrah's, I was primed to take on the giant mirror ball.

It was still light out by the time I left the trailer, so I decided to walk the ten, short blocks to the church gym. On my way out the door, Uncle Slim yelled from his La-Z-Boy, "Just give us a call when you want a pick-up, okay?" Aunt Cindy teased, "And, don't let any of those John Travolta wannabees smooth talk you into anything!"

I giggled and waved, then said, "Bye, now. See you tonight."

I was among only a few other kids who'd shown up early for free dance lessons. I paid my two bucks at the entrance in the hallway then got my hand stamped with red ink that said "Disco Inferno."

The first lesson of the evening was a sultry, sexy number aimed at couples. I played it safe and skipped that one. The remaining lessons were fast and funky, requiring everyone to form a singular line and follow a precise protocol of body movement. I easily picked up the groove and added a few extra butt wiggles to make the dance my own.

After that evening's lessons, the band teacher began testing his sound system, dismantling then reassembling an array of cords and wires hooked to a large control panel labeled

"Mr. Faith's Laser Light Show." I leaned back against the faded, yellow-tiled wall and mouthed the words to a song that was playing on an overhead speaker. The adrenalin of anticipation was beginning to pump.

By the time 7:00 rolled around, several kids had started lining up at the entrance. I hovered nearby and looked for the friendly faces of my buddies. 7:10 came and went. A Bee Gees favorite rolled through the air, one of their trademark slow numbers that made you tingle all over and left you with an inescapable urge to French-kiss the nearest boy. Tommy from Chorus class came sauntering over. I could tell he was going to ask me to dance, so I looked the other way and pretended not to see him. Tommy was the LAST person on the planet I wanted to French-kiss.

"Hey, Theresa!" he said, oblivious to my hint. "How deep is *your* love?"

I stared at his pale, freckled face, framed by a bowl-shaped haircut. "Tommy!" I piped up. "How awesome that you could make it tonight!"

"Yeah," he responded uneasily, eager to get to his point. "Wanna dance?"

My heart sank. I didn't really want to, but couldn't bear to hurt his feelings. I looked out over the crowd in a last-ditch attempt to locate my girls. They were nowhere in sight. I took a deep breath, then reluctantly followed Tommy beneath the multi-colored glow of the strobes. The song's slow rhythm forced me to nuzzle in, and I cringed as I wrapped my arms around Tommy's slender shoulders. "Where the hell were Dana and Cheyanne?!" I silently cursed. I tried to keep my eyes closed and concentrate on the song, but that made me dizzy so I reopened them. I spotted Frederick, and my heart started beating faster. Frederick was the cutest boy in my English class, and I'd had the hots for him since the moment I'd laid eyes on his baby blues. I welcomed the diversion and tried to catch his attention.

"You're such a good dancer," Tommy whispered as he pulled me closer, then bent his head and breathed into my ear.

"You too," I awkwardly whispered back. "UGH!" cried my head.

He leaned in to smell my freshly washed hair. "What'd you say?" he asked.

"I saiddd . . . you too!" I shouted back, annoyed with his advances.

While distracted, I'd lost track of Frederick's whereabouts and anxiously scanned the dance floor, spotting him a few feet away. Sweet victory! I cocked my head to one side and charmingly smiled then sent a flirtatious wave his way. He smugly nodded and mouthed the words, "How's it goin'?"

The song ended after what felt like eons, and I politely thanked my dance partner before backing away. K.C.'s "I'm Your Boogie Man" started blasting from the loud speakers just as I was free and clear. Tommy turned toward me and roared, "Ah, man, I am s-o-o-o-o-o fired up! This is like *only* my favorite song!" He then rushed beside me and grabbed my hand, pulling me back onto the dance floor. "C'mon," he said excitedly. "Let's get it on!"

"Ahhh . . . ," I stammered, trying to think of a good excuse. Lucky for me, one of my best friends happened to be walking past, giving me an easy out. "Oh, you know what?" I said. "I so promised Jody that I'd save this song for him."

I discreetly glanced at Frederick, who was still on the dance floor and beginning to shake his groove thing at his girlfriend. "Hmmmm, I'll show him what a groove thing really is," I thought to myself then raced over to Jody, looped my arm in his and begged, "You gotta dance with me! Please? I'll explain later."

I was a good dancer, and I knew it. In fact, if ever there had been a bona fide disco queen, it was yours truly. I'd already won the Yearbook Awards "Best Dancer" category and

197

was now eager to justify my title to the one and only person who mattered to me that night . . . Frederick; the one with the silky, blond hair and surfer smile; the one with eyes as blue as Calgon bath water; the one who didn't even know I was alive.

I quickly captured the electrifying rhythm, letting it flow through me. I snapped my fingers, twisted my hips and shook my booty as poetically as possible. Jody stayed in step, and grooved right along with me, snap for snap, beat for beat. Each time the chorus played, the two of us fluidly moved together and bumped the sides of our hips with as much sexual prowess as any 14-year-old could muster. In between booty shakes, I monitored Frederick's reaction, only to discover I'd been bested by his girlfriend's low-cut blouse.

As the disco lights faded away, so too, did The Sunshine Band. Jody warmly patted the back of my shoulder and told me, "Thanks for the dance, Girl!"

"Yeah thanks, You! Let me know when you want to get down again," I replied as I slipped back into the crowd. Dana and Cheyanne had been waiting for me on the sidelines. They started clapping their hands and hooting at me, as if I'd just won an *American Bandstand* contest.

"Now, you know I know I'm good!" I teased, then kissed my forefinger and let it sizzle on my backside.

"Oh, What . . . ever!" said Cheyanne as she laughed at me.

"Where've you guys been?" I asked. "I mean, it's almost seven-thirty."

"Cheyanne's sister borrowed her favorite pair of jeans so we had to go to Plan B," explained Dana as she surveyed the dance floor's inhabitants.

"What's Plan B?" I asked.

Dana didn't hear me. "Have you seen Chip yet?"

"Not yet," I replied. "Hey, Dane, guess who came looking for me since *you* weren't here.

She snickered underneath her breath.

"Ohhh Theresa, we saw your *sweet thing*," Cheyanne teased in a slow, southern drawl.

"I know," I said dismally. "I saw him, too. He's too busy with his stupid girlfriend to even notice me."

"Not true!" Dana said encouragingly. "You look cute tonight."

But, it was true. My adorable, surfer boy was no longer in sight, most likely trying to steal second in the bushes outside.

Just then, several kids scrambled into the center of the dance floor to groove to the sounds of "Ring My Bell." "I'm not going to let Frederick ruin my night," I defiantly decided and strutted back beneath the strobes with Dana and Cheyanne in tow. "Let's get funky, Girls!" I shouted with my arms stretched above my head.

With Mr. Faith's Laser Light Show now in full swing, the mirror balls spun wildly from the ceiling like tiny, flashing lightning bolts. I was once again safely stowed within the confines of my secret spaceship, lost in the magic of music. Nothing could hurt me here, not Frederick, not Mom. Nothing . . .

Hanging out at the high school outdoor running track was second only to Saturday night disco parties as one of our favorite pastimes. Running wind sprints or competing in the 100-yard dash was the furthest thing from our hormone-drenched minds. Oh no, no, no! The track's main attractions were the two gigantic, overstuffed mats, a few feet thick, typically used by the high jumpers and pole vaulters to cushion their fall. Unbeknownst to the school officials, and all of our parents, for that matter, those tarp-covered mats became a magnet for an alternative sporting event beneath the moonlit stars . . . at least, for some of us.

Many times after a Friday night movie, Dana, Cheyanne and I would wiggle our way to our clandestine hideout, undoubtedly followed by a group of boys. Typically arriving first, we girls would jump up and down on those massive, blue marshmallow puffs, telling stupid jokes in mid-flight and giggling like crazy by the time our counterparts arrived. Before long, I'd be jabbering away at one end of the mats, alone and unaware, while Dana and Cheyanne were tucked beneath the weather tarp at the other end with their respective beaus, getting their apple flavored lip gloss sucked off.

"Hey Guys! Watch this!" I'd obliviously shout before realizing that I was the ridiculous, solo acrobat. "Guys . . . ?"

After a while, I tired of my third-wheel status and began looking for a kindred spirit of sorts, someone who wasn't tied down; in other words, another old maid such as myself. I found that someone in a girl named Sasha who I'd recently met in Mr. Wegge's music class. I didn't know what to make of her at first. She was unlike anyone I'd ever known; the daughter of one of the town's few bluebloods, a lawyer's child. She rarely wore blue jeans like the rest of us, preferring designer silk blouses and long, linen skirts. Her biting wit and confident expression enticed anyone who looked her in the eye to engage her intellect.

Sasha took a shine to me, perhaps for no other reason than that I was somebody different, a new toy to amuse her. Whatever the motive, I was delighted to take on the role of this privileged cat's fresh mouse. I will never forget the first time Sasha invited me to her house. It was better than winning the Golden Ticket. We entered through a side door into the most gorgeous kitchen I'd ever laid eyes upon. Refined, maple cupboards with gleaming, glass panels seemed to float above expensive, black granite countertops. Perfectly matched appliances, the best money could buy, were strategically positioned, and a Jetson-like dining set sprung from the middle of their modern breakfast nook. Just beyond the kitchen lay more elegantly appointed rooms, a formal dining room in rich, Scandinavian woods, a sunken living room in black leather, a library bathed in imported, Chinese silk and a music room designed to accommodate their prized, baby grand. This kind of splendor was in vast contrast with any existence I'd ever known and seemed to lay bare the fragile foundation of my daily life.

Sasha's room was located in the lower level, past the computer room, past the entertainment room, past Sasha's own, private bath, but just before the sliding glass patio doors that overlooked the banks of the swelling Rainy River.

We poured ourselves a couple of ginger ales and decided to hang out in the entertainment room. Sasha flipped on the Harman/Kardon sound system, then put on a Stones album. We sank back into the heavenly softness of the sofa, Sasha on one end and I on the other, and gossiped about the prevailing topic that seemed to consume us like a narcotic . . . boys, the most "well-equipped" boys in our music class, to be exact.

I took a sip of my ale and silently toasted my luck. So . . . this is what the good life was all about.

So far, Good Life Lane was looking mighty fine.

As the Canadian jet stream winds turned from frigid to subzero, the lake's ice quickly froze into a giant slab of solid rock. Our community once again welcomed any type of distraction until spring's arrival, often opting to pass the bone-chilling nights by celebrating with friends. It just so happened that Sasha's family hosted the fanciest party in town. Only the chosen few would be lucky enough to receive an embossed, burgundy and silver invitation to the annual Wagner Cotillion.

201

Given that every fancy party requires plenty of servitude, I was a natural choice of Sasha's mother, perhaps for no other reason than to make up for all the Sunday evening dinners to which I'd invited myself. Despite my lowly role, I was downright ecstatic to be invited. The only problem was that I hadn't any clothes remotely nice enough to fulfill my role, so I begged Sasha to lend me something fun and elegant. One day after school, when we were lounging on her sofa in the entertainment room, she casually said, "Let's go see what I've got on hand for you to wear to our party," and then led me to the walk-in closet in her bedroom.

"Pick out whatever you want," she instructed.

Overwhelmed by such generosity, I asked, "Are you sure?"

"Sure, I'm sure," she replied, as though that were a silly question.

I scrutinized the multi-layered racks of clothes that hung before us, then selected a Calvin Klein denim number. Just as I was about to lift the dress from its hanger, Sasha stopped me. "Wait, no. Not that one," she said decisively and handed me a trendy sweater dress. "Let's wear black."

On the evening of the cotillion, I showed up a few hours early to help with some of the mundane but necessary chores like slicing fresh carrots, ironing linen napkins and arranging delicate, snack sandwiches onto polished, silver platters. When I asked Sasha's mom, "So, where are all the green olives? You know, the ones with the little, red thingies in the middle?" she responded with a bewildered stare, leaving me with the impression that she didn't know they were part of the food chain.

Slightly before the seven o'clock kick-off, I wandered over to Sasha and fretfully asked, "Do I look okay?" then licked the palm of my hand and used it to smooth down some of my stray hairs.

"You look fine," she replied in impatient, high-pitched tones. "Relax, it's no big deal. You're just 'the help,' remember?" she said, reminding me of my proper place.

I wanted to relax but couldn't. I was convinced that the "beautiful people" would see right through me and somehow detect an imposter, one who had no regard for fine art, literature, or Chopin. When the distinguished guests finally arrived, I was grateful to find that most didn't even notice me as I meekly relieved them of their lifeless minks and expensive woolen coats.

Before long, each room on the house's main level was filled with conversation and laughter as the bubbly bubbled high in sparkling, crystal glasses, and the miniature sandwiches were devoured faster than we could supply them.

As part of the staff, my primary role was to carry trays of refined delights from the kitchen out to the masses. In other words, I was Platter Girl. Things were running smoothly at first, and I was pleased with my performance until Sasha threw me off course by handing me a tray of raw oysters. I stared at the slimy, ashen blobs, still floating in their shells, and hesitantly asked, "So . . . you want me to go out there with these things?"

"Go, go, go!" Sasha replied while swishing me away with an impatient hand gesture as she kept the kitchen humming by loading up another tray for the back-up Platter Girl who was waiting in the wings.

I swallowed back nausea before bravely slipping into the crowd of adorned guests, extending my tray as far out in front of me as possible as I made my appointed rounds. Soon, only two oysters remained. In the corner of the living room stood a tanned, bespectacled guest sporting fancy cufflinks and a diamond-encrusted watch, presumably one of those literature loving hot shots from the city. He was standing alone at the moment, so I approached. "Oyster?" I asked timidly.

"Don't mind if I do, now, Missy," he replied in an accent unfamiliar to me.

I courteously smiled, then attempted to slink away.

"Now, hold on," he said to me. "There's one more left."

Thinking that he intended to finish it off himself, I politely stepped closer and held out my tray.

"No," he said with a mischievous smile, "I think *you* ought to try one."

"Me?" I asked, temporarily paralyzed.

"Yeah. Why not?"

"Oh. Well . . . ?" I stammered nervously. "I already had one earlier in the kitchen," I lied.

"Well, now's your chance to have another," he said.

I was stuck. I wanted to yell, "Keep that god awful thing away from my virgin lips!"

Mr. Cufflinks held the tray for me.

"Okay. Just pretend like you know what you're doing," I said to myself.

I eased the oyster from the tray then self-consciously brought it to my mouth. A phrase from French class conveniently popped into my head, "Bon Appetit!" I said, trying to sound sophisticated.

"Down the hatch!" he responded, clearly amused.

I momentarily stalled, then tipped up the back of the shell, allowing the dead, gray matter to flop onto my tongue. With squinted eyes, I began to chew. Mr. Cufflinks disapprovingly shook his head from side to side, "Don't chew, Missy, just slid 'er down."

I tried really hard not to close my eyes, but when that thing hit my throat I knew my expression was screaming, "I'm gonna blow chunks!"

"Hey, hey! There she goes!" said Mr. Cufflinks as he intently gauged my reaction, then took another sip of his champagne.

I grabbed my tray and tried to eke out a polite excuse before rushing back into the kitchen.

"Sasha! Oh my God! You'll never guess what just happened!" I shouted at my friend.

Before I could explain any further, she put a finger to her lips and urgently whispered, "Shhhhh," then grabbed my wrist and pulled me closer.

"Did you see my mom and dad out there," she asked in muffled tones.

"Yeah, they're in the library. Why?"

"Were they talking to anybody?"

"Uh huh, some old broad in a silver-sequined dress," I told her as I wiggled my fingers in the air to imitate things that sparkle.

"Good," she said. "That should keep them occupied for awhile." She retrieved two low balls from the cupboard and filled them with ice from a nearby bucket, then grabbed a can of cola from the fridge and poured its contents evenly into each glass.

"Man, am I thirsty! I didn't even realize it until just now," I said as I gratefully reached for one of the sodas.

Sasha stopped me in my tracks. "Wait a minute," she said before suspiciously surveying the room, then grabbed hold of the nearest bottle of booze from the vast collection on the countertop, hastily opened it and topped off our drinks. She handed one of the full-fledged cocktails to me before lifting the other in the air. "Cheers," she impishly whispered.

"Clink," went her glass against mine before she knocked back a mouthful.

My eyes got big and round. "Holy crap, Girl!" I said. "Are you sure we're not going to get busted?"

"Do you think I would *let* us get busted?" she slyly asked, making it obvious that this wasn't the first time she'd listened to that pitch-forked, little red man on her shoulder.

"*We* deserve to have some fun, too, you know," she added, her brown-eyed expression as sharp as a knife.

I had just been inducted into the Jack Daniels hall of fame and was ready for more when Sasha's mom came waltzing in. "Oh, Sasha," she said melodically. "There you are. I need you to fix Bjorn a Manhattan. Use dry vermouth, not the sweet stuff and make it on the rocks, would you, Darling?"

While Sasha was expertly fixing the drink, her mom eyed our lowballs and said suspiciously, "I see you girls have found the soda."

Sasha and I exchanged wary glances.

"Next time, don't use our nice glasses," directed Mrs. Wagner, then pointedly glowered at my friend and added, "You know how expensive they are, Sasha. Be sure not to break any, won't you." She took the cocktail from her daughter's hand. "We need more cheese puffs, too, Darling," she said over her shoulder, her authoritative command colored in musical tones.

After Madame returned to her loyal subjects in the library, Sasha rolled her eyes and quickly fixed the two of us a second round before preparing a fresh hors d'oeuvres tray, sending forth her favorite Platter Girl to deliver the goods.

As the clock struck midnight, Sasha peeked out from the kitchen door into the thinning crowd and determined that our services were no longer needed. We rinsed out our lowballs to dispel any sign of foul play, then disappeared into the depths of the lower level. We were relieved to find some much needed solace, and sank into the comfort of the couch, switched on the TV and wrapped thick, cotton blankets around our shoulders. I leaned back against the armrest and gazed through the glass, patio doors. Droves of shiny, metallic snowflakes glittered like fairy dust in the halo of the backyard spotlight, elegantly mesmerizing as they danced toward the river below.

Sasha impatiently changed channels with the remote until she came upon a *M*A*S*H* rerun while I nestled deeper into my blanket and rested contently, becoming drowsier by the minute as the inner warmth of the liquor released me from my earthly bonds. Corporal Klinger, madly frolicking about in a frilly, white gown, was the last thing I remember as that enchanted evening drew to a close.

Each February at school, we celebrated Valentine's Day by expressing our varying degrees of passion for one another with a simple, colored carnation. Cupid offered one of three colors from which to choose: white was for friendship, red was for love, naturally, and purple was for that in-between, uncommitted gray area.

It was obvious which colored carnation Dana would be sending Chip that year, but I decided to ask her anyway while we were standing next to her locker one day after school.

"If I send him a red one then he'll know for sure that I'm whipped," she ruminated.

"Yeah. But, you are," I reminded her.

"Maybe I should send him purple."

"Why send him purple when that's not how you really feel?" I asked.

She thought about it for a second as she was kneeling down on one knee, tying the shoelace of her hiker boot, "I guess you're right," she conceded, then looked up at me and asked, "Are you going to send one to Frederick?"

"Yeah," I told her. "But I don't know if I'm going to put my name on the card."

"What do you mean?" she asked.

"I might just say it's from Your Secret Admirer or something."

Just as if he'd known we were talking about him, Frederick started walking toward us down the hallway. I quickly turned my back to him and yanked on my best bud's sleeve, "Dane! Oh my god! Look who's coming!"

"He's got those cute Levi's on again," Dana teased. "The cream ones that you think are so foxy.

"Dammit, it drives me crazy when he wears those." I started to panic. "Hey Dane, is he with his girlfriend?"

"No, he's with Mick."

Feeling like I'd just been handed a golden opportunity, I turned around and faced my cute, surfer boy. Our eyes met briefly before he leaned toward Mick and whispered, "Watch this."

As soon as he was a mere arm's length away, I perked up. "Hi, Frederick! How's it going?"

He looked straight ahead and didn't answer.

"Frederick?" I said again, confused by his complete disregard.

A smirk began forming across his lips.

I started to trail him, knowing full well that I was about to make a fool of myself. "Frederick? Are you mad at me or something?"

He kept ignoring me, as if I were invisible. I glanced at Mick, who was about to burst out laughing.

"C'mon, Frederick, I thought we were friends," I implored, far more concerned with acceptance than pride.

He and Mick picked up the pace as they walked toward the exterior double doors that led to freedom.

I tried to think of a clever way to engage him but all that came out was a pitiful, "Hey, I know a secret about you." I was groveling now. "I know someone who's going to send you a carnation. Don't you want to know who?" I could tell that he didn't care less.

He and Mick reached for the doors and forcefully pushed them open, leaving me standing alone on the inside as they swooshed back into my face.

Dana came up behind me and consoled, "What a loser! Don't let him get to you, Ther." She looked over at my wilted face and added, "Guess you won't be buying him a carnation after all."

I stared down at my trampled heart that was lying in pieces on the ground and quietly confirmed, "Yeah . . . guess not."

Mom finally came back from New York in early March of 1980, and hugged the hell out of me as soon as Uncle Slim and Aunt Cindy dropped me off at the duplex. I hugged her back but with less conviction; the hole in my heart was still raw from her extended absence.

My goodbyes to my uncle and aunt were sweet but short, knowing that I would see them again soon. It wasn't that I was glad to be rid of them, not in the least; it was more that I openly welcomed returning to my own turf.

"Where's Arthur?" I asked.

"He decided to stay in New York for a while," she replied.

"Why?"

"Oh, who knows. I guess he just wanted to be by himself for a while," she answered, unfazed, never lingering on any one topic for too long.

I lifted her left hand and stared at her one-carat diamond, then complimented, "Nice rock, Mom."

"Huuhhh?" she asked, confused by my slang.

"Nice rock. You know . . . nice ring," I explained.

She looked me straight in the eyes then gently laughed and said, "Oh, now Theresa, you say the darndest things."

After I'd taken my bath that evening, I crawled into bed and lay on my back, then looked up at the ceiling and thought about how my life had changed so drastically in the span of a single day. I was really home again and back in my own room. Sure my space was tiny, just a fraction the size of Sasha's, but hey, it was mine and mine alone. As I started to doze off, Mom breezed into the room then sat down beside me on the edge of my bed, drenched in her wonderfully familiar scent of Jean Nate. She looked down at me and affectionately asked, "How are you doing tonight, Sweetheart?" Before I could answer, she gushed, "Mother loves you, so!"

I looked up at her with eyes that saw only a tangled labyrinth, then tried to smile, not really sure of what to say. I was overjoyed to see her, to be near her, to once again experience the full force of her love. I just wished with all my might that she would try harder to be the mother I so desperately needed, and to be aware of the impact her actions had on me. I wanted her to live for someone other than herself, to muster the strength to keep me by her side forever and never let me go again.

She reached down and tenderly stroked my forehead with her palm as only she could do, then softly began to sing, "You are my sunshine." ♫♫♫

As the melody ran its course, it was as if Mom were bathing me in a pool of holy water. With each soothing word sung, the hole in my heart got a little bit smaller and all my pent-up anger faded into the blackness of my room.

~♦♦♦~

As fate would have it, my homebound journey turned out to be merely an interlude. After a handful of weeks back at the duplex, I came home after school one day to find Mom seated at the kitchen table, wrapped in her favorite fluffy, pink bathrobe, the one with all the cigarette burns.

"Hi, my little Honey!" she cheerfully greeted when I walked in the door. "I'm off to New York again!" she

210

exclaimed as she flung a hand into the air to emphasize her excitement.

I was standing in the entryway still holding my books. "What?!" I sneered. "You just can't even be serious."

"Yup!" she said. "Next week."

I moved in her direction, set my load aside, then placed both arms rigidly onto the table and leaned intimidatingly close. "Mom," I began, foolishly thinking that I could reason with her. "I've only been back home a month now."

She seemed taken aback by my hostile response. "Well," she said submissively, almost in a whisper, then took another sip of her Kool-Aid.

I began pacing the floor as my ire ignited. "Who do you think you are anyway?!" I bleated. "You shuffle me around like I'm some kind of fucking rag doll that you can just throw away when you get sick of me! Be a responsible mother for once and take care of me!!!"

"I have my own life, too, Theresa," she said, as if her lack of parental care was justified.

That's when my deep-rooted anger transformed into full-blown rage. Turning my hateful eyes away from her, I frantically scanned the room, then strode over to the buffet and picked up a framed picture of Mikie and me that had been taken when we were toddlers. I hastily removed the photo then gave Mom another searing glance before deliberately ripping it in two. I crumpled up the half that held my image and threw it at Mom as hard as I could. "Are you happy now?!" I screamed at the top of my lungs. "Is that what you want from me?!

Mom flinched as the photo went flying past her head, then sat helplessly as she watched my tantrum unfold. "Stop it, Theresa. Don't do this to me," she said feebly.

"Don't do this?! Don't do this?!" I shouted over and over again. "How 'bout you don't do a few things to *ME* that *I'm* not too happy about. How 'bout you get off your ass once in a while and stop smoking all those fucking cigarettes and drinking all that goddamn Kool-Aid and how 'bout you learn to be a real fucking mother for a change!" I couldn't stop glaring at her.

A haunting song started playing on the radio, and Mom easily fell prey to its melody, her eyes clouding with despair. "Ahhhhh . . . Ahhhhh, I can't take this," she moaned, as if she were about to collapse, then got up from the table and began sluggishly walking toward her bedroom. "You're an awful child," she whimpered. "Just awful. I don't know what I'm going to do with you." She went into her room and closed the door.

Less than a week later I was packed up and sent half a block down the street to live with my Uncle Willie and Aunt Mae.

Life at my uncle and aunt's agreed with me from the very beginning. The eldest of their four grown children had recently vacated the roost, leaving behind plenty of elbowroom and an empty bed just for me. By the time I arrived on the scene, Uncle Willie and Aunt Mae were already well versed in the ways and means of adolescents and easily integrated me into their family.

The shyer side of my personality returned, just as it always had whenever I found myself living away from Mom, but this time it failed to engulf me completely. The members of my new family were far too involved with the details of their own active lives to be overly concerned about the new arrival, leaving ample space to shed my cautious ways.

I continued to maintain my busy lifestyle. If I wasn't at school or track & field practice, I was undoubtedly goofing around with my friends somewhere. Each time I'd leave the house for my next engagement, I'd holler my farewells from the back door. "Write when you find work!" my uncle and aunt would often tease. I found that to be such a peculiar thing to say, but in time I grew to love it . . . *really, really* love it, realizing that it was a catchphrase unique to their own family circle, to what was now *my* own family circle. It didn't take long for me to decide that I was never going back to live with Mom, no matter what. I'd finally landed on solid ground and prayed that my uncle and aunt would have no reason to send me back from whence I came.

After I'd been away from the duplex for a number of weeks, I received a call from my stepfather.

"Theresa? Hello."

"Hi Arthur," I politely responded.

"How's everything going with Willie and Mae?"

I told him things couldn't be better. "How are you and Mom doing?" I inquired, not really caring but feeling like I had to ask.

"Well, that's why I'm calling. I'm going to have to take your mother to the Mayo Clinic for medical treatment."

"Okay," I coolly replied, wondering why he'd even bothered to inform me.

"Theresa, did you hear what I just said?"

"Yeah," I responded, a little confused. "You said Mom's going to some clinic."

"That's right. The doctors here in New York have found a cyst on her ovary; however, you needn't worry. Mayo is one of the best hospitals in the country, and your mother is going to be in good hands," my stepfather explained in a paternal sort of way.

"Oh, I'm not worried," I told him matter-of-factly.

There was such a long pause after my response that I thought Arthur had hung up the phone, and I was about to do the same.

"Theresa," he said for the third time, "Do you realize the seriousness of this situation?" I didn't know how to respond so he kept speaking. "You seem a bit callus, to say the least. Pardon my frankness, but it needs to be said."

"Um, I'm sorry Arthur. I guess I'm not really sure what you mean," I told him.

"Well. You don't seem the least bit concerned about your mother's well being."

I weakly defended myself, "Mom's been in and out of hospitals the whole time I've known her."

"I would've expected more from you, but that doesn't appear to be the case," replied a clearly disappointed Arthur.

My stepfather's dissatisfaction was not readily understandable to me. After all, what was the big deal? Mom was merely cycling through her life's seasons, just as she always had . . . 1) get sick 2) go to the hospital 3) get better 4) resume life 5) falter 6) repeat. Why should I to be overly concerned this time? My frame of mind, right or wrong, was simply the manifestation of my mother's endless rotation through illness, and I'd been conditioned to take it all in stride. To me, it had become no more than an unpleasant stain on my life.

"I'll be calling you from Rochester to let you know how the surgery went," Arthur said tersely.

"Okay. Thanks for calling, Arthur," I robotically replied.

"Goodnight, Theresa."

The long and dreary winter was ever so slowly replaced by lengthening days of sunlight, a clear signal that school would soon be in recess. One last disco remained on the season's roster, a gathering no one would fail to miss, except for Mademoiselle Sasha, who refused to have anything to do with that "disco nonsense." Lucky for me, I had a few backups and opted to go with my favorites, Dana and Cheyanne.

It was now mid-May and just a few days before the final disco party. A hushed buzz was going around school claiming that the Andersons were heading out of town for the weekend, leaving their two teenage boys at home and in charge. Seeing as how their eldest son was a not-so-secret member of the Blatz Beer Boyz Society, it wasn't hard to figure out where Party Central was going to be.

On Saturday night, we three chicks moseyed over to the pre-disco bash in our tightest jeans and purple letterman jackets. By the time we arrived, the house was crawling with so many kids that it looked like a colony of ants on a downed sucker. As soon as the three of us had ponied up the two-buck cover charge, we walked inside and were quickly swept away by the current of the crowd before eventually being deposited into the center of the kitchen. Dana craned her neck around, searching for Chip. After a few restless minutes she said, "Let's go check out the basement." I loyally followed my buddy downstairs, while Cheyanne stayed in the kitchen with her sister's boyfriend.

Chip was near the bottom of the stairs clutching a tapped Blatz. He smiled as soon as he saw us and lifted his plastic cup to toast our arrival. "Hey you Girls!" he said in a highly pronounced party mood as we moved toward him. "How goes it?"

Dana and I sauntered over.

"You want some beer or something?" he asked. Before we could answer, he handed his half empty Blatz to Dana and told her, "Hold this. Be right back."

While waiting for Chip's return, I confessed to my friend, "Man, I feel like a third wheel. Are you sure it's okay to hang out with you guys?"

"Yeah, why not? Don't worry about it," Dana replied reassuringly.

When Chip came back, he handed each of us a cold one, then downed the remainder of his own. The three of us were in

215

the middle of making small talk about why the boys had to swim naked in gym class when I suddenly spotted Frederick across the room. Oh, joy! My beloved surfer boy was at the party.

"Chip?" I asked sweetly and free of ulterior motives, "Do you know if Frederick's girlfriend is going to be here tonight?"

"You mean Sue? I think I heard Frederick say that she had to babysit or something."

"Solid!" I thought to myself. "Here's my chance. But, what to do? Hmmm . . . drink more? Yeah, that's it. I definitely need to drink more beer. Then I'll go over to Frederick and say something cute, yeah, or something really sexy. And if things get cookin', I might even let him get to second base with me." I pretended to brush away a piece of lint from my chest and used the opportunity to glance down at my assets, wishing I'd worn one of my aunt's fancy bras stuffed full of Kleenex.

Yeah, I had a plan all right, but it was filed in the Fiction section of my brain, right next to those spicy images I'd often conjured up after reading a romance novel just before bed. The truth of the matter was, I was scared to death to get to second base. I wasn't even yet practiced in the art of first. But, that's what it took to get a guy's attention, at least according to the girls in the locker room.

I started guzzling my beer, hoping to speed up the relaxation process. Within the span of about thirty minutes I'd polished off two of those puppies and was headed well into number three. I felt so carefree, so calm . . . so surprisingly content.

"Slaphappy" is the word I'd use to describe my next phase. I turned to face Dana and Chip, then slurred, "You two make such a coot couple!"

Dana looked embarrassed as she quite simply replied, "Oh, Ther."

216

"No, man, no," I went on, "I'm cereal. You guys are both tho good-looker. If you ever had a baby, I know it would be a super-vodel in Mogue magazine or thumbthing."

Dana plowed an elbow into my side to get me to shut up.

I could feel my eyes becoming heavier as I droned on and on. "I hope that thumbday Frederick and I can be a couple, too. Do you think we'd be as coot as you guys? No, man, tell me the truth. Do you? Oh Chip, don't tell Frederick, okay man? I don't want him to know about my crusher. It's our widdle theecret, okay?" I tried to wink at Chip, then brought my forefinger to my lips and spit out a "Chh-hhh-hhh" when I'd really meant to say, "Shhhhhhhh." At that point I felt my eyes close completely as though little miniature weights had somehow gotten fastened to the tops of my lids.

Dana grabbed my arm to steady me and nervously demanded, "Open your eyes, Theresa. You're freaking me out."

"I'm trying, but I can't . . . I can't . . . I just can't, man." That's when I felt something go terribly wrong down below. I hastily turned to my best bud and screeched in a panic-stricken voice, "Dana?! I don't feel so good."

"Uh-oh, you drank too much, didn't you?" Dana paused for a moment, trying to think of what to do next. "Here," she said as she handed Chip her beer. "Let's get you over to this bedroom where you can lay down." She took hold of my arm and gently led me across the room and into the dark, quiet space that was to become my detox headquarters. "Maybe you can sleep it off," she encouraged.

"Don't weave me, Dane!" I begged, feeling confused and wanting to go home.

"I'll just be outside the door only a few feet away, okay? I promise."

"Can you get thumbbody to give us rides home?" I whined.

217

"If you go home now, we're both going to get our butts kicked. Trust me. Just try to sleep it off."

Deciding that Dana was right, I took her advice and cautiously eased down into a fetal position on the bed. I could feel the potent, carbonated beverage sloshing around my stomach. Then, the oddest sensation hit me straight between the eyes, one that I hadn't planned on. The bed began to spin! OH NO, what was happening?! "Just lay here and don't move," I tried to tell myself. I began to breathe as evenly as I could, hoping my system would soon calm down. Just when I started to feel like it was safe to open my eyes, I heard the bedroom door creak, and someone flipped on the light switch, sending a flurry of piercing arrows straight into the center of my pupils.

A couple of older guys from the party burst into the room. "Well, well, what do we have here?" I heard one of them cluck.

I tried to lift my head, then said as loudly as I could, "Turn off the light, man! I don't feel so good!"

The first Bad Boy turned to his buddy and evilly snickered, "Did you hear that, Rod? Poor, little girl doesn't feel so good."

All of a sudden I felt extra weight on the bed, and before I knew it Bad Boy Numero Uno had begun jumping up and down.

"No!" I cried. "You don't underthand!"

I was utterly helpless as Bad Boy Dos decided to get into the game.

"Stop . . . stop . . . stop!" I cried, in sync with each bounce, my protests going unheeded. Before I knew it, I'd abandoned my fetal position and moved into a doggie pose, up on all fours. With each bounce on the bed came a massive, malted barley wave that angrily roared through my stomach then up, up, up and finally . . . out! Thick, gooey liquid erupted from my mouth as though I were some kind of possessed, Italian water fountain.

Having achieved their twisted goal, the two Bad Boys began laughing their asses off.

By that point, I'd not only lost track of my big romance strategy, but couldn't even remember what day it was. All I wanted was to get the hell out of there as fast as possible and home to my nice, warm bed.

I slithered away from the defiled mess I'd just made and managed to find my way back to my friends.

"Dane!" I gurgled. "You gotta get me out of here. Fast. Please?"

"Oh my gosh, Ther, are you all right?"

"I don't think so," I told her. "I just need to get home."

Chip, being one of the more popular boys in school, knew one of the seniors at the party and managed to arrange a ride for me.

"Do you want me to go with you?" asked a concerned Dana.

With strained eyes I assured her, "No, you go on to the disco. I'll be fine." I wasn't really sure I would be.

When I got home, I thanked my lucky stars that no one else was there. I crept through the dimly lit living room as best I could, accidentally bumping an end table before plodding back to my brown-paneled bedroom in the farthest corner of the house. I closed the door behind me, shed my puke-stained clothes, and crawled beneath the covers. With my head still pounding and my body relieved to have purged its unwanted burden, I rolled sideways then flipped on the clock radio. The Sledge Sisters were singing "We Are Family."

In the darkness, safe and secure in my soft cocoon, I reflected on the words of that song, and was filled with a fleeting moment of elation. I felt lucky and grateful for what I now had. At long last, I could leave behind an unsympathetic stepfather, an absentee brother and a mother who lived on the dark side of the moon.

"I finally have a real, normal family that I can call my own," was the last thought I had before sleep won out and tugged me to the land of serenity.

I was awakened the next morning, or at least what I'd thought was still morning, by a soft knock on my door. It was my aunt informing me that I had a phone call.

"Be right there," I said in a practiced, high-pitched tone, trying to sound as chipper as possible.

I hugged my pillow a bit closer, not really wanting to leave its familiar comfort, then reluctantly released it and sat up. I let my eyes acclimate to the daylight and lingered momentarily at the edge of the bed before getting up and putting on a t-shirt and a pair of sweatpants. I opened my door and walked over to the phone that was hanging on the wall at the opposite end of the living room.

"Why are you squinting your eyes?" my aunt asked as I walked past her.

"I guess I must still be tired," I lied.

"Boyyy, how can you sleep for so long? Half the day is gone," she teased.

"What time is it, anyway?" I inquired.

"A little past 11:00."

I picked up the phone, "Hello?"

"What's going on, Chick?"

I could hear soft giggling.

"Cheyanne? Oh, hey. Not much, I just got up."

"I heard you got pretty wasted at the party last night," she said.

"Yeah . . . about that." I looked around to see if my aunt was in earshot. "You know, I didn't really mean to. It just sort of happened," I explained.

"Did you talk to Frederick?" she asked.

"I wanted to, but it's like I ended up on Mars or something," I explained as I rubbed my throbbing forehead.

Cheyanne laughed.

"I'll tell you about it later," I added.

"Are you doing anything for lunch today?" she asked. "Dana's coming over around noon then we're going out for pizza."

Normally I would have been all over that idea, but on this particular Sunday morning it didn't have its usual appeal. Regardless, I felt like I needed an excuse to get out of the house. "Sounds good to me," I said.

"Oh, and Theresa?" Cheyanne said sweetly.

"Yeah?" I naively replied, taken in by the innocence of her voice.

"Bring some Blatz, would ya?!"

"Very funny. Just remember . . . your turn's coming," I jokingly warned.

"Later Girl!"

I hung up the phone and headed toward the bathroom to wash my face.

"Are you going over to your friend's?" asked my aunt.

"Yeah, we're going out for pizza."

"How 'bout I give you a ride?" she offered.

"Oh, that's okay," I replied, not wanting to impose. "It's not that far. I can walk."

"No," she insisted, "I'll give you a ride."

"Okay," I said, trying to avoid any possible conflict.

On the way to Cheyanne's, my aunt told me that her oldest son would be returning home from med school for the summer. At first I thought she was just trying to make small talk so I asked, "Really, when's that?"

"In a few weeks, at the beginning of June," she answered.

"It'll be good to have him around the house," I said with a "the more, the merrier" attitude.

"Well, I need to talk to you about that, Theresa," she said, never one to beat around the bush.

That's when I realized what this ride was really all about. Giant butterflies, the size of those that dwell in the Brazilian rainforest, started fluttering about in my stomach. As tears welled up in the corners of my eyes, I prayed they wouldn't betray me by splashing down onto my cheeks.

"Steven needs his room back," she told me without mincing any words. "I'd really like you to continue staying with us, but it's just no longer possible. There's not enough room, Dear."

By that time, we'd arrived at Cheyanne's house. My aunt pulled up to the curb and shifted into park, leaving the engine running. I knew there was nothing I could say to change the outcome, so I mustered all my remaining courage, swallowed back my sadness, then finally looked my aunt in the eyes. "Oh. Okay," I softly said. "Yeah, that's okay. Um. I understand. Really. I mean, he's your son and everything."

"I'm sorry, Dear," she said sincerely. "I really am. We'll talk more about it later, okay."

I nodded my head up and down then quickly turned away as I felt another surge of tears. "Thanks for the ride, Aunt Mae," I said. I sat there for one last, brief moment and added in a hushed whisper, "And, thanks for everything else, too." I got out of the car and gave a quick wave before turning and walking toward the front steps of Cheyanne's house.

I was in a daze at lunch and barely spoke to my two friends. I couldn't believe I had to go back to Mom. Sure, it was a life that would be spent with someone I genuinely loved, but the constant, bizarre drama was often more than I could handle, and I knew I'd have to once again spend my days on the run simply to stay sane.

That night while I was lying in bed, I could hear the wind blowing so hard against the trees that it sounded like ocean waves roaring onto a sandy beach. When slumber finally overcame me, I dreamt I was the most beautiful mermaid alive. Around and around I swam, freely spinning and twirling, light as a feather, no troubles weighing me down. The water felt so safe and warm. Down, *way* down below the surface I swam, where only those whose hearts truly belonged to the sea were allowed safe passage, past the whale's house and the octopus' den, behind the stone wall that appeared forgotten, the one covered in thick, sprawling fingers of seaweed. There, hidden behind that wall was my secret, crystal palace where no one would ever again be able to find me.

A fully recovered Mom was soon summoned back to Minnesota, and much to my surprise, returned with my stepfather in tow. Despite the many downward spirals in our dying relationship, Mom was thrilled to see me and didn't appear the least bit upset about having to reclaim me from the Lost & Found.

"Well, how's my Little Baby?" she cooed in the entryway of our duplex, then wrapped me in her arms and gently rocked our combined bulk back and forth.

"I'm not a little baby anymore, Mom. I'm almost fifteen years old," I said irritably as I pulled back, trying to discourage her infantile image of me.

"My Honey," she replied in gentle, baby talk tones as she looked innocently into my angry eyes, "You'll always be mother's Little Baby." She continued in a more adult-like manner, "I can remember when we lived with Daddy and I was so sick. You'd toddle over to me as I was crying on the couch and wrap your tiny, little arms around me. 'Mama,' you'd say, 'don't cry, Mama.'" She looked away and faintly smiled at the thought of such a bittersweet memory. "You were the darlingest, little, toe-headed thing in town. Just darling!"

223

"That was a long time ago, Mom. I've grown up since then," I said rebelliously, then gave her the evil eye and added, "In case you haven't noticed."

Unfazed, she sat down at the kitchen table while I picked up my suitcase and began hauling it back to my old bedroom. I abruptly stopped in my tracks when I noticed all the cardboard moving boxes cluttering our tiny living space.

"What's all this?" I asked, clearly perplexed.

"We're moving. Oh, didn't I tell you?"

"M-o-m-m-m, you never tell me any . . . thing!" I screeched as I rolled my eyes and looked toward the ceiling.

"Yaw," she said, once again dismissing my annoyance. "There's a nice apartment building over on, ah . . . ah . . . let's see. What's the name of that street?" She rested one of her elbows on the table then continued. "I don't remember. Anyway, Arthur decided that we should live over there, instead."

My jaw dropped open as I set down my suitcase and contemplated yet another turn of events. "You mean those new ones on Shorewood Drive? Right across from the mall?" I asked.

"Yaw, that's them."

I was no less than completely overjoyed. Ever since Daddy had died, Mom was barely able to scrape by, never capable of providing a decent lifestyle. At long last, we'd be residing somewhere lovely, somewhere respectable . . . somewhere I wouldn't be ashamed of.

My pulse raced at the prospect of my new life. "Will I get to have my own room?" I excitedly asked.

"Yup," replied Mom. "There's, ah, three bedrooms, one for each of us. Just right, huh?" She smiled in a way that showed her pride in having pulled off such a feat then added, "What do you think of them apples?"

I was no longer angry or annoyed. I was no longer anything but just plain happy. I rushed over to my mother and threw my arms around her. "Oh, thank you, Mom! Thank you, so, so much! This is the best news I could've ever had!"

She embraced me in her gentle, loving way and softly murmured one last time, "My Little Baby . . ."

Summer came upon us like a sacred kiss from the gods, beginning a new chapter in my young life. It didn't take long for me to settle into the well kept, freshly painted apartment with Mom and Arthur.

How I dearly loved that apartment, especially my bedroom. It was located at the farthest end of a single hallway, right next to Mom's. The best thing about it was the closet, the first one I'd ever had that was large enough to hold all of my clothes and didn't come with a broken door handle. An oversized window near the corner of my room faced west and looked out over the heavily wooded, winding road of prestigious Shorewood Drive, the same road on which many of the town's upper crust lived, including Sasha's. Sometimes I'd stare down at it from my third story vantage point, and wonder if all the doctors, lawyers and paper mill executives really knew just how fortunate they were to live somewhere other than on the ever-changing, unpredictable Ghellow Road.

By that time in my life, I'd been tossed into so many different living situations that I felt as if I were peering at the world through a thick, black veil, desperately trying to understand my volatile circumstances for what they truthfully were, yet never certain which pieces were illusion and which were not. Now I was faced with yet another new circumstance . . . living with Arthur. Instead of being resentful of my stepfather's inability to fully embrace me, I wanted him to like me, I wanted us to be friends, but he was so different from Daddy, and I understood his ways just about as well as he understood mine. I tried to remain agreeable as best I could,

225

and even pretended to like *Lawrence Welk* reruns just so we'd have something to talk about, trying to appear enthralled as the show's stars whirled around a ridiculous explosion of soap bubbles. My strategy paid off, and the increased comfort level between the two of us was my reward. Before long, our conversations evolved into something greater than primetime TV. When I wasn't inquiring about Arthur's life in New York or his career there as a pharmaceutical salesman, I was editorializing about the daily events that filled my own existence. Arthur, in turn, would often look at me with wise, calm eyes and try to coax my ego from its cracked, fragile shell. "You're a smart, young lady, you know that, Theresa? Don't waste your talents," he'd encourage. "Think about going to college. It's really the only option for you." It was comforting to finally have a believer.

On the wings of warmer, summer days came the season's greatest gift, freedom from the bondage of our confining winter wardrobes. Bulky ski jackets and multiple layers of clothing were gratefully cast aside for nothing more than shorts and a cotton t-shirt. That was about the only thing I ever wore when cruising around town on my black and yellow striped Huffy ten-speed, the one Mom had bought me for my 14th birthday. That crazy looking, second-rate bike was one of my best friends, and I rarely left home without it, often peddling down the old truck route past numerous hobby farms where gentle horses grazed in the afternoon sun, or wheeling it out to Frederick's house up on Jackfish Bay just to see if I could catch a glimpse of my cute surfer boy.

On one the most glorious summer days imaginable, I decided to phone Dana and invite her to one of my favorite warm-weather haunts.

"Dane? What are you up to?" I asked.

"Nothing, why?" she replied.

"Wanna hit the beach?"

"Um, yeah. Sure," she said.

226

"I'll be at your house in half an hour," I told her. "Call Cheyanne, okay?"

"Okay. See ya," she replied.

I was about to hang up when I heard her say, "Ther? Wait a minute."

"Yeah?"

"Which bathing suit are you going to wear?"

"That new one I bought when you went shopping with me last week," I told her. "See you in a little while."

I hung up the phone and went to my bedroom, then changed into a teal, Hawaiian-themed one-piece and an old pair of white shorts. I pulled a small backpack out of my closet, walked over to the hallway linen cabinet and fumbled through a stack of folded towels until I found my favorite, sun-faded orange and brown one, wrapped it around a bottle of Hawaiian Tropic, then stuffed it into my pack. After hoisting the load onto my shoulder, I carried it into the living room, then sat down on the couch and put on a pair of sneakers. "I'm going to the beach today," I told my stepfather, who was quietly reading the paper at our kitchen table. "Say bye to Mom for me."

My trusty steed was locked to the community clothesline just outside our apartment building's back door. I unfastened it and hopped on, destined for Dana's house where my two buds were waiting for me on the front steps, backpacks affixed and raring to go. After our quick hellos, the three of us began our five-mile trek on the bike path to City Beach, stopping only once to add a can of Orange Crush and a pack of Reese's Peanut Butter Cups to the indispensable contents of our backpacks.

Upon arrival, we wrestled our bikes into the metal rack and surveyed the heavily populated beach for any remaining sunning spots. Then Dana and I followed Cheyanne to a vacant patch of shoreline next to where her older sister was catching some rays. We threw our backpacks down on the sand, extracted our beach towels and fussed over them until they

227

were positioned for maximum sun exposure. Discarding our shorts, Dana and I plopped onto our towels while Cheyanne headed straight toward the water for a quick dip. I dug out my can of Orange Crush from my pack and twisted it just far enough into the sand so the wind wouldn't blow it over.

Turning toward Dana, I asked, "You going into the water now?"

"No, I think I'll wait a while," she replied while slathering suntan oil onto her winter-weary flesh.

I remained in a seated position facing the water, my arms locked rigidly behind me. I looked northward across the bay at the pine-speckled Canadian lakeshore, then closed my eyes and listened to the distant sound of hungry, white seagulls searching for their next meal. It wasn't long before I heard laughter nearby followed by sharp, high-pitched squeals. I opened my eyes to find Cheyanne in a water fight with two boys from our junior high clique.

"No! Stop it! I don't want to get my hair wet!" I heard her shriek with feigned conviction in the waist-high water.

I slowly sipped my Orange Crush while watching from afar before making the bold decision to get into the game. I set my pop down and wiped my mouth with the back of my hand, then hesitantly headed into battle. As soon as I got to Cheyanne's side, I tried to divert some attention away from her by attacking the boys from behind. Initially a bit timid, I began slapping the water lightly with the palms of my hands. When this had no effect, I began splashing with more force. No luck. The boys didn't seem to notice I was even there. I tried splashing them with one hand, with both hands, with what I'd call a "super splash" by using the entire length of my arm. I even plunged head first into the water and used my thrashing legs as a weapon. Nothing worked. I soon felt like that fat kid in gym class who nobody ever wanted to pick for their kickball team. I finally gave up and plodded back to shore, then sat down on my beach towel and jealously stared at my friends who were having so much fun without me.

In every class there is a standout beauty, and ours just happened to be Cheyanne. All the other girls wanted to look like her, to talk like her, to *be* her; all the boys just wanted to be with her. Cheyanne had always been one of my best friends. After all, we both carried a permanent VIP pass to the same club of sisterhood. But, she was forever the Farrah to my Kate Jackson in this underaged game of Charlie's Angels where beauty never failed to trump brains, especially in the meat department. It wasn't that Cheyanne was dumb, far from it; she'd simply never been forced to reveal that much of herself.

"Why did I wear this stupid bathing suit?" I moaned out loud with no intention of anyone else hearing me.

"What was that?" asked Dana.

I looked down at her relaxed, sand-cradled body and noticed that she still had her eyes closed. "Oh, these stupid one-piece bathing suits were Cheyanne's dumb idea," I complained.

"I thought you loved that suit. Why did you buy it if you didn't like it?"

"I don't know," I whined. "I guess because Cheyanne bought one and said that they were the "latest thing," then you bought one, so then *I* bought one. I'm just too short and stumpy to wear a one-piece."

"I think you look cute," said Dana. "Besides, you know how short summer is around here. You can always get a bikini again next year."

"I guess you're right," I replied.

Feeling sorry for myself, I looked down at my flat chest and bacon-thick thighs and wondered why I hadn't been blessed with Cheyanne's athletically slim, well-proportioned body and richly crowned head of hair.

229

"Maybe someday I'll grow out of this dumpy, Ugly Duckling disguise to become that Beautiful Swan who every boy wants," I wished to myself.

Yeah maybe . . . but it was looking like a long shot.

Summers in northern Minnesota were far too short and this one seemed to speed by faster than most, leaving me at August's end with a half empty bottle of banana scented suntan oil. But just as the lovely, warm days were slipping away, anticipation on a different front filled the air as my friends and I prepared to enter the tenth grade, forever leaving behind the days of jumbo asphalt playgrounds in exchange for a world where eye makeup was no longer considered a four-letter word, and the prospect of dating older boys became more than just a fantasy.

I was more than ready to travel down this thrilling, new path toward adulthood, but there was one twist I hadn't anticipated. One that I'd completely overlooked until the very day I came face to face with it, and that one twist was my brother, Mikie. Never before had we shared the same school. In fact, my brother and I had rarely spoken since the day he'd abandoned ship all those years ago, and Mom simply lacked the will to ensure that her two children remained united. During his absence, I'd learned not to miss him. I'd learned not to care. And he, in turn, had done the same. As the years passed, only the cursed German/Irish blood that ran through our veins linked the two of us together. My brother had his gig, I had mine, and there didn't appear to be any good reason to alter the status quo.

I can clearly remember the first time I saw Mikie on my new stomping grounds. He was walking toward me in the hall, his five-foot-nine, athletically fit frame clothed in a pair of tan corduroys and a plaid, cotton shirt with the sleeves rolled up.

230

Eager for attention from anyone, including my older brother, I beamed at him and sped up. As I neared, I tried to catch his eye, but he wouldn't look at me. He just stared straight ahead. I chirped, "Hi, Bro! How's it hangin'?" in my squeaky, juvenile voice. He rigidly marched past without even the slightest acknowledgment, eyes forwardly aligned as if in an army platoon. My stare followed. I slowed my gait to a dead stop and turned to watch him somberly round a corner at the end of the hallway. I stood transfixed, unsure of what had just happened and looked down at the ground to let my mind rewind. "Was my brother mad at me? What had I done to piss him off?" I wondered to myself. But I couldn't answer my own questions. "What a loser!" I sneered underneath my breath, then turned back around and began walking to my next class.

I didn't think about that exchange again until I was walking home from school. No matter how many times I replayed the scene in my mind, I couldn't figure out why Mikie had ignored me. It was true that the two of us hadn't spoken in months, maybe even longer, but there had never been a time when we hadn't acknowledged one another with at least a wave. This time was different, this time was strange, and it hit me hard. I was used to being distant from my brother, even disengaged, but I was simply unprepared for being cut completely out of his life.

I walked along the dirt, service road past the Holiday Inn, reflecting on the times that my brother and I had shared together. He and I had once been friends. Not good friends, not close, but friends nonetheless. And instead of establishing a unified front in the presence of the ever-looming Medusa, we'd unknowingly let her petrify us. It now seemed as if we were permanently divided, destined to drift farther and farther apart.

Before that day, I'd never realized that the only other face in this world that was sketched so similarly to mine was becoming no more than a complete stranger.

231

~ ◆ ◆ ◆ ~

I chalked up my brother's bitterness toward me as just one more thing to get used to. Later that same day, I asked Mom what was bothering Mikie. "Ahhh. Why, I don't know *what*'s gotten into your brother," she predictably replied, never quite sure how to interpret either one of her children.

I pushed Mikie to the back of my mind and forged ahead, embracing senior high and all it had to offer. I found salvation in my academic world, just as I always had. Striving to be well liked, I continually pushed myself to be all things to all people. Never did I let a soul pass by in the hall without shouting a bubbly "Hi there!" Never did I let a day end without sowing something lovely and sweet, like a maiden in a meadow sprinkling seeds of Forget-Me-Nots onto the fertile soil, hoping they'd one day blossom into a returned favor. It was as if I'd sacrificed who I truly was so that others would care about me. It was as if, in some absurd way, any ounce of kindness bestowed upon me by each of the many could somehow make up for the lost love of but a few.

Cooling northern temperatures produced the thick, morning frosts that clung to browning lawns and fading vegetable gardens. October had arrived. Within a few, short weeks, my classmates and I would be casting our ballots to elect the ever-popular Homecoming king and queen. Dana and Cheyanne had been nominated the preceding year while I had been voted the girl with the Best Personality. And although it was a treasured recognition, indeed, my dreams now envisioned a far loftier goal.

I didn't bother reading the special edition of the school newspaper on the day the royalty nominees were announced. I just didn't feel like looking at everyone's name in the limelight . . . except for mine. I was sitting with my two best buds at lunch that same afternoon, and had no choice but to listen as

232

the two candidates chatted excitedly about what they were going to wear to the coronation ceremony.

"Cheyanne?" asked Dana as she tore open her snack pack of Doritos. "Can I borrow that dress you wore to Snowball last year?"

"Which one was that?" Cheyanne replied.

"You know, that Laura Ashley knockoff?"

"Sure. I'll see if I can find it."

Cheyanne then casually looked at me and asked what I'd be wearing.

I scooped a blob of cream filling from the center of my Hostess cupcake and let it linger on my fingertip, "Me? Jeans, I guess. I haven't really thought much about it."

"You're wearing jeans?" asked a surprised Dana.

"Yeah. What's wrong with wearing jeans?"

"Nothing, except . . ." Dana began, attempting to steer me in a different direction.

"Don't you want to look a little sassier than that?" asked Cheyanne. "I mean, everyone's going to be watching you walk across the gymnasium floor."

My face contorted into a look of complete bewilderment. "Why would they do that?" I asked.

Cheyanne and Dana exchanged surprised glances.

"Don't you know?" asked Dana.

"Know what?"

Dana gave my shoulder a friendly slap, then explained, "Ther, you got nominated for Homecoming Queen. I mean . . . duh."

She looked at Cheyanne, and the two of them said "Duh-uh" in unison.

"What?!" I said in disbelief, my round, blue eyes enlarged with excitement. I sat there for a moment in complete amazement, utterly speechless. That's when the light bulb went off, and I realized that my friends were playing a practical joke

233

on me. I furrowed my brow, narrowed my eyes, then suspiciously asked, "Are you guys funning with me?"

"No, we're totally serious," said Cheyanne. "Didn't you read the announcement in today's paper?"

I shook my head "No."

"You're in there. You got nominated, Girl," Cheyanne said lightheartedly.

I looked at Dana who was nodding her head up and down, then said with a mouth full of fresh banana, "You totally did. I swear."

"Shut up!" I said with bona fide zeal as Dana and Cheyanne laughed at my stunned response.

Later that day, congratulations seemed never ending. "You totally deserve it!" said a track teammate. "I hope you win!" said a friend whose locker was right next to mine. I couldn't help but secretly revel in all the heart-felt attention.

Deep down I knew I wouldn't win. After all, I'd be competing against some of the prettiest girls in school. But the truth of the matter was, I didn't really care about winning. The nomination itself was my dream come true.

On the morning of my big day, I dressed myself in the form-fitting, pink skirt and matching floral blouse that Mom had bought for me out east, then sprayed a generous plume of Love's Baby Soft onto the sensual spot between my small, budding breasts. I fooled around with my hair and makeup in front of the bathroom mirror for several more minutes, trying to get it all just right. After finally feeling ready, I leaned in a bit closer toward my reflection to study the young girl who was peering back. I ran my fingers through my long bangs, pushing them farther away from my eyes, then rubbed my lips together to even out my gloss. Somehow I looked brighter than usual, more comely. Was it my outfit? My new shade of blush? Or

234

was I just getting better at mimicking the pages of my *Mademoiselle* mag? Whatever the reason, I wanted to bottle that fleeting moment of self-assurance.

I was strangely anxious yet excited at school that day, and found it hard to concentrate on my studies. Just before the two o'clock bell, the principal's voice crackled over the loudspeaker, announcing the beginning of our Homecoming festivities. The instant the bell rang, we all sprang from our seats like a herd of jackrabbits and dashed down the halls toward the gymnasium. When I reached the gym's main entrance, I wasn't sure where to go next, so I asked one of the teachers in the hallway. "Just follow the arrows," he instructed as he pointed to several white pieces of paper taped on the wall behind me that said, "Nominees This Way" in bold, black ink. I followed them around a corner to a little used corridor on the backside of the gym. Dana and Cheyanne were already mingling with our male counterparts. "Hi Guys!" I shouted, grinning uncontrollably. As I stood nearby listening to my friends chatter, my thoughts began to drift toward the reality of the situation. Before I knew it . . . Bam!! There it was, staring me straight in the eye. My insecurity had resurfaced and was stalking me like a hungry alligator in shallow, muddy waters. Sweat began pooling underneath my arms, and I was now absolutely terrified. Terrified of all the glaring attention. Terrified of doing something stupid and embarrassing, like tripping over my new high heels and crashing to the ground in front of all my classmates.

I was losing confidence by the minute when I felt a brisk tap on my shoulder. "Theresa, you're next," the voice urged. It was Dana prompting me to move forward into the gymnasium. I took a deep breath, then walked over to a fellow nominee, looped my arm in his and followed the couple in front of us out into the center of the vacant basketball floor. Once my partner and I reached the court's sideline, we parted ways and I took my place in the lineup of female hopefuls. As I faced the

235

bleacher full of restless students, I took another deep breath . . . and waited.

As soon as all twelve nominees—six boys and six girls— were finally in place, the purr of the drum roll signaled that a new king and queen would soon be chosen. I clenched my fists and nervously smiled as my eyes darted around the room. The reigning queen walked up to each girl from behind and dramatically floated an ornamental, paper crown above of our heads. I didn't dare look anywhere except straight ahead. I didn't even look at Dana or Cheyanne. "Swoosh!" went the crown past the top of my head. A few minutes later, it fluttered by a second time. "Just get the damn thing over with!" I thought to myself, no longer enjoying the suspense. And that's when the crown plopped right smack dab upon my golden locks. I couldn't believe it! A jury of my peers had picked me! Me?! Me!!! To be their queen! Both of my hands flew over my mouth as my jaw dropped open with stunned surprise. All the other female contestants rushed to my side to congratulate me, and I hugged them back with heartfelt gratitude as genuine tears of joy welled in the corners of my eyes.

The hoopla soon subsided, and the reigning queen presented me with a beautiful bouquet of long-stemmed, cream roses adorned with purple ribbons that matched the jerseys of our football team. The drum roll began anew, and a second crown was placed upon my royal husband's head. He took my hand and led me to our matching, crepe paper thrones next to the wall where we resided until the ceremony's completion. Afterwards, the two of us posed together for photos that would be published in the next edition of the *Daily Journal*.

Before I knew it, my moment of glory was over, and only a handful of people lingered in the hallways. I walked to my locker and dug out my backpack, then filled it with that weekend's homework assignments. I put on my coat, closed my locker then began my journey home to the apartment. I couldn't wait to tell Mom the amazing news and was already basking in the radiance of her delight.

When I opened our front door, I saw Mom's purse lying on the kitchen table. I hurriedly set my roses on an end table and laid my backpack on the floor. "Mom?! You home?!" I shouted, barely able to contain my excitement. Only silence greeted me back. "Mom?" I said again before walking down the short hallway toward her bedroom. Her door was closed, so I turned the knob to open it. At the far end of the room, Mom was tucked beneath her comforter, facing the wall, and all I could see was her freshly frosted, short, brown hair. "Mom?" I loudly whispered as I began my approach. "You'll never guess Wh . . ."

I was now close enough to look down upon her ashen face. Her eyes were clearly open yet unseeing, closer to comatose. My broad, triumphant smile instantly vanished. "Mom?" I said again, feeling wounded. She rolled toward me as if stirred by the sound of my voice. As she began to speak I quickly realized it was not my voice she was answering. She stared up at the ceiling with agonized eyes and strained her neck so that her head levitated just above her pillow.

"Why have you forsaken me?!" She asked the invisible spirit that hovered above her. "What have I ever done to deserve this?" she sneered. The dark circles beneath her eyes seemed to deepen with each tortured breath. "I have been eternally loyal to you, and this is the thanks I get! I've turned to you for refuge, but you continue to persecute me. Can't you see how you've brought me to my knees? I need your love, Jesus. Can't you see? What will it take to show you? Your cross is my cross, Jesus. Your burden, mine." She then paused, and I thought she was going to lie back down, but she remained motionless, silently searching the eyes of her savior. Suddenly, her jaw clenched, and she obediently shook her head back and forth, as if answering "yes" to a question only she could hear. Her verbal conversation resumed in huskier tones, "Jesus?

Please bring me closer to the throne. Please. I'm begging you . . ." Her head fell gently down onto her pillow, and all the muscles in her body relaxed. She lay there for a few more moments with her eyes wide open in telepathic conversation, the pained lines on her face now smoothing. Peace eventually came upon her, and she closed her eyes to drift away. Her body shifted slightly, sending a limp arm dangling off the side of the mattress, the palm of her hand open and extended skyward, like that of a priest at Sunday mass when he somberly declares, "Let us pray." I could tell she was nearing the other side. "I love you, Jesus," was the last thing she whispered before giving up her earthly burden until another day.

The sting from Mom's never-ending, delusional episodes and total lack of involvement in my life combined with the onslaught of the harsh Minnesota winter blues brought forth the darker side of my personality. I became even edgier than ever and began bickering with Mom and Arthur on a daily basis, trying to break away from any remaining oversight. Arthur's endless inquiries into my complete disregard for household chores and reasons why I so foolishly wasted my allowance on candy and Pac-Man games only worsened the problem. "For God sakes, just leave me alone, would you?!" I'd shriek with indignation.

On one particular Friday evening in the middle of January, the outside temps plummeted below zero. An enlarged regional map blanketed with animated icicles filled the expanse of our TV screen as the local news station warned of the pressing dangerous weather. "Don't leave home unless it's absolutely necessary," advised a concerned weatherman. At that time in my life, being with my friends was one of my few remaining pleasures, and I wasn't about to let a little thirty-below windchill stand in my way.

After spending more than an hour getting all dolled up for that evening's high school hockey game, I walked over to our living room closet to fetch my coat.

"Theresa," said my stepfather from his roost on the couch. "Now, you're not planning on going outside in *this* weather are you?"

"Sure. Why not?" I asked while zipping up the front of my sky blue ski jacket. "The ice arena is only a half-mile away. I can walk it in ten minutes. And besides, you shouldn't live in The Falls if you can't deal with a little cold snap."

He looked back at me as if I'd completely lost my marbles. "It's bitter cold out there. If you'll just take a moment to watch this weather report with me, you'll see what a foolish idea that would be."

"I wasn't being denied release, was I?" I fretted to myself. I started feeling tense and a bit claustrophobic. "I'll be fine," I said convincingly. "It's no big deal, anyway. I mean, I've lived in this town for a long time, and I think I can handle the weather by now."

"Now look here, Young Lady," Arthur sternly stated. "You're not about to go anywhere. It's brutally cold out there, and I don't want anything to happen to you.

I haughtily placed my hands on my hips then snarled back, "Well, if you *really* care about me, then why can't you just get off that couch and drive me to the arena?"

"Because I don't know if our car will start, and frankly I don't particularly want to go outside tonight!"

"I want to be with my friends!" I screeched then turned to open the apartment door, despite my stepfather's clear order.

"I'm warning you, Theresa," said Arthur. "If you leave this apartment, you *will* be grounded."

Being stuck in that cramped, smoky apartment with Arthur and Mom for any length of time was nothing short of imprisonment. "Gotta Keep Moving" had always been my tried and true mantra, and was the only way I knew how to remain

239

sane and survive. I sure as hell wasn't in the mood to lounge on the sofa all night and watch TV with my stepfather. On the other hand, I wasn't in the mood to get my ass grounded either. It was checkmate, pure and simple.

My hand rebelliously reached for the doorknob and lingered there momentarily before I clenched it in defeat then let it go. My anger flared from within, erupting before I could stop it. I turned to look at Arthur with freshly cocked and loaded eyes, then screamed, "I hate you! You're not even my real dad!" I tore off my ski jacket and threw it onto the carpet before running down the hallway to my room and slamming the door behind me.

I spent the remainder of that evening lying on my bed and bawling my eyes out as sappy, 80s love songs played on my transistor radio in the background.

The next Tuesday afternoon, as I was heading to the school lunchroom, I heard the secretary page me over the loudspeaker. "Theresa Waters, please report to the principal's office." My shoulders slumped. "What in the world could I have possibly done now?" I wondered to myself as I walked down the hallway. I'd been hauled into the principal's office only once before when I'd skipped study hall on a double dare, a king-size Snicker bar on the line, but ever since then I'd made damn sure to keep my nose clean.

"You're in trouble now!" teased my friend, Bobby, as I passed him along the way.

The school secretary was typing at her desk when I walked into the office. "Hi, Miss Johnson," I said politely. "I thought I heard my name paged. Did you want to see me about something?"

"Yes, Theresa," she replied matter-of-factly as she repositioned her reading glasses farther down the bridge of her nose then stood up to meet me on the opposite side of the counter. "Mr. Ky would like to speak to you."

I stood silently for a few bewildered seconds then said, "Um, okay. But, I don't have an appointment with him or anything." I cautiously looked Miss Johnson in the eye, "What's this all about?"

"You'll have to ask the counselor, Dear," she replied, then smiled at me and said, "Have a seat, and I'll let him know you're here.

I weakly smiled back then walked over to one of the square, plastic chairs pressed against the glass wall that separated the principal's office from the public corridor. I sat down and began to chew on the end of my pen, then craned my neck around to look at all the kids passing in the hallway behind me.

Mr. and Mrs. Van Ky were a young Asian couple who had recently moved into our apartment building directly across the hall from us and had stopped by one evening to introduce themselves. Mr. Ky, instantly recognizable, was the new counselor at our high school. Since his very first day on the job, the all-Caucasian student body naively speculated on the poor man's unfamiliar ethnicity. "Is he Japanese or Chinese? Japanese or Chinese?" we wondered, as if those were the only two viable options, oblivious to the possibility that he was neither.

Mr. Ky was now approaching me in the principal's office. "Theresa?" he called out, then opened the entry gate to let me pass onto the administrative side of the room. "So glad that you could come," he said as I walked toward him. He led me down a very short hallway to his office, then cordially stepped to the side of its threshold. "Please, won't you come in," he directed while gesturing toward the room's interior with his hand.

I entered the sparse but artistically furnished office, then sat in a chair on the visitor's side of his desk. He closed the door and took a seat across from me, then picked up a manila folder with my name on it from one of the many stacks of

241

paper on his credenza. He flipped it open then briefly perused its contents as I sat in suspense. After he was finished, he laid the folder back down and smiled warmly at me then asked, "And how are you doing today, Theresa?"

I grinned back with expert timing, "Great! I'm doing just great!" I told him, comfortably shifting into my preferred, happy-go-lucky, public persona.

He relaxed and eased back into his chair then looked at me with intelligent eyes through sleek, black-rimmed glasses and asked, "School going okay?"

"Yeah, school's great. I love school!" I told him honestly.

"Uh-huh," he replied then commented, "I see that you were nominated by the sophomore class as their representative for Homecoming Queen."

"Yes! Yes, they did!" I proudly responded, then began to babble. "I just couldn't believe that *I* was the one who got crowned. I mean, man! Me, of all people! I just thought that there was no way. I mean *NO WAY,* " I exclaimed as I fumbled nervously with my hands.

"Uh-huh. That's a most impressive accomplishment, indeed," he said as he smiled warmly again.

I cheerfully nodded my head up and down, then expanded the grin that was already permanently affixed to my face.

Mr. Ky then took on a more serious look. He leaned slightly forward and folded his hands together, resting them in front of him on top of his desk. "Theresa, there's something important that I'd like to talk to you about," he explained in a somber manner.

"Oh . . . kay . . ." I replied, now very confused about where this conversation was heading.

"It's about your home life," he began. "Since my wife and I moved in across the hall from you and your family a few months ago, we've heard much arguing." He then looked at me with caring eyes and asked, "Is there anything you want to talk about? Anything at all you'd like to tell me?"

The direction of this meeting was completely unexpected, and I was clearly unprepared. I tried to keep my smile intact, but couldn't help but let it fade. My eyes drifted downward as I defensively folded my arms in front of my chest. I could feel that dreaded lump in my throat rising, the one that was too easily seduced by genuine kindness and concern, the one which I'd tried so hard to outrun.

"Please keep in mind," he continued, "that anything you tell me will be held in the strictest confidence."

Over and over again, I glanced up at Mr. Ky then back at the floor, trying to decide how to respond. Here in front of me, in the body of a gentle soul, was a chance I'd never before had. For the first time in my life, someone was asking me to present *my* version of the truth and coaxing me to lay bare my feelings about all the unsolicited turmoil that floated around my life like an evil, dark wind. No one before Mr. Ky had ever dared shine an investigative light upon my unhealed, emotional wounds.

Finally, I said softly, "Um, I didn't know you could hear us fighting."

The counselor patiently waited for the balance of my thoughts.

I nervously looked around the room then back at Mr. Ky, "Things are sometimes hard, but you learn to deal with it."

"Do you feel comfortable in your current living situation," he persisted.

"Well. Most of the time I guess I do," I replied while my gaze focused on the framed O'Keeffe behind him. "It isn't always so bad. It's just that mostly I can't relate to my mom very much . . . and my stepdad, um, he's pretty old and sick of dealing with kids, so I just try to stay out of his way."

"Why is it that you can't relate to your mother, Theresa?"

I looked down at my hands that had made their way onto my lap as the untold number of reasons competed with each other in my head to be the first to step forth and be heard. I desperately wanted to reveal the truth, but the fact of the matter was that I simply couldn't. I was its prisoner. To reveal the truth to Mr. Ky, or to anyone else for that matter, would have exposed all of the severe oddities of my existence. For all of my life, my instincts had taught me to blend in, to appear normal, to be happy and act like nothing was wrong. And it was that exact formula that had led me down the path to popularity and acceptance. I simply wasn't strong enough to stray.

I looked over at the manila folder with my name on it and softly replied, "Lots of reasons. I can't relate to my mom for lots of reasons."

"I have plenty of time to discuss those reasons if you would like," he offered.

Another chance had just landed in my lap, begging me to take it, but I had to look the other way and pass it by. I shook my head from side to side and quietly replied, "No, that's okay."

Mr. Ky paused briefly and then expounded, "Whenever I see you with your friends here at school, you always look so happy, as though your troubles are few. I've learned a little about you in my short time here in The Falls and know that it must be impossible for you to be truly happy *all* of the time, given everything that has gone on in your life."

He was dead-on. I was trying so hard not to look into his eyes because I knew they were a mere stone's throw away from my river of tears. I swallowed hard then softly mumbled, "Honestly? The honest to God's truth izzzz . . . izzz . . . that I don't know how to be any other way."

Mr. Ky let my emotion settle into the room then gently said, "It's okay to be sad sometimes, Theresa. That is human nature. No one can expect you to be happy all of the time. Please remember that." I didn't respond at first so he rephrased his guidance into the form of a question, "Will you promise me that you will try to remember what I said?"

I was dangerously close to crying, so all I could do was shake my head "Yes" before squeaking, "Is it okay if I go now?"

Mr. Ky patiently looked at me and then replied, "Of course."

As I stood up to leave, he offered, "Stop by again if ever you'd like to continue this conversation. I'm here to help in any way I can, okay?"

Again, I shook my head "Yes," then walked toward the door and opened it. Before passing through, I turned around to look at the counselor, gave him a wobbly, Charlie Brown-style smile and said, "Um, Mr. Ky?"

"Yes, Theresa?"

"Thanks for every . . . everything," I stuttered. "I mean, it was really nice of you to talk to me about all this stuff."

"It's really not a problem. I'm just doing my job."

I headed out the door and back down the hall when I faintly heard him say, "Take care of yourself."

Mr. Ky never knew what a profound effect that meeting had on me. For all the years since Daddy died, I'd been treading water in the middle of a monsoon, sometimes going under, trying so hard to invent and reinvent survival strategies. Until that day, I'd never before taken a hard look at the girl I'd become, one who was so far from the daughter Daddy had left behind. I was now no more than a juvenile version of a CIA operative, armed with a suitcase full of disguises to aid in whatever mission I needed to accomplish.

I will forever be indebted to kind Mr. Ky for caring about me. On that day, he planted within me a divine seedling schooled in the healing arts that would lie dormant for many years, becoming buried beneath layers of uncertainty and self-doubt. It would bravely gather the strength to survive and one day reemerge to offer me one of life's greatest gifts . . . the gift of self-respect.

It was nearing the end of March when I received a phone call out of the blue from a woman I'd never met.

"Is this Theresa?" she asked.

"Yeah," I apprehensively replied as I tried to place the voice.

"My name's Shelly. I'm your brother's guardian," she told me.

"My brother's guardian? What?" I suspiciously questioned. "He lives with Buck and Sarah on the other side of town."

"No," she corrected. "He *used* to live with Buck and Sarah. Now he lives with me out on County Road Nine."

"Okay, now I'm confused," I replied.

She brushed aside my pursuit of an explanation and told me, "Never mind that for now. Why don't you have your mom inform you later. Anyway, the reason I'm calling is because your brother would like to meet with you."

"Well, why didn't he just call me himself?" I asked, sincerely wanting to know.

Shelly ignored my question, "Will you be around this weekend?"

I sat down on a nearby stool and considered my availability. "I'll be here for a while on Sunday," I answered.

"Fine," she said. "That'll work. I'll bring Mikie over around two or so."

"Can't I even talk to my own brother?" I asked, mystified.

"It really would be best if you'd wait until the weekend," Shelly replied.

Feeling the obvious presence of a brick wall, "Okay" was all I had left to say.

246

"See you next Sunday at two then," she confirmed before disconnecting.

After hanging up the phone, I stood up and walked around the corner into our kitchen.

"How ya doin', Baby?" Mom asked brightly as I passed her on the way to the fridge.

Purposefully ignoring her, I pulled out a carton of orange juice and took a few, deep swigs, wiping the excess liquid from my lips with the sleeve of my flannel pajama top. I placed the carton back onto the top shelf and closed the fridge door, then drifted over to the kitchen table where I sat across from Mom.

"How's my little Lambie Pie?" Mom asked again before taking a sip of her morning coffee.

I yawned then replied, "Good. What's going on with Mikie?"

"Well," she said slowly. "I don't know what you mean?"

"Why is he living with this Shelly chick?" I clarified.

"Oh that," said Mom languidly before shrugging. "Sarah called and told me that Mikie got into a big fight with Buck so they had to kick him out of their house."

"What?! Mikie got kicked out of their house?"

"Yup," she replied. "Sarah was just sick about it."

I sat across from my mother, silently criticizing her as I searched her face for signs of sympathy toward her firstborn. "Mom, why didn't you say something before?" I scolded.

"Ah . . . well," she stuttered. "I guess I just didn't think to tell you."

"Don't you even care about your own son?" I asked with a scowl.

"Well, of course I care! But what am I suppose to do about it?" she demanded in a loud, piercing voice.

I switched to a different line of questioning. "Why would Mikie want to see me?" I asked.

"How should I know?" replied Mom, now visibly agitated.

"Well, maybe you should know because, for one, you're his mother," I replied.

"Well I don't, Theresa. That's enough. I don't want to talk about it anymore."

Frustrated by having learned nothing from this conversation, I stared at Mom a bit longer with the small hope of getting more answers out of her. I shifted positions in my chair while studying the empty expression on her face as she gaped at an overflowing ashtray on the table next to my arm. I had seen that same look a million times before; it was Mom's signature salute to the myriad of prescribed medications that had slowly and destructively eaten away her mind. I sighed, knowing I'd reached a dead end, then got up and left the table to get myself ready for the day.

When the following Sunday afternoon rolled around, I sat alone in our living room and watched a Kung Fu episode on TV while anxiously waiting for my brother to arrive. Shortly after two o'clock there was a quick rap on the door. I stood up and opened it. "Hi Mikie," I said cheerily, then stepped aside to let him pass.

He was deep in the clutches of that weird militia mode, the same one I'd witnessed at school. He didn't greet me or even so much as look at me when he passed, he simply walked over to the stereo console in the living room, then rigidly rested against it. Shelly followed, briefly introduced herself, then hoisted her haunches onto the console next to my brother and parked herself there as if it were a perfectly normal place to sit. I closed the door then hurried over to the couch where I sat across from the two of them.

Mikie turned to stare out the apartment's picture window that overlooked a vacant, grassy field, his blank look revealing nothing.

At first, I patiently waited until too many awkward moments filled the empty space. "Sooooo Bro, you wanted to talk to me about something?" I asked lightheartedly, still pretending nothing was amiss.

Mikie kept staring out the window without answering. I looked at Shelly. She had this peculiar grin on her face, as though she were hiding a devious secret. The strange attitude of my brother's companion only added to my confusion, leaving me with no other alternative but to dismiss her. "Yoo-Hoo, Mikie?" I said, still trying to capture my brother's attention.

Shelly assertively placed her hand on my brother's shoulder and gently shook it. "Mikie," she said as she leaned in closer to his ear. "Tell your sister why you're here."

Her influence had an obvious effect. Mikie slowly turned his gaze in my general direction but not directly upon me, letting it rest in a safe place on the coffee table in between us.

Although I remained clueless as to my brother's true intentions, there was now one thing I knew for certain. Whatever he had to say was not going to conquer the great divide that had severed us.

"Mikie," Shelly prompted again.

Finally my brother began to address me. "I came over to tell you how much I hate you," he stated, still looking at the coffee table.

I reactively twisted my face to reflect my disbelief. "What . . . did you just say?" I spit out.

"I said I hate your guts!" His tone was now gutsier and more defined.

I started to laugh nervously, hoping this was merely some kind of strange joke. "Mikie," I said, "What are you even talking about?"

He continued to keep his distance while the venom rose in his throat. "You ruined my life! You used to get me into trouble with Dad all the time . . . on purpose, too. You were his favorite, and you knew it. Dad beat the crap out of me all because of you!"

I couldn't believe what I was hearing. "Mikie," I began, shedding any remaining conciliatory pretense. "What in the hell is wrong with you? That was years ago! We were just little kids. I can't help it that I was Daddy's favorite. What do you expect me to do about it now?!"

"I wish you'd never been born!" he yelled.

"Well, too fucking bad!" I snapped back. "I'm here and there's not a goddamn thing you can do about it!" Then I turned the tables on him. "You know, what is your problem anyway? You're the one who got to live with a nice family while I got stuck back here with Mom. How great do you think *that's* been, huh?! You bailed, asshole!"

"Fuck you!" screamed Mikie. "You think you're all high and mighty now just because you're some Homecoming Queen! Well, I've got news for you. I ain't never gonna take any shit off of you again! Got it!"

"It's Your Royal Highness to you, jerk!" I screamed back. "And by the way, I don't care if I ever see you again! I mean, it's not like you're really even my brother anyway! I don't even fucking know you anymore! You've NEVER been a real brother to me!"

Shelly sat silently on her little perch and smirked during the entire argument, as if reveling in the brutal barbs that exploded from our mouths, pushing us ever closer to the edge of our family's abyss.

Finally I'd had enough. I wasn't about to single-handedly take the blame for the hijacking of my brother's childhood, of *my* childhood. I stood up and marched over to the door then angrily opened it. "Get out!" I screamed. "Get the fuck out! Now!"

Mikie's voice became menacingly grave, and he said, "Don't you EVER fucking tell me what to do!"

Shelly calmly addressed my brother, "Mikie, let's go. You've said what you needed to say."

My brother lingered for several more seconds, as if contemplating his next move, then strode toward the door. Right on cue, Shelly hopped down from the console to follow him out.

As Mikie was about to pass me, he looked directly into my eyes for the first time since his arrival. "It's a long life, bitch!" he sneered, his hatred searing clean through me.

I defensively narrowed my eyes as if to say, "See if I care," then turned my glare upon Shelly.

"It was nice meeting you," she cooed with the sincerity of a whore.

I slammed the door behind them as hard as I could then stood absolutely still, as though I'd been transformed into a stone statue. I didn't scream, I didn't cry, I simply stood there with my jaw clenched, thinking about my brother and the terrible things he'd just said to me. It was at that very moment when I solemnly vowed that I would never again give Mikie my friendship. The camel's back had been broken.

That day was one of the many turning points in my life. It would prove to be the last time I'd ever talk to my brother until several years later, after he'd graduated from high school and told Mom about Shelly's inappropriate sexual advances, after he'd been discharged from the army for erratic behavior and suicidal tendencies, and after he'd been diagnosed with one of humanity's cruelest and most debilitating mental disorders . . . schizophrenia.

The fragrant lilacs of spring had long since wilted away by the time June arrived, no longer perfuming the air with the scent of renewal and promise, now giving way to boisterous cricket concerts on warm, summer evenings.

Once again in need of summer employment but tired of working the fast food gig, I decided to try my hand as a bookkeeper for a local fish house. I hadn't foreseen the downside until I went home smelling like Long John Silver after my first day on the job. As if that wasn't bad enough, I'd somehow managed to become the preferred target whenever the fish processors in the back warehouse got bored and felt a burning desire to chase someone around the office with a live, freshly trapped lobster. Even so, it sure beat the hell out of wearing itchy, polyester pantsuits and asking rowdy teenagers if they wanted an order of fries to go with their super deluxe country fried chicken sandwich.

When I finally had a day off from work one bright, sunny morning, I decided to pay Sasha a visit and hopped on my trusty steed, then peddled the few, short blocks down Shoreview Drive. The Wagner residence, typically full of life, was now completely deserted, and I realized that my friend's family had packed up their belongings and moved to their summer cabin out on Rainy Lake, just down the road from City Beach. With nothing on my hands but a whole lot of time, I turned my bike around and headed east.

Twenty minutes later, I turned off Beach Road into the circular, dirt driveway that led to the rear entrance of the Wagner's lakeshore property. I leaned my bike against the trunk of a nearby maple, then strolled over to their back door and knocked. "Hello?" I called through the screen. "Anybody home?" Sasha's mother pranced toward the entry, dressed in a crisp white, cotton outfit and bathed in a fragrance far more exotic than your typical drugstore perfume.

"Oh. Hello, Theresa," she said as she opened the drawbridge. "Sasha . . . company!" she called to her eldest daughter. When my friend didn't readily appear, she ushered me toward the front of the house and instructed, "Why don't you go into the kitchen. I'm sure she's in there somewhere."

"Okay. Thanks a lot," I replied as I began ambling my way through the stylishly rustic living room, past the stone fireplace and into the room with the million-dollar view where Sasha was at the sink washing the last of the breakfast dishes.

"Hey, Sasha," I greeted as I opened the refrigerator and helped myself to a handful of red grapes.

"Hey, Ther. What's up?" she asked while peering back at me over her shoulder.

I sat down on a thick, wooden bench at the kitchen table and gazed out the bay window into the cloudless, blue sky. "Man, what a perfect day!" I exclaimed. "Wanna go hang out on your dock?" Before giving my friend ample time to respond, I added, "Oh, that's right. I didn't bring my suit. Hey, can I borrow one of yours?"

"Sure," she answered as she carefully set a white, porcelain plate into the drying rack. "They're in the top drawer of my dresser. Pick out whichever one you want."

I momentarily lingered at the kitchen table while holding the diminishing cluster of grapes in my hand and stared past the tall pines that flanked the front yard, past the private dock where a brand new Crestliner patiently waited to serve and out over the silvery, black water that danced in the breeze. "How could anyone be unhappy here?" I silently mused.

After changing into my bathing suit of choice, I waited for Sasha to join me on the dock. She appeared minutes later carrying a brimming crock-pot of miniature, barbequed appetizers and a plate of cheese and crackers. The two of us basked in the midday sun while consuming our gourmet snacks, and discussed the summer's forthcoming social agenda.

"Guess where I'm going next week?" Sasha asked with an air of mystery in her voice.

"Vegas!" I shouted, sure that there was no other place a girl like her would rather be.

"Nope."

"Okay, okay, I've got it . . . Paris!" I said, thinking that perhaps she'd decided to satisfy her more sophisticated side.

"Nope, not Paris."

253

Realizing this little game could go on forever, I decided to throw my friend a curve ball, "I don't know . . . The Blue Ridge Mountains?"

"Wrong again," she jokingly chided. "I'm going down to Atlanta to visit a friend I met in Aspen last year."

"When your family was out there skiing?" I asked.

She nodded.

Oh cool!" I replied, secretly wishing I could join her.

Sasha then gave me a sly, come-hither look and cooed, "And if I'm lucky, maybe I'll even get my Georgia Peach plucked."

I returned her bedroom-eyed stare with one that was comically quizzical. "What exactly does that mean," I asked, having a pretty good idea.

She tilted her head slightly to one side while looking directly into my eyes, then gently scolded, "Oh, *come on!* You know *exactly* what that means."

"You mean . . . it means what I *think* it means?"

"Theresa," she said to me in the tone of an older sister. "We're sixteen years old. We've got to figure out how to do *IT* sometime."

"I suppose," I replied, then casually looked away to conceal my inexperience.

"Right?" she asked, urging confirmation.

"Yeah, you're right," I said, trying to appease her, then quickly added, "But, Chick, don't be asking me for any advice because you know that I'm so not ready for *The Big Nasty.*"

"Don't worry, I think I can manage to find my way around just fine all by myself," she said with a naughty smirk. Then her eyes began to twinkle. "Let's make a deal. I'll find myself a sweet, southern boy, then dish all the juicy details after I get back."

I wanted, at the very least, to *appear* to be on the uninhibited, sexy side of the Cool Chicks' fence, so I replied with false certainty, "Yeah, man. Go for it! You'll be like my

Dear Abby, except for sex questions . . ." I cleared my throat, then elevated my pitch to a higher level, and pretended I was conducting a serious interview, "Dear Abby, how will I know when my boyfriend has a boner?" I nervously giggled at the thought of a "boner," then looked over at my friend who appeared mildly amused, enough to keep me rolling. "Dear Abby, should I be the one who puts the saddle on his wild stallion or should I let him take care of his own damn business? Dear Abby, what should I do if his wing-ding isn't long enough to give me some sweet satisfaction?" Then I laughed my usual, "I think I'm so funny!" laugh.

Sasha knowingly smiled at my naiveté, then reached over and clasped one of my hands in hers and gently patted the top of it. "I'll get you up to speed, Little Dearie, just you wait and see," she devilishly assured.

The two of us lounged on the dock and sipped raspberry juice spritzers for the remainder of that afternoon, our bared skin embracing each golden ray of sunshine. Those moments were a treasure in my life, filling the dark void. I wanted to drink them all in, to savor them, never sure of what lay just around the bend.

Summer fades quickly in the North Country, and that's when Sasha broke the bad news. "I'm leaving in a few weeks to attend prep school out east," she told me one evening while we were drinking watered-down Mimosas and preparing a dessert tray for yet another one of her parents' lakeside parties.

"What?!" I screeched, absolutely horrified. "You've GOT to be joking. Please tell me you're joking," I ordered.

My friend glanced at me before skillfully slicing another patisserie. "It's true," she said indifferently. "My parents want me to go, and I'm not exactly opposed to the idea."

"Sasha, you've got to fight them," I demanded. "C'mon. You can't leave me!"

255

"Don't be silly. I'm not leaving you," she insisted. "I'll be back at Christmas. And . . . who knows, maybe I'll even get kicked out of school." Then she looked at me with mischievous eyes and added, "Let's hope so, anyway."

On the day of her send-off, I hugged her tighter than she would have preferred and told her with tear-stained eyes how much I was going to miss her. "It's not that big of a deal, Theresa. Really," she said, trying to deflect my sorrow.

The loss of my friend and all her eccentricities was most certainly going to put a huge hole in my life. She would be hard to replace. But, deep down I knew that Sasha, ever the consummate cosmopolitan, wasn't really cut out for a horse and buggy town like ours anyway. It was time for her to move on.

Luckily, I still had Dana and Cheyanne. But, as newly issued drivers' licenses spread like wildfire, they began spending more and more time in the backseat of their boyfriends' cars, leaving me with little choice but to scour the playing field for yet another lone comrade. And, that's when I hooked up with Paul.

Paul was the type of guy who could get along with just about anyone. He was easy going, and as lovable as a giant teddy bear. We'd been acquaintances for quite some time, but it wasn't until later that fall, in eleventh-grade study hall, when we became fast friends. We were talking to each other in class one afternoon when he asked me if I wanted to join the boys swim team.

"You mean the *girls* swim team," I corrected.

"No, I really do mean the boys swim team," he insisted in his distinctive, raspy voice. "Coach has an opening for a statistician. Are you game?"

I looked back at him with a hint of distrust in my eyes, then asked, "Well, what *exactly* would I be doing?"

"You know, statistician stuff," he replied matter-of-factly, as if I knew perfectly well what that entailed.

"Such as . . ." I prompted.

"Oh, timing us guys in the pool, going to our swim meets, doing errands. You know, stuff like that." When I hesitated before giving an answer he coaxed, "You'll get to see a bunch of sexy guys walking around in their skimpy, little Speedos." Then he laughed and added, "An extra bonus."

Blushing, I gently swatted his arm and joked, "Oh, shut up!"

I considered his offer for a few more minutes, then told him, "Okay, I'm game. I'll do it. But, not because of the Speedo thing. I swear!"

Paul turned out to be the brother I'd always wanted but never had. When I wasn't with Dana or Cheyanne, I was with Paul . . . at the movies, or driving around town on Saturday nights in his dad's rusty Suburban. Sometimes we'd just hang out in his family's modest rec room and eat popcorn and M&Ms all evening. I felt completely at ease with my new friend. Sure, he was no Sasha, who ever could be? But I loved him just as much.

In early December of that same year, on a snowy, Saturday morning, I was sitting with Mom at our dining table, eating a plateful of French toast she'd just prepared. I glanced at her in between mouthfuls and noticed she was looking at me with genuine affection. She seemed to be in an unusually good mood, particularly considering that Christmas was merely weeks away.

Her soft chuckle broke the silence between us. "Wanna hear a joke?" she asked.

"Sure," I replied as I shrugged indifferently, knowing that she would tell it regardless of my opinion.

Her eyes twinkled with a bit of mirth as she began her tale. "There was this older gentleman who went to a barn dance all by himself one Friday night . . ."

"Oh no," I interrupted. "Not this one again."

Mom ignored me and continued. "He'd served in the army when he was just a young fellow, and his leg had gotten blown to bits in combat so the doctors replaced it with a wooden one. He was shy and terribly conscientious of his disfigurement and wouldn't ask any of the pretty girls to dance. So, he sat in one of the chairs next to the wall and watched from the sidelines as everyone else whooped it up on the dance floor. Now he didn't know it at the time, but there was a young woman who'd had her eye on him ever since he'd walked in the door, and she was trying to muster the courage to ask him to dance. After most of the evening had gone by, the attractive brunette made her way across the room and over to where he was sitting. "Excuse me, sir? Would you like to dance with me?" she asked sweetly. The man was so flattered that he immediately stood up and blurted out in front of everyone, "Well now, would I!" The attractive brunette gave him a dirty look and hollered back, "Peg leg! Peg leg!" then stormed away. The man turned to the woman seated in the chair next to him and asked what he'd done wrong. And, the woman said, "That poor gal has a wooden eye, you big dummy!""

My mother then laughed her rat-a-tat laugh, as though she were funnier than Johnny Carson himself.

"Oh, Mom," I gently scolded, "That joke is so corny."

My unfavorable comment didn't seem to bother her. "Whatcha up to today, Honey?" she asked.

I gnawed off another chunk of my toast then began talking with my mouth full, "Um, I don't know. I guess I hadn't really thought much about it. Why?"

"There's a Christmas boutique in the church hall today. I thought I'd go on over."

"Sounds fun," I replied.

"How 'bout you go with Momma today?" she suggested. It'd been a long time since Mom and I had done any real bonding. I'd typically spent most of my waking hours trying to run in the opposite direction. For some reason, accompanying her to the church bazaar sounded refreshingly appealing, perhaps even normal. I decided to jump at the chance.

"Yeah, sure," I replied. "What time do you want to go?"

"I've got to put my makeup on and get dressed first, but we'll leave after I'm done," she answered. "How does that strike your fancy?"

"Sounds good," I told her before polishing off the last of my morning meal.

The church hall had been temporarily transformed into a Christmastime bazaar and was buzzing with activity by the time we arrived. Shoppers perused neatly arranged buffet tables, each stocked with an assortment of goodies ranging from Saran-wrapped stacks of homemade lefse to intricately crocheted Christmas ornaments.

Mom and I hung our coats on the community rack in the entryway, then she opened her purse and pulled out a ten-dollar-bill. "Go buy something nice for yourself, Honey," she directed, then tendered a wet kiss on my cheek before losing herself in the swelling crowd of gray-haired old ladies.

I scanned the contents of the hall, trying to decide where to begin, then drifted over to the closest table. The woman sitting on the other side asked me how I was. "Good, thanks," I replied as I smiled at her. I looked down at the colorful, woven wristbands she was selling, then reached for one that had the letter "T" intricately sewn into its center and positioned it on my wrist before snapping it into place.

"My husband makes those in his workshop behind our house," she offered.

I nodded in reply, then lightly caressed the bracelet with my free hand. "How much is it?" I asked.

"Five dollars."

259

I kept my new prize on my wrist and handed over the money. After the woman returned the change and courteously thanked me, I walked to the next table of wares. Delicately knit, pink and white booties and hand-sewn, gingham bibs did nothing to spark my interest, and I scurried past.

The lady behind the third table stood out in the crowd of plainly clothed women like a catholic priest at a bar mitzvah. She wore a colorful, multi-layered gypsy dress and sported a flock of brass bangles around each of her wrists. A black bandanna tied around her head accentuated the diamond-shaped, scarlet tattoo on her forehead, just between the eyebrows.

"Would you like to have your palm read today, Mademoiselle?" she asked me in a phony, Bulgarian accent.

I reached into my pocket and pulled out my remaining five-dollar-bill, then considered whether or not I wanted to part with it. "How much is it going to cost me?" I asked.

"Free of charge," she boisterously replied. "Have a seat."

Intrigued by what she had to offer, I sat down in the folding chair opposite her and studied the details of her face. She looked oddly familiar. Was she a cashier at the Piggly Wiggly? A waitress at Bridgeman's? Or had she been a customer of mine last summer at the fish house? I couldn't be sure.

"Give me your hand," she insisted as she took hold of my limp limb and pulled it toward her. "Now then, let's have a look, shall we?" She scrutinized the lines that ran along the inside of my hand as she lightly caressed them over and over again with the tip of her forefinger. "This is your lifeline," she instructed as she traced its route diagonally from the top to the bottom of my palm. "You will have a very long life." Without looking at me for any kind of reaction, she continued searching and stroking to reveal more signs of my future. "You will travel often," she said mysteriously.

"With who?" I asked, my interest peaking.

"Men," she stated. "There will be many lovers in your life." She then looked up at me without hesitation and told me, "You will break many hearts one day, my Dear. Be prepared for this."

I snorted and said sarcastically, "Me? No way. I've never even had a boyfriend."

"Joke if you must, but the palm never lies," she answered in all seriousness.

I considered the oversized Dickens' Snow Village globe next to her arm, a pseudo crystal ball of sorts, and weighed the gypsy's authenticity, then looked her directly in the eyes. "What are their names?" I asked hopefully.

"Names? I have no names. I only know what I know, and I know that you will break many hearts," she repeated with conviction.

"Can you tell me where I will go with all these, um, lovers?" I asked timidly, uncomfortable with the image that the word "lovers" conjured up.

She gently clasped my hand in between the two of hers and leaned closer, her tone becoming almost maternal. "My Dear," she began softly, "it doesn't matter what a man's name is or where it is that he may take you. The only true force in life is l-o-v-e . . . love. Look for the man who has love for you in his heart, and it is there that you will find the meaning of happiness on this earth."

I stared back into her mesmerizing eyes, waiting for more of my story to be told. She affectionately squeezed my hand before letting go, then rapped the top of the card table with her knuckles and abruptly said, "Time's up, my Dear! I have another customer waiting."

I'd been so lost in her magnetism that I hadn't even realized someone was standing to the side of me, patiently waiting for their fortune. I looked up at the stranger and apologized, then turned to the palm reader and said with sincere gratitude, "Thank you. Really. That was great. I mean,

261

thanks so much!" I pulled the chair back for the next patron and went searching for Mom to share the secrets that had just been revealed to me.

I found her next to the choir girls who were selling freshly brewed coffee and Christmas cookies. She was standing completely still, staring across the aisle at a well-dressed woman who was preoccupied with inspecting a variety of fresh, evergreen wreaths.

"Mom, Mom!" I said excitedly as I approached. "You'll never guess what the fortune teller just told me!"

Mom didn't hear, or even see me, for that matter. She was fixated on the woman with the elegantly coiffed hair and sparkly, diamond ring. As soon as I saw the animosity in Mom's eyes, I knew she'd once again crossed over to that unreachable place in her mind, a parallel world to which only she held the key.

"Mom?!" I said again, anxious to get her attention.

"She thinks she's better than me," Mom hissed.

I followed Mom's scorching stare, then asked, "Mom, what in the world are you talking about?"

"Just because she has all that money and a big house doesn't mean that I don't measure up!"

Despite knowing full well that the battle had long since been lost before I'd even reached my mother's side, I foolishly attempted to pull her back into my world anyway. "Mom, stop it," I insisted. "That lady doesn't even know you."

"I'm not riff-raff, I'm not on welfare. I have a job, and I earn my own way in this world!" she pointlessly argued.

"Mom, you haven't had a job for years now. And, what does it matter anyway?" I argued back.

Mom's piercing gaze remained trained on the unsuspecting target of her delusion. "Why does she keep staring at me then?!" Mom demanded.

"I don't know. Probably because you're staring at *her*," I shot back. "Besides, Mom, she's not even staring at you. She probably just keeps looking at you because you're creeping her out!"

"I'm creeping *her* out?! *Her* out?!" Mom ranted.

I folded my arms in front of my chest. "Yes, you are creeping her out!" I snapped, then ordered, "Stop it right now, Mom. This is really getting embarrassing."

But, she wouldn't stop. She simply couldn't stop. She kept going on and on about what an upright citizen she was and how she refused to be treated like dirt. As the minutes passed, it was becoming clear to me that Mom was once more far beyond my reach, just as she always had been, and I was suddenly filled with disappointment and sadness. The enchantment infused by the gypsy began to vanish. I looked at my mother's unheeding face one last time, then did the only thing left in my power. I turned and walked away.

My mother . . . forever the delicate rose of spring, the youthful flower caught in a late, unexpected frost before she ever had the chance to unfurl her velvety petals and become the beauty she was meant to be. She remained eternally lost in the prison of her own mind . . . she remained eternally lost to me.

Later that winter, Dana decided to try out for the hockey cheerleading squad and had somehow managed to talk me into going with her. Her boyfriend, Chip, was a starter on the varsity team, and she never strayed far from his side. Although I didn't even know how to skate, loyalty was far more important than succumbing to my own inadequacies.

On the day of cheerleading tryouts, my heart just wasn't into it. My ice performance turned out to be nothing short of disastrous, illuminating my true feelings about donning a skimpy, purple and gold getup, then skating around a frozen sheet of water while shouting, "My back aches, my pants are tight, my body shakes from the left to the right . . . Go

263

Broncos!" The judges were about as enthusiastic toward me as I was toward them and were swift in handing me my walking papers. Dana, on the other hand, blew her competition away, guaranteeing herself a permanent seat with Chip on the traveling hockey bus.

Dana now had less and less free time, considering her many distractions—a boyfriend, an after-school job and cheerleading practice—so it seemed only logical to shift my semi-permanent home base from her house to Paul's. My newly acquired friend was so popular that his house constantly hummed with social activity, forcing his parents to relinquish full control of the basement family room to their second child.

Whenever Paul and I were hanging out together, somebody else was usually in the mix. Sometimes it was a good buddy from the swim team, sometimes it was a friend from Student Council and sometimes, if I got really lucky, it was Paul's best friend and neighbor. Don, a.k.a. "The Italian Stallion," was tall and athletic with wavy, brown hair and flawless, olive skin. His shy, brown eyes would twinkle whenever he smiled, sending my heart dashing straight for the Emergency Room. He was smart and sweet, and I'd soar on the wings of his sincerity whenever he laughed at my peculiar sense of humor. Spending time with Don excited me in ways I'd never felt before. He was someone who seemed to truly enjoy my company, so different from my cute surfer boy, Frederick. It didn't take long for my ardor to blossom into a full-blown crush.

But, I knew deep down that his price tag was more than I could afford and was convinced he'd never return the intensity of my feelings. Ever the guarded one, I kept my secret yearning to myself.

By the spring of '82, I was becoming more headstrong than ever. Having been in possession of a valid driver's license for several months, which seemed like eons in the teenager time continuum, I'd somehow made up my mind that I deserved to have a car of my own. I shamelessly begged Mom and Arthur for what I regarded as rightfully mine, "I want a sports car, a red one. Won't you please, please buy one for me? Pleazzze?"

"You don't need a car," they told me repeatedly. "What on earth are you going to do with a car anyway? This town is small enough for you to walk from one side to the other in about half an hour."

But, a car is what I wanted, and a car is what I was determined to have. Since Mom and Arthur weren't willing to budge on the matter, I decided to pull out my ace in the hole. I'd have to go see Grandpa.

Grandpa was the guardian of my meager inheritance, the keeper of the purse strings, so to speak. Our humble house in the city had been sold after Daddy died, and the resulting profit had been tucked away in an account belonging to my brother and me until our respective eighteenth birthdays. Never before had I asked Grandpa for an early dividend, but never before had I been so desperate. I was convinced he'd eventually come 'round to see my reasoning.

One day after school, I decided to pay him an unexpected visit. Knowing that he'd be in the middle of his afternoon nap, I opened his bedroom door, then quietly crept to his bedside and whispered, "Grandpa? Grandpa? You awake?" I impatiently shook his shoulder. He continued snoring, unaffected, while frozen in his typical napping pose on his back, his arms tucked close to the center of his chest and his hands balled into tight, little fists like that of an alert ground squirrel.

Several more minutes of my intense prodding eventually brought Grandpa back to life. He tried to open his eyes but one wasn't yet ready to cooperate, giving him the fleeting appearance of a man who'd had too much to drink. As he slowly brought a hand to his face in an attempt to wipe away the sleep, he had that familiar expression of "Where in the hell am I?"

He squinted as he looked up at me, trying to discern who'd just turned off the power to his dream factory, then pointed in the direction of his dresser and groggily requested, "Bring me my glasses, would you, Theresa?"

"Grandpa, I've got something that I really, really need to talk to you about," I said as I fetched his spectacles, bubbliness oozing from every pore of my body.

"What is it that you need?" he calmly asked. "I'm listening."

"Well," I hesitantly began. "Is there any way you could get up so that we could talk about it?"

"Is it something so important that it can't wait until later?" he evenly questioned.

"Um, sort of," I replied.

I could see Grandpa staring up at the ceiling in the faint darkness of the room, as if he were trying to muster any remaining strength, then he swung his legs over the side of the bed and onto the floor.

"All right then, I'm coming," he told me as he slowly followed me into the living room.

We sat on the couch, and Grandpa groaned a little while stretching one of his legs so that it rested on top of the coffee table.

"Now. What can I do you for?" he asked, looking across the room at a picture on the wall as he patiently waited for my answer.

"Well Grandpa, I have a plan," I said, trying to control my emotions.

"Ha!" he responded then chuckled out loud. "That's certainly nothing new." He grabbed a nearby pillow and placed it behind his head, as if foreseeing a taxing conversation at hand. "What sort of a plan?" he asked.

"Okay, Grandpa," I began. "I was driving around with my friends last weekend, right? And we went by Second Bridge Auto. And Grandpa, they had the coolest car *ever* in the whole, wide world for sale. I'm not even kidding!" I shifted my position on the couch so I could look my grandfather squarely in the eyes. "Grandpa. I'm planning on buying it."

"You want to buy it, huh?" he repeated skeptically while analyzing my expression, trying to determine whether or not I was actually serious. Then he asked, "So, what did your mother have to say about all this?"

"She said she wouldn't buy it for me," I hastily replied in an effort to get that pesky, little detail out of the way. "BUT . . ." I continued, "this is where my plan comes in. The plan is that I can withdraw some of Daddy's money and use it to buy the car." I then leaned back into the softness of the couch and looked at Grandpa as if I were some kind of damn financial genius.

My grandfather was far from being anybody's fool and took little time before giving me his answer. "Oh, no you don't, Young Lady. You'll be doing no such thing," he firmly stated.

"But Grandpa . . ." was all I could say before the Wise One quickly interrupted me.

"Don't you know that you can't go about foolishly spending your money on things like that. How much do you think it takes to run a car?"

I gave him a blank look then shrugged my shoulders.

"Exactly. You *don't* have the money for a car," he said, emphasizing the word, "don't." "And furthermore, you've got a few expenses that I still need to take care of, like health insurance for one, and anything after that is to be used for your college education."

"I don't need health insurance!" I rebelliously declared. "I'm perfectly healthy! Never been sick a day in my whole

267

life." I folded my arms in front of my chest and sassily argued, "Can't you understand that I'd rather be spending my money on something worthwhile like a cute, little sports car?"

Grandpa looked at me as if I'd lost my marbles. "So . . . you think you don't need health insurance? Well then, I'm afraid you have a lot yet to learn there, Young Lady," he said, trying to rationalize with me.

But I was not in a rational state of mind. "It's my money, Grandpa! You really should hand some of it over."

"I'll do no such thing," he insisted, trying to save me from myself.

I was angry now and couldn't think of anything better to do than stand up and stomp my feet, "Yes you will!" I demanded. "You *will* give me my money! It's not yours! It's mine!"

"Now listen here. Stop being so doggone pig headed," Grandpa said while sternly looking me in the eye. "I have a job to do, and that job is this. I am here to make sure that you don't blow what little inheritance you have. You need to get yourself to college. Don't you understand that? And if my decision means that you're going to be upset with me, well then, you'll just have to be upset."

At the time, it wasn't important for me to understand that Grandpa was simply trying to do right by me. All that mattered was getting my own way, and I was furious at the thought of losing this argument.

Grandpa then leaned back into his pillow again and stated in his signature, levelheaded way, "You know, Theresa, you seriously ought to think about studying law and becoming a lawyer. You love to argue like *nobody* else I've ever known."

I wasn't in the mood for Grandpa's levelheadedness, and I wasn't in the mood for his opinion, either. Realizing I wasn't going to get what I'd come for, it was pointless to remain. "Fine!" I shouted. "You can keep my money! But, it's *my* money, Grandpa. Mine!" Then I turned and stormed out of his house.

And that was how I thanked Grandpa for all he'd done on my behalf.

~♦ ♦ ♦~

Another summer brought with it the inevitable job hunt. I was tired of the greasy-face syndrome that the fast food joints had to offer and couldn't bear another day of smelling like rotten fish, so I went in search of an employment opportunity that better suited my personality. Dana happened to be working at the local health club at the time, and gave me a tip that her boss was hiring. "You should apply," she encouraged. "I'll talk to Bear and put in a good word for you."

Ben was his real name, but most people called him "Bear" because of all the curly, black hair that sprouted from his body like that of an over-watered Chia pet. I'd seen him at the club on occasion when I'd stopped by to chat with Dana, but he never said much and always had this wary look upon his face. I never let it bother me, assuming it was just part of his odd personality.

Dana had mentioned that the job would entail nothing more than making a few racquetball court appointments and picking up a towel or two in the locker room. "What could be so hard about that?" I thought to myself. It was time to have a meeting with Bear.

I headed over to the club one bright, June morning, then made my way down the murky, windowless corridor that led to the customer service desk. Bear was there when I arrived, spraying the countertop with a bottle of disinfectant. He glanced up at me but didn't say anything, he just kept spraying and wiping, spraying and wiping.

"Hi Bear!" I said, trying to sound upbeat.

He set down the bottle but kept a firm grip on its neck. "What's up?" he asked without the slightest hint of emotion.

269

"Um," I stuttered, starting to feel nervous. "Dana said that you had a job opening, and I wanted to pick up an application."

"No job openings here," he curtly stated before returning to his task.

I was not to be so easily dismissed. "But, Dana said that you needed some extra help," I insisted as the pitch of my voice rose higher.

"Well, Dana's wrong," he replied.

I looked at the typed message on the bulletin board behind him and pointed at it. "But . . . you have a Help Wanted sign right there on that wall," I timidly argued.

When he failed to respond, I decided to try a different method of persuasion. "I just want you to know, Bear, that I'm a real hard worker, and I can put in extra hours whenever you need me to." Wanting to showcase my complete skill set, I added, "And, I love working with people, if that helps any."

Bear plunked his cleaning bottle onto the counter and looked me squarely in the eyes. "Look," he began, clearly agitated. "I told you, I don't need any help. Got it?" He stared at me until he could sense that I was becoming uncomfortable, then turned around and pulled the Help Wanted sign off the bulletin board. "We've already hired someone," he stated, then tossed the sign into a nearby garbage can.

The weight of his unprovoked animosity bore down hard, and I felt like bursting into tears. I knew Bear was lying. "But, why?" I wondered to myself. A revelation suddenly hit me right between the eyes like a racquetball off the back wall, and I now understood what this strange exchange and all of Ben's wary glances were about. He didn't see Theresa Waters when he looked at me. The only thing he saw was the daughter of that crazy lady who argued with invisible spirits in the middle of the supermarket aisle. The dark walls of the health club were now beginning to close in, and all I wanted to do was get out of there, pronto. I backed away from him, trying hard not to let my disappointment show, and meekly thanked him before hastening toward the exit.

I would return to the infamous grease mines for yet another summer, scarred by the extensive reach of my mother's dark shadow.

The winter season in the town where I grew up was like a bizarre kind of frozen hell. But the summertime? Man, there was nothing like it anywhere. It never rained much, and the temperature rarely rose above eighty degrees. Just about every day was like being in paradise. On some of those perfect summer days, I'd grab my tennis racket and bike to the community courts across the street from Lucca's Grocery. Hour after hour, I'd slam my ratty, yellow ball into a green wall of plywood that had been constructed for single players such as myself . . . and I was rarely alone. At least one other kid at the courts was lucky enough to have his own car and gladly provided the background music, cranking up his stereo so that the rockin' tunes of Devo, AC/DC and Michael Jackson blared across the asphalt parking lot through his opened front door speakers.

Occasionally, this amazingly cute guy with perfectly feathered, sun-kissed hair would drive past in his baby blue Toyota. Although I'd never talked to him before, I still knew who he was. He'd graduated from my high school a few years earlier and was now considered one of those "forbidden fruit" boys from the community college. His name was Jake, and damn was he sexy. Was it because he owned his own car . . . or simply that he was post-adolescent? I can't say for certain, but whatever the reason he sure knew how to ring *my* bell. Whenever he drove by the courts and slowed, I'd stare and frantically wave like some kind of crazed groupie.

271

I'd finally kissed a guy or two by that time in my life, but they were usually drunk, horny, and in desperate need of easing their boyhood desires. I'd even made-out with Frederick once, my ever-elusive heartthrob, but he'd made it perfectly clear that he wasn't at all interested in the inner workings of my mind. All in all, my lips were still fresh and unschooled in the mysterious art of romance.

If you were a teenage girl back in those days and had your eye on a particular boy, you'd tell two friends then they'd tell two friends and so on and so on. The rumor mill would eventually make its way around town and, if everything worked in your favor, he'd ask you out on a date. Since I was in desperate need of a summertime fling, I decided to make one of my boldest moves ever. I told two friends about Jake.

A few weeks later, Jake drove by the courts and did something he'd never done before. Instead of passing by, he stopped his car and let it idle just beyond the other side of the fence, turned down his stereo and beckoned me over. I couldn't believe he was waving at me, so I looked around only to discover that I was, indeed, the lucky recipient of his attention. I set down my racket and ball then trotted over to him.

I was a little nervous as I bent down to his eye level, almost close enough to plant a juicy one right smack dab onto his luscious lips. "Hey," I said with a combination of delight and surprise. "How's it goin'?"

"You're not bad out there," he told me as he nodded toward the practice boards.

I waved his compliment away, "Oh, I'm all right, I guess."

We talked for several more minutes about things that didn't matter, like the weather and our summer jobs, then he asked me if I had any plans on Friday night.

"I don't have to work until Saturday morning so, um, nothing, I guess," I said, trying to sound like I was fully immersed in the dating scene.

"Some friends of mine are having a kegger up on Boy Scout Island. Wanna come?"

"Yeah, sure," I bubbled, not really caring that I was under the legal drinking age. "What time?"

"Great," he said then charmingly smiled. "Pick you up around seven." I was about to give him my address when he asked, "You live over in those apartments by the mall, right?"

I giggled nervously. "Yeah, how did you know?"

He just smiled again and said, "See you at seven," then put his hand on the stick shift and slowly pulled away.

I raised my arm in the air and waved goodbye as I watched him putter down the dirt road that led to the main drag. "See you at seven, then," I shouted, giddy with triumph.

And that was the beginning of my first expedition into the unknown world of S-E-X.

Just about every weekend after that was a carbon copy of itself. Jake would pick me up on Friday night, wearing one of his many, *many* black, concert t-shirts, then we'd drive to some hidden party location in the woods and drink beer with his friends. Jake would glance at his watch around ten o'clock, then look at me and comically exaggerate, "Whoa. Look at the time, would ya? Why, it's way past your bedtime, Young Lady. I've gotta get you home." I wasn't the only one at the party who knew we weren't exactly going back to my place. The two of us would hop into his Toyota and cruise over to an unoccupied make-out spot. After a little small-talk, he'd lean over and pick up a Journey cassette from the front dash then ever-so-smoothly slip it into his tape deck. That was his little way of saying, "Let's get it on, Baby." He'd ease the backrest of the driver's seat down into a horizontal position, and I'd crawl on top of him, sloppily returning his kisses. Before I knew it, he was petting me in places where I'd never before

273

been touched. It was all so heady at first, so exciting to finally be a player in this grown-up game. As the weeks flew by, our little routine became exactly that . . . a routine, and I quickly began to tire of it. There was only so much sexual fondling I could handle in the dead of night while Steve Perry howled in the background.

Near the end of that summer, after several weeks of misbehavior in my wake, I came home from the tennis courts one Saturday afternoon to find Mom and Arthur seated in their usual chairs at the kitchen table, taking turns filling up the ashtray with their half-smoked cigarettes.

"Hi Mom. Hi Arthur," I said innocently as I set my racket in the living room closet and began to walk down the hall toward my bedroom.

Mom looked at me with piercing eyes and asked, "Where were you last night?"

I stopped in my tracks. Given all the sleeping pills that escorted her to dreamland on a nightly basis, I was surprised she'd even noticed my extended evening escapades.

"I was here . . . in bed," I stated, trying to sound legitimate.

"You didn't come home until after midnight, you little shit," she hissed. "You know you're not allowed to stay out that late."

"Mom, don't be so crazy," I told her, trying to remain calm and unaffected. "It's no big deal, anyway."

"You're out late all the time these days, and I'm sick of it," she continued.

By this point in my life, my patience with Mom had worn paper thin, especially when it came to parental rights. I'd waded through most of my life's trials and tribulations with little help from her, and felt she was out of line whenever she played the "authority figure" card. As far as I was concerned, Mom had long since forfeited her right to govern me.

"Oh, you're sick of it now, are you? *You're* sick of it?!" I yelled, losing my cool. "Well, I got news for you, Dearie. I'm sick of a whole lot of crap you do, too!"

"Listen, Sister," she shot back. "Don't you dare mouth off to me. I'm your mother and don't you forget it!"

"I don't care if you're my mother or not. Half the time you're not even around, and when you *are* here, you're in that damn bed," I fumed, pointing down the hallway toward her room. "So don't you sit there and act all high and mighty and tell me what to do. Got it . . . Sister?" I stood my ground and glared at her with my hands firmly resting on my hips as if I were daring her to challenge me.

Arthur intervened. "Now you listen here, Theresa," he said sternly as he repeatedly pounded his forefinger on the kitchen table. "If you don't toe the line right now and show some respect for your mother, you are going to be grounded for a week. Do you understand me?"

Now it was now two against one, and I became more infuriated than ever. "I'm so sick of this place! I hate it here! And I hate you, too!" I screamed at both of them, then ran to my room and slammed the door. I flopped onto the floor and let the tears race down my cheeks as I knelt there with my head in my hands, wishing with all my might that I were eighteen—a legal adult—and could leave once and for all. But I wasn't eighteen, and I couldn't leave. I was stuck in that excruciating middle ground between Smoldering Hell and Blazing Inferno Hell.

Mom and Arthur were upset, and I could hear them trashing me through my closed bedroom door.

"The girl is incessantly irresponsible," said Arthur.

"She won't behave. No matter what I tell her, she just doesn't listen," replied Mom.

"We've done everything possible to give her a good life," justified Arthur.

"I do and do for that girl," Mom bleated. "I just don't know what more she wants! Is she out for my blood?! My soul?! What on earth could she want from me?!"

"Maybe you should call your friend, Sheila, and see if she'd be interested in taking Theresa for awhile," Arthur suggested.

"She needs some sense knocked into her, that's what she needs," replied Mom.

I couldn't believe what I was hearing; I couldn't believe that I had to live in a world that never made any sense to me. I felt like I had a permanent pass on the Crazy Train and didn't know how to get off. I couldn't stand it any longer, so I stood up and angrily wiped the tears from my cheeks then opened my door and marched into their midst. "Since neither of you gives a damn about me, I'm leaving for good! Getting the hell out of here!" I shrilly proclaimed before dramatically exiting through the front door and slamming it behind me.

I had no jacket, no extra clothes. The only thing of value on my person was a little cash. I didn't even know where I was going until the moment I unchained my bike and hopped on.

I rode to Paul's house as fast as my legs would take me, my streaming tears seeking asylum in the hard blowing wind. I hastily set my bike down on my friend's front lawn then raced to the front door and rang the bell, lowering my eyes to hide the pain. Paul's mom answered. "What is it, Dear?" she asked, sensing that something was wrong. She gently put an arm around my shoulder and led me inside. "Are you all right?"

I swallowed hard as I looked into her eyes and tried to smile through my tears. "Yeah, I'll be okay. Th-th-thanks for letting me come in," I stuttered.

"Do you need anything?" she asked, still concerned.

I shook my head from side to side.

"Why don't you go into the family room, and I'll get you some Kleenex. Paul will be there in a minute," she told me.

I cried on my friend's shoulder for the next several hours. "I wish I could live like you do," I confided as I repeatedly blew my nose. "I wish I could have parents who weren't so weird and wanted to take care of me." My friend sympathetically listened as the glut of my animosity oozed from my pores like a thick, black tar.

By the time my tears had dried, Paul's mom came into the room and unexpectedly said to me, "Your Aunt Mae is here to see you, Dear."

"My Aunt Mae?" I replied, puzzled. "Are you sure it's my Aunt Mae? I mean, how did she know that I was here?"

"She said she's come to take you home," replied Paul's mom.

Now I was scared. I didn't want to go back home. "Back home?" I feebly reiterated.

"Yes, Dear," she answered before smiling sympathetically then leaving the room.

I closed my eyes and heavily sighed then shook my head from side to side in disbelief. "I don't want to go back there," I told my friend.

"I think you should talk to your aunt about it," Paul advised. "I know she'd try to help you."

"Yeah, maybe you're right," I replied. I caressed the fleshy part of my cheeks, trying to wipe away any remaining dew of my distress then stood up. "Thanks for being my friend, Paul. I mean, I don't know what I would have done without you."

"Forget it," he said. "That's what friends are for." He got up and gave me a big bear hug before following me into the living room.

As soon as Aunt Mae saw me, she asked in her upbeat way, "How are you doin', Kiddo?"

I tried to sound as strong as possible. "Hi Aunt Mae," I said then shrugged my shoulders and glanced at the floor. "Okay I guess."

"Your mom called," she explained.

"How did she know I was here?" I asked, clearly mystified.

"Don't know. She must be aware of how much time you spend here at Paul's," she stated in a lighthearted voice, trying to ease the tension. "Get your jacket, and I'll take you home."

"Um, I don't have a jacket," I answered.

"Oh, okay. Well, that's fine. Then we'll just go."

I hesitantly walked toward her then turned to wave goodbye to Paul before stepping outside.

"Okay. Bye, now. Thanks," my aunt said to Paul and his mom, then closed the screen door behind her.

We'd settled into her car and were driving away when she glanced at me and asked, "Why the long face?"

I intently looked back, trying to decide if I should tell her what was actually on my mind. That's when I noticed we were traveling in the opposite direction of Mom's apartment. "Aunt Mae? We're going the wrong way."

"What do you mean?" she asked.

"Well, my apartment is the other way," I said while pointing toward the west.

"We're not going to your apartment," she stated frankly.

"We're not? But I thought you said that you were going to take me home."

"Yes. I am taking you home," she told me. "*My* home."

I was stunned, momentarily speechless. "Your home?" I quietly repeated in disbelief.

"Yes, of course," she said matter-of-factly. "Why would I come and pick you up if I wasn't going to take you back to *my* home?"

"I . . . well? I guess I don't know," I replied.

She looked over at me and asked, "Is that all right? Do you want to come to my house?"

"Yeah, sure I do," I said earnestly, still trying to comprehend this new turn of events.

"I've told your mother that you can stay with me for as long as you'd like."

"Wow, really?" I said, not believing my luck. "You mean . . . I don't have to go back and live with Mom and Arthur?" Before giving her a chance to answer, I added, "Ever?"

She chuckled then replied, "Not if you don't want to."

I stared out the windshield for a moment as I thought about it, then said, "I'm pretty sure that I'm not going to want to."

That evening, my aunt treated me to a meal at one of the nicest restaurants in town, just the two of us. We talked about light subjects, things that were uncomplicated. After we returned home, she showed me to my new room, then told me she had to drive to the grocery store and pick up a few things.

After she left, I took out whatever remaining cash I had in my pocket and laid it on her bedroom dresser with a note that said, "Thanks for the great vittles."

Later on that night, as I was comfortably tucked beneath my freshly washed sheets in one of my aunt's nightgowns, she came into my bedroom and sat down beside me.

"What's this?" she asked gently but firmly as she held up the money I'd left for her.

"It's my contribution," I explained.

"You don't owe me anything, Dear," she told me. "I took you out because I *wanted* to. We'll be going to dinner occasionally, and you need to know that you don't have to pay for it. Okay?" she said, then looked down at me with an expression that implied there was no other correct answer than "yes."

"Okay," I confirmed, then timidly smiled. I looked away as I tried to think of how to express my utter gratitude for all my aunt had just done for me. "Thanks for everything, Aunt Mae. Really. I mean, thanks for coming to pick me up and for dinner and for everything," I said. Somehow my words sounded tinny, unable to convey what I was truly feeling inside.

My aunt lovingly patted my arm and told me, "We'll talk more about everything later, okay. Sweet dreams." Then she stood up and gently closed my bedroom door on her way out.

A day that had begun as one of the bleakest in my seventeen years had miraculously turned out to be one of my best. That Saturday was the beginning of a whole new life for me, a life that I'd always dreamt about but never thought possible.

I was there to stay and would never live under the same roof with my mother again.

By that time in her life, Aunt Mae was a middle-aged woman who was living alone. The River of Love that she and my uncle had once floated upon had become a River of Tears, flooding the shared beating of their hearts. The four children they'd raised together were now on their own, and my aunt was an empty nester in every real sense of the word.

I'd been living with her for just a few short weeks when she came home one afternoon with something completely unexpected. I was watching TV in the living room when I heard the back door open. "I have a surprise for you!" she yelled. "Come on into the kitchen." Having no earthly idea what to expect, I stood up and began walking toward the sound of her voice. As I rounded the corner, I saw a large, cardboard box resting on the kitchen counter.

Still in her jacket, Aunt Mae was standing directly beside the surprise. "Go on, open it," she encouraged, her poker face revealing nothing.

I unfolded the flaps and peered inside. "Mew, mew," cried the little, orange fluffball who jumped toward me, frantically trying to escape the confines of the package. "Oh my gosh! Aunt Mae!" I gasped. "You got me a kitty! My very own kitty!" I scooped up the ten-week-old mini-tiger and cradled him against my chest.

"Well! What do you think?" asked my aunt, seemingly pleased. "Do you like him?"

"Like him? Oh, so much more than that. I absolutely *love* him!" I shouted. "Thank you! Thank you so much, Aunt Mae!"

And that was how my new life began. Many more days spent with my aunt were filled with unbelievable joy and a newfound peace I'd never before known. There was no more arguing to contend with, no more crying, and the only thing left for me to fear in the middle of the night was a wild and unruly tiger kitty who delighted in pouncing on my feet. I raised my aunt higher and higher on her pedestal with each passing day, and thanked the blessed stars above for all that she'd provided. I knew she wasn't a saint, at least I was pretty sure she wasn't, but she had come closer than anyone else to saving me from my darkest days. And, the only means I had of expressing my gratitude was through love, sheer love, for I had nothing else to give.

Since I now had a strict curfew and was no longer allowed to rendezvous beneath the midnight moon, Jake predictably lost interest in me. Whatever lust for one another we'd once had now fizzled out faster than a joint during a police raid. It wasn't that we broke up exactly, it was more that he just stopped calling. Truth be told, I was actually relieved to keep my blouse buttoned up for a change.

During my last year of high school, Mom would often call. "Stop by and visit me once in a while, Honey," she'd beg, but I never wanted to, so I never did. I resented her sudden interest in wanting to become friends now that she no longer carried the burden of raising me.

My aunt and I became closer and closer as time passed, and I began to confide in her about concerns I'd long since buried. During dinner one evening, I decided to initiate a

281

conversation regarding some of the things that were tumbling around inside my head.

"Aunt Mae?"

"Yes?"

"What would you think of me if I told you that I was afraid I might turn out like my mom?"

"What do you mean?" she asked.

I looked down at my plate, trying to decide how to reveal myself, then looked back at her and cautiously explained, "I'm scared that I'm going to become a schizophrenic."

"Now, why would you think that?" she asked without hesitation.

"I guess, well, mainly because it's a hereditary thing. I mean, I think it is. Isn't it?"

She set her fork down then asked in all seriousness, "Have you been hearing voices?"

I shook my head from side to side then explained, "I don't want to be like her, not *anything* like her, and I'm just scared that I might be."

My aunt took her time in arriving at a response. Finally, she said, "I know some of the counselors at the mental health clinic. How would you feel about setting up an appointment to talk with one of them?"

I silently contemplated her proposition. The more I thought about it, the more it seemed like a reasonable thing for me to do. "Sure. Yeah, sure," I replied. "I'd like to do that. I think that's a really good idea, and it might help me understand my situation a little better."

On the morning of my appointment with the mental health counselor, my aunt asked, "Would you like me to go with you? If you'd rather go by yourself, that's fine. You can take the car."

"No. No, I want you to go with me," I told her sincerely. "Actually, I'm a little nervous to tell you the truth."

Later that morning, Aunt Mae drove me to the counseling center located directly behind the town's hospital. I could feel my heart trembling at the thought of what the counselor might say. I had so many dreams out there waiting patiently for me to arrive and was terrified that the heavy hand of mental illness would shatter them to bits.

My aunt escorted me into the austere building where we checked in with the receptionist, then sat down in a small, dimly lit waiting room. After a few minutes, the counselor appeared in the doorway and graciously smiled at my aunt and me. "Theresa? Right this way."

Aunt Mae and I followed her down a short hallway into a small office that was bathed in pinks and mauves. "Please have a seat," she suggested, pointing to two cushioned guest chairs. She pushed her own closer toward the two of us, opened her notebook and said contemplatively, "Now then, Theresa, I understand you have some questions for me?"

I looked at my aunt for reassurance then back at the counselor. "Well, yes," I began. "There are a few things I'd like to ask you. I don't know if you know who my mom is."

"Yes, I know your mother very well," she interrupted. "She comes here regularly to meet with a colleague of mine . . . about once a week. She is such a dear spirit, always telling jokes and making everyone laugh."

"Yeah, that's her," I said, slowly shaking my head up and down while my eyes darted around the room. I found it odd that the counselor didn't mention Mom's dark side. "Then I guess you know that she's a schizophrenic and has a lot of mental problems."

The counselor nodded, "Yes, I am aware of that."

"I wanted to talk to you about how that might affect me," I explained while fidgeting in my chair. "What are my chances of having that same type of illness?"

"Before I answer your question, I'd like to ask a few of my own. I think it's important that I get a better idea of who

283

you are, Theresa, and what *your* personality is like," she explained then waited for a response. I didn't have one. "Now then," she continued as she studied me then glanced at the notebook in her lap, "Do you ever hear voices? Any kind of voices? At any point throughout the day or night?"

I vigorously shook my head "No!" as if I were trying to expel the very thought from my mind.

She wrote something down then asked, "Have you ever blacked out and couldn't remember a specific period of time?"

Again, I vigorously shook my head "No!"

"Do you ever feel paranoid? As though someone were out to get you?"

"Do you feel like everyone else is better than you are?"

"Do you ever have prolonged periods of depression for seemingly no reason?"

"Do you ever have hallucinations of any sort?"

My answer to all of her strange and probing questions was an honest and resounding "No!" The more questions she asked, the more I felt as though I had somehow miraculously made it through the gauntlet after all and might have a good shot at a normal life.

The counselor patiently listened for the next several minutes as I talked in depth about my relationship with Mom. Near the end of our meeting, she closed her notebook and slid her reading glasses from her face then looked directly at me. "Well then, Dear," she said, "I don't think there's anything more you really need to worry about, at least for the time being. You currently seem to be in good mental health." She then lifted her hand slightly into the air and molded it into a warning symbol. "I will caution you, however, that schizophrenia often does not manifest itself until later in life. Sometimes it sneaks up on a person, not revealing itself until after they've been out in the world on their own for a while. Because, you see, that's when a person begins to experience most of life's troublesome burdens." She then gently tapped the side of her forehead with her free hand and stated, "The mind of a schizophrenic simply can't handle the responsibilities that come with adulthood." The counselor paused and patiently waited for me to say something. When I didn't, she looked down at her wristwatch and said, "Looks like it's almost time for my next appointment." She stood up and walked toward the threshold of her office, then opened the door. I shyly smiled at her as I passed and told her how beneficial the meeting had been.

"Call me if you have any other questions," she said. "I'll be happy to help in any way I can."

On the drive home, I didn't say much to my aunt; I was too busy replaying my meeting with the counselor. She'd struck a tender chord by suggesting that I wasn't completely out of the woods yet because I hadn't lived on my own. But then again, hadn't I? Hadn't I already endured more than most? I vowed right then and there that I would ***never, ever*** let mental illness take me down, ***no matter what***. It had already destroyed the lives of my entire family, Mom, Daddy and now my brother. One of us had to make it out alive and, GODDAMN IT, it was going to be me. It . . . was . . . going . . . to . . . be . . . ME!

That final year of high school was bittersweet. For once, my life seemed to be falling into place, and I wanted to savor every day before it all changed after graduation. I remained close to my dear friends, and even managed to capture the attention of the "Italian Stallion," who seemed sincerely interested in the inner workings of both my body *and* my mind.

Graduation arrived in late May and, before I knew it, I was getting ready to leave for college. I went over to Grandpa's house to say my goodbyes. "I'm going to major in Poli-Sci, Grandpa," I proudly told him, trying to sound sophisticated with my cool talking lingo.

"Poli, what?" Grandpa asked with a perplexed, crinkled expression on his face.

"You know, Poli-Sci . . . ," I said again. "You know how you're always telling me to become a lawyer, right? 'Cuz you say I like to argue so much and everything? Well, I decided that you're probably right, so I'm going to major in Political Science, and then go on to law school." I shrugged my shoulders. "Don't know where just yet, but I'm sure I'll figure it out."

Grandpa chuckled knowingly and said, "Oh I'm sure you will, Theresa. You always do." He then looked me straight in the eyes and quickly changed the subject. "You know, your mother called me. She'd really like to see you before you leave."

I bit my tongue, trying not to say something sarcastic and disrespectful about his daughter.

"She's your mother. You know that. And the right thing to do is to go and say goodbye," he urged.

I looked up at the ceiling, lips tightly pursed, then exhaled an annoyed sigh and begrudgingly conceded, "Yeah, I guess you're right, Grandpa. You're always right."

I talked a little longer about my excitement for what lay ahead, then Grandpa told me to look after myself. "Just you be careful out there," he warned. "It can be a mighty cruel world."

I walked over to where he was seated, leaned down and squeezed him tightly, then told him how much I was going to miss him. "I'll write to you a lot. I promise," I said truthfully. He quietly nodded in reply. "I love you, Grandpa. I'll see you at Thanksgiving," I told him, then kissed him lovingly on the cheek. I felt the gaze of two liquid brown eyes staring up at me from the floor near his feet, so I knelt down and nuzzled the aging beagle then cooed, "And you take care of yourself, too, Bucky, you old hound dog, you." I steadied my hand on the coffee table and eased myself up, drinking in the familiarity of the timeless living room I had known for so long before letting myself out one last time.

The late autumn winds were blowing once more, signaling the kind of change you can only feel deep within if you listen with nothing more than your soul. For me, it was a change far more pivotal than anything before and was something that I had waited for just about all of my life.

The night before my aunt was to take me to college, I laid in my room surrounded by darkness and stared out the window into the layered depths of the creamsicle moon. It got me thinking about what Daddy had said all those years ago . . . "You're going to twirl with the moon, Twink." The distant sound of his voice started reverberating through my head and hot tears soon followed. So many of my childhood moonbeams now lay melted at my feet.

My thoughts slowly drifted to Mom. I hadn't visited her as Grandpa had suggested. In fact, I hadn't talked to her for weeks. I rolled toward my nightstand and looked at the alarm clock. It was 11:30. I wasn't sure if she'd still be awake, but I decided to call anyway. I got out of bed and put on my slippers then tiptoed through the living room and picked up the phone.

"Hello?" she answered sleepily.

"Mom," I said softly.

"Oh, how are you, Honey?" she asked, unmistakably happy to hear the sound of my voice. "I've been thinking about you so much. You never come to visit me."

"Yeah, I know," I answered sheepishly.

"When are you leaving for college?" she asked.

"Tomorrow morning."

"Oh dear, tomorrow? Already?" A few seconds of silence passed before she continued. "I suppose I won't get a chance to

287

see you before you go, then," she said, her disappointment readily apparent.

"I guess not," I answered, trying my best not to get emotional.

"Well, then, my Little Honey, just know that Mother loves you. You've always been my Shining Star, my Little Superstar. That's what you are! And you are going to be a superstar in college, too."

I was suddenly overcome with sorrow and didn't know what to say. For some unknown reason, all I wanted to do at that very moment was rock in my mother's arms one last time. I took a deep breath as I gathered the strength to compose myself then said modestly, "Oh, I don't think I'm going to be any kind of superstar, Mom."

"Write to me, will you, Honey?" she asked sweetly.

"Sure. I mean, yeah, of course I will," I replied. Not knowing what else to say I decided to bring our conversation to a close. "Well, it's late, Mom, and I guess I should be going now."

"Okay, my Darling. You just take such good care of yourself and know that I love you ever so much."

"Okay Mom," I replied.

"I love you, My Sweet Little Girl."

"I love you, too, Mom."

Bright and early the next morning, my aunt and I loaded up the car with all my school necessities. After placing my last suitcase in the trunk, I realized I'd forgotten one final task, so I turned around and went into the house. "I'll be back before you know it, Little Buddy," I whispered as I hugged my tiger kitty close then kissed him on the head. "Take good care of Aunt Mae." I gently set him onto the carpet then took one last look around and snapped a photo in my mind.

It didn't take long for us to pass the city limits sign that read, "International Falls, Population 10,237." "Better make that 10,236," I thought to myself. I looked out at the colorful clusters of birch and maple trees that had made their home next to the side of the road, their yellow, orange and crimson leaves silently falling to the ground, bidding adieu to the only life they'd ever known. It somehow seemed so fitting.

The white stripes on the black, paved road ahead caught my attention as they flashed past us faster than a white tailed buck. They were merely painted lines on federal highway 53 to anyone else, but they represented so much more than that to me . . . they were a radiant symbol of my freedom. I was nervous about my future and even a little scared, but I was damn ready for it to begin.

I eased back into the softness of the passenger's seat, slipped on my headphones, closed my eyes and pushed "Play."

Dear Daddy,

It has been so many years since you left me. Did you think I had forgotten you? Sometimes I wish my voice could reach up to the heavens so that you would hear how much I miss you.

I am eighteen years old now and have just started college. When I was packing my things before I came here, I found that letter you'd written to me on the night you died. It was in my old jewelry box. When I opened it up, this is all it said:

My Dearest Twink-
We are all but vessels of those who have come before us. Don't let me down.
Your father,
Rick V. Waters

About the Author

T. H. Waters lives in the charming city of Minneapolis, Minnesota, where she resides with her significant other and their two adorable kitty cats. She spent the first half of her childhood in Minneapolis before moving to International Falls, Minnesota, in 1975. Compelled to write this book based upon the unique experiences of her youth, she is grateful for the privilege of finally being able to live out loud.

www.ingramcontent.com/pod-product-compliance
Lightning Source LLC
Chambersburg PA
CBHW031252170626
46807CB00001B/114